Hamilton (Mrs.) Madden

Memoir of the Late Right Rev. Robert Daly, D.D., Lord Bishop of Cashel

Hamilton (Mrs.) Madden

Memoir of the Late Right Rev. Robert Daly, D.D., Lord Bishop of Cashel

ISBN/EAN: 9783744661249

Printed in Europe, USA, Canada, Australia, Japan

Cover: Foto ©Andreas Hilbeck / pixelio.de

More available books at **www.hansebooks.com**

MEMOIR

OF THE LATE

RIGHT REV. ROBERT DALY, D.D.,

LORD BISHOP OF CASHEL.

BY

MRS. HAMILTON MADDEN,

AUTHOR OF 'PERSONAL RECOLLECTIONS OF THE BISHOP OF CASHEL.'

LONDON:

JAMES NISBET & CO., BERNERS STREET.

1875.

PREFACE.

SOME time having elapsed since the death of the Bishop of Cashel, and no Memoir of this eminent man having appeared, the Author determined to try what she could do. She had the advantage for many years of an intimate acquaintance with the late revered Bishop. She has received much valuable assistance from several of his clergy, who love his memory, and wish to have it perpetuated. She has also, by the kindness of a member of his family, been put in possession of some of his manuscripts, and of many letters preserved by him. Some persons expressed their fears that it would not be practicable to collect a sufficient quantity of material for the work, as none of his early correspondence has been preserved; but, on the contrary, she has been obliged to omit a great deal of valuable matter, in order to confine it to the limits usually prescribed,—amongst other things, his speeches at the controversial meetings at Carlow, and in the House of Lords on the subject of National Education; also correspondence carried on at some length on various important subjects. These she will reserve in case of an

enlarged edition being called for at some future time. It
has been her humble desire to endeavour to represent him
such as he was; and if in any degree she has been enabled
to do so, she trusts that it may be both interesting and
instructive, and lead some in these days to obey the command of the Lord by the prophet Jeremiah: 'See, and ask
for the old paths; where is the good way? and walk
therein, and ye shall find rest for your souls.'

CONTENTS.

CHAPTER V.

PASTORAL CARE.

CHAPTER VI.

' HERE A LITTLE, AND THERE A LITTLE.'

CHAPTER VII.

A BISHOP.

CHAPTER VIII.

EPISCOPAL WORK.

CHAPTER IX.

CORRESPONDENCE.

CHAPTER X.

PARTING DAYS.

APPENDIX A.

APPENDIX B.

APPENDIX C.

MEMOIR

RIGHT REV. ROBERT DALY, D.D.

CHAPTER I.

EARLY DAYS.

'Lord, with what care Thou hast begirt us round !
Parents first season us : then schoolmasters
Deliver us to laws ; they send us bound
To rules of reason.'

GEORGE HERBERT.

ROBERT DALY was born at Dunsandle, in the county of
Galway, the residence of his father, the Right Honourable
Denis Daly, on the 10th of June 1783. The Dalys were an
old Irish family. His mother was Lady Harriet, only child
of the first and only Earl of Farnham, and a great heiress.
His father was a gentleman of considerable property and
influence, which he made use of in the cause of his country,
joining in the patriotic exertions of Grattan, Flood, and
Curran, to endeavour to raise poor Ireland in the scale of
nations. His career of usefulness was cut short at an
early age : he died young, leaving two sons and six
daughters, the youngest of whom was born after his death
The eldest son, James, was only fourteen months older than

A

his brother Robert, the subject of our Memoir, and was raised to the peerage as Baron Dunsandle the same year that Robert was appointed to the bishopric of Cashel. They were the two eldest of the family, and were a striking contrast to each other in character and disposition, though equally clever in the acquisition of learning. James was remarkably gentle, and was easily led and influenced by others, while Robert possessed qualities which were exactly the opposite. James was his mother's favourite; while Robert resembled her in many respects, not only in looks, but in a healthy and vigorous constitution both of mind and body, in strength of mind, and habits of regularity and punctuality, and a certain plain common sense which is a very uncommon thing. There were not to be found in those times photographers in every country town; consequently we have not interesting memorials of the brothers in the shape of photographs, taken every year in various attitudes, and treasured up by foolishly fond parents. We are left very much to our imagination to fancy what they must have looked like while playing about in the demesne at Dunsandle, in those days when he remembered his nurse, on losing her husband, coming into the nursery, and saying in a triumphant tone of voice to the children, 'Wish me joy! I'm *shut* of my bargain,'—a circumstance which his great sense of humour, no doubt, made sure not to be forgotten by him. His reminiscences of the universal spelling-book were also very amusing. It seems to have been at that time the chief elementary book of English teaching; and the moral story of 'Tommy and Harry' was imprinted

on his memory, together with the reckless exclamation
of the latter,—'I don't care for that neither,' said the
hardened wretch. We have no record of his sayings, or
of many of his traits of character when a child ; all who
remembered him at that time have passed away. Perhaps
he was not a very wonderful child—wonderful children,
he said himself, were never heard of in after life, except as
oddities, who gave you the idea of 'worn-out wonders.'
On the death of her husband, Lady Harriet Daly went
with her children to reside at Bromley, near Delgany, in
the County Wicklow, a place which had belonged to her
mother, Lady Farnham, and now came into her possession.
It was a comfortable, substantial house, in a well-wooded
demesne, in the vicinity of some of the loveliest scenery of
the County Wicklow. In this and the neighbouring parish
of Powerscourt, Robert Daly spent the greater part of his
life. They were highly-favoured spots, remarkable not
only for the beauty of their scenery and their genial
climate, but for their moral beauty, and for the fruits of
righteousness which were brought forth by many who
resided there in after times. Here he was favoured by
many of the advantages of a good home education ; and no
doubt, his earliest associations of happiness being connected
in his mind with the beauties of nature, gave him that
thorough taste for the country which he preserved to the
last, and which is perhaps the most innocent, and at the
same time the most elevating to the mind, of all our natural
tastes. The road by which he so often rode or drove back
and forward from Bromley to Powerscourt Glebe is one of
the loveliest in Ireland. After passing through the richly

wooded glen of the Downs, which forms part of the beautiful demesne of Bellevue, at the end of which there is a fine view of Great Sugarloaf, the road winds for some miles through a defile called 'The Rocky Valley,' where the scenery is of a wild and sublime character—the mountains rising precipitously on each side of the road, while large boulders of rock seem to overhang your path, and bright little streams enliven the grey gloom of the valley. It is the great variety of scenery met with in so short a space of time that gives its great charm to the County Wicklow.   On coming out of the Rocky Valley and ascending a hill, a prospect meets the eye which can hardly be surpassed in beauty,—the demesnes of Powerscourt, Charleville, and Tinnahinch, surrounded by an amphitheatre of mountains; the wooded glen, so well known as the 'Dargle,' or the 'Glen of Oaks,' winding along; and a view of the sea in the distance, with Bray Head on one side and the Killiney Hills on the other. To return to our subject, there was one important ingredient wanting in Mr. Daly's education, a want which was at that time existing, though perhaps not felt, in almost every family,—a want of religious teaching.

Sunday schools had not then been thought of, or classes for catechizing and instructing young people in the Holy Scriptures, as the only book able to make them wise unto salvation through faith which is in Christ Jesus; while catechisms and the 'Week's Preparation' were thought to contain sufficient instruction for candidates for confirmation.   His mother, though an excellent woman, and most conscientious in the discharge of what she felt to be her duty, was not at that time under the influence of true religion. He was not given to the prayers of a Monica; but his mother in after times learned from him in the school of Christ, and was no doubt given to his prayers. Children were in those days kept in great order, and not encouraged to think too much of themselves. His mother used to say that her children were the worst children in the world, probably from her great anxiety that they should be the best. He afterwards spoke of it as being a trait peculiar to her character to undervalue everything that belonged to her, while many others are found to overrate their possessions. Her children, accordingly, secretly rejoiced one day at overhearing her (while looking at her bees in the garden) say, 'My bees are the worst bees in the world; they never swarm when they ought.' She seems to have succeeded in giving her sons a thorough abhorrence of everything that was low and wicked; the reason given for their removal from Dr. Moore's school at Donnybrook, after a very short stay there, was Robert being so much shocked at what he witnessed among his schoolfellows, who were not probably worse than other schoolboys at that time. At an earlier period, he and his brother were for a few months at Dr. Stock's school at Delgany. The exact date of his going there is not known, but it is likely to have been soon after his mother's removal to Bromley; he was then more than twelve years of age. Dr. Stock was rector of the parish, and kept a school in the glebe-house for a small and select number of pupils. Their uncle, Colonel Daly, was joint guardian to the brothers with Lady Harriet. Judge Daly (who never

married) seems also to have taken a great interest in the
education of his nephews.   He for many summers resided
at the church cottage in Delgany, and when in his old age
he became infirm, his nieces all took their turn in nurse-
tending him, particularly the eldest Miss Daly, who lived
with him for some time before his death.   Robert was very
much attached to this uncle, and often told a story of his
saying to him when a boy, ' Two and two are four, Robert ;
can you contradict that ?'   This love of contradiction
remained with him, however, through life ; it was a strong
characteristic of his nature, a high development of the
organ of combativeness, which, phrenologists tell us, is the
quality that gives energy to a character, and enables it
to surmount the difficulties that come in its way.   In his
case this quality was well directed, by the influence of
divine grace, and helped him in those times, when he met
with much which he thought it his duty to oppose, to fulfil
his baptismal vow to fight manfully under Christ's banner
against sin, the world, and the devil, and to continue
Christ's faithful soldier and servant until his life's end.
Lady Harriet was assisted in the choice of a tutor for her
sons by Dr. Cleaver, then Bishop of Ferns, who was married
to her first cousin.   The person chosen was a highly educated Englishman, Mr. Hordern, under whose care they
pursued their studies at home, reading all the morning till
about two o'clock, when they went out to walk or ride.
They were very fond of shooting, and their mother kept
a gamekeeper to accompany them in their excursions.
When the rebellion broke out, in 1798, Mr. Hordern
returned to England.   On hearing of the dangerous

illness of her step-mother, Lady Farnham, with whom her second daughter, Charlotte, had always lived, Lady Harriet went to London, where she remained for several months, bringing three of her daughters with her, and leaving the two youngest with their grandmother, Mrs. Daly, in Dublin, who had a house in Cavendish Row, Rutland Square. It was probably this interval that was spent by the brothers at Dr. Moore's at Donnybrook, who took pupils to prepare for College. On the death of Lady Farnham, Lady Harriet returned with all her family to Bromley, where her sons pursued their studies during their College course under the direction of their tutor, Mr. Eyre, who was, as Mr. Hordern had been, recommended to Lady Harriet by her cousin the Bishop of Ferns, and who remained with them until they took their degree. Robert Daly and his elder brother entered Trinity College, Dublin, together as fellow-commoners in 1799, under Mr. Davenport, and obtained first and second place. Robert distinguished himself highly, and won the gold medal in the year 1803, which was at that time only awarded to those who got *Valde in Omnibus* at every examination during their whole course, the exception of one *Bene* being allowed, and whose conduct had been throughout correct and unblamable: only one gold medal was given in each class. As Robert was but twenty when he took his degree of B.A., in 1803, Colonel Daly thought him too young to give up his studies; he therefore advised his going to Oxford for two years. He accordingly entered at St. Mary's Hall, from whence he took an *ad-eundem* degree in 1805. His brother, on coming of age in 1803, visited

Dunsandle, and was much amused but rather affronted at the tenantry, who had not seen him since he was quite a child, preparing jam to regale him with on his arrival. After this period, Robert seems to have very often visited his native place, and to have enjoyed his favourite sport of shooting over the Galway mountains ; which he afterwards spoke of as ' a time when I thought that God had sent me into the world for no higher purpose than to slaughter grouse.' He remembered one rainy day, while the general elections were going on, asking the gamekeeper if he thought the weather would soon clear up, and being amused at the answer of the old man, who looked very wisely up at the clouds, and said, ' Not till the perjury's over !' In speaking of his early days in after life,—of the time when he was, as he termed it, an ' unconverted sinner,'—he was apt to be more severe in his judgment of himself than others would feel disposed to be. He was always remarkably well-conducted, and there are few who would condemn a young man whose time was not fully occupied for spending his leisure hours in shooting. We find Sir T. Fowell Buxton, in the beginning of a letter of most valuable advice to his son, saying, ' I particularly regretted being away last week, as I think I might have done something for your shooting before you went to College.' It was Robert Daly's nature to follow up whatever pursuit he undertook with energy ; and accordingly he entered into it *con amore*, and, we must confess, continued to go out occasionally with his gun for some time after he was ordained. It was not very long, however, until all the energies of his nature and powers of his mind were absorbed in the pursuit of a higher and nobler occupation,—that of winning souls to Christ. Mr. Daly, afterwards Lord Dunsandle, was returned, in the Conservative interest, for the County Galway at every election during his life. These contested elections called for the expenditure of large sums of money. Their grandfather, Lord Farnham, had a property in Kent, which, as it did not go with the title, he left to be divided between his two grandsons. It was afterwards sold, and Robert, with his share of this fortune, to convenience his brother, bought from him a portion of the family estate, which at that time was probably worth nearly £1000 a year. When the disturbance occurred in Dublin, in 1803, called Emmett's Rebellion, in which Lord Kilwarden was killed, volunteer corps were organized by those who were loyally affected in various localities, to assist the Government in putting down rebellion, as the number of military in the country at the time was not sufficient for that purpose. Amongst other places, the village of Kilcool, on the sea-coast, in the parish of Delgany, had its yeomanry corps, in which Mr. Daly enrolled himself on his return from Oxford, when his manly bearing made the peasantry all declare that 'he would make a fine soldier.' The military ardour so naturally called forth at this stirring time in the breast of an energetic, high-spirited young man, and the patriotic feeling which he inherited from his father, inclined him for a while to choose the army as his profession. The state of public affairs at this time, not only in Ireland, but in all parts of the kingdom, which was then threatened with invasion by Buonaparte, was well calculated to call forth these feelings. The influence of true religion never was so little felt in our country. A writer of that period observes: 'It is remarkable to observe the contrast between the parliamentary debates at the commencement of the last century and those of the present day. Then, scriptural allusions and illustrations were common, and no man seemed to be afraid of quoting the authority of Christ or His apostles in vindication of his opinions. Now it would be difficult for any one who should do the same to escape the brand of some opprobrious name.'[1]

Sir Jonah Barrington reveals unpleasant truths about the state of moral feeling among the nobility and gentry in Ireland at the time of the Union,—how almost every man had his price. We need not wonder that this book is now out of print, and that another edition of it was not called for. Mr. Daly's father did not, as we have seen, live to see his country's disgrace, and his son was a minor at the time of the Union. They were therefore not tried on this point; but if they had been, we do not think that a Daly would have been numbered among those who thus, as it were, sold their birthright. But God had His chosen people amongst them, and on their account, and in answer to their prayers, the punishment so richly deserved was averted from our land. It may be interesting to give an extract from a letter of a learned and pious Lutheran minister in East Friesland, dated Hatshusen, September 15, 1803:—'I fear not much for England from Buonaparte and the French. There are more with you than against you, because the Lord has a great multitude of children in your country. He will, doubtless, hear the

[1] *Christian Observer* for 1803, p. 765.

fervent prayers of His children, and for their sakes give security. There are also in Germany many of His people, who daily unite their prayers for England's welfare.' We read in the Holy Scriptures, that 'when the enemy shall come in like a flood, the Spirit of the Lord shall lift up a standard against him' (Isa. lix. 19). The enemy was now indeed coming in with a flood of ungodliness upon our land, but in answer to the prayers of His believing people, the Spirit of the Lord lifted up a standard against him. The banner of God's truth was now unfurled,—gospel truth as revealed to us in the Bible; and around it there gathered a goodly band of warriors, small in number at first, but all good men and true. Their numbers increased as they went on, and they determined, in God's help, to begin by circulating the Holy Scriptures, and endeavouring to teach them to the rising generation. It was under this banner that Mr. Daly eventually enrolled himself, as we shall afterwards have occasion to show.

When, by divine grace, his talents were enlisted in the cause of Christ, he was eminently fitted to fill the post assigned to him in the Church of Ireland at that stormy period of her history, when the zeal and boldness of a second Luther were required to take advantage of that short interval between the slumbering security of former times and the wily Jesuitism of the present day; when Roman Catholic priests could be induced to enter into controversy with Protestant clergymen; and men of fervent, heartfelt, practical piety were wanting, to thaw the ice of cold indifference on the subject of religion which had prevailed among Protestants for so long a time.

CHAPTER II.

'Lead, kindly light, amid the encircling gloom,
    Lead thou me on !
The night is dark, and I am far from home,
    Lead thou me on !
Keep thou my feet ; I do not ask to see
The distant scene ; one step enough for me.'
                Irish Church Hymnal.

IT does not appear what were the exact motives which influenced Mr. Daly in deciding upon taking orders ; he thought himself, when looking back upon them, that they were not what he would afterwards have considered indispensably necessary to one who desired to devote himself to the work of the ministry. He often said that he trembled to think how lightly he had undertaken such solemn responsibilities, and would tell how it was at a ball that he made arrangements about his ordination ; but God, who had called him by His grace to preach the unsearchable riches of Christ, was leading him by a way that he knew not. He never spoke of any particular period as one that he could look back to as the time of his conversion to God— his awakening to the sense of the realities of religion seems to have been a gradual one ; but every step that he gained in his Christian warfare he maintained manfully, and each doctrinal view of divine truth, as he came to see it clearly, was put forth by him and preached with a power which brought conviction to his hearers. He was ordained deacon at Kilmore, by letters dimissory, in 1807, when he was appointed to the curacy of Malrancan, in the County Wexford. His rector was a cousin of Lady Harriet Daly's, the Rev. Thomas Gore, and with him Mr. Daly resided during his stay in that parish, as the former was then unmarried. Mr. Daly was the first clergyman who ever preached in Kilturk, in which part of the union a church was built in 1809. He was considered, even at this early stage of his ministry, to be a good preacher, and was very much respected as a zealous, hard-working clergyman. It is evident, both from the sermon which we shall have occasion to allude to a little further on, and from some passages in his journal, that while here he established Sunday schools in the parish, and classes for the instruction of apprentices and servants on the Sabbath day. In this immediate neighbourhood some of the most sanguinary scenes of the Irish Rebellion of 1798 had been enacted. Bargay Castle, the residence of Bagenal Harvey, Esq.,[1] was in the parish of Kilturk, and only nine years had elapsed since its owner had been executed for high treason. We can easily imagine what a moral wilderness this must have been into which Mr. Daly was sent to minister to the souls of others, without an 'evangelist' to take him by the hand and point out the way to the celestial city. There were at that time no clerical meetings, no classes for young men

---

[1] We find an account of a very remarkable dinner-party at this castle given by Sir Jonah Barrington in his *Personal Sketches*, vol. i. p. 148.

preparing for the ministry. He was led by the teaching
of the Holy Spirit to feel his own insufficiency for these
things, and with earnest prayer to study the word of God.
What he learned there he might be said, like St. Paul, not
to have received from man, but by the revelation of Jesus
Christ. It was, no doubt, his own personal experience of
what the prayerful reading of the word of God, without
note or comment, could accomplish, that made him so
zealous in his endeavours to secure this blessing for his
fellow-countrymen, and to educate the young in the knowledge, from their earliest youth, of that blessed book. It
is deeply interesting to have opened up to our view most
unexpectedly, by the document from which we shall make
some extracts, the first workings of divine grace in the heart
of this most remarkable man, his strivings (agonizings) to
enter in at the strait gate. How encouraging to any who
may be in a similar state of mind, to find how fully these
precious promises were fulfilled to him : ' They shall know,
if they follow on to know the Lord ; ' and, ' They that wait
on the Lord shall renew their strength ; they shall mount
up on wings as eagles ; they shall run, and not be weary ;
they shall walk, and not faint ' ! This can hardly be called
a journal, as the entries are but too few and far between ;
but it will speak for itself :—

' *Malrancan*, 23*d December* 1809.—I have this day, by
the grace of God, determined at every festival carefully to
examine into my heart and my past life, and to write down
my thoughts which result from it, that I may thereby be
enabled to judge of my progress in grace and in religion, if
I make any ; and if not, that I may detect my errors or my

sins before they get too fast a hold on me. And I pray unto that God who has given me a desire to work out my salvation by watchfulness and care, that He will, in the first place, by the blessed influence of His Holy Spirit, open my eyes, that I may see the vices, the errors, the follies, and the unprofitableness of my past life; that He will, in the next place, give me a real, heartfelt aversion to whatever I find amiss within me; and in the last place, give me strength to desert my evil ways, correct and amend my heart, and grow daily in the love of Him and His true and holy religion: this I beg in the name of my Saviour, Jesus Christ. I do think, if I can believe my heart, that I have really a love for religion, and an earnest, sincere desire to improve in it. I do think that I look upon it as my best hope and joy in this life, as well as the only foundation of the life to come. This radical principle I think I have unabated, but I confess with sorrow that I have not felt it as lively during the latter part of this year as I have at other times. For this I ask pardon of my God, and for its cure I look to His assisting grace, to the conversation of pious persons, and to reading books of deep, practical religion. Of what are commonly called vices I have not been guilty, I have had no temptation to them; but I do not therefore think myself innocent in the sight of God (God forbid!). Many indeed are my sins of omission; grievous must be in the sight of my God the defects of all my services, the imperfections in all my duties. I have made many resolutions about the better discharge of my duty as a clergyman, but hitherto I have not put them in practice; and here I record against myself that I think myself bound to personal individual exhortation to those persons that are within my cure, to endeavour to assist my public instruction by private admonition. As to my private duties as a Christian, I find myself now, as I have found at all former examinations, very deficient in the duty of prayer; it is still cold, formal, and lifeless, but, I trust, not quite in as great a degree as formerly. I mean to assist myself by not adhering in my private devotions to set forms, but endeavouring to habituate myself really to speak from the overflowing of my heart to God. Let me ask my conscience, How have I used that greatest talent that God gives us all, and of which no doubt He will expect an account, I mean my time ? In this point I cannot greatly charge myself with sins of commission. I do not spend it on things sinful, or even on mere amusement; but how much better might I employ it, particularly by constantly getting up early, and getting more instruction for myself before breakfast ! Let me, then, resolve to do this constantly for the future, and not amuse myself with bad excuses for neglecting it.'

' 21st April 1810.—Thanks be to God Almighty, who has preserved me in health and strength since Christmas, when I last prepared myself for the holy communion, I come now again in His name to look into the state of my soul, and to write down the state in which I find it. May God disperse the clouds of self-complacency which may blind me, and enable me to see through that mist the sad number of my sins, my negligences, and ignorances, through Jesus Christ our Lord. Alas ! I have still pretty nearly the same account to give of myself which I had the last time. The most pleasing thing to my view is, that I flatter myself that religion is my greatest object, and that which I have most at heart; but when I look for proof of this, how little satisfaction do I get! In prayer, I rather hope than seriously think that I am improved. I feel great continued wanderings in public worship, which I know it is my duty to overcome. In private, besides wandering and inattention when I adhere to the words I am used to, I feel an almost total incapacity to pray from the momentary impulse of the heart, as if I did not know my wants, or believe that prayer to God was the most likely means to have them relieved. In short, my devotions are cold and lifeless, and, I fear, must rather increase the sum of my guilt in the sight of God. I must seek a remedy for this. My thoughts are not under due restraint; they are often vain. Was all right within, this could not be the case. Nothing will correct this but a more hearty devotion to God, which will so occupy the mind with things heavenly and pious, as to leave no room for the author of all evil to suggest such thoughts. What lies heaviest upon my conscience is, the dreadful deficiency in the performance of my duty as a clergyman. If nothing but a change of scene can change my habits, I am bound to go to any situation, however disagreeable, rather than remain incurring guilt. In the one I refused, I think, in the main, I acted conscientiously; but still I fear the Searcher of hearts must see that I had too great a regard to my self-gratification. I fear, upon the whole, I have not improved; my time is not better spent, though I am up more early; and I have much indeed for which to ask forgiveness, through

B

the merits of my Saviour.   At this holy sacrament, then, I
hope to get pardon for the past, and, what I equally stand
in need of, grace and strength for the future; for I well
know that the true Christian will not be stationary, but
always advancing towards higher degrees of perfection.'

'10th June 1810.—O Lord God, who didst as at this time
send the miraculous gift of the Holy Ghost upon Thy first
disciples, in fulfilment of Thy promise to them, and who
hast promised not to leave those that call upon Thee comfortless, but to give Thy Holy Spirit to those that ask it,—
most mercifully grant Thy Holy Spirit to me this day, to
open the eyes of my mind, and enable me to see where I
have erred from Thy ways, and how I shall return to the
paths I have deserted, through Jesus Christ our Lord.
Amen.

' This day is indeed a day of humiliation and sorrow to
me.   God grant that it may be useful, notwithstanding.   I
have read over my remarks on two former occasions, and
find, alas ! that even this exercise is likely to degenerate
into form, for I never spent a more unprofitable time than
the seven weeks since I examined myself last Easter.   I
have to make the same complaints, to offer up the same
wishes, and to make the same resolutions, which, if I were
to judge by their fruits, I must pronounce insincere.   How,
then, can I say that I am sincere now ?   I find myself as
bad a Christian and as bad a clergyman, and yet still
would say, I hope to be better.   I have but one comfort,
that I am not callous and hardened in my state, but from
the bottom of my heart I cry out, God forgive me, God be
merciful to me a sinner, and make that reformation by His

grace which I cannot make by my own strength. I wish, however, to write down that I have determined, before this next week is over, to visit those persons in the parish whom I ought long ago to have spoken to most seriously on the subject of religion. God grant that my next examination may not find me using the same words, and guilty of the same sins.'

'22d *September* 1810.—O good and merciful God, unto whom all hearts are open, from whom it is equally fruitless and sinful to attempt to conceal anything that passes within us, impress this day a saving conviction of this truth upon my mind, that I may know and feel, that whilst I am seeking for the sentiments of my heart and the secret springs of my actions, to Thee they are all known, and appear as clear as the day, with all their guilt and criminality. Let this teach me, that if I am not sincere and candid in the discharge of this duty of examination and confession to Thee, I am a deceiver not of Thee, but of myself. I do not lessen Thy knowledge of my sins whilst I neglect Thy appointed means of getting pardon for them.

' I think I can say that I have done my duty as a clergyman better than heretofore. I have gone more to my parishioners, and talked more in conformity with divine truth. I have seriously endeavoured to instruct the youth in the neighbourhood, though I cannot say that even here my conscience is clear: I neglected it too long; I began it too late. I am now going into an enlarged sphere of clerical duties; I am therefore more than ever bound to pray to the great God for His grace, that I may discharge my duty in a different manner from what I have ever heretofore done—that I may consider myself as the servant of God, bound to give up my *whole* time, my *whole* talents, my *whole* income, to the service of my heavenly Lord. I am still, alas! a stranger to true prayer; and it is the greatest source of humility to me, that the most probable means of reconciling myself to my God is so far from having that effect, that the most profitable part of the exercise is when at the end of my prayers I cry to God not to accept, but to forgive their guilt and imperfection. As to the use of my time, my mornings have been more profitably spent, but my evenings are almost totally thrown away. I have given up some entire days to amusement, but hope they have not dissipated my thoughts from their legitimate serious employment. Upon the whole, I fear to make any conclusion; but as my scene will now be totally varied, and of course my trial altered, I shall be enabled to judge how far my principles are sound; and may God Almighty dispose my heart towards the full performance of my duty, and enable me to profit by those singular advantages that I shall have, for if I do not, great indeed will be my account. Let me never forget, that unto whom much is given, from him shall much be required. My trust is in the undeserved mercy of my Saviour; but while I hold fast the liberty with which He has made me free, let me be on my guard lest I make it an occasion of the flesh, through Christ our Lord. Amen.'

Among the great number of manuscript sermons which Mr. Daly wrote, we find one which was evidently written under the influence of the feelings expressed in this last entry in his journal. It was preached in Kilturk Church on the 2d of September 1810. The text was, 'Jesus answered and said unto them, Ye do err, not knowing the Scriptures,' Matt. xxii. 29. In this sermon he most affectionately and earnestly impressed upon his hearers the importance and the duty of studying the Scriptures for themselves, and of teaching them to their children, and entreated of them to attend the classes which he held for their instruction. It was always Mr. Daly's habit to write upon the outside cover of his sermons the names of the different churches in which he had preached them, and the date. We very rarely find an instance of his delivering one a second time before the same congregation. The sermon of which we have been speaking was again preached by him at Newcastle, in the year 1811, when beginning his ministrations to the young people there. It is evident, from the sentiments recorded in his journal, that his principal motives in seeking another curacy at this time were dissatisfaction with the manner in which he had hitherto discharged his clerical duties, and a desire to be more entirely occupied by them than he had scope for in a parish containing such a small number of Protestants; though his reason for the change may probably have been generally supposed to be the more worldly one of wishing to remove into the diocese of his cousin, Dr. Cleaver, who had been translated from the see of Ferns to the Archbishopric of Dublin a short time previously. He also felt a desire for greater means of spiritual improvement to himself than he had hitherto been able to enjoy. In the year 1810, Mr. Daly was appointed to the curacy of Newcastle, in the County Wicklow, where he remained for four

years, residing with his mother and sisters at Bromley.
During his ministry there they attended the church of
Newcastle, which, though not in the parish, was quite
close to Bromley, and gave him their assistance in the
schools and singing class, and in visiting the poor people;
so that it was remarked that the parish must be very well
worked, as Mr. Daly had the assistance of six curates,
meaning his sisters. He now established the habit in his
mother's house of meeting for family prayers, which had
not been thought of before, and which was a very unusual
practice at that time. The next examination of himself
which he records is dated—

'*Bromley, 24th December* 1810.—I praise and bless the
Almighty God that I am still, by His grace, in a state of
trial—that He has not cut short my time before my work
is done. I pray to Him most fervently to open the eyes
of my mind, that I may see my real state, and to incline
my heart more than ever to embrace and ever hold fast
what appears to be my duty; and above all things, to keep
formality from destroying the utility of this exercise; and
let me remember that the business is between my soul and
my God.

'I cannot forget that I spent a great deal of time, since
my last examination of myself at Dunsandle, totally without any occupation belonging to my profession, and indeed
too much without that seriousness I so well know ought
to be inseparable from a true Christian. It is true I am
inclined to flatter myself by saying that I did all that
with the praiseworthy purpose of being useful in the most
material way to one I most sincerely love; and though I

am sure that I was not wrong in giving and spending time there, yet I was wrong in living, while there, in a manner that would countenance the idle life the men of this world live. I pray God, through Christ, to pardon me, and to enable me, when next I go, to live in a more edifying way to others, and more profitable to myself. Still I have to say that my clerical duty, according to the idea I entertain of it, and have last year recorded against myself, is still undone; but I have begun to get a personal acquaintance with every person in my cure, and I certainly can see no excuse for not having personally applied myself to every one within it before next Easter. May God give me grace to speak His truth with plainness and sincerity, and them to hear it to their souls' comfort. In prayer, I rather hope than really believe that I am improved; I still have much to deplore, and much to desire of God. I do think that God Almighty is most graciously pleased to open to me more exalted views of religion than I had heretofore; and if I may so say, I am beginning to believe more and more that it is indeed a most comfortable reality. I think I have read the Scriptures lately with more effect, but have most severely to accuse myself of having broken through my so long observed plan of reading a portion of them every day. I beg God's pardon for this most dangerous crime, and I strictly warn myself against a similar failure in future. I accuse myself of a very hasty, disrespectful manner towards my mother, which she little deserves, and which is certainly very wrong. I must seek for God's pardon through Christ, and His grace to assist me to correct this in future.'

'15th April 1811.—I come again, through the grace of God, through Jesus Christ, to look into and examine my heart and life, preparatory to going to the holy table of the Lord. I most heartily thank the Giver of all good for having preserved me by His providence, and prolonged my state of probation. God of His infinite mercy grant that I may improve the opportunities He is pleased to give me, and really and truly walk forward under the holy guidance of His Spirit in the way of His laws and the paths of His commandments, through Jesus Christ. Amen.

'I feel gratitude to God and comfort in the reflection, that since I last performed this duty I have devoted my whole time to clerical duties. I bless and praise my God that I have not neglected my parish as much as heretofore. I have been in the constant habit of making personal visits to the parishioners, though to my shame I must own I have not yet gone to *every* person within my cure, as I bound myself to do on the last return of this exercise. God forgive me my still continued remissness in this instance. As far as I have acted up to my resolutions, I feel most grateful to God that He has blessed me with success beyond my most sanguine expectations. May it produce real substantial good to the souls of God's people. I shall be most truly blamable if I do not go on in that strength of God which has enabled me to do some little of that glorious work of turning the hearts of the disobedient to the wisdom of the just. I am going to begin the instruction of the young within the parish; I look forward to it with pleasing hope as a means of usefulness.

May God bless my efforts with success! I hope I have gained some little in the contest over the world; I hope it sinks in my heart every day. I thank God for it, and pray to Him to sink it lower and lower, and to raise me above it, until He enables me to fix my heart on Him and His heavenly kingdom. My coldness in prayer is still a great source of trouble to me; but indeed I feel that I deserve to be left in this way by God, because, in spite of my last resolutions, I do not read the Scriptures as often as I did, though I never did as often as I ought. Let me now resolve, in the presence of God, never on any pretext, even of the most holy business, to spend a day without reading God's word. I pledge myself, with God's assistance, to more early study, and particularly reading the Bible in the morning. I feel at times temptations to pride, and consequent carelessness in the execution of my duty. God forgive me that vice of Satan, and give me grace to resist it. I cannot say that I have been guiltless towards my mother, though I strove one day to humble myself before her.'

'2d June 1811.—Once more have I to return my unfeigned thanks to the Almighty Disposer of events that He has not cut short my time of preparation for eternity; that I am still, through His merciful providence, in health and strength to serve Him. May His all-sufficient grace dispose my heart to do so, and give me strength to work out my salvation under His holy guidance. May His Spirit, whose first effusion on the day of Pentecost I am about to celebrate at His holy table, be now shed in my heart, and enable me to go through the work of self-examination with sincerity and effect, that this practice may not become a form, but be effectual to keep me steady in the path of religion, through Jesus Christ.   Amen.

'I am in the presence of God, that sees the heart.   May I not venture to dissemble before Him—to lie not unto men, but unto God!   I have not, since my last examination of myself, been absent from my clerical duties; I have had no other business, no other pleasure.   Would to God I could say that I had been as fervent, as constant, as useful, as I have been unoccupied by anything else!   But I cannot say that I have made progress in my great business. Weather has been in my way; but had I the zeal I ought, I should still have done much more.   I hope in this respect to give a better account of myself next time.   I have written too few sermons.   I have begun a system of instruction for the youth; it is indeed my bounden duty. I hope I may have the blessing of God upon my endeavours, and that I may keep anxiously on my guard against carelessness or remissness.   As to prayer, it still is not as it should be, but I hope not falling off.   Still I condemn myself seriously for not practising early rising, as I know I ought, and determined I would.   There is nothing pleasing in this picture,—a dull, sad mediocrity, which is a dangerous state if acquiesced in.   Blessed be God that I look with hope to His mercy, through Christ, for the pardon of my sins, weaknesses, and ignorances; but I pray that I may never cease to seek His grace for sanctification, and to ask for continual supplies of His Spirit, to promote continual advances in the divine life.   God humble me in my own sight, and strengthen me with His

Holy Spirit in the inner man, through Jesus Christ our Lord. Amen.'

' 28th September 1811.—O Lord, Thou hast searched me out and known me; Thou knowest my downsitting and uprising; Thou understandest my thoughts long before. Teach me, then, O Lord, how vain the attempt to pass a mere form on Thee for real service; teach me how vain even the duty of self-examination, unless, knowing that Thou art a heart-searching God, I open my heart to Thee. May God open it to me, through Jesus Christ.

' I have, since my last examination, been constant at my clerical duties; but I fear that God is showing me that I am not as I should be, by allowing no fruit to my labours. The people are not as constant in frequenting the Lord's house. May I take it as a stimulus to greater industry, and a ground of humility, which should make me feel that it is God alone that giveth the increase. In His strength, however, let me go on. I have attended some brethren in sickness; I hope I have been a faithful and true witness. I must still own myself with sorrow to be guilty as to personally visiting my parishioners. The Scriptures, I am sorry to say, go on but slowly; if I expect progress in religion, I must read them more. Let me no longer make excuses for the neglect of this chief business of one who would seek the Lord whilst He is yet to be found. I ought to read all the Epistles carefully, and make remarks upon them, before Christmas. Prayer, I do hope, is slowly improving, though most lamentably remote from what it ought to be. Would it not be an excellent method of kindling devotion to fix some time in the middle of the day for it, when I should neither feel in a hurry, as in the morning, nor sleepy, as in the evening? I still complain of not rising early. I am ashamed of myself. I must humble myself for it in the sight of God, and must correct this long evil habit. Yet, weak and wicked as I am, so as to make me think it indeed a good tiding of great joy that unto me is born a Saviour, still I hope I am not a stranger to the Spirit of God, but am at least a little led by it. I bless God that I have an abiding sense of His presence, which, I think, never escapes my mind. I determine to read this the first Saturday in every month, that I may see what resolutions I have made, and may set about performing them before I come again to examination. May God each day be with me, and give me strength.'

'24th December 1811.—O Lord God, I beseech Thee to let Thy Holy Spirit be with me now, when, by Thy mercy and undeserved providence, I am again come before Thee to examine my ways, and acknowledge my sins which I have committed against Thee. For against Thee only have I sinned, and done these evils in Thy sight; that Thou mightest be justified in Thy saying, and clear when Thou judgest. May Thy grace be with this ceremony, and make it profitable to my soul by leading me to self-knowledge and repentance. *First*, as to my clerical duties, I can say that I have been constant to them, and occupied myself with nothing else. I hope I have been inculcating, both in public and private, repentance towards God, faith toward the Lord Jesus Christ. I leave my success to God, and hope He will keep me from self-seeking and self-preaching. I do not find time sufficient for reading the Scriptures, and particularly I condemn myself for not rising early enough. The same complaint I have still to make on that head. I fear my excuses for it are not such as will appear good on the day of account. May God of His mercy lead me to more zeal, more love, and more faith, and then, no doubt, I shall not have to complain of sleeping when I should be praying and reading those Scriptures which can make me wise unto salvation. As I value my soul, let me not have cause to repeat this accusation on the next time. In the general state of my mind I am pretty nearly the same as at the last review. I think I can say my views of religion are not falling off, and prayer, I do hope, is rather gaining ground; but yet much have I to lament, and much to seek after before I can consider myself as a man of prayer, which I feel confident is essential to a true child of God. I never, I am sorry to say, felt so little alive at any previous examination as at this, something owing to a heavy cold, and something owing to having dissipated my mind this evening by company. I must contrive to be always, in future, quiet the evening of my examination. I most humbly beseech the Almighty God not to let my many sins and imperfections be a cause of His withdrawing His Holy Spirit from me; then, indeed, should I perish for ever.'

If ever there was a journal in which the real sentiments of the heart were written, this is one. How it shows the tenderness of conscience that is the result of the Holy Spirit's convictions of sin! We find him who had always been considered to be a dutiful son accusing himself of want of respect to his mother, and at an age when too

many cast off 'the law of their mother,' humbling himself
before her.   He felt the importance of becoming what he
afterwards was, a man of prayer.   He resolves to study St.
Paul's Epistles attentively.   This resolution was carried
into effect, and many profited by it when he came to
preach his beautiful courses of Sunday-evening lectures at
Powerscourt on the Epistles of St. Paul.   It is much to
be regretted that these records of his feelings on these
important subjects were not continued, or, at least, have
not been preserved.   During the short space of time which
they include, we can trace an evident growth in grace, and
in the knowledge of his Lord and Saviour Jesus Christ.
It would be interesting were we able to trace the gradual
process by which this man of God became thoroughly
furnished unto all good works ; no doubt by the prayerful
study of the Scriptures, which, the apostle tells us, are
profitable for instruction in righteousness.   None of his
early correspondence has been preserved, and the friends
of his youth have nearly all passed away.   It is not likely
that he learned much from many of them in religious
matters ; it is more probable, generally speaking, that they
learned from him.   One exception may be the following
extract from a letter which we are enabled to give.   It is
from a lady, a relative of his.   Who shall despise the
day of small things?   The Lord often makes use of the
weak things of this world to confound the things which
are mighty, and no doubt Mr. Daly profited by Lady
Lucy's excellent advice.   There is no date to this letter,
but it was evidently written during his residence at
Malrancan :—

'I am pleased to hear you have decided on establishing family prayer on your return home, as it assuredly is an indispensable Christian duty; and would beg leave to suggest your reading a chapter every day in the Bible, previous to your commencing them. It is the best mode of producing a preparation of heart suitable to the performance of that holy exercise, and of instructing the unlettered in Christianity. I also consider it as the most likely way to enlighten the Roman Catholic part of your little congregation. Those poor people having adopted a false standard, it must be our business to place before their eyes the true and infallible one, and to endeavour to draw their attention to it; for which purpose it might be well, perhaps, to read the heads of the chapter, and afterwards to add, in a solemn manner, "*This is the word of God;*" and also, when you come to any passage in which Christ is set forth as the *only* Saviour of sinners, or any other essential point of doctrine or practice is pressed, to repeat it, saying "Take notice of that." It does not strike me that it would be prudent to do more than this at first; but if you find any individual disposed to place confidence in you relative to their salvation, or beginning to feel an interest in the Scriptures, a plain Commentary, such as Doddridge or Burkitt, might be introduced, and I shall (please God) bring you a few copies of a valuable little work which I had republished a few years ago, and which contains a simple, a Christian, and a satisfactory refutation of all the errors of Popery. I am sure, my dear friend, I need not remind you that earnest prayer is the most effectual way of securing success to every effort we make for the benefit of our fellow-sinners. We may sow, we may water (and in our respective providential situations it is our bounden duty to do so), but let us never forget that God gives the increase, and therefore to Him is *all* the glory due. This consideration, I know, is sometimes perverted to justify inactivity and lukewarmness, but surely it ought to have the contrary effect; and nothing should discourage us, when we consider that, though to our eye the soil may appear hard and unkindly, yet to Him who worketh with us "all things are possible." Will you forgive this hasty and undigested scrawl, which is written with an aching head; and believe me, my very dear sir, most sincerely and affectionately yours in Christ,   L. BARRY.'

That Mr. Daly did not undervalue the influence for good that women are sometimes enabled to exercise, he shows us in the following extract from a sermon, preached by him in London, in the year 1840, on behalf of a female school society. He says: 'Were I by any circumstances forced to confine myself, in any movement for the moral and spiritual advancement of my country or any other country, to one of the sexes — if arbitrary power or irreversible circumstances said, "Choose to direct your exertions to one or other, either to the male population or the female,"—I should not hesitate to choose, and say, "Let me address myself to the female sex, as, when gained, the most influential for good." Give me, in a family, give me the mother, as the best instrument to gain the father, and the peculiar heaven-appointed instrument to train up the children in the way they should go.'

There was a lady in the neighbourhood of Bromley who seems to have exerted an influence for good over the Daly family, as well as in the parish of Delgany, at that time. This was Mrs. La Touche of Bellevue, who was very remarkable for her great exertions, both in the cause of benevolence and the advancement of true religion. Her house was the first at which Mr. Daly went to a dinner-party, when he was about seventeen years of age. He remembered his mother, who was always remarkably punctual, arriving exactly at five o'clock, the hour mentioned, and finding that Mrs. La Touche was still at her school in Delgany. It is recorded in the Memoir of Mr. James Digges La Touche, one of Mr. Daly's earliest Christian friends, that, going from Dublin on one occasion to dine at Bellevue, he had a most delightful drive in a gig, with a companion whose conversation was most instructive and edifying. This companion his biographer supposes to have been the Rev. Robert Daly. During the time that he was curate of Newcastle, Mr. Daly formed an intimate friendship with Mr. Alexander Knox, who, together with many other educated and pious people, frequently paid lengthened visits to Bellevue. He was a very talented and interesting man, the author of several theological works, and exercised a great influence over many young persons who were beginning to think seriously, but who had not sufficient knowledge in divine things to be able to discern the sweet from the bitter. Mr. Daly was not

C

one of these.   Though loving the man, he had discrimina-
tion enough to perceive from the first the dangerous
tendency of his views on religious subjects, which were
very much the same as those that were put forward
many years later by the Tractarian party at Oxford.   He
afterwards alluded to his friendship for Mr. Knox in a
letter to Archbishop Whately :—

'I sat long at the feet of the same Gamaliel. . . . I
loved that uncommon character as a friend, I admired
him for his talents, and I honoured him for his deep
tone of personal piety, but I feel very thankful that I
was delivered from the erroneous doctrines of his school.
But if there was one feature above another to be observed
and lamented in that school, it was determined aversion
to all religious activity, and a standing off from those
whose love for a Saviour led them rather to active exertions in His cause than to the quietism of contempla-
tive devotion.'

Lady Harriet Daly was a very benevolent person, and
did much good to the poor people about her.   The
cottages about her gate were in after times a chosen
locality for placing the children under the care of the
Protestant Orphan Society.   She had a school of her
own at Bromley, where, during the time that their brother
was curate of Newcastle, her daughters were in the
habit of assembling the girls after service on Sunday,
and of teaching them as well as they could.   One of
his sisters remembers a circumstance which proves that
at this period Mr. Daly was perfectly sound in his teaching upon the great doctrine of justification by faith.   He

had preached upon the text in Romans v. 1: 'There-fore, being justified by faith, we have peace with God, through our Lord Jesus Christ;' his sister was question-ing the girls in her class upon what they remembered of the sermon, to which one of them answered that Mr. Daly said we must be justified by faith. 'And by works too,' added Miss Daly; upon which her brother, who was walking up and down the room, listening to what was going on, interrupted her, saying, 'I did not say that we were to be justified by works.' 'Oh, no!' she answered, 'you did not say so, but of course every one knows that we are.' He then went on to explain how that works are the fruits and proofs of our faith, and that by them we are justified in the eyes of man, but not before God. On his entering on his duties as curate of Newcastle, his preaching created a great sensation. (These facts were communicated to the writer by one who at that time resided in the parish of Newcastle.) The congregation in that church, as in most others of that time, had hitherto only been accustomed to hear from the pulpit dry and cold moral essays. They were startled by the power and earnestness with which he sought to impress upon their minds the great saving truths of the gospel. Many did not like his sermons, and thought them too long. They did not like their foundation to be taken from under them, false as it was, until they were enabled by divine grace to believe the great truth, that 'other foundation can no man lay than that is laid, which is Jesus Christ.' We have before observed that the beginning of the present century found the state of religious feeling in Ireland that of lamentable deadness. The clergy, generally speaking, were as ungodly as those to whom they were sent to minister in spiritual things. Many of them spent their time in hunting and shooting, for which they were not even reproved by their bishops. Mr. Daly, while curate of Malrancan, was one day riding with his bishop; they met a number of his clergy following the hounds, when the only remark made by the bishop was, that they ought not to hunt in red coats. The dawning of a brighter day, however, for the Irish Church began now to be visible. The Union, though it had been brought about by means which were much to be lamented, was overruled for good, as the appointment of bishops, deans, etc., was now in the hands of those who were not likely to bestow them from interested motives; consequently men were chosen to fill these offices for their merits and personal character, and not on account of their family connections.

After a time a corresponding improvement began to be felt in the character of the clergy appointed by them, although a very gradual one. The Revs. W. B. Mathias, Peter Roe, and two or three others were made the means of much good, particularly to young men entering the ministry. They sowed the good seed of the word of God; and they sowed in tears, as they were exposed to much persecution. Mr. Mathias, who was the minister of Bethesda Chapel, in Dublin, was inhibited by the then Archbishop of Dublin from preaching in any of the parish churches in his diocese; and Mr. Kelly, the author of many beautiful hymns, was, by the opposition he met with, driven out of the Church. Many religious societies were the fruits of their labours. The first of these, and the fountain from which the others were afterwards supplied, was the Bible Society. Like a great river, it can be traced to a small source. It had its origin in the year 1800, when a few of those godly men that we have before spoken of met together in a small room in Grafton Street, Dublin, prayerfully to consult together as to the best means of circulating the word of God in their country. They began by purchasing second-hand copies of the Scriptures at Liverpool and elsewhere, and lending them to those who were desirous to read them. One clergyman in particular frequently visited England, for the purpose of collecting old Bibles and Testaments, being assisted in this undertaking by Mr. Wilberforce and other Christian Members of Parliament.

In this good work we find Mr. Daly giving his hearty co-operation while curate of Newcastle; and on the formation of the Wicklow Auxiliary, in the year 1813, he was appointed its secretary. In the year 1809 he was given a prebendal stall in St. Finn Barr's Cathedral, Cork, which he held until his promotion to the see of Cashel, in 1843. The parish that was attached to it (Christ Church) was a sinecure. In 1814 he was presented to the living of Powerscourt. The following extract from a letter of one of his former parishioners at Newcastle, who had emigrated to America, written about thirty years afterwards, shows how much his removal from that place was regretted by his people:—'I did not expect you would have any recollection of me at Newcastle, as I was when there but seven or eight years of age ; but I very well remember your farewell sermon.   I remember the sermon chiefly, I suppose, because during its delivery my poor mother shed tears profusely ; and for my part I thought Mr. Daly must have been very naughty to make mother, and some others there, " cry so." '   In the autumn of the year 1815 Mr. Daly made a tour in France for about six weeks, in company with his cousin and former rector, Mr. Gore, and another friend.   During the greater part of this time he kept a journal, from which we shall give some extracts, which show that he was not deficient in taste for or appreciation of the fine arts,—a taste which he had such an abundant opportunity of gratifying in Paris at that remarkable period of its history.   If afterwards he paid but little attention to these matters, it was because he counted all things but loss for the excellency of the knowledge of Christ Jesus his Lord.   We shall give the account of their journey in his own words :—

'*Monday, 21st August* 1815.—Left London at 4 o'clock P.M., and after a favourable passage of four hours, were landed at Calais at 5 o'clock in the afternoon of Tuesday, the 22d of August.   We left Calais at 12 o'clock on Wednesday, determining, in consequence of the lateness of the hour, not to go farther than Boulogne that night. The country between Calais and Boulogne is flat and uninteresting, but well cultivated.   As far as we could observe, the people at Boulogne were much attached to Buonaparte.

'*Saturday, 26th August.*—We entered Paris about 12 o'clock, by the Barrière of St. Denis, and settled ourselves before 2 o'clock in very comfortable apartments (for which we pay 250 francs a week) in Rue Neuve St. Augustin, near the Place Vendôme, which lies between our lodgings and the Tuileries. We walked out after dinner, and took the Place Vendôme on our way to the Tuileries. The Place struck me as magnificent, and the column in the centre, which was erected by Buonaparte to commemorate his exploits, as very beautiful. It is entirely of bronze, the base and shaft sculptured all over with his military achievements. His statue, which surmounted the column, has been removed, and is at present replaced by the white flag. We proceeded from hence to the Tuileries, which I thought a *tout ensemble* worthy of a great monarchy. It strikes me as superior to St. James' Park, as it is more of a piece. The exterior of the Palace is very noble; it makes me blush for St. James', and does not raise my opinion of Carlton House. We walked through the Palace into the Place du Carrousel, which is magnificent. L'Arc de Triomphe, on the side opposite the Palace, has a grand effect; but it appears to me to be too much loaded with ornament. There is also a good deal of gilding, which, I think, looks paltry. It is surmounted by four horses, wrested from Italy by the French Republic. They are said to be beautiful, but they were placed too high for my eyes. The car is empty, which has given rise to a pun on the ex-Emperor: " Le char l'attend "—" Charlatan."

'*Monday, 28th August.*—After breakfast our party went to the Louvre, which more than answered all my expectations, great as they were from everything I had heard.

We first looked at the statues, particularly at the Apollo Belvidere, the Venus de Medici, the Laocoon, and the Dying Gladiator. The Apollo struck me most; its grace and dignity are beyond conception. There is an expression of pain in every muscle of the Laocoon which is truly astonishing. Every one has heard, and of course must acknowledge, the Venus to be a *chef d'œuvre;* but to my taste it was not so striking as the Apollo, the Laocoon, or even as the Dying Gladiator. By what I hear, it grows upon you as you examine it attentively, and I mean to pursue that plan. We ascended by a noble staircase to the Gallery, which it is no exaggeration to call the first in size in the world. It is said to be 1300 feet in length, and still contains the choicest productions of the painter, though a few have been taken away by those to whom they of right belonged. Those taken away belong for the most part to the Flemish school. The "Transfiguration," by Raphael, is pointed out as one of the finest pictures there; and it is undoubtedly very striking, but, in my humble judgment, fails in an important particular. But it is a failure which must necessarily attend all attempts of mortals to represent the Divinity. The "Transfiguration" undertakes to show you the Second Person of the Trinity in all His glory; and what human power can perform that? I was greatly struck with the "Madonna," by Raphael, which stands next to the "Madonna delle Sedia," by the same artist (there is a doubt whether the latter is the original), but which in my opinion exceeds it. The expression of the countenance is more suited to the character of the Virgin than that of the "delle Sedia," which is that of a sprightly young woman, who does not seem conscious that she carries our Saviour in her arms. As we went from the Louvre, I had a full view of the four horses which stand on the Arc de Triomphe, in the Place du Carrousel. The figures of the horses and of their attendants are really admirable, but their effect is injured by the gilding.

'*Saturday, 2d September.*—We visited the Luxembourg. The gardens are fine; the exterior of the building is nothing striking, but the interior is noble. The staircase is extremely fine, but its effect is somewhat injured by a railing to assist those who go up and down. It is filled with the statues of the principal persons of the Revolution. In it the Chamber of Peers assembled; and perhaps there is no palace in France which exhibits the craft of Buonaparte more than the Luxembourg: it is filled with everything in sculpture and painting which can set him off to advantage, and throw the Bourbons into the background. To remedy this, it has been thought advisable to cover the pictures and take away Buonaparte's statue, which stood in the Hall of Audience, next to the Chamber of Peers. This seems bad policy. It is said, however, that it is done preparatory to their entire removal. It was not thought fit to suffer the achievements of the usurper to remain in a royal palace; but it is said they are to be preserved for the glory of France, and put up in some other place. The *conducteur* gave us a specimen of Buonaparte's impatience when giving audience; no excuse would be received when he gave his orders; his answer was, "Il faut aller, il faut aller."

'*3d September.*—Went to Versailles, which more than answered my expectations. It is indeed a most noble palace, and the gardens fully equal to it; the Opera House very fine; the Chapel equally so; the Grand Gallery most superb—though not the sixth part so long as the Gallery of the Louvre, it far exceeds it in symmetry. I shall not attempt to describe either the pictures or the statues, but I cannot omit to mention that the door was pointed out to me through which poor Marie Antoinette made her escape from the Parisian assassins. It is somewhat surprising that the Library, which is very fine, was untouched during the Revolution. The French claim the character of " savants;" I wonder they did not make that a pretext for plundering the books.

'*7th September.*—Saw the model of the elephant on the site of the Bastile. It is of plaster, and is 54 feet high; it is said to be well proportioned, but one cannot judge of that from so near a view. Buonaparte's plan was to make a canal for the distribution of water to the city. This canal was to pass under an arched pedestal, upon which an elephant of that size, and made of bronze, was to be placed, out of whose tusks the water was to play. The idea was certainly grand, and the figure, if well executed, when seen at the proper distance, would have been a most magnificent embellishment; but he should have secured to himself the empire of the world, or of Europe at least, before he did so. The notion which he must have entertained in determining on such a work was to place, instead of the Bastile, a monument of his benevolence to the public. He had the vanity to think that a work of art, the expense of which must have been a considerable pressure on the public, would efface from the minds of the people the various acts of tyranny and oppression of which he was the author. We proceeded from hence to the Louvre, and took a view of some of the statues; and from hence went to the Tuileries, to see the King pass to his carriage. His countenance is very benevolent, and his face had the appearance of health, but he is very infirm on his limbs. I observed he wore the Garter. As he passed along, some voices cried "Vive le Roi!" but some of the English determined, on my proposal, to substitute "God save the King!" for the French expression, which the King noticed by a gentle inclination of his head, and said, "I thank you." We afterwards visited the interior of the Palace. The Gallery is magnificent, and is hung with very fine Gobelin tapestry, representing some of the exploits in the reign of Louis XIV. The rooms were gilt and otherwise embellished by Buonaparte; and the "N" still remains, as also the eagle. There are some large pictures covered with silk, which I suppose relate to him; but there was no *conducteur*, so we got no information on the subject. I was glad of the opportunity of seeing the King in his proper place, having seen him, in November 1813, at Bath, getting into a job carriage to take the air.

'8th September.—We went to Notre Dame, where High Mass was celebrated, it being the feast of the Nativity of the Virgin Mary. The interior of the church is most beautiful; the Gothic arches are very fine, and the arrangement of the pillars, which are very beautiful, gives the church a grand and awful appearance. It is surrounded on the inside by private chapels, where we saw several persons paying their devotions. There was a private mass celebrated in another part of the church, and I believe many persons were communicating there. The grand altar is very fine, but I was disappointed at the High Mass. I had heard it mentioned as a magnificent ceremony, and expected to see something of that magnificence in the Cathedral of Paris; but the exhibition was paltry, and it must have fallen greatly from its former splendour. High Mass does not impress a Protestant with anything like religious feelings; at least it produced none such in me. The swinging of the censer during the service looks more like a juggler's trick than a Christian ceremony, particularly when two were swung at the same time; for they kept exact time, and caught it on their wrists at the same moment by some contrivance, as if they were exhibiting on a stage. The priest chanted the lesson of the day, which was one of the genealogies of our Saviour. This was performed before a large cross, with candles lighted; and when he came to the birth of our Lord, it was accompanied by a profound obeisance. On the whole, I admire the church extremely; the circular windows of painted glass are beautiful, and, I should think, of considerable antiquity; but I never desire to see such a ceremony again.

'*9th September.*—We went to the Gobelins, an establishment of great extent, the property of the King, and carried on at his expense. There is nothing sold there, but presents are made from it. The exactness with which paintings are imitated is wonderful; my eye could not distinguish the difference in several specimens. We saw them at work both in the horizontal way, which is the original, and the upright way, which has been introduced subsequently. They work from the back, and the workmen are the artists. It is not like scenery in damask, which is done by common weavers, who do not know what work they are performing.

'*Sunday, 10th September.*—Mrs. D—— and I, accompanied by Mr. Blacker, went to Protestant service. It was celebrated in a large church, in a narrow street which turns out of the Rue St. Honoré. We procured seats in the gallery, directly opposite the reading-desk and pulpit. The attendant procured us books, containing a very good French version of the Psalms and the prayers used there, by which it appears that the service is scriptural. The prayers are very good; I could discern nothing in which they differed from ours except in form. The minister gave an exhortation, and then read the three chapters which contain the sermon, immediately after which a psalm was sung—the singing very bad. After this there were some prayers and another psalm. The preacher (Mr. Morneau) then ascended the pulpit, and preached upon the text, "Blessed is he who shall not be offended in me," in French. He appeared to be eloquent and impressive; but his manner of pronunciation was so different from that which I have been accustomed to, that I could not carry away with me a connected idea of his discourse. I could understand detached passages, and they appeared good. After the sermon there was a general prayer for the Church, etc. Louis XVIII. was prayed for; some of the supplications were that the crown he wore should not long continue a crown of thorns. The whole concluded with a psalm and a blessing. There was a very numerous attendance at the sermon, so that I imagine Monsieur Morneau to be a popular preacher.

'11th September.—Went to the manufactory of Sevres. The porcelain surpasses in fineness of texture everything of the kind. They have made some good imitations of lace, which are merely for curiosity, and are not dear; but the fine porcelain is very expensive. Some of the services come to near 2000 louis, and some vases to that sum at least. The paintings are admirably executed, particularly a portrait of the present King; also flowers, fruits, and birds' nests; a porcelain table, value 32,000 livres; a beautiful miniature of Madame de Sevigné, with five celebrated ladies, on a set of tea-things; the tea-tray to contain these was also of china, most beautifully painted—the price of the whole, 3500 livres. There was a service of china, each plate containing one of Dinon's views of Egypt, price 32,000 livres. We saw a very pretty service, for which they asked a sum which would have amounted in English money to about £150; a Sappho, beautifully painted on glass, in colours burnt in, as in the china; several miniatures of celebrated persons, most exquisitely executed; and two magnificent candelabra, of the same price as the vases. We returned to town at four o'clock, and spent the evening at home, part of which I employed in writing my journal.

' *Wednesday, 13th September.*—We visited the Jardin des Plantes, to see the Museum of Natural History and the Amphitheatre of Anatomy. The Museum is a vast and magnificent collection, in which is to be found every animal which has as yet been discovered on the earth; an infinite variety of fishes, insects, shells, plants, gems, marbles, all arranged in admirable order; each species of animal so well preserved, and its posture so natural, that one can hardly suppose it not to be alive; the whole contained in a suite of apartments of great extent.'

CHAPTER III.

HEART WORK.

' Whose joy is, to the wandering sheep
    To tell of the Great Shepherd's love ;
To learn of mourners, while they weep,
    The music that makes mirth above.'

Christian Year.

WE have now come to that period in Mr. Daly's life in which he became rector of Powerscourt, a name associated with delightful and pious recollections connected with him by very many who are still alive, while some—not a few—have fallen asleep who will be bright gems in his crown of rejoicing in the day of the Lord Jesus, who learned from him to wash their robes and make them white in the blood of the Lamb. A goodly company of those whose dust now sleeps in the churchyard at Powerscourt will, with their pastor, be amongst the number of those of whom it is said, ' They shall walk with me in white, for they are worthy.'

To this living was attached the prebendal stall of Stragonil, in St. Patrick's Cathedral, Dublin. The income of the parish was not large—about £300 a year. Mr. Daly had a good private fortune, which enabled him to be very independent of pecuniary considerations ; and he has often said, that during the time that he held this parish he spent much more upon the schools, and the relief of

the poor, etc., than the income which he derived from it.
There was no glebe. This was a great want, and Mr.
Daly lost no time in taking measures to have it supplied.
His manners were not at all times very conciliatory, and
Lord Powerscourt, who at that time was not influenced by
true religion, was very much prejudiced against him, and
unwilling to give him ground to build his glebe-house on
the Powerscourt estate. He was consequently obliged to
fix upon a spot of ground which the liberality of Lord Rathdowne (then Lord Monck) placed at his service, although
it was farther from the church and from the village of
Enniskerry than he would have chosen. His first residence
in the parish of Powerscourt was at the Dargle Cottage, a
lovely spot at the entrance of that beautiful glen. This
cottage is now a very good-sized residence, but at the time
we speak of it only consisted of four small rooms,—a
sitting-room in front, with a kitchen behind it, and two
bed-rooms over them. The sitting-room was so small that
Mr. Daly would often tell how he managed during the
winter that he spent there. When one side was roasted,
—as he was obliged to have the table he was writing at
very near the fire,—he had to turn round so as to let the
other side, which was perished with cold by the draught
from the door, get fair play. It was here for the first time
that he lived quite alone, which he continued to do for a
great part of his long life. He does not seem ever to have
had any serious thoughts of marrying, though, as is always
the case when an unmarried clergyman of good fortune
becomes popular, there were some reports spread upon the
subject, which were quite unfounded. Perhaps those who

D

gave rise to them did not understand the tender nature of the feeling which exists between a spiritual father in Christ and one to whose soul he has been the means of bringing a blessing, and interpreted it as being of another nature. When rallied upon this subject by his friends, and asked why he never married, he would answer: 'To tell you the truth, I never had time to go about the preliminaries.' He said his parish was his wife, and upon it he certainly bestowed his time and affections. His brother had married, in 1808, Maria Elizabeth, second daughter of Sir Edward Skeffington Smyth, Bart.; and two of his sisters were married,—the second eldest to Mr. Godley of Killigar, in the County Cavan, and the third to the Rev. Horace Newman, afterwards so well known and so much beloved and respected as Dean of Cork. The family party at Bromley was now a good deal diminished; but as Mr. Daly had only removed a few miles from them, their affectionate intercourse continued to be frequent and uninterrupted during his residence at Powerscourt, as he was warmly attached to his mother and sisters. On his return home from France he took up his temporary abode at the cottage of Coolekeigh, which was more convenient to him than that of the Dargle, during the building of his glebe-house, as it was quite close, which enabled him to inspect its progress in person. This glebe-house was destined to be for many years the scene of happy, peaceful enjoyments,— not of that kind which is only as the 'crackling of thorns under the pot,' but foretastes of that happy time when the Chief Shepherd shall appear, surrounded by the sheep and lambs of His flock.

The house built by Mr. Daly was a small one, but there was a good-sized parlour at the back, with a large window at the end of it which looked upon his flower-garden, of which we shall say more by and by. The lawn was a very small one, and round it there was a walk leading to a schoolhouse, built at his own expense on the glebe ground, which school he continued to support as long as he lived.

The Protestant population of the parish at the time of his becoming rector was probably above 2000 (it is now about 1600, but has been diminished by emigration). Of these, a large number were of the better class of farmers,—a fine body of yeomanry, such as any landed proprietor might be proud of. Powerscourt has been in the possession of the Wingfield family for nearly three centuries. An interesting story is told of the first Viscount Powerscourt, who distinguished himself both in the civil wars in Ireland and afterwards on the Continent. He was appointed a Mareschal of Ireland in the year 1600; and on one occasion, when Queen Elizabeth gave him a commission to go over to that country for the purpose of putting down a rebellion there, she took off a scarf which she wore, and wound it round his shoulders with her own hand, as a token of her esteem and a badge of the authority with which she had invested him.

Over Lord Powerscourt's tenantry Mr. Daly exercised a most salutary influence, and was greatly beloved by them. The Buckleys, Burtons, Evanses, etc., were most regular in their attendance at church; and as many of their farms were located under the mountain, at the back of

Powerscourt demesne, the situation of the old church was convenient to them. They had perfect liberty to walk and drive through the demesne, and to put up their horses in the stable-yard belonging to the house, which was quite near.

It was indeed a pleasing sight on the Sabbath day, morning and evening, to see all the avenues of this beautiful demesne traversed by persons of all classes going to the house of God, the elevating and softening influence of the beauties of nature helping to lead the mind to holy thoughts.

It was feelings such as these which prompted one of this congregation to write the following verses during a walk from the top of Enniskerry Hill to the church, which comprised some of the loveliest views in the neighbourhood :—

> 'Sweet evening bells ! How sweet to hear,
> How pleasing to the Christian's ear !
> Ye whisper thro' the silent air,—
> " Come, serve the Lord with praise and prayer ;
> Attend the Bride and Spirit's call—
> Come ! all who thirst ; come freely all !"
>
> 'Sweet evening bells ! Thy voice is known
> To those the Shepherd calls His own ;
> And thus, rejoicing in the Lord,
> They flock to hear His saving word ;
> To drink of grace from living wells,
> Where ye invite, sweet evening bells !
>
> 'Sweet evening bells ! Thy rural chime
> Reminds us of the resting time,
> When pastors call their stragglers home.
> Come ! weary wanderers, haste to come !
> Come ! safe within the fold repose,
> Where pasture *ever* verdant grows.'

Amongst Mr. Daly's nearest neighbours were two ladies who were afterwards eminent for their piety. We have before mentioned that the ground granted for the glebe was given by Lord Rathdowne, and it was only separated by the road from Charleville, which was his residence. Lady Rathdowne, or Lady Monck as she was then, was one whose heart the Lord had already opened to attend to divine things, and she highly valued Mr. Daly's teaching, both for herself and for her children. He was, during the remainder of her life, her spiritual guide and counsellor in every difficulty; whilst she, on her part, gave him her assistance, in every way in her power, in carrying out his views for the good of his people.

He was indeed eminently qualified to be the guide and counsellor of those who required to lean on others for advice and support, and has been on this account not inaptly compared to Greatheart, the guide of Christiana and the children in Bunyan's *Pilgrim's Progress*.

Colonel and Mrs. Howard then resided at Bushy Park, which adjoined the demesne of Charleville. Some members of this family were among the first that the Lord vouchsafed to give him as seals to his ministry here.[1]

---

[1] In a sermon preached by Mr. Daly on the death of Theodosia, Lady Powerscourt, one of Colonel Howard's daughters, in the year 1838, he says :—' She always stated to me that she was converted to God in the year 1819. The dangerous state of health of her near relative, the former Lady Powerscourt, appears to have prepared her heart for receiving the word of the truth of the gospel ; and during the season of the last illness of that dear child of God, she conceived she was born again, not of corruptible seed, but of the incorruptible seed of the word of the living God. At that time I can testify that a great change took place in her views, in her tastes, in her life, in her conversation.'

Mr. Parnell of Avondale, in the County Wicklow, was married to one of their daughters, who had died a few years after their union. An intimate friendship existed between him and Mr. Daly, and very many affectionate letters passed between them. We shall here give some of them :—

To William Parnell, Esq.

'DARGLE COTTAGE, BRAY.

'MY DEAR PARNELL,—I thank you for everything in your letter but for supposing that you needed an excuse for the length of it. Is it an excuse for one of its perfections ? . . . Before I go to graver matters, I would tell you that Mr. K—— has gone off the bargain, and will not give me his place for this summer, so that I must put up with a little hovel beyond Charleville; unless I can persuade my uncle to take Bushy, and you can persuade the Howards to part with it; in which case I shall quarter myself upon him, and live very comfortably. . . . I cannot say that I should expect many converts to true religion from a book which should prove that rents would be raised by a large distribution of Bibles. Good certainly might be done to those who received them, but I could see no good in those who joined to distribute them on such grounds. I do not desire to see worldly advantage thrown into the scale on the side of religion; for my idea is, that if we do not get a firmness of principle and strength of faith which will make us choose God and His Christ in defiance of all the world, we get nothing. We cannot serve God and Mammon; we must choose, and it

is of every importance to our own comfort to have that
choice distinct and decided, and not to leave us thinking
we are serving God when in fact we are serving our
worldly interest. Wealth can do very little to promote
religion; it is very apt to pollute the very source. I am
very happy in thinking that you are reading the New
Testament, and with interest; for I cannot conceive any
one to read it without prejudice and not be made a real
Christian by it. I suppose, of course, that it is not
done out of formality; for I look upon formality to be
a greater enemy to religion than even scepticism itself.
Reason may beat a man out of his scepticism; but the
formalist does not alarm or offend reason, and he feeds his
pride in his way, perhaps, as surely as the sceptic does his.
The humbled mind that goes to God's word will, I am
convinced, find there instruction, edification, and consolation. He will find there what the soul longs for, for
himself and others,—a prescribed means of acceptance for
every sinner, an assured hope of an inheritance that will
not fade away, and the most comforting promise of divine
aid and assistance to carry him safely through the land of
his pilgrimage. He will find innumerable passages all
speaking in unison with that which says, "Fear not, little
flock, for it is your Father's good pleasure to give you the
kingdom." We shall find, then, that God desireth not that
we should perish, but striveth to bring us to repentance,
to turn us that we may live, and hath prepared a reward
for the righteous as surely as there is a God that judgeth
the earth. I am rejoiced to hear that Mrs. Howard is
become more resigned, and hope indeed that her amiable

daughters may be a comfort to her tender, affectionate spirit; but I hope she may ever keep in mind that they too are mortal, and mortality is a poor thing for the soul to rest upon: they, too, may go before her. My hope for her is, that she and they may live for eternity, and not have their happiness depending upon worldly prospects, which, we all know, are vain, and liable to change. "Delight thyself in the Lord, and thou *shalt have* the desire of thine heart." For you, who have suffered the greatest loss, I do hope you are resigned; and that when you join the spirits of the just, you will "rejoice in your tribulation," and say, "It was good for me to be afflicted; in very mercy has God visited me." You speak of your vacillation and my steadiness. I wish we had both more of the latter; but unsteady as I may be in my practice, I can say I never hesitate about the wisdom of the course I have adopted,—the wisdom of making this life totally subservient to the interests of a better, of living above this world with a hopeful prospect of a better. I wish I could live more up to my principles, for which I must watch and pray. These I recommend to you.—Yours most sincerely,   'ROBERT DALY.'

To the Same.

'DARGLE, BRAY, 11*th April* 1815.

'MY DEAR PARNELL,—Be assured that I should not at all consider it time thrown away to go at any time to Avondale to pay you a visit. I found there everything I could wish. I might spend my day as busily, as profitably as I wished; and when the usual social hours drew

us together, I might indulge the bent of my mind, and say
without restraint whatever was the real sentiment of my
heart. That is what I call society; not that unnatural
state where form and stiff civility freeze and chill what
should be warm and lively, and when the dread of saying
what may not be understood or relished confines your
conversation, and makes it anything but a flow of soul.
For large and promiscuous company I have neither taste
nor talents. I cannot, like Tom, raise my hand against
every one, and have every one's hand against me. And yet
I feel uncomfortable to sit silent when I hear principles
I condemn, or see practice I disapprove; whereas no one
enjoys more than I do the free and good-humoured exchange of sentiments, particularly upon the subject which
most interests me, and I am sure is most important.

'As to my preaching, I do indeed feel most thankful for
any power that God has given me of doing good; to be an
humble instrument in His hands is the greatest honour
I aspire to. It is a talent of which I feel so deeply the
responsibility, that I do not think I can be vain; and
indeed, when I look for the effects of it, I see nothing to
elate, but much to humble me. Could I do good by it, it
would make me happy, but, I hope, not proud. What is
any man that he should be proud?—The workmanship of
another, who, instead of acting up to the excellence that
is given him, is continually falling short of what he is
intended for; a being who, at the very time that others
are perhaps addressing him with praise, hears the voice of
God within him accusing him of defect and neglect. No;
the man that at one view sees his duty and his practice,

at one glance looks at himself and his God, never can be proud. I shall hope to see Tom in Dublin. I should offer to pay you a visit, but that both this week and the next I shall be obliged to go to town.—Believe me, yours most sincerely,   ' ROBERT DALY.'

To the Same.

' DUBLIN, 19th April 1815. '

' MY DEAR PARNELL,—I really am very sorry that it is not in my power now to fix a time to pay you another visit. I have upon me the complicated cares of house-building, which I am just beginning, and which will require my presence until fairly set a-going. I am now in town, to get the necessary papers signed, etc. But from these I should run away for a day or two, but that I am appointed by the Archbishop of Cashel to preach the Visitation Sermon on the 25th of May, for which I have made no preparation yet; and I must be among my books for a short time before I begin my sermon, in which I am very anxious to speak with force, and by citing authority with effect. As to the annoyance of children, you need never mention that to me, as I really am not annoyed by them; with yours I was amused as well as interested.

' As to yourself, it is with the most gratified feelings that I have remarked you so humbly bending under the afflicting hand of our common God. Yours has indeed been an afflicting visitation of no common kind. Was this world the only scene of our existence or God's operations, we should in vain seek for light or comfort; but if these mysterious providences raise our minds and make us shoot into the world to come, we can not only reconcile these things with God's goodness, but even see how in many cases it may have been good for us to have been afflicted. Perhaps with some minds nothing would have so powerful an effect in realizing the idea of another world as the removal of the object of one's affection. We feel then disposed to say: "She is not dead, but sleepeth; she cannot return to me, but I may go to her." We shrink with double horror from the idea of the soul's extinction; we get our wishes, our hopes, on the side of whatever revelation offers as a truth; this world appears in its real vanity, and our heart's desire is that we may walk with steady steps to a better. As to what you say of the plague of your own heart, I can believe it all and not think the worse of you. I am sure you are something much better than a good sort of a good-hearted man. "Those that be whole need not a physician, but they that are sick." And those that think themselves still whole will not seek or value a physician; whereas I do in my heart believe that those who feel their want, and seek, shall find pardon for the past and strength for the future. It is nothing to believe in providence, unless we believe in a particular providence suited to each particular case. I as firmly believe in grace, which is, in fact, providence for the soul. It is worth nothing unless there is particular grace,—a grace to be had by each individual person, suited to his particular case, sufficient for his particular wants. This, I think, is the great subject for prayer, and this the great source of my hope and confidence, that the grace of the Almighty, which He has promised to those who ask it, is able to make me a new creature, to stop open sin, and, what is more difficult, to reform those heart sins of pride, etc., which we had perhaps looked upon before as virtues and noble features of the soul. Should you leave Avondale before the end of May, I beg you will let me know when you are to be at Bushy. If you stay till June, I shall, please God, certainly pay you a visit.—Yours most truly,   ' ROBERT DALY.'

To the Same.

'DARGLE, BRAY, 21st *May* 1815.

'MY DEAR PARNELL,—I received your very kind and affectionate letter on Friday, and intended to have answered it yesterday, but was prevented by a friend, who came to see me at eight in the morning, and stayed with me until eight in the evening; so that, though I generally make it a rule not to apply Sunday to the business of letter-writing, I think I shall not misapply the interval between the two services by giving you some of my thoughts in return for yours. To dispose of comparative trifles first (although where I live is a trifle, the kindness about it is very far from being a trifle), I had a most kind letter from Mr. and Mrs. Howard, begging of me to make use of Bushy, which I shall certainly avail myself of until I can get my new abode comfortable.

'The next trifle is, that I shall, if possible, go and see you the week after next. And now to more important and most delightful subjects; for it is the most delightful sensation that the human mind is capable of, to think that one has in any way been an instrument in God's hands of leading a fellow-creature and a friend to what is his happiness here, and will be his never-ending happiness hereafter. To confer happiness is surely the happiest thing conceivable—that is, God's happiness, God's work; and to God let us ever give the glory. And with the most unfeigned sentiments of self-abasement, and the most sincere gratitude, should I return my thanks to the Almighty for having been pleased in any way, however low, to make use of me for His designs of love and goodness. If you look back, I am sure you will find many kind leadings of Providence, gracious warnings, and merciful, though, to human nature, severe discipline. See God in everything, and it will make the happy effect doubly happy, and the prospect full of hope. I do hope and trust that He that hath begun a good work in you will carry it on to the end. I was by this day's solemnity led to consider much the mysterious subject of the Trinity, and I viewed it not in a speculative but practical way. I hope you will view it in the same way; there is no thorough Christianity without it. It is not enough to believe in one God; we must for our salvation and our peace believe in one Saviour of sinners, as we have all sinned; and one sanctifying Spirit, as we, being unholy, all want the sanctifying influences of the Spirit. Our blessed Saviour is the great Emmanuel, God with us, partaking of the nature of both, the only Mediator between offended God and fallen man; the Holy Spirit, His successor, as it were, on earth, another God with us, dwelling in us, working in us, helping our infirmities. This truth, speculatively very obscure, practically very easy, very clear, very important; the manner of it not revealed, not necessary to be known; the fact revealed, and highly important and influential. I cannot say how obliged to you I am for your warm, affectionate advice about marrying. For your comfort I will tell you I am not in the least against it, if Providence (in whom I believe) should put it in my way; but I endeavour as much as I can to put my happiness upon something higher than any worldly connection. I should be very much afraid of endangering my happiness by joining myself to any person who, not having my views, could not be a partner of my spiritual as well as temporal happiness; and I have too deep-rooted a sense of the fallen state of every human being, and the averseness of the heart from the things of God, to presume upon my power to manufacture a lady after marriage. But if Providence should throw in my way any one that I had reason to think would help me on towards heaven, strengthen me when I am weak, warm me when I am cold, and soften me when I am harsh, I should consider it a great addition to the many mercies God has graciously poured upon me since I was born. I love, I admire the sweet charities of domestic life; though, perhaps, seeing an imperfect, partial specimen of them put forward, as if they hindered the possessor from standing in need of anything higher, has made me jealous, and rather too much afraid of giving them any praise. Besides, no duties of the second table are a substitute for the higher duties of the first; my wish is to see both put in their right place, and both kept. I have come almost to the end of my visitation sermon; to-morrow and next day I must revise it, and go to town.

I hope nothing will prevent me from seeing you the week after this. I mean to call, before I go to town, at Bushy, to settle about going there on my return.—Yours most affectionately, 'ROBERT DALY.'

In the valley between Bushy Park and Powerscourt a pretty little place comes in, called Tinnehinch, where old Mrs. Grattan (widow of the famous Henry Grattan) and her daughter lived. Lord and Lady Powerscourt were constantly resident, and were frequently visited by Lady Powerscourt's brother, Lord Jocelyn (afterwards so well known as the Earl of Roden), and his wife; also by her sister, Lady Anne Jocelyn. To all these persons (none of whom are now alive) Mr. Daly's ministry was made useful in the most remarkable manner; and among these high-born people was he allowed first to see the fruits of his faithful preaching and affectionate private exhortations.

St. Paul, in writing to the Corinthians, tells them that in the Christian calling 'not many noble are called.' The state of this parish at the time we speak of seems to have been an exception to this general rule. Amongst them were found many who, though not poor in worldly things, were rich in faith as well as poor in spirit.

There was something peculiarly genuine in the religion of the early Christians of this century; it appeared to be with them a principle never lost sight of, which guided their every thought and every action, and the tone of heavenly-mindedness breathed through their letters is truly delightful. Religion was not then fashionable, its language was not in every one's mouth, there was less temptation to profess what they did not feel; consequently those who did make a profession of religion were only those who were constrained by the love of Christ to live not to themselves, but to Him who had died and given Himself for them.

In the summer of 1818, a lady who was living at Bray, having heard much of Mr. Daly's preaching, drove over to Powerscourt Church to hear him.   His sermon that day is well remembered by her, and was a most impressive one, on Deut. iv. 29 : 'If from hence thou shalt seek the Lord thy God, thou shalt find Him, if thou seek Him with all thy heart and with all thy soul.'   At this sermon Lady Jocelyn was present, and was so much affected by the feelings which it gave rise to in her heart as to be obliged to leave the church.   That these feelings were not like the early dew, which passes away, was afterwards proved. Her husband wrote to Mr. Daly a short time afterwards :—

'I assure you Lady Jocelyn does not at all seem to me to have lost that thirst for the knowledge of God, or that sense of her own unworthiness, which you witnessed at Powerscourt.   It is a delightful state of mind for one to be in, as it is sure, if sincere, to be productive of the Christian's real comfort and unshaken hope.   I would give anything to feel as she has done, and does, as it is such a satisfactory test of the grace of God having come upon her.'

A short time after the date of this letter, Lord and Lady Powerscourt, with their two children and Lady Anne Jocelyn, went abroad for Lady Powerscourt's health : her complaint was consumption of the lungs.   She spent two winters at Madeira, and before leaving Powerscourt begged of Mr. Daly to keep up a constant correspondence with her on religious subjects, in order to be the means, under God, of perfecting that good work which she trusted had been begun in her heart. She seems to have possessed in a remarkable degree that first and last of Christian graces, as St. Augustine considered it,—humility, which is shown in her last letters. Just before setting out on her first voyage, she writes to him:—

'PORTSMOUTH, 26th October.

'As we are quite uncertain when we shall be hurried away, I take this moment to write a few lines to my dear friend. My heart was so full the last time I shook hands with you, I could not tell you what I felt for all your quite unmerited kindness, and for your anxiety for my ever-lasting happiness. But I know the best return I can make is to benefit by all the blessed truths you spoke to us; and I pray constantly that they may become rooted within me, and that I may be allowed to praise that merciful Saviour with you hereafter, who have worked indeed to lead a wandering ignorant sheep to His fold. . . .'

The change in Lord Powerscourt's feelings not only towards Mr. Daly, but (through the blessing of God on his ministry) on the subject of religion generally, is evident from his letters written at this time. Abundant evidence was given by him afterwards of his devoted zeal in the cause of Christ: to one religious society he gave in his lifetime £3000, and bequeathed a very large sum of money in his will, to be spent, as he expressed it, in His 'Master's service.'

E

Alluding to Mr. Daly's having been offered the Deanery of Cashel, Lord Powerscourt writes thus :—

'MADEIRA, 6th March 1820.

'MY DEAR MR. DALY,—   .   .   .   .

I am selfish enough rather to be glad that you should remain as you are, though I trust, if it were for the good of souls that any such change should take place, that God who watches over His true Church would still take a spiritual care of those who in your parish have been turned to Him. But even for your own sake, unless we are sure that God calls us, it must be painful for a minister of Christ to leave a scene where God seems to be continually blessing his labours, for a change which must always be uncertain. And when we consider how Church preferment is usually disposed of, the worldly chances are, that the want of a zealous spiritual pastor would be dreadfully felt. We must feel every day more and more how God overrules everything for our good, if not to our liking at the time, at least spiritually speaking. I remember perfectly well my *anger* and *pride* at the time of your appointment to the living of Powerscourt, having applied for it for a good-humoured, amiable person, whom I cannot be sufficiently thankful did not get it by my means, as all his accomplishments are utterly worldly; and the parish of Powerscourt would, in all probability, had I then been successful, not have possessed, or scarcely, one spiritual soul in it. When I reflect on the blessing that has evidently attended your labours, by the accompanying Spirit shed so much abroad in our very blessed parish, of which, under God, we ought to look to a conscientious clergyman as the means, how can I be too glad of the failure of my plans and worldly views? . . . —Believe me, my dear Mr. Daly, with the greatest truth, most affectionately yours, 'POWERSCOURT.'

On the 25th June, but a few months after the receipt of this letter, Mr. Daly was called upon to preach Lady Powerscourt's funeral sermon in Powerscourt Church. She died at sea on her passage from Madeira. The following was addressed at this time to Lady Powerscourt's brother :—

To the Earl of Roden.

'POWERSCOURT GLEBE, 12*th July* 1820.

' MY VERY DEAR FRIEND,—It may at first appear strange that you should not before this have heard a word from me about the sermon you expected, or about the heavy trial that the mysterious providence of God has sent to you. I am sure, though you may not have accounted for my silence, you have not suspected me of being either totally forgetful or unfeeling. It was on my return from Abbeyleix, just as I was going to write and send the sermon, that I heard the afflicting intelligence. I was not prepared for such a blow to my dear friends (for such I know you and Lady Anne allow me to call you). I trembled at the thought of their being oppressed with over-much sorrow. I did not know how or where a letter might find you. I knew it was no time to send you the sermon; I therefore have put it to the press here, and hope

to get it neatly done. I have also kept the prayers Lady
Anne was so good as to give me, until I was sure of your
movements. I have since been grieved to hear of the
effect of the very severe shock upon yourself and your
dear sister's delicate and weak frame. But why should
we not trust God? Why cannot we say, "He doeth all
things well"? Why not believe that word of Scripture,
as true as any other, "Whom the Lord loveth He
chasteneth"? I know no one to go to for comfort when
one feels low, or depressed, or sorrowful, like dear Lord
Powerscourt. He has such strong, such lively faith; he
feels such a reality in these things; he has such warm
affection for his friends; he loves you and Lady Anne so
dearly. And yet, merely through the power of faith, he is
not the least uneasy; he can say, as you did once to my
great comfort, "It is the Lord's work, and it must end
well." "And suppose," said he, with tears in his eyes,
"it did kill one of them, when are we so fit to go to
Christ as when we are most humbled and most looking to
Him?" In the map he looks at he sees the heavenly
country as well as the earthly, and he draws his reason-
ings from thence in a way that few can go with him; and
he can confide everything to the love of the heavenly
King, the King that is set upon the holy hill of Zion. Oh
that we may every day be more enabled to do so! The
Lord is working a great work in the world, He has a
glorious end in all He does; and shall we not strive to
subdue every thought to obedience to Him? We have
more than we can express to be thankful for, and shall we
not leave the little particulars that concern us to His

wisdom and love? I trust we shall; I feel assured you and
Lady Anne do. You feel severely, no doubt. The Lord,
who wept o'er Lazarus dead, intends you to feel; but He
will bless the feeling, though painful. I cannot say why
you two need such severe and repeated chastisement, line
upon line, line upon line, and such a cold-hearted wretch
as I am is left in comparative absence of all trial; but the
Lord knows. I hope we may all meet again this year at
Powerscourt, and speak of the great things the Lord has
done for us. Lord Powerscourt has been much interested
by, and was a great comfort to, the wife of one of his
tenants who has died of a consumption. He astonished
them by reading and praying with her, for two hours,
at two different times. Wingfield, Mackee, and I spent
two nights at the wake, reading, speaking, and praying
with a house full of Protestants and Catholics; we were
listened to with great attention by all. The Lord is doing
great things amongst us. May we bless Him as we ought,
and ascribe to Him all the glory! Remember me, with
every expression of Christian regard and affection, to Lady
Anne. I can say I sympathize with you in your sorrows.
My kindest regards to Lady Jocelyn.—Yours most affectionately,   'ROBERT DALY.'

This melancholy event seems to have deepened the tone
of religious feeling in the several members both of the
Wingfield and Jocelyn families, and at the same time to
have awakened fresh expressions of gratitude and affection
to Mr. Daly, who had been the means, under God, of so

much blessing to their souls. Their letters to him are most interesting.

The Hon. and Rev. Edward Wingfield, who was Lord Powerscourt's brother, afterwards an eminent Christian, learned much from him, and highly valued his advice and opinion. In an answer to a letter from Mr. Daly, dated 23d September 1817, in which the latter had endeavoured to show him the way of the Lord more perfectly, Mr. Wingfield says: '. . . Discussion such as this, between men " in whose hearts there is no guile," I think may be productive of much mutual advantage. Forgive me saying *mutual*, for I feel how like vanity in me it is, by such a word, to appear to put myself upon a level with one of so much more experience and power than myself. Believe me, however, most sincerely obliged to you for the kindness you show in thus communicating these objections to me, and most anxious that you should not cease informing me of your own sentiments, and of your sincere opinions with regard to mine. . . .'

In later years Mr. Daly was much pleased with an answer made to him by a poor man. He was about to leave home for a time, and said to his gardener, 'Well, John, I have found a good man to look after my poor people while I am away.' 'Oh!' replied John; 'but who will look after the *poor rich* people, sir ?'

The following letter from Lord Powerscourt, amongst many others received by Mr. Daly, proves that many of an humbler class than those we have yet mentioned had benefited by his instructions :—

'POWERSCOURT, 27*th February* 1821.

'MY DEAR DALY,—I received your letter a few days ago, and am happy to hear you found an opening at Abbeyleix. There is very little to communicate from here of any interest. Things are going on very well and smoothly, I hope still growing. Buckley's daughter of Glankenny, that was so ill, has gone to her last home, I hear in a very delightful frame of mind, both from Buckley of Knockbaum, and M'Kee; and, moreover, that the mother was in as good a way. When her daughter was dying, she took a prayer-book by the side of the bed, and said it was to pray for her daughter, who was not able to pray for herself, that the Lord would take her to Himself in peace, and give her strength to bear it. In Bill Keegan M'Kee thinks there is an improvement. I went to see Browning on Saturday. Poor fellow! the Lord has laid His hand heavily upon him; he is greatly afflicted, but in the midst of it all he said that God was very gracious and kind to him. . . .'

We find from the letters addressed to Mr. Daly at this period that he was actively employed not only in his own parish, but in various schemes for benefiting both the souls and bodies of the suffering poor in other localities. At the time of the famine, in 1817, his exertions were very great; and a short time afterwards he interested some of his friends in England about the Dublin Mendicity Institution, procuring, with their assistance, funds to improve and carry it on.

Amongst other useful things which his hand found to

do, was the superintendence of a school for the sons of
Irish gentlemen, which the late Lord de Vesci had established in the year 1817 at Abbeyleix, in the Queen's
County. It was planned on the model of Eton and
Harrow on a small scale; and as Lord de Vesci was most
anxious for the scriptural instruction of the boys, among
whom his own sons were numbered, he appointed Mr.
Daly as one of the governors. One of his frequent visits
of inspection to Abbeyleix is mentioned by Mr. (afterwards Chief-Justice) Lefroy, who was also a governor of
the institution. He writes :—

'ABBEYLEIX, *Monday.*

'We found Robert Daly here. He preached for us
yesterday in his usual excellent style, and has been our
delight and edification, as well out of the pulpit as in it.'

In April of the same year Mr. Lefroy dwells at length
upon a sermon which he had heard from Mr. Daly, in a
letter to his father :—

'LEESON STREET, 1*st April.*

'. . . I heard yesterday from Robert Daly—one of our
best men and best ministers—a sermon which I often
wished you could have heard. It was on that beautiful
Psalm (the 23d): "The Lord is my shepherd, therefore
can I lack nothing. He shall feed me in a green pasture,
and lead me forth beside the waters of comfort."'

It was about this time that Colonel Howard's brother, the
Hon. and Rev. Bullen Howard, besought of Mr. Daly several

times to sit for his picture, but always received the same answer, that he had not time. At last, upon his renewing his entreaties upon the subject, Mr. Daly said: 'Well, I am collecting money for the building of a church at Killegar, in a district where it is very much wanting. If you will give me £50 towards this object, I will sit for my picture.' 'Done,' said Mr. Howard. Accordingly the picture was painted. It is in the possession of the Howard family, and is the only likeness that was ever taken of him in his younger days.

To the building of this church at Killegar Mr. Daly gave £100; and to assist in providing an income for the clergyman, he gave a sum of money sufficient to endow it with £30 a year.

On the death of Mrs. Howard, Mr. Daly wrote the following letter, full of Christian sympathy, to her eldest daughter, who was married to Admiral Proby, afterwards Lord Carysfort :—

To Mrs. Proby.

'POWERSCOURT GLEBE, 17th *November* 1821.

'MY DEAR MRS. PROBY,—I feel that I am the person of all others the least qualified to write a word of comfort to a person in deep affliction, as I know nothing of affliction myself, as the Lord has dealt so graciously with me that He has never given me an hour of any real sorrow ; and I feel as if to everything I could say the mourning soul would be ready to answer, "You know nothing of my sorrows ; they are such as a stranger intermeddleth not with." But yet may I not be allowed to say, that I am not insensible to another's griefs; and that though I am sure I cannot adequately conceive what must have been your sufferings during the long time of awful suspense, and now when all suspense is over, yet you have friends who can weep with you when you weep, and sympathize with you in your loss ? In a worldly point of view, there is nothing to be said to alleviate affliction of this kind. There is a gap made in the world when a beloved parent is withdrawn which nothing can fill; and did we consider our friend as possessed only of worldly feelings, we could only look to the cold influence of time, or the colder influence of worldly occupation, to blot out both the object and the sorrow from the mind. But I rejoice to think, my dear Mrs. Proby, that this world is not considered by you as an abiding place; that it is not your all, and that therefore you can look at even such an affliction as the present with views and feelings drawn from other higher sources. You can consider her that is gone as translated, not destroyed; removed indeed from you, but only a little before you. Whilst you think of your loss, you can set against it her great gain; for indeed I should not know what to say to any person of Christian feelings upon the death of our beloved, if I could not speak with scriptural confidence of their safety. I am sorry that I but seldom saw dear Mrs. Howard, being most of the time of her illness absent from the country; but when I did, she always spoke of herself with the deepest humility, and of her Saviour as the only object of her hope. She was perfectly aware of her danger, and never deceived herself with false hopes, which is so common with those who dare not think of their latter end.

Her expressions of Christian faith and hope were more expressed to Lord Roden, who acted the part not only of a Christian friend but of a Christian minister, and who was in the time of trial a comfort indeed to the dying soul, as well as to her afflicted friends. "The Lord gave, and the Lord hath taken away; blessed be the name of the Lord." Christianity will not take away our feelings (God forbid it should!),—"Christ Himself wept o'er Lazarus dead,"—but it can chasten those feelings, and administer comfort in the midst of them. It can furnish us with many reasons why, when the Lord taketh away, we should say, "Blessed be His name." If families were all to live at the same time, and die at once, in what an awful state of surprise would death find them. If, with the warnings we have of one taken and another taken, we live so little in the expectation of death, and in the anticipation of another world, how should we be without those warnings? Would not the awful day come upon us unawares? Whereas I know nothing so calculated to join our souls to the invisible world as having a beloved parent or friend gone before us, by whose help we can realize another state of existence when we ask ourselves, "Where are they? Where is she whom, so short a time ago, we saw amongst us?" St. Paul had, I am sure, this idea when he said, "We are come unto Mount Zion, the heavenly Jerusalem, the innumerable company of angels, and *the spirits of the just made perfect.*" Is it not an alleviation of our sorrow to think she is now *made perfect?* Sin and sorrow are at an end, and God Himself has wiped every tear from her eye. Surely this will help us to have our conversation in heaven, where we know our beloved is gone, and where there is pleasure in considering her as ever with the Lord, in whose presence is fulness of joy, and at whose right hand there is pleasure for evermore. We feel our loss, but can we be insensible to her gain? It is my earnest prayer that the effect upon you and all your dear family, upon myself and all her friends, may be to impress us more and more with the uncertainty of life, to make us feel more and more that there is but one thing needful, which is "to be found in Christ; not having our own righteousness, which is by the law, but that which is through the faith of Jesus Christ." May it teach us to be always ready, with our loins girded about and our lights burning, like men that wait for their Lord. I got the other day a few lines, written upon a lady who died lately, which seem to me to be so applicable to the case of her whom the Lord hath removed from you that I think it might be gratifying to you to see them. I showed them to Miss H., and she was much pleased with them. I spent a very gratifying hour yesterday at Bushy, as far as I may say gratifying in the midst of sorrow. I read some favourite portions of Scripture, and it was gratifying to think they were received, and gave some comfort. All the party seemed more calm than I had expected to see them. Miss H. seems wonderfully supported, as indeed she was throughout the whole of her severe trial; but she knows Him who is a present help in time of trouble. I beg to be kindly remembered to Captain Proby.

'That you may be supported under your affliction, and have reason to say, " It was good to be afflicted," is the earnest prayer and wish of your sincere and faithful friend,   'ROBERT DALY.'

We shall give an extract from Mrs. Proby's answer:—
'. . . I do not consider it as one of the least of God's mercies to us to have made and continued you our minister, dear Mr. Daly, who always take every opportunity to warn and exhort us, and lead us in the narrow path that leads to eternal life ; and I trust I may in the end be able to thank God that you have proved such a blessing to us all.' The families of Wingfield and Howard had always been closely united, but were now more than ever drawn together by Lord Powerscourt's marriage with Theodosia Howard, which took place in the year 1822. During their absence from home on account of Lord Powerscourt's declining health, Mr. Daly wrote as follows:—

'POWERSCOURT GLEBE, 25th March.

'MY DEAR LADY POWERSCOURT,—I have been so long intending and delaying to write to you, that I will spend no more time in making excuses for not having done so sooner. I have been anxious to be able to give you some account of the progress of those things in which you took an interest whilst here. I am sorry to say that Captain Mason has been very ill for above a fortnight, which has prevented him from attending either Lord Powerscourt's class at the Sunday school, or your adult class, for some time. Colds have been very general, and he got a bad one, which has been particularly heavy

on him.   I fear he has not quite got rid of it, though
he was at church on Sunday.   The greater part of your
scholars attend well, and I trust will be found to make
progress.   I have given your class at the Sunday school
to Mr. Warren, who is very attentive to them, and being,
I trust, truly Christian, will, I hope, be blessed to them.
I was at the school at Bushy on Friday, and found the
children making progress.   Hessy Miller was able to
read along with the others, and seemed to understand
what she read very well.   I have been sometimes at
Bushy, and once or twice we had very pleasant reading
and conversation.   Affliction, so common in this evil
world, has visited some of the flock.   Dear Lady Rathdowne has been sorely tried by the loss of her brother,
Sir R. Trench.   She was particularly attached to him;
and his late opening to religious views, whilst it gives
comfort under his removal, yet endeared him the more,
and so made his loss the greater.   His end was very
peaceful; indeed more, it was triumphant, and has contributed much to support his bereaved widow.   All his
family, who are very affectionate and full of feeling, are
in great affliction.   They were expecting him in Dublin,
to take leave of them for a time on his way to America,
when they heard of his illness, and then of his death,
which has, I trust, only separated them for a season.
What a world it is! how full of disappointment and
vanity!   What a comfort that we have no abiding city
here, but are allowed to seek for one to come!   Oh that
we lived more as pilgrims do, and showed our faith by
our fruit, and had our affections fixed less upon that

which is perishing, and more upon that which is enduring!
I find the people still anxious to hear the Scriptures read,
and I am very well attended at the different places
where my little congregations assemble. I went one
Wednesday evening to hear Edward Wingfield preach on
the Roman Catholic controversy. I was much pleased;
the church was crowded beyond anything I could have
expected. He preached for an hour and a half, and kept
up the interest of the people. When he is more fully
acquainted with the subject, he will do it powerfully;
and I feel assured he has not preached in vain. One
woman, of a respectable rank in life, has come to him
and declared her renunciation of the errors of Popery.
He is anxious not to have the lectures entirely given
up; but finding that the subject, being new to him,
requires much study, he is anxious to get different
clergymen to assist him in a course once a month. I
have promised to give him a lecture against the Infallibility of the Church of Rome, which I conceive to be
the foundation-stone of their building; if we could pull
that from under them, all would soon fall. Edward looks
ill, having worked beyond his strength, but I hope he
may now recruit and take a little rest after Easter. It
is time I should say a little about yourself. I hope
your soul prospers. I have been just reading when
Barnabas went to Antioch; and when he saw the grace
of God he was glad, and exhorted the Christians with
purpose of heart to cleave unto the Lord. This is what
I feel disposed to exhort you to do. I need not, I am
sure, exhort you to turn unto the Lord, for that, I trust,

through grace, you have long since done; but surely there is every reason I should exhort you and every other Christian to cleave close unto the Lord. In change of scene and circumstances there is always trial to the Christian; there is something that, unless they are very settled, disturbs and dissipates the mind. I have always found the very act of travelling and changing place dissipating to my mind. This proves how very weak we are; but even this may, through grace, be profitable to us, by humbling us, and making us more watchful, and showing us the necessity of cleaving the closer and more simply to the Lord. I forgot to ask Lord Powerscourt how the young servants go on, how change of scene and circumstances agrees with them; I am sure they are under great trial. I trust they may receive no harm, but do their duty in that state of life in which it hath pleased God to place them. You have, I doubt not, great opportunities of hearing good sermons of experienced, judicious ministers. Mrs. Proby told me that she had an extract from some sermon you had heard; and I wanted her to let me see it, but she was so conscientious that she would not, lest you should be displeased, and send her no more. I used all my eloquence with her, but could not prevail. I trust you will give me leave, that I may profit by what you hear; you owe me this much, I think. Pray let me know how Lord Powerscourt's health is; he says nothing about himself. I hope he has consulted about that very teasing affection in his throat. I have at times been very uneasy about it, lest, by neglect, it should become more serious than he is aware of. I trust you do not forget your Christian, and, alas! too many unchristian, friends in this parish; and that you pray for us, that the Lord may be with us and give us an abundant measure of His grace. I hope on Sunday mornings that you plead for us, as part of the universal Church that has a claim upon your regards. I am sure there are many amongst us that follow Lord P. and yourself with their imperfect prayers, and pray for your domestic happiness, and your growth in every Christian grace, and your final and effectual triumph over every trial and temptation, until the time when the Lord shall present you blameless before the throne of His glory. Remember me most kindly to your little flock. I should like much to hear something of your Brampton visit. Farewell; I commend you to the word of grace, which is able to build you up, and give you an inheritance among them that are sanctified. Believe me to be, dear Lady Powerscourt, your very sincere and affectionate friend, 'ROBERT DALY.'

Upon receiving the sad news of the death of Lord Powerscourt, Mr. Daly, who knew how truly to sympathize with his friends in their time of affliction, and to 'weep with them that weep,' addressed the following letter to his sorrowing widow :—

'POWERSCOURT GLEBE, 25th August.

'MY DEAR LADY POWERSCOURT, — It is not because I did not feel for your situation, and sincerely sympathize in your sorrows, that I delayed writing to you till now.

F

It is not at the first moment of affliction that the mind
is able to bear even the consolation of a friend. The
Lord's dealings with you have been very mysterious.
We cannot comprehend them; but that is no reason that
we should not say: "It is the Lord, let Him do what
seemeth good in His sight." It is not in our power to
say why the Lord should in one year have subjected
you to so much suffering; why He should have married
you to dear Lord Powerscourt, to suffer with him and for
him during a short season, and then be forced to part with
him. I have no doubt that it was His will, His doing,
for some good purpose of His own, though inscrutable
to us. It was not your will, it was not your seeking,
and therefore more assuredly can we say, " It was from
God." It is He, too, who gave that has taken away; and
surely there is as much mercy in that blow, considering
all the circumstances, as could be in any such bereavement. We can have no doubt, that as to him to live
was Christ, to die was gain. How happy is his redeemed
perfected spirit now in singing the new song, which none
but the redeemed of the Lord can sing! . . . We performed the last melancholy office for him on Saturday;
there were then many, very many, sincere mourners.
They seemed, indeed, to know his value by the way in
which they appeared to mourn his loss. I never saw
so universal a tribute of respect as is paid to his memory
by the whole parish and neighbourhood. We have all
got a lesson that there is but one thing needful, which
is peace with God through Jesus Christ. I pray God to
give us all grace to follow after this pearl of great price

—to think ourselves rich with it, poor without it. I hope soon we may see you in this parish, where I feel assured your sphere of duty lies,—where the Lord first awakened your soul to the value of His salvation, and where He will open many channels in which you may show His praise. It would be a great pleasure to me to hear from yourself, when able to write, how the Lord deals with your soul, how He supports you in the hour of trial, and makes your afflictions work together for your good. I can say with St. Paul to the Corinthians, "My hope of you is stedfast; for as you have been made partaker of the afflictions, so shall you be also of the consolations of the gospel." That the Lord, who has suffered the clouds to hang over the morning of your life, may give you light out of darkness, and make your path like the shining light, which shineth more and more unto the perfect day, is the earnest prayer of your most sincere and affectionate friend, 'ROBERT DALY.'

Lady Powerscourt, in many of her letters to Mr. Daly, dwells upon the fact that he had been, under God, instrumental in leading her to know and love her Saviour. In one of them she says: 'Strive hard for me in your prayers; I owe you more than I can say, humanly speaking, and I would not write to you this way, did I not feel that you are the only person who feels for my soul as I feel for it myself, for we have both to give account of it. This I can say, that you are pure from my blood. Oh! may I still be your joy and crown of rejoicing in the last day; and may all your instructions not cast me deeper into hell.'

In another letter she says: 'What a thing it is, dear Mr. Daly, even for *this life*, to have a hope full of immortality! How sweet for you to have been made the communication of this bud of happiness to one destined to tribulation, the unfolding of which has been so unspeakably sweet and sustaining!' And again: 'I shall yet be a very great joy to you, and I joy to believe it. In the day of His appearing I may have many masters, but only one father.'[1]

Lady Powerscourt, after the death of her husband, came to reside at Powerscourt House, where she spent the greater part of her time during the minority of her stepson. Her life was spent in doing good; but the most useful, and no doubt the happiest, period was that in which for many years she continued under Mr. Daly's ministry and teaching, working with him for the good of her people at Powerscourt.

The manner in which the Sabbath day is observed in a country may be looked upon as the pulse by which to judge of the state of its health and vitality with regard to religious matters. We must therefore infer, from the manner in which Mr. Daly speaks of the desecration of that holy day, in a sermon which is to be found in the library of Trinity College, Dublin, that the state of society in Ireland in the year 1817 was that of much ungodliness. It was preached by him on Sunday, the 23d of March, in St. Anne's Church in Dublin, in aid of the funds of the Sunday-School Society for Ireland. In this respect, as well as in many others, a great change for the better

[1] See Letter 74 of Lady Powerscourt's letters.

took place in our country a few years after the time we speak of.

It is beautiful to be enabled to trace the way in which God condescends to carry out His great purposes through the instrumentality of human means ; how He appoints His servants their respective work in His Church, and at the same time makes it plain that it is He which worketh in them both to will and to do of His good pleasure. In the *Life of the Rev. James Haldane Stewart* we read that, in the year 1821, when laid aside by bodily weakness from public ministrations, he felt his mind forcibly impressed with the importance of calling upon all the ministers of our Church, in England, Scotland, and Ireland, to unite in prayer for the outpouring of the Holy Spirit upon themselves, their parishes, and the country at large, and to direct their attention and that of their congregations to the work and offices of the Third Person in the blessed Trinity. Besides publishing a circular letter to all the clergy, he wrote individually to many of them on the subject, and amongst others to Mr. Daly, who cordially responded to this invitation, as he afterwards did to that of Mr. Stewart to hold prayer meetings on the first day of each year, for the purpose of entreating the Lord to pour out His Holy Spirit in an especial manner during the ensuing year. It is a remarkable fact, that from this year (1821) might be dated the great revival of religion in the Irish Church,—a revival, not merely a display of excited feeling, such as is sometimes associated with the term, but a steady increase through the land of true religion, and of the knowledge of our Lord and Saviour Jesus Christ.

Mr. Stewart was a remarkably happy-minded Christian. Mr. Daly would often relate an anecdote of him, on the occasion of a visit which he paid to him at Powerscourt some years later. When choosing which hymn should be sung, Mr. Daly proposed, ' Why those fears,' etc., to which Mr. Stewart replied, ' Do not talk of fears; Christians have no fears!'

It was also Mr. Daly's privilege to ' rejoice in the Lord alway;' and on no other occasion do we find him expressing feelings so much bordering on what might be called ' low spirits' as in the following letter, written at a time when he was recovering from, and still suffering, the effects of an illness. It is, however, most interesting, as showing his deep humility, as well as his honesty and faithfulness to his friends :—

' KILBROGAN GLEBE,
' BANDON, 17th February 1824.

' MY DEAR ——,—Your very kind and acceptable letter followed me to this place, where I am paying a visit to a most Christian person, my sister Mrs. Newman, and am taking some little relaxation from parochial duties. I feel very much obliged to you indeed for the great interest you take in my health, and for the very affectionate sermon you have given me upon the duty of taking care of it. I agree with all you say, only that on the foundation you are, I am happy to say, misinformed. The very great kindness of some of my friends has led them to magnify my illness, and at the same time not to give me credit for taking the care of myself which I have done. I assure you my conscience has rather accused me of taking too much care, and neglecting my parish too much. I have done nothing this winter in Powerscourt but preach my turns, and carry on my services in my own house. I have done nothing in going from house to house. Your letter has humbled me to the very dust, to have you speaking so highly of me when I know my miserable deficiencies, to have you praise me when I know that if you knew me you would not do so. Nothing so humbles me as the thought that I would not for the world that you or any of my Christian friends knew me as God knows me, or as I know myself. When I think of myself as a minister of the gospel, I do wonder that the Lord should have spoken by me. I understand something of what St. Paul says: "The treasure is in an earthen vessel, that the excellency of the power may be of God, and not of man." "Poor, yet making many rich."

'One effect of the bilious attack I have had has been to make me heavy and stupid, and to disable me from improving by reading the time which, had I been well, I should have devoted to the active duties of my parish. I have, I hope, been very much humbled, and yet enabled still to hold fast to Him that loved me and gave Himself for me. You ask me if I think your confidence presumptuous. I am very far indeed from thinking so; on the contrary, I consider it just, and that it gives honour to God. I think you express it in rather stronger language than we are used to hear, when you say that Abraham in glory is not safer than you. I recollect no passage in Scripture as strong,—none that tells a human being so plainly that he cannot destroy himself,—and yet I cannot say it is anti-scriptural. May that sweet assurance be ever yours to the end of the race, when the angels shall carry you into Abraham's bosom! I find it sweetly expressed in the last verse of Psalm xxiii.

'I could have no greater gratification than going over to you for a short time, and speaking with you upon God's dealings with you, but I fear it is not the path of duty. I cannot be in Dublin sooner than the 10th of March. I think I must stay for the meeting of the Irish Society on the 17th; and then your departure comes so quickly. You grieve me by what you say of your friends, and what I thence conclude of one so near and dear to you as he that is now with you. If I was disposed at all to find fault with you, it would be for not being able to be all things to all, that by any means you might gain some. I sometimes thought you did not make allowances enough for persons not awakened, and that you did not go enough towards them to win them to their true interests. You have, I have remarked, an unbending honesty in your nature which it is difficult to make suit itself to the prejudices of unconverted persons; and it is very hard to steer a middle course, between hard austerity on the one hand,—which seems to say, Stand by, I am holier than thou,—and sinful compliance on the other. To steer a right course requires much wisdom from above, much heavenly guidance. May God direct and guide you, and let you see those you love walking in the truth, and acknowledging you as the honoured instrument of leading them right.—Your most affectionate friend in Christ,   'ROBERT DALY.'

The next letter was addressed to a Christian friend in deep affliction, and suffering much distress of mind :—

'BALLINASLOE, 6*th* October.

'MY DEAR ——,—I received your letter when I was in a peculiar hurry, having engaged in a controversy with the Roman Catholics, and being likewise on the eve of leaving home on a tour to my native county; and this is the first moment I have had when I could hope to give my mind to your case, without interruption, as I could wish.

'I was certainly much distressed at finding you so overwhelmed with grief, and unable to take the comfort which I really thought might be found in your case. The Lord has certainly grievously and heavily afflicted you. It would indeed be Satan that would tempt you to say, "What black thing have I done which makes my tender Father so angry with me?" It by no means follows that those who are most afflicted are guilty of any peculiar sin. It was the great fault of Job's friends that they would fasten upon him some peculiar crime as the reason why he was suffered to be afflicted; but we know from the story that the Lord had other reasons—grander reasons than any which merely respected Job himself. There was the same error in the case of those who asked our Lord about the blind man, "Who had sinned, this man or his parents, that he was born blind?" Our Lord told them it was neither on account of that man's sins or his parents' that he was born blind, but to answer God's purposes for His own glory. It is indeed mysterious why you should have been made such a sufferer; the reason we cannot tell.

We are not authorized or led to look for it in any peculiar declension on your part; but this we may be assured, that all is right. May all our hearts be led to feel and know this! I know that, never having suffered affliction myself, I am disqualified from doing the office of a Christian minister to those who are afflicted; but I know you have a tender and merciful High Priest, who can be touched with the feeling of your infirmities and sufferings, having been in all points tempted as well as you. He will remember mercy in the midst of His chastisements, and when you have suffered awhile, will perfect, stablish, strengthen, settle you. I cannot but wish greatly that you were amongst us again. I know you would suffer bitterly at first, but I think our parish is your providential place, where God would mark out to you your duty, and in the path of duty would give you the measure of His comforts.

'I have been led, by the public way in which the priests have preached against the Protestant religion, to preach, both in Bray and my own church, publicly against the doctrines put forward by them, especially on the subject of miracles. I have not yet had an opportunity of judging of the effect of this course, but I felt it to be clearly marked out as my duty, and therefore I trust that God will give it a blessing. We are going on very prosperously with our plan for employing the women, and I trust the intercourse we thus are led to have with the inhabitants may be productive of spiritual advantages. Our schools still prosper, and I hope that more real good will be done in them than ever. I am going to attend some Bible meetings in this dark quarter of the world. You can have no idea of such a gloomy, fearful state of ignorance as this quarter of the world is in. It is a darkness that may be felt. Oh, may the Lord's light shine speedily upon it!

'I commend you most affectionately to God and the word of His grace, which is able to build you up and give you an inheritance among the sanctified.—Your most sincere and affectionate friend, 'ROBERT DALY.'

CHAPTER IV.

THE BIBLE SOCIETY.

'The Bible! That's the Book. The Book, indeed;
  The Book of books;
  On which who looks,
As he should do, aright, shall never need
  Wish for a better light
  To guide him in the night.'
                        GEORGE HERBERT.

MANY of the religious Societies which arose as adjuncts to the Bible Society, and of which it was the foundation, were fostered in their earliest and most tender years by Mr. Daly's care. On referring to the first report of the Hibernian Church Missionary Society, established in the year 1814, we find that he was one of the speakers at its first meeting, held in the Rotunda on the 22d of June 1814, when a deputation came over from London, consisting of the Rev. Josiah Pratt, the Rev. Daniel Wilson, afterwards Bishop of Calcutta, and the Rev. William Jowett. The origin of the Scripture Readers' Society is told in a very interesting manner in a letter from the late Chief-Justice Lefroy, in which, after speaking of the lamentable and degraded state of the peasantry in the South of Ireland, brought before his notice while on circuit, he says:

'It therefore occurred to me to try the experiment of Scripture readers,—to endeavour to get a number of humble, pious men, well versed in the Scriptures, to go from house to house reading and praying with the people. I wrote to the late Lord Powerscourt, the Rev. Robert Daly, and some other Christian friends on the subject, offering, in order to stimulate an effort on a large scale, to give a thousand pounds towards the formation of a Society for this purpose. The friends I applied to responded nobly to the call. Lord Powerscourt put down his name for two thousand pounds; Mr. Daly and his uncle, the late Judge Daly, and other friends to the cause (whose names you will find in the list of original subscribers, either in our own books or Messrs. La Touche's), put down their names for large sums, and we raised at once near £4000, if not more. We got up a committee of good men, men of faith and prayer, and endeavoured to steer our course by simple scriptural principles; and as the Lord put it into our hearts to begin the work, so I think He has guided us most graciously in carrying it on to where it has now reached.'

The Irish Society, established in 1818, was very dear to Mr. Daly's heart. His connection with it began very soon after its birth. He never failed to attend its committee meetings, of whose operations he and the honorary secretary[1] were the mainspring. Their object was one of beautiful simplicity—namely, to teach the Irish-speaking peasantry to read in their native language those Scrip-

[1] Henry J. Monck Mason, Esq. He published a history of the Irish Society and its origin, which gives a most interesting account of its proceedings. He was one of the friends of the Scripture Readers' Society, mentioned by Chief Justice Lefroy, who took an active part in working for it and many similar associations.

tures which had been printed and were circulated amongst
them by the Bible Society.   This they effected by employing any persons among the peasantry, whatever might be
their creed, who were able to read Irish, to teach their
neighbours, paying them so much a head for every pupil
they could produce at their quarterly inspections who was
able to read a chapter in the Irish Bible; and by sending
readers among those who were willing to hear it read to
them.   The necessity for a Society of this sort was shown
very strongly by Mr. Daly in a sermon which he preached
in the year 1828.   He says:

'I would mention a place lately become the object of
the Society's care, from which you may judge of the great
need of such an instrument, and the immense good likely
to be effected.   On the north-west coast of Donegal lies
the island of Tory, about 12 or 14 miles distant from the
land.   It contains 500 inhabitants, all but about three or
four speaking Irish alone.   There is no resident minister
of any denomination in the island.   A Roman Catholic
priest occasionally visits, to collect fees and give absolution.   There is no place of worship, no school, no copy
of the Scriptures of any kind in the island; and amongst
the majority of the inhabitants, it is said, the very existence of a God is not known.   An awful tempest in the
winter of 1826, which did immense damage in the island
by covering many of the fields with sand, brought the
case of these poor fellow-countrymen before some of the
zealous Christians at Donegal.   This led them to consider their spiritual destitution, and this Society, with the
assistance of a zealous individual, has established a per-

manent schoolmaster, and has also sent a circulating master into the island, for the purpose of teaching a few, in different places, to read the Irish Scriptures, and employing them to teach others. Both these masters have been kindly received by the inhabitants; and what a subject of gratitude will it be for the existence of this Society if that solitary place shall be glad of us, and that wilderness shall blossom as the rose!'

Mr. Daly's conviction of the expediency of making use of the Irish language as a means of instructing these poor people is put forward by him in a letter addressed to the committee of the Bible Society in the year 1824, from which we shall make an extract :—

'I should have readily written to you on the subject of the Irish language, but that I considered my testimony not worth having, as coming from quite a partisan. I can only say that I have returned from my tour through Connaught *strengthened* in *all* my views on the subject. My cousin James Daly, the Warden of Galway, stated to me the preference of the people, taught to read both Irish and English in the jail, towards the Irish language, and so strongly towards the Irish character, that when, from being without a supply of them, he has given a Testament in the Roman character, he has been obliged to promise to exchange it, and has frequently been called upon to do so after a long interval.'

Mr. Daly did not take up his opinions second-hand; we find by a journal which he kept during one of his visits to his brother's house at Dunsandle, that he took some trouble to come at the truth on this subject. He was through life a consistent supporter of the principle that the human family cannot be really benefited, either temporally or spiritually, without religion, and that all true religion must be based upon the truths only to be found in the written word of God. On the 19th of March 1823, we find him attending a large and influential meeting at the Rotunda in Dublin, which was convened for the purpose of taking into consideration a philanthropic plan for the amelioration of the miseries of poor Ireland, which was proposed by Mr. Owen, a Scotch gentleman. His idea was to found a settlement, similar to one which had been established by him at New Lanark, where all classes were to live together in habits of industry and harmony; but as religion, which alone could ensure good conduct, was carefully excluded from the scheme, Mr. Daly raised his voice, in conjunction with some of his Christian friends, both clerical and lay, in opposing the godless plan, which eventually fell to the ground. When, in the year 1825, Mr. Daly was appointed corresponding secretary for England to the Irish Society, he from that time, as long as he remained at Powerscourt, visited England every spring for three months, for the purpose of advocating its cause. This unfortunately deprived the April meetings in Dublin of his presence for several years, which was a very great loss. It however proved salutary for him, as he was a good deal annoyed by what is called 'a clerical sore throat,' which the constant use of his voice in preaching and lecturing, etc., had brought on. It was the only ailment that he seemed to suffer from. If, after his winter's work at Powerscourt, he had spoken at all the Dublin meetings in spring, he would probably have been incapacitated for, and laid aside from, using his voice in summer, for which he had so many and such important calls. In a well-written little pamphlet by a very talented clergyman, entitled, 'The Rotunda; or, Characteristic Sketches of the Speakers at the Religious Meetings held there,' published in 1826, Mr. Daly's absence from them is lamented in the following terms :—

'SUNDAY-SCHOOL SOCIETY.—*James.*—Where is the Rev. R. D—, of whom I have heard so much? I thought *he* never deserted his post; I thought he could not be absent from his favourite Society, to which, I hear, he has given the tribute of his gratitude, as being his best help in his walk of ministerial usefulness.

'*Edward.*—Ah, he is absent against his will; and sure I am, that though absent in body, his master-mind is this day with the Society, and we have his wishes, his prayers, and his whole heart. Unfortunately he is not well. Much against his will, he is forced to absent himself from those meetings, which he was so much accustomed to delight and control. Strong and stout as his body looked, it is not equal to the working of his stronger mind; though the scabbard be of iron, the Damascus blade, in the sharpness of its temper, can work through it. And Daly has preached, talked, lectured, catechized, disputed, and controverted, until (as it is said) the organs of his voice have become relaxed, and he is ordered to England to escape from the pulpit and platform. The Roman Catholics say that Priest M'Sweeny's question, at the discussion at Carlow, stuck like a burr in his throat, and he cannot

G

extract it; but we would say with more truth, if the
result of that meeting had any effect on his health, it must
have been caused by seeing men who call themselves
Christians exciting an uproar, acting as craftsmen, and
bringing a whole town into confusion, as, full of wrath
and fearfulness for the falling off of their gain, they cried,
" Great is Diana of the Ephesians." Concerning R. D—,
we only hope that Heaven will send him home safe and
sound, restored to all his health and all his powers; and on
this day twelvemonths may he be found here in his place,
to gladden and invigorate the Sunday-school meeting.'

While Mr. Daly loved and worked for other Societies,
the one which required his assistance the most at this
time was the Bible Society. Its annual meeting in the
Court-House at Wicklow was always a most interesting
one, and numerously attended by all the neighbouring
gentry, some of whom went from a great distance to attend
it. The speakers chosen were men of ability, but amongst
them Mr. Daly was always considered the ' great gun;' and
though he had continued for so many years to address
pretty much the same audience on the same subject, he
never seemed to have exhausted it. One of his parishioners at Powerscourt, who never failed to drive over with
all his family to the Wicklow Bible meetings, gave expression to this feeling in rather an amusing way. On his
return from one of them, after giving an account of the
other speeches at the meeting, he said: ' Mr. Daly was
himself to-day, as *indeed*, I *must say*, he *always* is !' He
went frequently on deputations to advocate this cause,
and in one of the printed reports of meetings we find a

speech of his mentioned thus :—'Mr. Daly, who *exceeded* himself on this occasion,' etc. etc. In the year 1816 a very clever but very mischievous pamphlet was published by a clergyman, the head master of one of our endowed schools in Ireland. It had for its object opposition to the principles and to the work of the Bible Society. This attack, though ably answered by the friends of the Bible Society, had a great effect in damping the ardour of many of its supporters, and of making all the bishops in Ireland, with one or two exceptions, not only to withdraw their patronage, but strongly to oppose it, although one or two of them had before that time allowed themselves to be appointed its vice-presidents. At this important crisis Mr. Daly, equally uncompromising in his support of truth and in combating error, became its champion. He, however, while he felt that he must conscientiously differ from those in authority on this subject, did so in the most respectful manner. The following letters, from which we shall give extracts, prove this. They appear to have been written in answer to communications from the then Archbishop of Dublin, advising him to withdraw from the Bible Society :—

' MY LORD,— . . . I take this opportunity of expressing my sincere regret, that in supporting the Bible Society I should be dissenting from the opinion expressed by your Grace, and of assuring you that I am influenced by no want of respect for your Grace, either personally or as regards your exalted station, but by a conviction with regard to the nature of the Society which leaves no choice as to my conduct. I feel that, as a servant of God, I dare not desert it. It would be a sacrifice of my conscience which no man could have a right to expect from me, and which I am sure that your Grace would not desire. I regret much that there should be any divisions and differences amongst us and those who profess to be servants of one Master. Praying that in our several stations we may acquit ourselves as to the great Head of the Church, I remain, my Lord, with much respect, your Grace's humble and obedient servant, 'ROBERT DALY.'

To the Same.

'MY LORD,—I had the honour of receiving your Lordship's letter. I cannot deny myself the pleasure of expressing my thankfulness that my former letter should have been received by your Grace as it was intended by me. I feel much honoured by your Grace's taking the trouble of writing to me so fully on the subject, and you may be assured the topics you have mentioned shall meet from me most serious consideration, with, I trust, earnest prayer that the Lord may direct me right. As it is not your Grace's wish that I should answer to you any of the questions you have put to me in your letter, I shall not attempt to do so; but allow me to say, that an humble individual like myself, who goes into the houses of the middle orders and the cabins of the poor, has a peculiar opportunity of knowing the hold the Bible Society has upon the affections of the country; and, in my humble judgment, it does so recommend itself to the thinking part of the community, it is so firmly fixed in the hearts of the religious part of the population, that even could I admit the expediency of our Church never having lent a helping hand to its formation, I cannot but tremble at the probable effects, not to the Society, but to the Established Church, of her now abandoning such a powerful machine to unfriendly hands. Even could I admit the full extent of the evils you mention, some of them never would have existed but for the neglect of the Society on the part of those who lent their names to promote its progress, but took no part in its management. Others might have been reminded and counteracted by their exertions. All, on the other hand, are likely to be aggravated by the abandonment of the Society by those whose influence, if really and steadily exerted, could have done with it as they pleased. This certainly appears to be a very awful crisis for the Church, when the word of God, which should have been the bond of its union and the source of its strength, has become the subject of division and the cause of its weakness. . . .'

Some of the bishops went so far in their hostility to the Bible Society as to inhibit any clergyman from preaching in their dioceses who took any part in its proceedings. It was now a common saying in the religious world, ' Robert Daly against all the bishops, and all the bishops against Robert Daly.' At a meeting of the Bible Society in the Rotunda in Dublin, he compared their opposition to the proceedings of that Society with the conduct of Sanballat the Horonite, and Tobiah the servant, the Ammonite, and Geshem the Arabian, in endeavouring to stop the building of the temple in the 2d chapter of Nehemiah; and in a

most humorous speech, constantly alluding to them as
Sanballat, etc., made an impression upon his audience
which at least one of the hearers (the writer's informant)
remembers to this day. His answer to them was the same
as Nehemiah's,—'The God of heaven, He will prosper us.'
He had promised that His word should not return to Him
void; and looking for the fulfilment of this promise, they
went forward. On the withdrawal of the Primate from
being president of this Society, which he had until now
countenanced and assisted by liberal contributions to its
funds, the Archbishop of Tuam took his place, and continued through life to be its warm advocate and valiant
supporter through all its most stormy campaigns. It was
natural that the rector of Powerscourt should have his
spirit stirred within him to endeavour to wipe off the
dishonour which had been heaped upon that blessed Book
within the walls of his church at the time of the great
rebellion. 'In the Church of Powerscourt, in the year
1641, the Papists burnt the pulpits, pews, chests, and
Bibles belonging to it; others of them took the Bibles,
etc., and wetting them in dirty water, dashed them several
times in the Protestants' faces, saying, " I know you love
a good lesson; here is one for you; come to-morrow and
you shall have as good a sermon." They took the Bible
of a minister named Master Slack, and opening it, laid it
in a puddle of water, and then stamped on it, crying, " A
plague on the Bible! it is it that has bred all this quarrel;
we hope in a few weeks all the Bibles in Ireland may be
used in this or a similar way." ' [1]

[1] Clark's *Martyrology*, p. 338.

In the year 1824 all the energies of Mr. Daly's mind, and his talents for controversy, were called forth to defend the cause of the Bible Society, and even of the Bible itself, from formidable attacks in various parts of Ireland, made upon it simultaneously by enemies of another character from those we have mentioned before. On these occasions two of his leading characteristics were brought very prominently forward. One of these was the remarkable influence which he exercised over the Church, and the power which he possessed of putting down opposition; the other was the beautifully Christian spirit in which he always conducted any arguments in which he was engaged on religious subjects, never losing his temper, or being betrayed into showing personal feeling towards his opponent. The minds of the Roman Catholic priesthood in Ireland seem to have been worked up to a pitch of frenzy at this time, which induced them to forget themselves, and to depart from the wise line of conduct they had hitherto followed, and have ever since adopted, of refusing to enter into controversy with Protestant clergymen on scriptural subjects. The cause of their making such violent attacks upon the advocates of the Bible Society in various parts of Ireland was their feeling that the craft by which they had their wealth was in danger from the circulation of the Scriptures among the Roman Catholic population. In the year 1825 the Irish Reformation had proceeded so far, that in the parish of Askeaton, in the County Limerick, 170 adults became converts to the Protestant faith, and 300 young persons. They first made an effort to bring back their wandering flocks to their faith in the doctrines and power of their Church by pretending to perform miracles; and for this purpose, in the year 1823, brought over Prince Hohenlohe, who was supposed to work miraculous cures upon sick people,—the only one of which that appears to have been substantiated having been afterwards proved to be merely the effect of great mental excitement, upon a young woman suffering from a nervous disorder, enabling her to make exertions to which she had not before felt equal. As the Protestants in his parish were invited in a particular manner to inquire into these things, Mr. Daly felt it to be his duty to put them on their guard. He consequently preached a sermon on the Scripture doctrine of miracles, in Powerscourt Church, on Sunday, the 21st of September 1823.[1]

This and other controversial sermons which were preached at this time, seem evidently to have had the effect at least of putting a stop to any efforts on the part of the Roman Catholic party to gain over Protestants to their erroneous views on this subject, as Mr. Daly rather triumphantly says, in his letter to Dr. Doyle, dated September 5, 1825: 'The public well know that you were behind the scenes, and the principal actor, in the discussions of 1824, as you were in the miracles of 1823. You and your party have been beaten out of the field in both.' This assertion was not answered or denied by Dr. Doyle. The Roman Catholic party, we find, were the aggressors, not only in this controversy on the subject of miracles, but in the

---

[1] This valuable sermon was printed, and is still to be found in some volumes of miscellaneous sermons. We regret not having space to insert it here.

more lengthened one which followed on the reading of the Holy Scriptures by the people.

The Bible Society had gone on quietly for nearly twenty years, when in various parts of Ireland its hitherto peaceful meetings were interrupted by angry opposition from priests of the Roman Catholic Church, who said they were come to express their disapproval of the sacred Scriptures being circulated amongst their people. In every instance the deputations of the Bible Society pursued the same wise and judicious course. They told the priests that it was contrary to the rules of the Society to allow any persons to speak at its meetings except those that were members or subscribers to it, but that if they would patiently wait until the business for which they had met together had been gone through, they would be most happy to discuss fairly and dispassionately the points at issue between them. In some cases the Roman Catholic party did not consent to this without first creating a good deal of disturbance. At Loughrea their conduct seems to have been more violent than on any other occasion.

These 'Biblical Discussions,' as they were called, created a very great excitement throughout the South and West of Ireland at this time. They continued from August till November of the year 1824, and were ably conducted by several talented and pious ministers of our Church. The most remarkable of these meetings took place at Carrick-on-Shannon, Carlow, Cork, Waterford, Kilkenny, New Ross, and at Easky, in the County Sligo.

Mr. Daly took part in many of them, particularly in two, which were held in the Presbyterian Meeting-House

at Carlow, Colonel Rochford in the chair. At the first of
these, on the 18th November 1824, he was joined by
the Hon. and Rev. Edward Wingfield and the Rev.
Richard Pope. Their opponents were the Revs. Mr.
M'Sweeny, Mr. Clowry, and Mr. O'Connell. The subjects
under consideration were :—The indiscriminate reading of
the sacred Scriptures ; whether the Scriptures interpreted
by every man's own judgment is a safe rule of faith;
whether their copy of that sacred Book is not adulterated,
or, if genuine, whether they or the Church of God have a
right to distribute it to the faithful. Mr. Daly was an
able controversialist : he was well read in the Fathers, but
still better in the sacred Scriptures ; he had a logical mind,
which made his reasoning unanswerable ; and seemed to
have a peculiar facility of arriving at once at a common-
sense view of a subject, which it was difficult to controvert.
There were, however, many qualities which he possessed
as a speaker which a written report of his speeches can
give no idea of, — his forcible, energetic manner, his
powerful voice, the touches of humour with which they
were interspersed, and which were always so happily
directed, that they told with thrilling effect upon his
audience. At the close of this meeting such a scene of
riot and confusion took place, that the officer commanding
the police having intimated to the clergy of the Established Church that, from informations of which he was
in possession, as well as from his own personal observation, he could not undertake to be answerable for their
lives unless they immediately retired, the Rev. Messrs.
Wingfield, Daly, Pope, and Jamieson were obliged to scale

a wall eight feet high, by which they escaped the insults and attacks of an infuriate rabble. Three days afterwards Mr. Daly addressed a letter, which appeared in the *Carlow Morning Post*, to the Rev. Mr. Clowry, repeating a challenge which he had given at the meeting at Carlow, when he called upon any six priests in Ireland to meet six Protestant ministers at the Rotunda, or any other convenient place in Dublin, early in January, to dispute for two days on the sufficiency of the Scriptures on the one hand, as maintained by Protestants, and on the authority and infallibility of the Church on the other, as held by Roman Catholics. A correspondence then ensued between these two gentlemen, which continued for some months, and which was afterwards published with notes by Mr. Daly in the form of a pamphlet, and circulated throughout Ireland. At the conclusion of the Carlow discussion, the clergy of the Roman Catholic Church had declared their determination to be present at the succeeding anniversary of the Bible Society, in order to oppose the circulation of the Scriptures. Their hearts failed them, however, and they did not appear. Their retreat was covered by their bishop, Dr. Doyle, who published a letter forbidding any further controversy. To this letter Mr. Daly published an answer, addressed to Dr. Doyle, in which he triumphantly proved that the victory had been gained by the friends of the Bible, an assertion which has never been publicly refuted. This letter, which is a very long one, concludes thus :—

'May this Book, which we would circulate, reach in all the power and demonstration of the Spirit to you, sir, and to your people, and be a light unto your feet and a lamp unto your paths. I entertain towards you no worse wish than this, and I cannot desire for you or myself a greater blessing.—I remain, sir, your humble servant,—ROBERT DALY.'

The proposed meeting was held in the Presbyterian Meeting-House at Carlow; and as the champions of the Roman Catholic Church did not come forward, Mr. Daly and his friends may fairly be said to have remained masters of the field.

Much good arose out of these 'biblical discussions;' and it is probable that, if they had been allowed to go on for some time longer, the errors against which they were so ably directed would have been shaken off by a large majority of the population. As it was, it must have been encouraging to Mr. Daly to receive such letters as the following, telling him of some individuals to whom they had been made useful:—

'MY DEAR DALY,— . . . I had a long conversation a few days since with C. D., who, you know, is not an enthusiast on the subject of discussion meetings, etc.; yet he told me two anecdotes which seemed to intimate that he felt strongly how great a spirit of inquiry had been excited even in neighbourhoods where there are no readers, etc., to push it forward. An old man, a herd of a gentleman in a remote part of his parish, came to his master: " I have a favour to ask, your honour." "What is it, Tom ?" "The loan of a Bible." "Why, Tom, you know if you had one you would not read it ; and if you did, the priest would take it from you." "No, your honour, he would not; and I will read it." "What put it into your head, Tom?" "I want to look at some points in it, your honour." "What points?" "Oh, your honour, I have them all here," pulling out of his breeches pocket a paper as brown as dirty hands, tobacco, and smoke could make it, and showing the account of one of the discussion meetings, with the passages of Scripture all marked. His master therefore lent him the Bible, on condition that he would not destroy it, nor give it up except to him. The poor man, thinking it too good a thing to be kept to himself, assembled ten or twelve of his neighbours at night to examine the points. The priest came in and demanded the Bible. On the man telling him that he had got a great deal of knowledge from it, and wanted to get more, and would therefore keep it, the priest threatened to *damn* him. "Oh, your reverence, that's only human breath." "Well, I will turn you out of the chapel, and cut you off from the Church." "Perhaps, your reverence, you would only be doing now what I would be doing myself in three weeks or a month." Here it ended. The poor man kept his Bible, and was still reading it when D. left the country. The other circumstance occurred respecting a girl of about sixteen, who up to the age of twelve had been educated a Protestant, but, her parents dying, had soon gone to mass. She came in, a few days ago, to the parish school, and the mistress began to remonstrate with her on the subject. While she was doing this, a Roman Catholic schoolmaster came in, and the mistress stopped. "Oh, Mrs. Kelly," said he, "you may go on; I know what you are at. You want to persuade that child to go to church." The mistress acknowledged it was so. "Well," said he, "I am called a bigoted Roman Catholic, and I will give her advice: Child, go to church, and never go to mass as long as you live." On seeing the woman stare, "Yes," said he, "and if I were not afraid of my life and my livelihood, I would never go near them again. The priests, if they wanted to keep us with them, would never have entered into those arguments with the Protestants." This was said openly in the school. The girl has ever since gone to church; and this, you know, was in the County Tipperary, where the Roman Catholics claimed a triumph. I have left myself little room to say I hope you take care of your health, both spiritual and bodily. May the Great Shepherd of the sheep be with you, and bless you. Believe me always your truly affectionate friend and very unworthy fellow-servant,

'JAMES DIGGES LA TOUCHE.'

The Roman Catholic priests seem after this date to have only come forward on one occasion for the purpose of controversy in connection with the Bible Society. This was probably at the meeting mentioned in the *Memoir of the Rev. Godfrey Massy*. 'When another of these agitators denounced the Bible as the author of sects amongst Protestants, the Rev. Robert Daly—now and for many years the zealous Bishop of Cashel — so admirably retorted, by showing up the multiplicity of rival sects in the pretended "centre of unity" at Rome,

and by detailing the deadly feuds between Jesuits and
Jansenists, Dominicans and Franciscans, on the doctrines
of grace and immaculate conception, etc. etc., and the
comical modes in which some of the Orders vented their
" holy malice " against one another, that the denouncer
of the Bible retired in confusion, amidst peals of laughter
at his folly.' About this time the Reformation Society
sprang up, and with it Mr. Daly was at first for some
years connected. Deputations were sent all round Ireland,
inviting Roman Catholic priests to enter into discussions
with them, but without success except in one instance.
In the year 1827 the Rev. Richard Pope and the Rev.
Joseph Wolfe were challenged to enter the lists with the
Rev. T. Maguire, P.P. of Innismagrath, which challenge
was accepted by Mr. Pope, and a most spirited controversy
was kept up daily during the entire season of Lent,
which excited an interest in the religious world which
was not soon forgotten. The proceedings of the Reformation Society were afterwards looked upon by Mr.
Daly and his fellow-workers as bearing too much of a
political character, and they did not, in consequence, continue very long their connection with it.

The Bible Society passed through many other stormy
scenes besides those we have mentioned in this chapter.
It was too good an institution to be allowed to go on
without interruption from the enemy of souls ; but it
has outlived them all, its internal divisions as well as
its outward fears, and it still remains the great armoury
from which all the other religious Societies may furnish
themselves with the sword of the Spirit, which is

the word of God. In the year 1825 Mr. Daly and the whole Irish Church sustained a severe loss in the death of the Hon. and Rev. Edward Wingfield (Lord Powerscourt's brother), who was intimately associated with Mr. Daly in all the labours in the cause of truth which we have mentioned in this chapter, as well as in the bonds of Christian friendship. The latter was his companion during his last tour for the Bible Society, when the tone of heavenly-mindedness in his speeches forcibly struck all who heard him. He was greatly beloved by all who knew him; and though it is now nearly fifty years since his removal, his memory is still green in the hearts of many. An obituary notice of him published in the *Christian Examiner*, probably written by Mr. Daly, concludes with these words: 'Thus hath the Lord taken to Himself, in the prime of life, and in the very meridian of his usefulness, one of the brightest luminaries of our National Church.'

CHAPTER V.

PASTORAL CARE.

'Go with the name of Jesus to the dying,
  And speak that name in all its living power.
Why should thy fainting heart grow chill and weary?
  Can'st thou not watch with me one little hour?'

IT was during the next ten years of Mr. Daly's ministry at Powerscourt that he might be said, so to speak, to have reached the zenith of his usefulness and influence, not only in his own parish, but in his more public ministrations both in England and Ireland. He was singularly blessed in being allowed to see so much fruit of his labours, and, even during his lifetime, in having so many seals given to his ministry. This more than usual degree of success, we would in all humility suggest, might be attributed to the following characteristics of his manner of working:—In the first place, whatever he did, he did heartily to the Lord, and not to men; his motives were those of the most fervent love to Christ, and the most affectionate love for the souls of his people; he could appeal to the Searcher of all hearts, and say with Peter, 'Lord, Thou knowest all things, Thou knowest that I love Thee,' and he was ready to show it by feeding His sheep and His lambs; he watched for the souls of those committed to his care as one that must give account. In the second

H

place, he was eminently a man of prayer. The numerous lectures in the different parts of his parish were all begun and ended by earnest extempore prayers; and for the last ten or twelve years of his ministry at Powerscourt he held special meetings for prayer one morning in every week at one or other of the schoolhouses in his parish; and on New Year's Day, to ask for the outpouring of God's Holy Spirit at the beginning of the new year. At these meetings his prayers were so fervent as to melt the hearts of all present. His manner was as if addressing himself to one that he exceedingly loved. Besides this, he interceded individually in his private prayers for many of his parishioners, especially the young people, about whom he felt a particular anxiety. He has said to many of them that they were remembered by him before the throne of grace. Then, in the third place, his teaching was all founded directly upon the word of God. This was particularly the case with regard to the instruction given to the young people in his parish. The number of young people who seem to have profited in after life by the instructions they received at Powerscourt was quite remarkable. Many of those who emigrated to America and other places wrote back letters full of gratitude and thankfulness for what they had learned there; besides numbers of others, whose progress in the Christian course he was able personally to watch over in this country. He refers to this in a charity sermon for a school society, which he preached in London in the year 1840. The following is an extract:—

‘There is nothing in which there is a larger or surer

return to the workman than in education. I have been much engaged in the education of the youth in my neighbourhood, and there is no field in which the Lord allows me to see so much fruit. I bless God that I could give many instances of young women, who had laboured under every disadvantage that could flow from the ignorance and the bad example, in every way, of their families, and who had no counteracting advantage but the privilege of attending a school in which they were taught the word of God, to be a light to their feet, and also taught such other things as put them in a way of respectably earning their bread, and who are now useful members of society, and heirs, through grace, of Christ's heavenly kingdom. I have got heart-cheering accounts of such young persons, snatched as brands out of the burning, from the various quarters of the globe,—from Australia, from America, from various parts of England and Ireland. They never forget to mention with gratitude the school in which they were taught things pertaining to life and to godliness.'

The following is an extract from a pleasing specimen of these letters :—

'. . . The children of Powerscourt may and have wandered far, far from their friends and home, but never, no never, have I heard of one who forgot that parish of mountains, glens, valleys, and waterfalls, and thee—thee, its beloved minister, benefactor, and instructor of our childish days. True it is, we were wild and wayward when we were under your care, and gave you much pain instead of pleasure ; but the good seed sown by you in our early days has, I trust, taken deep root in the hearts of many. For my own part, this blessed word of inspiration now lying beside me, that you placed in my hands in the days of infancy, has been my chief and only comfort through many a dark and gloomy day. Indeed, I never felt its real value till I was separated from you and all— yes, all I love and value upon earth. Oh, would to God you would end your days amongst us all! We all love you very much. We have wandered to other parishes, as I said before, but we claim no other shepherd; no, nor never will. When they talk to me here of my minister, I say, " No, no; he is not my minister. Mr. Daly is my minister. I am a poor strayed sheep from his fold. I only tarry here for a while; but never shall I call any one else my minister." '

'. . . Dear sir, if you are not too busy, will you write to me? You promised long ago to " write to me now and then." A letter from you makes me very happy; it gives me to feel I am not as yet forgotten by the best of friends. But farewell, my beloved friend and minister; and although we never meet again in Powerscourt, we shall meet where there are no farewells, where parting is never known, and where the tear of sorrow is never dropped; for " God Himself shall wipe away all tears." '

His love for the souls of the Roman Catholic children in his parish led him to address a letter to their parents, in consequence of opposition being made to their education by the Roman Catholic clergy. In this letter he expressed his affectionate anxiety for their welfare, concluding it thus :—

' A better day will yet dawn upon our parish and our

country, preparing for those predicted times when the Lord will put His law in men's hearts, and write it in their minds, and they shall teach no more every man his neighbour, and every man his brother, saying, " Know the Lord ;" for all shall know Him, from the least unto the greatest, saith the Lord. That those times of the universal spread of the knowledge of the Lord may quickly arrive, ought to be the prayer of every Christian. You shall have my constant prayer for you, that the word of the Lord may run and be glorified among you, and that you may " be delivered from troublesome and evil men " (2 Thess. iii. 1, 2¹).—I can subscribe myself, with great truth, your sincere and affectionate friend,—ROBERT DALY.'

This letter was printed and circulated amongst them; and he also wrote one of remonstrance to the parish priest on the same subject. Mr. Daly has sometimes been accused of harshness in his manner of speaking of Roman Catholics, but any unprejudiced person reading his letters, speeches, and sermons addressed to them, will acknowledge that their tone is full of affection. In his controversies with their clergy, he always addressed them with courtesy. Two or three of these were carried on about this time, of which, perhaps, the most important was a lengthened correspondence on the infallibility of the Church. It arose out of a conversation which took place at Mr. Daly's house, and is mentioned by Archdeacon Brien in his *Reminiscences.* Speaking of the strength of Mr. Daly's character, he says :

' He was a man of great moral courage, which indeed is

¹ Douay version.

the highest order of that distinguished virtue. I heard
him say once, " I am not a bit afraid of the devil." And
yet it was not that he in any wise underrated the wisdom,
and power, and energy, and subtlety of that deadly enemy;
but he had clothed himself in the panoply of heaven, and
he leaned evermore upon the grace of Him who had
fought and conquered, and was able to succour the
tempted because He Himself had been tempted and
triumphed. He was strong in the grace which is in Christ
Jesus, and exercised himself to have a conscience void of
offence towards God and man; and that gave him courage,
as the Scripture says, " Who is he that will harm you, if
ye be followers of that which is good ? " It gave him
courage, and invigorated the energy of a naturally bold
and determined character.

'He shrank not from controversy, as the incident which
occurred in Carlow in his early ministry, and which is
well known, sufficiently testifies; but he carried it on in
private as well as public, and managed it with skill and
the exhibition of a friendly spirit. Soon after he went to
Powerscourt as rector, he invited the priest of the parish
and his coadjutor to dine with him. As soon as dinner
was concluded, and colloquial conversation commenced, he
proposed a question to the priests,—"Whether we are to
prove the Scriptures from the Church, or the Church from
the Scriptures ? " The coadjutor, being, I suppose, less
established in the Papal doctrine, and perhaps speaking
in the integrity of a sound judgment, replied: " The
Church from the Scriptures; " but the parish priest,
highly displeased at such a scandalous admission, sharply

reproved his coadjutor, and the issue was a vigorous controversy, prolonged through the evening, partly between the priests themselves, and partly between the priests and the skilful and adroit host. At last the parish priest, anxious to depart, as feeling probably that the controversy had become too hot, begged to be allowed to call for his horse. Mr. Daly proposed that he should remain for prayers, the time for which was just at hand; but it was all in vain. The priest was in the excitement of Richard the Third when he cried, " A horse! a horse! My kingdom for a horse!"—only the King was going to fight in desperation, but the priest, in desperation, was flying from the fight. I need not say, that as soon as he could obtain his horse, he departed with incontinent speed.

'But though Mr. Daly was valiant for the truth and earnest in controversy, and entirely opposed to the pernicious corruptions of truth which exist in the Church of Rome, yet he could act with Christian kindness even towards a priest.

'A storm having occurred on an occasion in Powerscourt, considerable damage resulted. Among other things, the priest's house was much dilapidated. It was necessary to raise a subscription to repair it. Application was made to Rev. Mr. Daly for help, and he responded to it by a donation, saying, that if the application had been for a chapel to build or repair, he would not have contributed towards it, but as the priest was a man, and must have a house to live in, he saw no objection to giving for the repair of the house; and so he contributed, showing in that act that he knew how to distinguish between helping a system and helping an individual, and that he was ready to respond with his means where the interests of charity demanded it.'

The Bible was the only book made use of by Mr. Daly in his classes for giving religious instruction to the young, except when preparing young persons for confirmation : on these occasions he explained the Church Catechism from Scripture.   He often, in after times, spoke of the importance of having the memories of young people stored with passages of Scripture, mentioning, to show the value of it, the case of a little boy who died in Enniskerry of a lingering illness.   Being too weak to be able to read, he said to Mr. Daly, when visiting him one day, ' Now I feel the good of those chapters in St. John's Gospel that you made me learn by heart; I can repeat them to myself when I have not any one to read for me.'   And another anecdote of an old lady, who had not been religiously brought up, but whose heart was turned to the Lord in later years. She one day said to him in an earnest manner, ' Oh! teach the little children verses of the Bible, and hymns, that they may have comfort in thinking of them when they are old, as I am so tormented by the silly things learned when I was a little child, that come into my head now when I wish to think of better things.'

His habits of order and punctuality enabled him to get through with ease to himself an amount and variety of business which would puzzle and overpower those who have less method in arranging their hours and particular times for each duty.   The morning was his time for writing; and the number of letters that he received and answered about the orphans and foundlings located in his parish were sufficient in themselves to occupy a large portion of his time. We have before said that the Saviour's injunction, 'Feed my lambs,' was one that was particularly obeyed by him. Of these there was a larger proportion in his flock than is generally to be found. He was one of the governors of the Foundling Hospital, which then existed in Dublin, and as there were numbers of most desirable locations for the children in Powerscourt parish, within reach of good schools, he had them placed there; and so tenderly were these children cared for by the persons to whose charge they were committed, that it frequently happened, that when the time came for delivering up the child, though the nurse was entitled to receive a sum of money on the occasion, it was not produced, but continued to reside as one of the family in the house where it had been educated.

Mr. Daly was careful to appoint a better class of schoolmasters and mistresses in his parochial schools, fully competent to give a good education to the children of the respectable farmers, who paid something to the master or mistress quarterly, by which means he kept them under his own care for religious teaching, and was enabled to give a superior education to the poorer ones, who could not pay for it. The schools were most excellent and well worked. Besides those supported by him, there were several on the Powerscourt estate belonging to Lord Powerscourt, two of which were in the village of Enniskerry; and Lady Rathdowne had both a daily and a Sunday school opposite the gate of Charleville, which were superintended by her and her daughters.

Mr. Daly held various weekly classes for the young people, among whom the children of the gentry were included. The younger classes were called the ' Miracles,' the next to them the ' Gospels,' while that intended for the elder ones was called the ' Epistle' class. The two former were taught by the curate of the parish before service in the church on Sunday mornings, when a great number of little ones were gathered on the forms, placed outside the rails of the communion table, appropriated to them during church time, where they were watched over by one of their schoolmasters. The ' Epistle' class was taught by Mr. Daly himself every Saturday; and in all these classes, but more particularly in the latter, it was the privilege of the writer of this memoir to receive instruction for many years. This last was a most interesting one, and as we were, generally speaking, sure to have him for our teacher, was highly prized by us; great was the dismay if we saw the curate coming in his place. The subject was taken from the portion of Scripture which he had lectured upon the preceding Sunday evening, about six or seven verses from one of St. Paul's smaller epistles. The substance of these verses was written by him each week upon a piece of paper, divided into six or more clauses, to prove each of which we were to find three references. The chapters in which they were to be found were marked by him, while we were expected to find the verses in them that applied, and to learn them, as well as the verses to which they referred, by heart. We were also expected to be able to tell him the meaning of the passages we were considering; if we failed in this he never reproved us, but would say pleasantly, 'Ah! that is the hard thing, when we come to ask for the meaning. Cannot you give me a verse to prove that? Why, I thought that if I had asked you for a hundred, you would have given them to me.' These classes were only held for about six months in summer and autumn. At the beginning of this season, in the year 1828, on the 11th of May, he preached a sermon, in which he dwelt chiefly upon his anxiety about the young people in his flock who were not mere children, but had arrived at that age when the world had most attractions for them. His text was Deut. vi. 6–9, 'And these words, which I command thee this day, shall be in thy heart: and thou shalt teach them diligently unto thy children, and shalt talk of them when thou sittest in thine house, and when thou walkest by the way, and when thou liest down, and when thou risest up. And thou shalt bind them for a sign upon thine hand, and they shall be as frontlets between thine eyes. And thou shalt write them upon the posts of thy house.'

Mr. Daly was very fond of children, and was greatly beloved by them; he had always something funny and cheerful to say to each child, and these little words were watched for and treasured up by them. Sometimes, when one of the poorer children would hang down her head bashfully when he was speaking to her, he would take hold of the leaf of her old straw bonnet, and pull it up to make her hold up her head, when the leaf has been seen to come asunder from the crown in his hand. The answers of the children at times to his familiar way of catechizing them were rather amusing. He was one day explaining

the parable of the rich man and Lazarus to a class in the
Sunday school, and having tried to make them feel how
much more really happy Lazarus was than the other, he
said to one little boy, 'And now, come, my little fellow,
tell me honestly which would you rather be—the rich man
or Lazarus ?'   'I'd rather be the rich man, sir !'   A
teacher was one day engaged with her class in the Sunday
school, when she observed that the girls, who were generally very attentive, were looking about, and not minding
what she was saying to them.   'What is the matter with
you to-day, girls ?' she said.   'Mr. Daly's mamma, ma'am;
Mr. Daly's mamma is coming up the school !'   The teacher
had been sitting with her back to the door, and did not see
Lady Harriet Daly coming in.   They thought that Mr.
Daly's mamma must be a being of a very high order
indeed.

Once a year, just before Christmas, all the children in the
parish, of all classes, were gathered together at the Glebe
Schoolhouse for examination, when those whose answering
was good enough were given premiums, while at the same
time Mr. Daly distributed clothing liberally among the
poorer ones.   These were called by the children the 'Great
Examinations,' and great was the excitement felt amongst
them in watching his progress round the room, when many
a little heart would flutter with anxiety to repeat their
verses correctly, valuing quite as much *his* approbation as
the book that was to be the token of it.   Their grief was
sometimes inconsolable when the premium was missed.
On these occasions, as the number of children to be examined was so great, there was only time to hear them

repeat the portion of Scripture appointed, which they were expected to be able to do very correctly. Several chapters were given to be committed to memory; and as Mr. Daly, as he went round the room, asked each child to repeat a portion of the lesson, they did not know what part they would be taken in, and consequently were obliged to know it perfectly, as the mistake of a word would lose them a good mark, and three bad marks would forfeit the premium.

They were all collected together for another purpose,— the 'Waterfall Dinners,' the first of which was described in a letter, published in the *Christian Examiner* for 1827, in the following words :—

'I have seldom been more gratified than by being present at the school dinner given to the children of the schools of Powerscourt parish, on Monday last, September 17. About 530 children, among whom were many Roman Catholics, all attending the schools in various parts of the parish, and all receiving spiritual instruction, assembled in Powerscourt demesne, near the waterfall, and partook, with gratitude and cheerfulness, of the abundant meal provided for them by the principal patrons of the schools,— the Countess of Rathdowne, Viscountess Powerscourt, and the Rev. Robert Daly. About half-past one o'clock the children, having assembled, were conducted across the rustic bridge in the order of their schools, and placed at tables spread for them on the lawn of the banqueting-house. Before the repast, a hymn was sweetly sung by the children, and grace said most solemnly by Mr. Daly. After a substantial repast of roast beef, followed by a plentiful supply of plumpudding and apple-pie, the entertainment concluded by another hymn, sung by the children and their friends. The day was most favourable, being mild and warm, but without the sunshine that might have incommoded the children. The richness of the foliage of the trees, the clear blue sky, the roar of the cataract seen through the spreading branches, under whose shade the happy little ones enjoyed the kindness of their friends,—all gave a physical enchantment to the moral feelings which were associated with the view of so many hundreds showing in one parish the blessings of scriptural education. The simplicity of the entertainment, and its admirable arrangement, prevented that excitement on the part of the children which might arise from a consciousness of their being part of an exhibition ; and about four o'clock the whole separated, gratified at what they had seen and enjoyed. Such scenes, if not too frequent, must be productive of good ; they may serve as a reward for attention and industry, and may therefore stimulate ; they arouse an attention to the feelings of the lower classes which must bind them closer to their superiors ; and every poor man who saw the titled lady, or the benevolent rector and his associates, busy in attending on the inmates of his little cottage, must have felt that such persons valued him and his for their own sakes, and regarded rank and wealth but as the accidents of time, and nothing in the eye of Him with whom is no respect of persons. If Providence spare me life and health, and that the Powerscourt school dinner be repeated another year, I shall certainly make an exertion to attend it.'

During the summer months Mr. Daly held meetings every Wednesday evening, for the purpose of practising singing for the church. These were called the 'Wednesday evenings;' and to them all the parishioners who wished to attend were welcome without being invited, as well as any of the school children who were capable of joining in the singing. They were greatly enjoyed by young and old, and were looked forward to by the children with great delight; while the others prized them as opportunities of enjoying Mr. Daly's society in a more unconstrained manner than they did at any other time. When the clerical meeting interfered with this engagement on one evening in the month, it was generally whispered through the parish, 'There will be no "Wednesday evening" this week.' It was his custom on each of these occasions to invite some to take an early dinner with him,— an excellent repast, though served up on his dinner-service of plain white delf. After dinner they adjourned to the Glebe Schoolhouse, where the party assembled at 6 o'clock P.M. Miss Daly (who always came over from Bromley for the occasion) gathered the school children around a pianoforte, and taught each child separately the simple tune of the psalm and hymns to be sung the following Sunday, after which all joined in singing them together. When the practising was over, the party walked through the shrubbery to Mr. Daly's garden, where the school children had tea and excellent hot cakes, prepared for them by his good old housekeeper, who poured out the tea for them.

He would sometimes pleasantly relate how, when pre-

paring for these tea-parties, he went into a shop and asked
for the largest teapot and the smallest that they could
supply him with,—the latter to be made use of by himself
when alone. The forms and tables were arranged on a
beautifully smooth grass plot in his flower-garden, just
opposite the large window of the parlour. He took great
pride in the fine sod, and would tell those that admired it
that he had it mown every second Wednesday. He enjoyed greatly seeing the children at their tea, and would
sometimes give a piece of their cake to one of the company, which was always very good. When they had
finished, all joined in singing the evening hymn, 'Glory
to Thee, my God, this night,' while standing on the grass,
after which the children went home. The rest of the
party then walked about his beautiful garden, a favoured
one being now and then presented with a full-blown
cabbage-rose, or a bunch of lily of the valley, or some of
his excellent strawberries.

The writer met with a touching instance of the way in
which these little gifts were sometimes treasured. When
looking over the papers belonging to one who has passed
into the heaven to which he taught her the way, she
found a withered bunch of lily of the valley, wrapped up
in a piece of paper, inside which was written, 'Given by
Mr. Daly in his garden at Powerscourt, June 8, 1835.'
He took great delight in his garden, and when asked once
by an officious visitor, 'What do you want with a gardener?' he made the characteristic answer, 'I do not want
a gardener, but my gardener wants me.'

When it began to get dusk, all went in to tea, after

which he had prayers and a short striking lecture, when all went home. The young people were also very much interested by the 'Penny-a-week' meetings, which were held quarterly, in the schoolhouse at Enniskerry, for the purpose of collecting subscriptions for, and giving information concerning, four of the religious Societies,—the Bible, the Church Missionary, the Jews, and the Irish Societies. Mr. Daly's speeches at these meetings were particularly lively and interesting. In one of them, when contrasting the great interest taken in the education of the black children to the apathy that existed with regard to our poor Irish children at home, he said: 'People are very much interested by hearing of little black children with white shirts, while they care very little about poor white children without any shirts at all.'

While Mr. Daly fed the lambs of his flock, he did not forget the sheep; and while distributing the sincere milk of the word to the babes among them, he also prepared strong meat for those who were of full age. Like St. John, he had his varied teaching for the 'little children,' for the 'young men,' and for the 'fathers,' varied only in strength and in quantity, but not in quality; to all he preached the same gospel, the unsearchable riches of Christ. Every second Monday evening was devoted by him to the instruction and edification of a class of young men preparing for the ministry. Many of them came from a considerable distance to attend it. They dined with him, and spent the evening so profitably, that not a few who have grown grey in the service of the Church look back with thankfulness to

what they were privileged to learn at those meetings.
He also gave a practical kind of training for the duties
they were about to enter upon to those amongst them
who lived in his parish, by employing them as district
visitors and Sunday-school teachers, sometimes asking
them to undertake a cottage lecture in some remote part
of the parish. He and his curate held several lectures
at the various schoolhouses, some of them in the mountain district at Glenchree and other places. These
lectures, some of which have been published, were admirably suited to arrest the attention and to gain the hearts
of the class of people to whom they were addressed.
Mr. Daly did not intend that all these various means of
grace should be attended by the same people; he rather
rebuked one lady who went to every lecture or prayer
meeting that was held by him almost every day in the
week, telling her that he did not like to preach to people
that were 'stuffed;' he preferred that they should have
time 'inwardly to digest' what they heard. On Sunday
mornings, while the curate was engaged in teaching the
'miracle' and 'gospel' classes, Mr. Daly had a class for
the old men, in the vestry-room of the church, in which
he was assisted by one or two of the laymen among
the neighbouring gentry, when they encouraged these
poor men to converse in an unconstrained manner upon
religious subjects. One of them, who, though only half-
witted, had been made wise unto salvation through
faith which is in Christ Jesus,—a labouring man, who,
though a fool, had not erred therein,—showed his affection
for Mr. Daly on one occasion in a very characteristic

and amusing way. It was generally known that the Deanery of Cashel had been offered to him, and that he had gone to Cashel before making up his mind whether he would accept it or not. There was great anxiety among high and low to know the result of his decision; and as Mr. M'Kee, the curate, was riding along the road, this poor man, who was working in the next field, put his head over the hedge, and called out, 'Is he *made?*' 'No, he's not,' answered Mr. M'Kee, riding on without stopping. 'Lord be praised!' said the man, going back quite cheerfully to his work. Mr. M'Kee was a great contrast to his rector, being remarkable for the childlike simplicity of his character. Mr. Daly used to call him his little wife, and was very fond of him, but was sometimes provoked with him for being so easily imposed upon. He one day lent him an umbrella, as it was raining when he set out to walk to Enniskerry from the Glebe. When he got half way it stopped, and Mr. M'Kee meeting a beggar woman, he gave her sixpence and the umbrella, which he desired her to leave at the Glebe, but which she did not do. The umbrella was never heard of again, and Mr. Daly made him pay for it, to punish him for his folly. In describing Mr. Daly as he went about his parish of Powerscourt, we cannot omit making mention of his horse, which he rode during the greater part of his residence there, and which is so much associated with remembrances of him. Alexander the Great's ' Bucephalus ' was thought worthy of mention in the pages of history, and surely 'George the Fourth ' has quite as good a right to be mentioned here. Mr. Daly gave him this name

because he bought him just at the time of the King's
visit to Powerscourt; he was a tall, handsome bay, with
very high action. His master would often tell a story
of one of his poorer parishioners saying to him, 'Whenever I see your reverence, I'm sure to see a great baste!'
He never rode any other horse until after he went to
Waterford, when 'George the Fourth' was turned out
to grass for the remainder of his days,—a picture having
first been painted of him, which was hung up in the
landing-place outside the drawing-room door at the
palace. 'A merciful man regardeth the life of his beast;'
and as he could not bear the idea of a horse that had
served him being ill-treated as a hack, he often preferred giving one that he no longer required to a friend
who would take care of it, to getting a few pounds for it
from some one who might work it too hard.

In the year 1829 a District Society was formed in
the parish, for the purpose of benefiting the poor in
temporal as well as spiritual matters. They were encouraged to put by a small sum, a penny or more, according
as they could spare it, which the district visitor received
weekly, and marked down upon a printed card furnished
by the Society; upon this they received a considerable
premium at the end of the year, when they were given
clothing, blankets, or firing, according to their wants.
The visitor was expected to embrace the opportunity of
trying to do them good in a spiritual way also.   Lady
Powerscourt alludes to this Association in one of her
letters, written to Mr. Daly during his absence in London.
She says: 'The District Society goes on flourishingly.

All satisfied in hearing you are to be the treasurer, for *they know you*. Great lesson for us! Let us be satisfied in depositing body, soul, and spirit in the hands of Him who has undertaken to lose nothing the Father has given Him to keep, but to raise it up at the last day. Surely He will return all with a rich premium.' The poor in Powerscourt had indeed a right to know Mr. Daly as their friend.

The District Society was afterwards followed up by a Loan Fund, for the assistance of the poorer farmers. During the latter part of his stay at Powerscourt, he built at his own expense a large room in the village of Enniskerry, where the business of this loan fund was carried on, and meetings held for religious purposes. His various occupations did not prevent him from being at all times ready to give advice and afford comfort to parishioners of all classes who called to see him. One poor man, who from his eccentricity was not likely to do well in this country, he had given money to for the purpose of going to America, where he had hoped he was doing well, when, to his great consternation, Pat appeared one morning at the Glebe, when the following amusing conversation took place between them: 'Well, Pat, I thought you were in America; why did you not stay there?' 'Och, your reverence, it was too cowld, *too cowld entirely!*'

Pat then informed his reverence that on his passage home he had been very nearly shipwrecked, when Mr. Daly asked him, in a solemn tone of voice, whether on that occasion he had any serious thoughts. 'Indeed I had, sir,' said Pat. 'Well now, tell me, my poor fellow,' said Mr. Daly affectionately, 'when you saw the waves rising over your head, and only a plank between you and eternity, what did you think?' 'I thought I'd be drowned, sir!' was the reply. Mr. Daly always complained, that when any one came to ask his advice about their intended marriage, they had always made up their minds beforehand; if he saw fit to advise them against it, they would very quietly say, 'Thank your reverence; well, what day could you marry us?'

When any of his 'tithe children' applied to him on an occasion of this sort, he supplied them liberally with clothes, and gave them a little money in hand, provided it was a match which he thought desirable. These 'tithe children' were the tenth child in every very poor family, to whom he said he had a right as rector of the parish. He provided for them, putting them, when old enough, in a way of earning their bread by apprenticing them to trades, or training them as servants under his housekeeper, and afterwards procuring situations for them.

He was very fond of simplicity in dress, and would often say that it was no reason, because the 'wicked women in Paris' wore a particular fashion, that we should imitate it. He one day reproved one of the farmer's wives because her daughter wore flounces on her gown. 'Oh! no, your reverence, I assure you they were only bias tucks.' 'Well,' said Mr. Daly, 'all I know is, that she had double muslin on her knees.'

It was remarkable how his opinion on these matters influenced the whole neighbourhood, as great simplicity of dress and manners prevailed throughout it, though the society consisted chiefly of people of the higher orders, many of them of high rank. Very many of these were pious people. Several of them had been attracted to Enniskerry and its vicinity by this very fact, and the desire of profiting by Mr. Daly's ministry. This was especially the case with regard to invalids; the climate being mild, many came there seeking health of body, and were by him directed to the Physician of their souls. He visited them most assiduously, and had reason to trust that not a few amongst them would thank God through all eternity for having been sent there.

One of the most eminent Dublin physicians of that time, being himself a Christian man, encouraged his patients to go there, that they might have the privilege and consolation of Mr. Daly's visits.

A most interesting and remarkable instance of his usefulness in this way has been recorded in the journal of a Christian lady, with the following extract from which we have been favoured. Mrs. Arthur Wolfe, the mother of the two children whose memoir has been written by Canon Stevenson under the title of 'Perfect Love,' was sent for from England in the year 1826 to attend her brother, Mr. Hamilton, in his last illness. She thus writes:—

'Very little time was spent in talking of the wants or ailments of the poor body. His whole soul was filled with anxious concern for the welfare of his children and the safety of his soul.

'*Mercy, pardon*, were the subjects of his never-ceasing cry; deeply he regretted his want of knowledge of the

Scriptures. He said he felt assured his sins were too great to be so easily washed away as by receiving the sacrament, which a clergyman had been desirous to administer to him. He wanted something more, he said; he wanted to speak to the Lord Jesus, but he did not know how to do it. Feeling my own incapability in every way to satisfy his soul's inquiries, and finding no pious person to whom we were known beyond the poor soldier that had been reading and praying with him before I came, we sent to his physician in Dublin, to ask if we might remove to Enniskerry, in the County Wicklow, where I knew many of the Lord's people; but before the messenger returned with the answer, my beloved brother, who in reality was seeking his blessed Saviour, determined he would go, and at an early hour next morning we set off on his jaunting car. The day was fine, and we reached Enniskerry about five o'clock. As we approached the town (beautiful for situation), and were driving slowly down a long winding hill, we perceived a gentleman on horseback walking as slowly after us. We turned to the hotel; he turned also, waiting, as it appeared, to see if the poor invalid would enter. As soon as he saw the carpet bags going in he approached a little nearer, and when he saw the tottering steps of my dear brother needing further help, he came forward, helped him in, and left his card upon the table, on which was written, " *The Rev. Robert Daly.*"

'Oh, what a moment to give praise to God! What a fulfilment of His gracious promise, " He that seeketh me shall find me!" Yes, we found Him! Before the next hour was over, Mr. Daly was at the door again, and heard

from the lips of the sufferer the anxious state of his soul,
borne down as it was by a sense of sin; while, in return,
he heard from the man of God the message entrusted to
his keeping by the merciful lips of Jesus. Soon was this
dear servant of the Lord on his knees, in earnest supplication for blessings from above to be poured on the suffering
soul before him. Great was his agitation, and the agitation
of all present. My dear brother cried out, " What shall
I say to the Lord for neglecting to read the Bible? I
am sure I would believe it all if I knew it, but I don't
know it."

'Mr. Daly replied, " Cast that sin, with every other, at
the foot of the cross."

'Shortly after he got up to go away, saying he would call
on the morrow; and so he did, at an early hour. From
that time we were visited by kind and pious friends all
the day long, anxious to do everything that could be done
to render comfort both to the soul and body. One week
passed, or perhaps more, when my dear brother said to me
he felt his end fast approaching, and that he wished to
return to his children. Sad, yet beautiful, I may say, were
the parting prayers that flowed from the lips of all. The
Lord seemed bent on all sides to grant to the departing
soul the needful change of heart, and inspire it with the
holy confidence it needed. Mr. Daly spoke more encourag-
ingly, and said " he wished he could see all his parish
lying at the foot of the cross as the suffering soul before
him lay; it was there he wanted to see them." '

During the summer months, at this period, every available cottage in the country or lodging in the village of

Enniskerry was sought after. Mr. Daly and his curate preached on Sunday mornings alternately, when his sermons were always written, though he delivered them with all the warmth and freshness of an extempore preacher; although he had the manuscript in the pulpit, he did not appear to read it. They were most striking and powerful; and so affectionately did he beseech his hearers in Christ's stead to be reconciled to God, that the words seemed to go from heart to heart, and you felt as if the last sermon was the best you had ever heard him preach. He has been heard to say, that he never gave the finishing touch to his sermon till Sunday morning, just before setting out to go to church, ' So I gave it to them hot.' He spent the whole of the previous Saturday in preparing it; if any visitor came in then to interrupt him, he would say, ' Are you going to preach for me to-morrow ? if not, I must bid you good-bye.' He never wrote a new sermon except for Powerscourt, but never preached an old one there. His eloquence was persuasive and impressive; it was of that kind which chooses the best and most forcible language to express its meaning. There was nothing flowery, no attempt at bursts of high-flown oratory, but they commended themselves to the hearts and consciences of the hearers.

His subject was handled in a masterly style, and his sermon so well arranged that there was no difficulty in carrying it away. In his own parish he seldom preached controversial sermons; his time was too much occupied by telling them how that, ' without controversy, great is the mystery of godliness,' etc.

The Roman Catholics did not offer him any opposition; on the contrary, many of them allowed their children to attend his scriptural schools. Protestant Dissenters there were none: a Methodist preacher once came to hold a meeting in a remote part of the parish, but finding that he had Mr. Daly as one of his audience, he did not come again. Mr. Daly said to him, 'I heard that you were come to feed my people, and I came to see what kind of food you were giving them.' He lectured every Sunday evening himself in the church during the summer months, going through one of St. Paul's smaller epistles each year. These were extempore, and were by many preferred even to his written sermons; they were so much valued in his later years by Lord Powerscourt, that he offered to light up Powerscourt avenue with lamps hung from the trees, if he would continue the evening service in the church during the winter. Mr. Daly, however, thought it better to have (during that season) service in the schoolhouse near the Glebe, while his curate, who lived in Enniskerry, held one there.

No man ever possessed less vanity, or cared less what people thought of him; though in one sense he was proud —proud towards his fellow-man, but humble towards his God. A characteristic anecdote of him shows these qualities of his mind. A stranger, on hearing him preach for the first time, went round after service to the vestry-room, and complimented him in high terms upon his very eloquent discourse, when Mr. Daly quietly looked at him and said, 'With me it is a very small thing that I should be judged of you, or of any man's judgment. He that judgeth me is the Lord.'

Mr. Daly was very happy at Powerscourt. His heart was in his work, his health was excellent, and his time fully employed. The lines were fallen to him in pleasant places; he was surrounded by friends with whom he could sympathize, who were like-minded with him, with whom he could take sweet counsel; his warm heart and cheerful disposition made this a subject of enjoyment to him. Though he lived alone, he seemed never to feel lonely. His sister, Lady Crofton, lived close to him, and she and her son spent two or three evenings every week at his house. Some of these evenings were spent in preparing the *Powerscourt Calendar*, which was drawn up under Mr. Daly's superintendence, and printed by him for the use of his parish. He continued to use and circulate it after he became a bishop, and it was sought after by many in other places.

This calendar divided the portions of Scripture so that the whole Bible was read through in the course of three years, three references being given to each chapter. When reading the Old Testament, the references were to the New, and *vice versa*. The curate of the parish, Mr. Wynne, gave his assistance in this work; and they were sometimes joined by some of the parishioners, who thought it a great honour, particularly the young people among them, to be invited to a 'calendar evening.' The writer remembers one of these evenings at which she was present, when each person suggested whatever verse occurred to them as being applicable to the chapter that had been read by Mr. Daly, from which he selected the three that he thought best, and marked them down. The evening closed with family prayer. He was lecturing on the parable of the ten virgins, and when he came to the passage, 'Our lamps are gone out,' the lamp on his table began to flicker, and he was soon left to finish his lecture in darkness. He did not, however, make any remark upon it, though it was long remembered by those who were present. One or more of these calendars were given to every family in the parish, and the desire expressed that they should read each day the chapter appointed for it, thus securing the attentive reading of a small portion of God's word daily by all his people, amongst whom, in his constant visits, the chapter of the day often furnished a topic for profitable conversation; while he often chose the text for his morning sermon on Sunday from some portion of Scripture which had been read during the preceding week.

Mr. Daly told a story remarkably well. He had a great many very good ones, which he brought forth occasionally out of his treasure-house, but they were never dragged in by the head and shoulders. He was a most agreeable and at times entertaining companion; he knew how to vary his conversation 'from grave to gay, from lively to severe.' In talking over his parochial visits among the poor people, he related an interview which he once had with one of his cottagers in a very amusing manner. This poor woman lived in a remote part of the parish, so that he was not able to go to see her very often. However, on one of these occasions, he found that twins had been born a short time before; and as nearly a year elapsed before he could visit her again, a second set of twins made their appearance in the meantime. On entering her cottage, he said to her, 'Well, Anne, how are the twins?' 'Which twins do you mean, sir?' said the poor woman in a most melancholy voice. 'Oh, Anne, Anne, you're a fruitful woman!' 'Och! your reverence, I'm the *unfortunate* woman!'

He had also a great quickness in repartee, and, like a thorough Irishman, was never at a loss for an answer. When staying at the house of the late Duke of Manchester (who was an intimate friend of his) at Tanderagee Castle, on his appearing at the breakfast-table the morning after his arrival, the Duke (who sometimes indulged in a pun, though in this case not a happy one) held up his watch and said, 'Good morning, Mr. *Delay* (which he meant as a play on his name); fifteen minutes late for breakfast!' Mr. Daly, who never was guilty of being late, produced his watch, and answered: 'I was told that breakfast was to be at nine o'clock, and I am here to the minute by Dublin time.' 'Yes,' said the Duke; 'but our clocks are always fifteen minutes fast.' 'Well,' said Mr. Daly, 'I was not aware of that arrangement; and I certainly never dreamt that a good Christian man like your Grace would teach his clocks to tell lies!'

One of his friends, when showing his little boy to him for the first time, thought that Mr. Daly's praises were slow in coming, and said to him, 'That's a fine little fellow!' 'I'm *glad* you're *satisfied* with him,' said Mr. Daly, bursting out laughing.

He was on another occasion showing to the same friend one of his curious books of old divinity; and on his remarking that he knew who it was written by, although the author's name was not given, his friend asked him, 'How could you be sure of his style of writing?' 'How do I know that's *your* nose?' answered Mr. Daly; 'because I never saw another a bit like it.'

After he was made a bishop, he was visiting Mr. M. at his country parish; and looking at the view from his glebe, which was quite bare of trees, but which commanded a splendid view of the Ghaltee Mountains on one side, and Knockmeladown on the other, 'Now,' said Mr. M., 'you can see the mountains!' ' *To be sure* I can; the difficulty would be *not* to see the mountains!'

Mr. Daly published a collection of hymns for the use of Powerscourt Church, which was afterwards enlarged and generally used in his diocese. He wrote a preface to it, and amongst other things, dwelt upon *standing* as being the proper attitude while singing the praises of God. He gave a copy of this hymn-book, bound in leather, to every person, while the mothers of families had their names printed on the outside cover in gold letters.

He was very happy in his curates. In after life he remarked that he felt it to be a blessing which he had from the Lord, that he had never had any painful differences with any person with whom he was closely associated, but was always enabled to get on well with them. He was singularly fortunate in those who were his fellow-labourers in the ministry at Powerscourt. On the promotion of Mr. M'Kee to the incumbency of Mellifont, he was succeeded by the Rev. Arthur Wynne, Mr. Daly's cousin, and one whom he had known and loved from his boyhood. They were like-minded in their views on religious subjects, and warmly attached to each other, though differing greatly in their turn of mind and natural dispositions.

Mr. and Mrs. Wynne were both very much beloved at Powerscourt. Though of a delicate frame, she was very energetic. As she was a very good musician, and had a fine voice, she so much improved the singing in the church, that during her stay there it was quite of a superior character, although there was no instrument. Her clear voice led the choir, which was composed of the clerk's family, who were all excellent singers. They were joined very generally by the congregation, Mr. Daly's hearty notes of praise being heard very distinctly among them.

The celebrated Robert McGhee might also be said to have been a fellow-labourer with Mr. Daly in his parish. Although not his curate, he was for many years employed as a moral agent on the Powerscourt estate, and resided in the house, his health not being good enough at that time to allow of his undertaking much clerical duty. He had a weekly lecture at Powerscourt House, which, though only intended for the servants and work-people belonging to the place, was regularly attended by many of the gentry in the neighbourhood.

Mr. McGhee did not at that time preach very often, as he suffered from a nervous affection of his throat; but he always took part in the prayer meetings, which were held every Tuesday morning from ten to eleven o'clock. These were very delightful meetings. They were begun by singing a hymn; then followed a prayer for the wants of those who were present; after which, a chapter having been read by Mr. Daly, an intercessory prayer was offered up, in which any persons who were in sickness or trouble of any kind in the parish were pleaded for at the throne of grace, as well as for blessings upon the Church at home and abroad; another hymn was then sung, when the concluding prayer was one of thanksgiving, after which the meeting was ended by a short dismissal hymn.

In the neighbouring parish of Delgany Mr. Daly had many Christian friends, with whom he enjoyed having intercourse. Some of them are mentioned in a letter addressed to the writer of this Memoir, of which the following is an extract:—

'. . . It is at Bromley that I like to think of him best, sitting with his dear old mother and sisters, and in the sweet social circle of near relations and friends—Cleavers, Scotts, Wynnes, and many others now gone. I can remember some of the pleasantest, happiest evenings of my younger years spent there. I loved Lady Harriet very much, and enjoyed a large share of her love and friendship for many years.

'One evening, as we sat round the fire, the stopper of a smelling-bottle, belonging, I think, to Mrs. Newman, was so close that no one could open it. The Bishop (as he was then) said, "Give it to me; I have a *strong* hand." I said, "*Strength* will not open it." He then handed it to me, saying, "Well, try *your* hand." I tapped it round quietly with a key, or something of the sort, and the stopper loosened. He took it from me with a beaming look, saying, "Nothing like gentleness."'

Probably it was this feeling that 'there is nothing like gentleness' which caused Mr. Daly to be peculiarly

K

drawn in the bonds of Christian affection towards his cousin, Mr. Cleaver, who was at that time rector of Delgany. The warmest friendships often exist between persons of the most opposite dispositions, each perhaps admiring in the character of the other those points in which they differ from themselves. They were both of them entirely devoted to the work of the ministry, but their manner of working was not in every respect the same. Both parishes were models of highly-cultivated spots in the Lord's vineyard, and the work was the same in both; but the exact way of carrying it out, and the arrangement of the two parochial systems, were different. Mr. Daly strongly resembled Luther, not only in character, but even so much in personal appearance, that a print of that great Reformer, which he had hung up in his study, was often thought by strangers to have been intended as a likeness of himself. Mr. Cleaver was as frequently compared to Melancthon. He was of a gentle and tender nature, of a sensitive and nervous temperament, which led him to shrink from entering into the stirring controversies in which Mr. Daly was engaged; and on one occasion, when the latter returned triumphant from one of these conflicts, Mr. Cleaver said to him, ' Robert, you were born to command, and I to obey.' His retiring disposition, however, did not make him indolent; he was most untiring in his efforts for the good of his people. He was possessed of great talents as a preacher—his sermons were models of beautiful and elegant composition; yet he was remarkably humble. We have heard it stated, and we believe with truth, that he was offered a bishopric, which, after lying awake a whole night thinking over it, he refused, not considering himself suited to the post.

An intimate friend of his communicated to the writer of this Memoir the following most touching and characteristic account of his last moments :—'He spent most of the day preceding his death in singing hymns, asking his sister to accompany him on her harp. When near his death, he was observed to look up with an astonished and delighted countenance to heaven, and was heard to say, in a tone of voice which expressed much surprise as well as joy, " *Well done, good and faithful servant !* " He then entered into the joy of his Lord. It appeared to those about him as if in his dying moments he had heard these words addressed to him, of which he felt himself unworthy.'

At the Wicklow clerical meetings, which were held the first Wednesday in every month, Mr. Daly showed himself, as Mr. Cleaver had represented him to be, 'born to command.' They were very numerously attended, and were held in the different parishes in the district in rotation, and several Christian laymen were admitted. One or two of them had the meeting at their houses when the clergyman of the parish could not conveniently do so.[1]

[1] One of these meetings, held at Mr. Daly's house, is thus described by the Rev. William Sandford, incumbent of Clonmel:—'Amongst my earliest recollections of him is one in connection with a clerical meeting at Powerscourt rectory, to which, though only a divinity student, I was introduced by a clerical friend. The man and the scene are even now as vividly before me as if it were an event of yesterday. The room crowded with clergymen, several of them eminent evangelical leaders of the day, and the rector, the Rev. Robert Daly, in the chair. Topic after topic came up for discussion. For a while some two disputants would engross the con-

In the parish of Nun's Cross the clergy always assembled at Glanmore Castle, where they were sure to have a large meeting, on an average about forty, who were hospitably entertained by Mr. Synge. These meetings were highly prized, and felt by all who attended them to be very profitable. Mr. Daly always took the lead; his opinion was bowed to, and his judgment depended on by others, in any difficulty which arose. On one occasion a discussion arose whether a clergyman ought to go into the parish of a neighbouring clergyman to officiate if sent for, one of the curates present saying he had been placed in a difficult position by being asked to do so, and not feeling sure as to what was the path of duty. Mr. Daly turned to him, and said very solemnly: 'Young man, never refuse to go to any one who sends for you as a minister of Christ.' His advice was often asked for, even by persons who were not very well acquainted with him, and was generally found to be sound. We read an instance of this in the Life of Rev. Frederick Robertson of Brighton, when, as a young man, he felt it difficult to make up his mind as to what profession he would go into. Not liking to oppose the wishes of his father, who urged him to choose one to which he felt a repugnance, he asked Mr. Daly's advice, which

versation, waxing warmer as the debate advanced, without adding much towards the solution of the question. At the right moment the chairman would interpose, with some weighty observation on the point at issue. It acted like magic. The mists clear away, and the subject stands revealed, clear and simple, in its own light. Never was I more struck with the superiority of one man above his fellows than on that occasion—in all but in name a bishop among his brethren. Not afterwards, when surrounded by some forty of his clergy at his Waterford clerical meetings, was this pre-eminence more conspicuous.'

was as follows: 'Do as your father likes, and pray to God to direct your father aright.' What wisdom is here! If he had advised the young man to pray that he himself might be influenced by God to make a right choice, it might have laid him open to the temptation of self-deception, and perhaps of rebellion against his parent's wish.

A clergyman who knew him well writes thus about him: 'In private, when his advice was asked (as I once had occasion to do), he was most useful.'

Mr. Daly was very fond of the study of prophecy; and about the time that we are now speaking of, Lady Powerscourt invited all who were interested in the subject to spend every second Tuesday evening with her at Powerscourt House, when most interesting and profitable hours were spent in reading and conversing on those parts of Scripture which bear upon it. Mr. Daly always presided, and Lady Powerscourt would, as he expressed it, 'prove him with hard questions.'

She had, during her visits to London about this time, gone frequently to hear Mr. Irving, and (though not agreeing with him in his more peculiar views) had entered warmly, and even enthusiastically, into his desire for the study of prophecy. Mr. Irving had been led particularly to consider this subject by the reading and translating of a Spanish work by one 'Ben Ezra,' who considered that the second coming of our Lord must be so near, that Christians ought not to entangle themselves in any worldly engagements.

These ideas were taken up very warmly by some Christian people in England, amongst others by Mr. Drummond, who was well known in the religious world at that time. An interesting account is given in the Memoir of the Rev. Edward Irving of some meetings which were held in the year 1826, at Albury, the seat of Henry Drummond, Esq.

Lady Powerscourt was present at these meetings, as appears from a letter to Mr. Daly, of which the following is an extract:—'I am going to the prophets' meeting at Mr. Drummond's. . . . No arguments are to me stronger than yours, so much so that I always conclude I have strong grounds for an opinion if it is not shaken by your arguments to the contrary.' They appear to have suggested to her the idea of holding similar 'discussions' at Powerscourt House, which she did in the autumn of the year 1827, on which occasion she invited to her house the most remarkable men, of whatever Christian denomination they might be, who were interested in the study of prophecy, from all parts of England, Scotland, and Ireland, and entertained them at her house for a week; during which time meetings were held morning and evening, to which every one in the neighbourhood was invited. Mr. Daly took the chair, and they were conducted uniformly on his part in a spirit of Christian love, and in a very judicious manner. A subject was arranged for consideration for each day, and a copy of the paper which contained them given to each person. The meetings were begun and concluded with prayer. In his closing address on one of these occasions he expressed himself as follows :—

'As to the grand outlines of threatenings to sinners, and promises to the people of God, and as concerns the personal glory of the Lord Jesus Christ, I feel pleasure and comfort in dwelling on them; and I feel obliged to the students of prophecy for having led me to a more clearly defined view of glory, as connected with the glory of Jesus. I find something upon which my mind rests with more security than upon a vague idea of the happiness of a disembodied spirit, with which for many years I was content. I have only to add, that I thank my Christian brethren for the edification and comfort which I feel grateful for having been allowed to enjoy amongst them; and if at any time I have said anything that was unsuitable, and that should not have been said, I feel assured they will overlook it, and consider it as the infirmity of man. I am thankful for their communications; and I pray for them as for myself, that the Lord may enable us all to minister His word "as to the Lord and not to men," as workmen of the Lord that need not be ashamed, out of whose treasures we may bring things new and old, and rest our souls upon the Rock of Ages.'

These discussions were held annually at Powerscourt House for three or four years. They were much enjoyed by many, but they became latterly a source of great anxiety to Mr. Daly, who felt that he was set as a watchman over the souls of his parishioners, and feared lest the many strange doctrines which were propounded then might disturb the simplicity of their faith, and alienate them from their scriptural Church. Unfortunately these students of prophecy (although the interest they felt in that study was shared by him) held, and brought forward, on other subjects very erroneous opinions. Amongst these

was that celebrated and truly pious though mistaken
man, Edward Irving. Mr. Daly's opinion concerning the
doctrines held by the Irvingite party is expressed in a
letter to a Christian friend :—

'DUBLIN, 29th April.

'MY DEAR MISS P.,—I return you the letter. I feel
a great deal for the state the Lord's Church is in, yet I
cannot think that really Christian people will be long left
in the fundamental errors of Irvingism. In the conversation I had with my dear friend H., I said to him, "I
ought first to know your doctrines before I inquire even
into your pretensions to gifts ; for if an angel from heaven
should come and preach any other gospel than that which
the apostles preached, I ought to hold him accursed." He
assented to this, and I asked was it true that they denied
the imputed righteousness of Christ. He said it was ; that
it was a gross mistake to suppose that God accounted a
man to be anything but what he really was; that God
accounted no man righteous but just in proportion as the
man really was righteous. . . . I said, "Let us go to texts
of Scripture—Phil. iii.; do you consider that the righteousness there spoken of 'as being of God by faith' is
an imputed or an imparted righteousness ?" He said, an
imparted righteousness. He went so far as to say that the
manifestations in their Church were the testimony of
God to their holding that holy truth. Nothing could be
plainer than his language. As a body they have departed
from the gospel of Christ. Mr. Baxter's tract, which I
gave you, will furnish Mrs. P. with full materials for

those failures of prophecies which she wants to show among them.

'May the Lord defend His own truth, and deliver His Church from error.—Yours, in the love of the truth,

'ROBERT DALY.'

The Plymouth Brethren also gave expression to their peculiar views on religious subjects. All that Mr. Daly felt to be dangerous he thought it his duty, as the minister of the parish, manfully to oppose; while the Christian spirit in which he did so is shown by the following extract from one of his speeches at the conclusion of the discussions in October 1832, which was taken down by one of those who were present:—

'I must say in truth that I do feel my mind so harassed with all that has passed, that instead of saying anything more, I think it best to ask one of my brethren to entreat the Lord's pardon and forgiveness for all the evil that has crept in among us through our defilement and infirmity; to ask for more of the Holy Spirit, for more light; to return thanks for the privileges that we enjoy, and to pray that our meeting together may be blessed; that though there may have been error brought forward, the Lord may be pleased to lead us into all that is truth, all that is holiness; and if, in the various observations which have been made (this evening particularly), there have been great differences of opinion upon what appear to be fundamental points of doctrine, to pray that we may be enabled to exercise towards each other a spirit of love and of interest for one another. For myself, I earnestly desire to ask that all should remember me as a Christian friend, and especially when they think I have erred, that they should ask the Lord to lead me into all truth. I would desire grace to say, in the spirit of one who was inspired to be a writer of Scripture, " God forbid that I should sin against my brethren in ceasing to pray for them." May a spirit of mutual love and interest be promoted; and may a deep feeling of our own sinfulness, of the sinfulness of our brethren, of our own ignorance and error, and the error and ignorance of our brethren, produce amongst us tenderness and a forbearing spirit towards one another, accompanied by an ardent looking up to the Lord, that He would cleanse us from all sin, and bring us into the unity of the Spirit. For myself, I never felt in spirit so much inclined to say, " Oh that I had the wings of a dove, that I might flee away and be at rest!" When my soul is forced to dwell in such an evil world, when I see before me the prospect of such divisions in the Church, when I think of those being so separated upon earth who I do hope are joined together in the Lord, there is something within that causes me to say, " Better to depart and be with Christ;" *that* is the wish of my heart. I once heard one much loved by many here pray that he might remain on earth until the coming of the Lord; and I did feel (though perhaps it might have been sinful) that I would not wish to be left to witness all the evil, the separation, and the variety of errors with which it seems as if the Lord is beginning to allow the Church to be tried even now. I certainly felt this evening a more awful sense of coming evil than I ever did before; whilst I trust at the same time

I felt, though something that was suggested by a brother did grieve me, that he was right in speaking of personal responsibility, and in saying that it was a small thing to be judged of man's judgment. I felt that I stood before my God; and whilst some of my Christian brethren might say that I was blaspheming against the Holy Ghost, I could go to Him and say, "Lord, Thou knowest all things; Thou knowest that I love Thee." One good effect at least that our meeting together this evening may have produced is, a more simple seeking after God; if we have not sweet fellowship with one another, that we may be led to seek more " fellowship with the Father, and with His Son Jesus Christ, till we all come, in the unity of the Spirit, unto a perfect man, unto the full measure of the stature of Christ." '

While considering this spirit of Christian love, we shall give an extract from the letter of a friend, which discloses to us, as it were, 'the reason of this;' as Christian was enabled to see in the Interpreter's house the man behind the wall with the vessel of oil in his hand, which he cast secretly into the fire :—

'*Thursday, 4th October.*

'MY DEAR MR. DALY,—I longed so much to write to you on Saturday, that as I could not do so then, I must now, and hope it will find you at Tanderagee. You seemed to feel still much of your former interest in us when we dined together at your house, but, as you said, "you mourned over us because we had gone so far." I was afraid you would think last week would do such *wild* people much harm, so I want to tell you the impression left by it. But first I must indeed tell you what I think will comfort your heart. I remember your prayer after dinner at your house, in which you prayed that your " spirit might be kept," and that *we* might get good and not evil from the meeting. I am *sure* the first petition was heard. It was delightful to me to see how the Lord was answering you ; and I felt, that though your spirit must indeed have been tried to the very utmost, you were graciously with-held from saying one word, I think, to wound any one. The prayer which you uttered, but which I am sure the Spirit dictated, on Friday evening, went to the hearts of very many, and the few words you said at last called forth many a tear and much sympathy for you. May the Lord ever thus, my dear friend, give you the victory through His own strength! I do bless God indeed for this His great mercy. When I saw one poor brother, Mr. M., so left to his own spirit, I felt doubly thankful that you were kept, though sorrowful indeed, yet " meek and lowly" in the strength of our dear Master. I did not hear your last address, but dear little Kate Wingfield came into my room after it, quite melted in tears. I slept in the bed-room next Lady Powerscourt's dressing-room, and know from herself that most of that night was passed *in tears*, she was so very much distressed for what you must have felt. Early in the morning I saw her, and she told me this; she felt as if all had gone wrong, but especially she felt for you. . . .—Ever, my dear Mr. Daly, most sincerely and faithfully yours, ' L. M.

' I went to Aungier Street, but do not feel the least

disposed to leave our own Church from what I saw there.'

So faithfully did he discharge his duty in watching over his people, that, with the exception of Lady Powerscourt, not one amongst them was led away from the Church, even though they had what might appear an example worthy of imitation in her. It showed strikingly the influence that Mr. Daly possessed over their minds, and their respect for his opinion, that no one in the parish of Powerscourt followed her example when she joined the Plymouth Brethren; but all lamented the fact, and wondered how she could take herself from under *his* ministry, to whom, under God, she owed so much. He had not, however, the slightest feeling of jealousy on the subject, as he was remarkably free from such little-minded feelings on religious subjects; but he must have felt it deeply, though he never spoke about it. All this is plainly exhibited in the sermon preached by him on the occasion of Lady Powerscourt's death, from which we shall make an extract :—

'What she thought right, that she did, with a single eye, regarding neither the censure nor the praise of men. In the only step she took which we could not but disapprove, and which could not but grieve us, we feel no hesitation in saying, we are assured she had a single eye to God. In quitting the communion of the Church of England, and separating herself from those in connection with whom her soul had received life and strength and comfort, we feel assured that she was only actuated by a desire after more holiness, more perfect purity. She did it with much pain, much personal suffering and struggle, and never in a spirit to lessen her love to those whom she valued as fellow-disciples of Jesus.'

When Lady Powerscourt told Mr. Daly that she had determined on joining the Plymouth Church, which at that time held its meetings in Aungier Street, he said to her: 'You expect to meet with perfection, and you will be disappointed; it is not to be met with among any body of Christians in this sinful world. After a little time you will separate yourself from some whom you will find not to be as perfect as you thought them to be; others will be added to the number; at last you will be left alone; and when you look into yourself, you will not find perfection there.'

Lady Powerscourt was a very remarkable person. In the preface to the volume of her letters, which was published after her death, in the year 1838, by Mr. Daly,[1] he says:

'She, of all the Christians I have been privileged to know, came nearest to that which she has, in such strong, uncommon terms, stated to be her idea of a Christian: "Not one who looks up from earth to heaven, but one who looks down from heaven on earth." She appears to have ascended a high and holy eminence, and from thence to have looked down upon those earthly scenes with which too many are entirely engrossed, living up to that high spiritual requirement of the apostle,—" Set your affections on things above, and not on things on the earth; for ye are dead, and your life is hid with Christ in God." '

[1] These letters were afterwards translated into French, and had a considerable circulation.

Mr. Daly's love for souls was very great. A Christian friend said to him one day that she wished that he would visit her more frequently. His reply was: 'You and I are on our way to our Father's house, where we shall be always together. Now my work is to seek the lost.' Many and various were his engagements with this work in view. He exerted himself very much about founding the Episcopal Chapel in Baggot Street in the year 1834, and was trustee to many other proprietary chapels in different places.

Having a prebendal stall in the Cathedral of St. Patrick's, he took his turn in preaching there, and was generally called upon to preach the annual sermon for the schools in connection with it, as he brought large congregations and good collections. He frequently preached charity sermons in Dublin. Many of them were in aid of parochial schools, scriptural education being well known to be a subject that he had much at heart, and with which he had long been experimentally acquainted, as we shall have occasion to notice more at length in our next chapter.

CHAPTER VI.

'HERE A LITTLE, AND THERE A LITTLE.'

> ' It is the index to eternity.
> He cannot miss
> Of endless bliss
> That takes this chart to steer his voyage by ;
> Nor can he be mistook
> That speaketh by this book.'
>
> GEORGE HERBERT.

IT is not our intention to go deeply into the much-vexed question of National Education ; but as it was a subject which, during Mr. Daly's whole lifetime, occupied so much of his thoughts and attention, and in connection with which he was so well known both in England and Ireland, that a memoir of him which did not touch upon it would be incomplete ; as in becoming the champion of scriptural education he was obliged both to controvert the opinions of his diocesan and to oppose that system of education which was supported by the Government of his country, we are desirous to show that he was not actuated in this matter either by party spirit or by a feeling of personal opposition ; that it was not a new idea or whim taken up suddenly, but the settled conviction of a lifetime,—a principle which he felt to be of such importance that he acted upon and advocated it through life.

With this in view, it may be interesting again to refer to a sermon preached by him, about three years after he entered the ministry, strongly advocating those principles in defence of which he would afterwards have laid down his life.   To these he continued faithful until death, as we shall have occasion to show in the records of his later years.   The two great objects upon which he laid such stress in this, one of his earliest sermons,—namely, the benefits of scriptural instruction for the young, and the blessing to be expected from the circulation of the Holy Scriptures among the people,—these two objects were to the last dear to his heart, and were the last subjects of his public ministrations.

All must then acknowledge that he was a consistent supporter of scriptural education.   Archbishop Whately himself felt this in his later years, when experience taught him that Mr. Daly had been right; and he learned to show much respect, and even affection, for him whom he had formerly only looked upon as an adversary, and to feel that he was not his enemy because he had told him the truth.

At the beginning of the century, the only Society for scriptural education was the Incorporated Society, established in 1783.   Besides this, there were a few parochial boarding-schools, which were not found to effect much good in proportion to the money expended upon them. The hedge-schools were very bad, those supported by private means were few, and Sunday schools had not been thought of.   When the importance of vital religion and of scriptural instruction began to be fully realized,

L

many and successful were the means used to bring it about. The Kildare Place School Society was so generally felt to be useful, that in the year 1815 it obtained a large grant of money from Government annually. The Sunday-School Society spread its influence over the whole of Ireland so universally, that before long there was not a parish to be found without a Sunday school. The number of Roman Catholic children who attended these scriptural schools became so great, that the prelates of that Church began to fear for its stability in this country if the rising generation were to be brought up as Bible Christians. They consequently signed a petition, asking for a Parliamentary grant to enable them to educate the Roman Catholic children according to their own views. What followed is well known to our readers.

The Commissioners appointed to inquire into the state of education in Ireland gave a very favourable report of the efficiency and usefulness of these scriptural schools.

We cannot be surprised that Mr. Daly, to whose heart the cause of religious education was and always had been so dear, was deeply grieved when the Parliamentary grant was withdrawn from these institutions, and upon their ruins was built up a godless system, the practical result of which was the withdrawal of all the Roman Catholic children from the scriptural schools, and the funds granted by Government for the purpose of general and united education through the country being applied almost exclusively to the assistance of the Roman Catholic priesthood in maintaining their schools, from which the word of God was excluded.

Mr. Daly was not one to grieve over an evil without trying to remedy it. He accordingly—ever ready, unlike Meroz of old, to come to the 'help of the Lord against the mighty'—raised his voice and used all his influence to oppose what he felt to be so prejudicial to the best interests of his countrymen. In this he was joined by a very great majority of the Irish clergy, who were not to be tempted, either by the pecuniary assistance offered to their schools, or by the prospect of promotion to Government livings, deaneries, or bishoprics, to join in what was against the convictions of their consciences. They have been but ill rewarded for this by the blighting in many cases of their earthly prospects; but their reward is on high. Christ will bring it with Him,—a crown of glory, in which will shine as bright gems those souls to whom their faithfulness had secured the knowledge of the truth as it is in Jesus. He says: 'Behold, I come quickly, and my reward is with me.' May his ministers still prove faithful to this trust committed to their charge, 'Feed my lambs.' At this time, when the subject of scriptural education again agitates their minds, may they be enabled to be 'faithful unto death,' and, contemplating the character of one who, in this respect as well as in many others, 'fought a good fight,' may they go and do likewise. On the 10th of January 1832, one of the most respectable and influential meetings ever known in Dublin was held in the round room of the Rotunda by the friends of scriptural education in Ireland, for the purpose of petitioning Parliament on the subject. They took as their motto, 'The Bible, the whole Bible, and nothing but the Bible.' The meeting was very largely attended, and the platform crowded by laymen of the higher orders as well as clergymen, many of the speakers being laymen.

The Archbishop of Tuam was in the chair, and Mr. Daly was called upon by him to open the meeting with prayer. His speech on this occasion was a most powerful one, and the expression of feeling at this meeting was one of unprecedented warmth and earnestness. Finding that the expression of their feelings upon this all-important subject had not the effect upon the measures of the Government that they might reasonably have expected, and that they were not likely to procure any aid from that quarter for the support of their schools, the friends of scriptural education determined upon forming a Society, for the purpose of collecting subscriptions and seeking for help in the good cause which they had at heart. An address was issued in the year 1832, signed by seventeen of the prelates of the Established Church in Ireland,—two archbishops and fifteen bishops,—recommending this course to their clergy.

At the first annual meeting of the Church Education Society for Ireland, held in the Rotunda, Dublin, on the 24th of April 1840, His Grace the Lord Primate in the chair, Mr. Daly declared his intention to continue as long as he lived to raise his voice against a system of education without the Scriptures.[1] That he carried this intention into effect we shall afterwards have occasion to show. A letter was about this time addressed to Arch-

[1] See Appendix A.

bishop Whately, signed by a very large majority of the clergy of the dioceses of Dublin and Glandalough, of which Mr. Daly was one, stating their reasons for not being able conscientiously to support the National Board of Education, as he had recommended them to do. At a great Protestant meeting held in Exeter Hall, London, on the 11th July 1835, for the purpose of proving to Protestants of all denominations, by authentic documents, the real tenets of the Church of Rome, Mr. Daly gave his reasons for not thinking it desirable to entrust the Roman Catholic priesthood with the education of the youth of our country. He also proved that the National system had failed in the matter of promoting united education among the various sects in Ireland. We regret much, from its length, not being able to insert this speech, which has been very well reported.

In the spring of the year 1830 Mr. Daly went as usual to England, and kindly undertook the charge of a little girl of twelve years old, whom her aunt was sending to school in London. On their arrival an interesting incident occurred, which the little girl (now the mother of a family) thus describes in a letter to the writer of this Memoir: 'Having taken charge of me to leave me at school, he had to get out of the Liverpool coach (for in those days there were no railroads, and we were two days going up to London) at the corner of Regent's Park, instead of going on to the office. Mr. L.'s servant happened to be passing, and saw him by the light of a lamp seeing our luggage taken out. On that night Mr. L. was dying, and his family wished him to see a clergyman; he refused, saying there was but one clergyman on earth who could do him any good, and he was far away. Some one asked who it was; he replied, "Robert Daly of Powerscourt." The servant, who had returned to his master's room, stepped forward, and told how he had 'seen Mr. Daly get out of the Liverpool coach at nine o'clock that evening. The family knew the hotel at which he always stayed, so he was sent for immediately. . . .'

We find this interesting circumstance respecting his friend recorded in a journal which he kept during this visit to London and Paris :—

'*Monday, 8th Feb.* 1830.—I sailed from Dublin, and though the evening had been very boisterous, yet, encouraged by the rising of the barometer, I went aboard, and had a very good passage of about fourteen hours to Liverpool. Tuesday I slept at Birmingham, and on Wednesday I went by Warwick and Leamington, and arrived about nine o'clock in London. On my arrival at my friend Hewitt's, I heard of the severe and dangerous illness of Mr. L.

'*Thursday.*—At four o'clock I was called up to see Mr. L. I found him very ill, but entirely in his senses. I spoke to him of the salvation of Jesus, and he expressed his sole and only hope to be in Christ. I prayed with him, and he seemed to join with his whole heart in the prayer I offered. I remained with him till six o'clock. I returned again at eleven, and found him much sunk; he could not speak, but when I spoke of Jesus he pressed my hand, and expressed in that way much gratification.

He lived till half-past one o'clock, and then quietly breathed his last, and I trust entered into his eternal rest. Poor Mrs. L. was wonderfully supported under her unspeakable calamity. She wished me to dine with her poor bereaved children, which I did, and prayed with them in the evening.

'*Friday.*—I dined this day again with the afflicted L.'s. It was very gratifying to see the young people feeling so much and so properly their afflictive dispensation. They seemed very much affected at the exposition and prayer.

'*Sunday*, 28*th Feb.*—In the morning I called on Lord Roden and Lord Le de Spenser. It was quite improving and edifying to see his state of mind after recovering from a fever at Nice—so grateful, so alive. We went to Long Acre to hear Mr. Howells. On Thursday I went to Brompton Park, to pay a visit to Lady O. Sparrow, and found her much better than I had seen her before. I had much conversation with her upon some of the heresies in Irving's books. Lord Roden came on Tuesday, and we had a very pleasant and I hope profitable time.

'*Tuesday*, 16*th March.*—I left London at half-past ten, in company with Mr. Mayers, and arrived at Dover at half-past seven. We met a gentleman in the coach who was going a few miles to see a brother, who had broken his thigh by a fall from his horse, he having lost another brother about a week before. He was an old sailor, and had a great deal of feeling, and we took an opportunity to put before him the comforts of the gospel of Christ, of which he seemed to know little, but was glad to hear. We embarked on Wednesday, the 17th, in the *Crusader*, English packet.

'*Paris.*—We felt very thankful to the Lord for having brought us so far in safety. My friend and myself returned thanks to Him together for His mercy, and besought Him to bless us during our stay in Paris.

'*Sunday.*—This has been a day of pain and real grief to me. In the morning, after having read some Scripture and prayed to the Lord not only for myself, but for my dear flock and the world at large, I went with Mr. M. to a café to breakfast. We then went to the Post Office, and it was most afflicting to see the shops open, and everything going on just as if there was no Sabbath. Having got no letters, we proceeded through the Tuileries gardens and the Champs Elysées to the English Church; and it seemed as if the whole world were assembled to amuse themselves,—reading newspapers, playing plays, dressed in their good clothes. But the most extraordinary thing was to see some at work; they were carting the dirt off the street as if it was a common day. This last was not Popery, but Infidelity. Oh, how this people seem ripe for destruction! I felt so thankful that I lived in a different country. We reached the church, and found it quite full of most respectable English persons. What a blessing that there is a place for them to get a little food in this wilderness! Mr. M. preached from Heb. vii. 24, 25. I met at the church J. Daly. He had been very much pleased with two sermons he had heard from Mr. M. before. He told me of a very instructive epitaph he had read at Le Père de la Chaise,—"Il vécu court, il vécu Chrétien, il a assez vécu."

'*Tuesday.*— We visited the Louvre, and were much delighted with it, far beyond my expectations. I was particularly pleased with a Rubens of Christ on the cross, and a Titian of Christ being crowned with thorns. I expect often to go again, for it is impossible to enjoy such a crowd of beautiful pictures on first sight. The gallery itself is well worth seeing. I spent the evening with ——, and talked very freely to her about her conduct at Brussels. She appeared in a very humble state of mind, and I hope will not be led to put herself forward as a public teacher again.

'*Wednesday.*—I went to hunt among the back shops for some valuable books. I bought two Greek Testaments for 6½ francs, but saw no valuable divinity books. We visited the Church of Notre Dame. It is a beautiful building, well worth seeing, bringing mournful ideas to the mind of a Christian.

'*Thursday, Friday, and Saturday.*—We continue to read some Hebrew together, and I have found it very profitable. I have as yet seen but little of Paris, neither of my companions being able to walk much. I have gone through many of the booksellers' shops; there are very few good books—those few very cheap. I passed through many very wretched streets, where the people appeared very poor and very dirty. I think Paris a wretched town, except a few grand spots, which make the other parts appear the worse. We drank tea with ——, and had some pleasant conversation. J. Daly read from Jude, and prayed. It struck me that verses 20 and 21 would make a good subject for a sermon, contrasting the mercy in verse 21 with the judgment in verse 15.

'*Sunday, 28th March.*—What a blessing that there is a Sabbath, and how wretched those who know not its blessedness! It is not known in this country. I went, after having engaged in prayer with my companions, to ——, who took me to Faubourg de Mt. Parnasse, No. 41, to hear Mr. P., who preaches at the mission-house there. We mistook the hour, and were too late, coming in at the end of the sermon. We heard, however, a very sweet psalm sung, and a very nice prayer, which made me regret not hearing the sermon, much more animated and more catholic than Mr. Oliviet. There were not forty persons in the room, and if it was ever so crowded, it could not contain a hundred. It is most grievous to the soul to think that those who know the Lord are so few; may He increase their number! I was much pleased in hearing —— say that certainly there was no place, she believed, in the world where there was so much religion as Powerscourt. I feel every day more thankful that my lot hath fallen unto me in that pleasant place. Oh that I may be a faithful pastor to my dear flock there! In returning, I went into a chapel in Rue St. Honoré. It was most melancholy to see the crowd of people walking backwards and forwards, whilst some were in the midst of all the confusion repeating prayers, and the priest going on saying his Latin mass. "Father, forgive them, for they know not what they do." In the evening we went to the chapel in the Oratoire, and heard a good French sermon from Mr. —— of Bordeaux. We had hoped to have heard Mr. M. It was pleasant to hear the sound of the same precious gospel coming from Bordeaux.

'*Monday, 29th March.*—Daly and I, after reading a chapter in Hebrew, went to the Bibliothèque Royale. It is a magnificent establishment, without any outward show or ornament. There were a great many persons reading and comparing manuscripts. Mr. Mayers and I dined with Mr. Waddington, 88 Faubourg St. Martin. Mr. and Mrs. Waddington are Christian people, and seem to be engaged in all the Christian activities of Paris. They had to meet us, Mr. and Mrs. Montagu, Mr. M., Mr. Cook, a Wesleyan preacher, Mr. —— of Bordeaux, and Mr. Fernandez. They all spoke English perfectly well, and gave us a pleasing account of the progress of the Lord's work in France. They say there is a desire to hear, and more among Roman Catholics than nominal Protestants. Many call themselves Protestants merely because they laugh at Popery. What is wanted in France is a greater liberty of preaching. No man can assemble more than nineteen persons without a licence under a penalty. Many English works on divinity are being translated into French ; part of Scott's Bible has been translated, and 1500 copies sold. I read and expounded a portion of Scripture.

'*Tuesday.*—I walked for a time in the Luxembourg Gardens, and read there two psalms. I went through the palace, saw the Chamber of Peers, which is very handsome, and a room which Buonaparte had prepared for the young King of Rome, ornamented all round with tapestry representing different parts of Rome. The young King of Rome's picture was in the room, but has been removed

by the present King, and replaced by a tapestry map of
Rome. I bought a manuscript Bible for 96 francs. I did
not feel quite right in laying out so much on a book that
is curious, but useless; but I can, I am sure, get more
than my money for it at any time. We dined at Mr.
Montagu's. We met Mr. and Mrs. Waddington and Mrs.
Wilks. Mrs. Wilks is very active in promoting the
Lord's work; she keeps two readers continually employed.
She gave a very interesting account of finding in Paris
and elsewhere many descendants of the Jansenists, who
had parts (leaves) of Bibles, and who knew the truth, and,
though they held many Roman Catholic errors, rejoiced in
hearing the doctrines of grace. Also many descendants of
Huguenot families, who are coming out in various places.
In Orleans there is a congregation of 500 collected, and
two places of worship built for them.

'*Thursday.*—After reading a chapter in Hebrew, we
went to see Mr. Olivict, and had some conversation with
him. He told us of his having been turned out of a Protestant state for preaching the gospel, and received in a
Roman Catholic one. We went then to the most extraordinary sight we have seen, the Cemetery of the Père de
la Chaise, said to be 100 acres given up as a burying-
ground. It is a most singular-looking place, with tombs,
and cypress trees, and little gardens of every possible
variety, upon a hill which commands a view of the whole
city of Paris. Some features of it struck me much. I saw
but one Christian inscription; I literally saw not the name
of Jesus but on one English tomb. There was generally
the language of much affection, but it was sorrow with-

out hope. One very striking feature was the Jews' bury-
ing-ground, entirely separated by a wall from all the rest.
How strange that infidel France should be overruled to
make them a separated people, even in their graves!
"They shall not be reckoned among the nations." No
people but the French would ever have thought of making
their burying-place an inviting scene for the pleasing of
the eye. It was very hot this day, the thermometer was
72 in the shade; in the sun it was as hot as it is usually
with us in July.

'*Friday.*—We went with —— to see Versailles. It
had rained in the morning, but turned out very beautiful
in the afternoon. There is much grandeur and finery
about the palace, but it has a gloomy air of desertion. We
had some pleasant conversation both going and coming.
I went to the Jews' synagogue, Rue Notre Dame de Naza-
reth, where there was to be an installation of a new rabbi.
It was a melancholy sight, and plainly taught us that
"Ichabod" was written over that people. There was much
that resembled Roman Catholic ceremony,—reading in an
unknown language. There was some good singing, but no
devotion exhibited by any persons, with the exception of
one young man, who caught my eye, and seemed devout.
It was interesting when they went for the law, and brought
from a chest at the end of the synagogue a roll, and
opened it, saying, "This is the law which God gave to
Moses." It looked so strange to see all the people with
their hats on. In conversation with Mr. Cook, a Methodist
minister, I heard a circumstance of a rent in the Roman
Catholic Church which deserves to be remembered. A

portion of them, now called " La Petite Eglise," have protested against the spoiling of the Church at the French Revolution, and against the concordat made between Buonaparte and the Pope, and have excommunicated the Pope and all the French clergy concerned in it. They call themselves the true Church, and all the others schismatics and apostates. They are a numerous body in North and South.

' *Sunday, 2d April.*— —— very kindly gave me a seat in her carriage to the mission-house, 41 Boulevard de Mt. Parnasse, where Mr. P. preached at ten o'clock, in French, from Gen. xi. 27. He spoke of the moral image of God, described well Adam's original state, then contrasted man's present state, and spoke of the Redeemer that could alone bring man back to think from whence he had fallen. I had got a ticket to go to the Royal Chapel at ten o'clock. I could not bring myself to give up Protestant worship on the Sabbath to gratify my curiosity by seeing the King and the forms of Popish worship; I therefore determined to take my chance of being in time after Mr. P.'s service. I was, however, too late, as they would not let me into the gallery after the King had entered and service begun. This was a great Sunday, being Palm Sunday ; I did not, however, feel myself disposed to witness their mummeries, though I must try to be present at high mass before I return home. At half-past two I went to Mr. Oliviet's, and heard a good sermon from Rom. viii.: " For I reckon that the sufferings of this present time," etc. He spoke much of the destination of Christ's believing people being to share the glory of their Head. He said he would mention only one qualification which marks the way that leads to a share in that glory, and that was a willingness to endure the shame,—shame from the world, who will think believers fools; shame as sinners, as heirs of hell and destruction, ready to take everything as of pure grace. The singing was very sweet; and his prayer for the edification of believers, and the conversion of sinners, and confirming those not yet ready to endure shame, was very beautiful. There was the best congregation that I had yet seen in his room. In the evening I went to the Oratoire. It turned out a very bad night, yet there were a few there. Mr. M. lectured in course upon the 7th chapter of Romans. He went rather too generally through the chapter; he showed, however, that he knew the evil of the human heart, and the only remedy for it in Christ Jesus. He dwelt exclusively upon the first elements of the Christian truth in a manner much calculated to impress the ignorant, and to confirm those who knew the primary elements of the gospel. His manner is impressive and earnest.

'*Monday.*—In the evening I went to a missionary meeting at the Oratoire. Mr. P., the secretary, expounded part of John xvi., "When He is come," etc.

'*Tuesday.*—I hired a carriage to go to Brussels for 100 francs. It would have been dearer but that it was a Brussels carriage.

'*Wednesday.*—Mr. Mayers and I set out on our journey at a quarter before seven. We found the posting better than we expected. We got to Compiègne, where we dined, at a quarter before two. We had an accident by

the breaking of one of the springs, which we had to tie
up, yet we reached St. Quentin at nine o'clock. We found
the French very civil when we wanted their help to tie
up the spring; they seem very attentive to strangers. We
stopped at the Hotel d'Angleterre. At first the hostess
did not seem inclined to give us the accommodation we
wanted; but when I said I should look for another hotel,
we got a sitting-room and two bed-rooms. After reading
a psalm and thanking God for His mercies to us, we
went to bed, which we found cleaner and better than we
expected: I slept very well. Mr. M., to whom we had
an introduction, came to see us; we had some pleasant
conversation with him. There are near 1000 Protestants
in St. Quentin—many very ungodly, a few truly pious.
Since real piety has sprung up among them, they have met
with more jealousy than before. There is at present a
case in trial as to the right of persons to meet for worship,
the settling of which may promote the cause of truth very
materially. Having to preach this evening and to-morrow,
he could not give up much time to me. He therefore sent
a pious young man with me, who took me to see a Mrs.
Kite, a pious English woman, but rather depressed in her
spirits. I spoke to her, and prayed with her and her
husband, who is a man by all accounts not under the influence of religion. I went then to see a poor family converted from Popery. There was a very old woman, who
seemed quite alive to spiritual things. Her son, who had
been himself converted lately, was the means of bringing
her to the knowledge of the truth. She had been a great
devotee, and had images and crucifixes, which she gave to

Mr. M. She gave me a Popish book, which she used to prize. Her son seemed a very happy Christian. They seemed poor, and their house was very dirty. They said their Roman Catholic neighbours never molested them; that the majority of the Roman Catholics never went to any place of worship. I went then to see another. Christian convert, who seemed to understand well the freeness and gratuitousness of the gospel. Mr. M. dined with us at half-past three. He seems indeed a good man. He described his situation, so like that of ours in Ireland, between Roman Catholics and nominal Protestants. He has in his congregation about 20 real Christian converts from Popery. He is a man of prayer and faith, and great determination. He spoke most highly of the good effects produced by the Continental Society in the North of France; he spoke particularly of a very interesting congregation, entirely formed and kept up by Mr. Gambier, an agent of that Society. He spoke very highly of Mr. Coligney. Before we parted that he might prepare his evening discourse, he begged I might pray with him. His spirit seemed refreshed, and I hope mine was also. "As iron sharpeneth iron, so doth the countenance of man his friend." At eight o'clock we went to the Protestant Church, which had been a Roman Catholic one before the Revolution. Many of the churches were at that time taken from their original purpose; some turned into manufactories, and this one into a Protestant temple. It is large enough to hold any that would assemble in it these times. There were about 150 persons, many of whom were Roman Catholics. Most of the Roman Catholics did not stay out

M

the whole service, but got up and went away before the sermon was half over. There was nothing in the sermon to offend them, and I understood from Mr. M. that it arose most probably from their habit of running in and out of their churches during divine service; they never think of going at the beginning and staying to the end. He said they were all Roman Catholics who thus went out, and I am sure there were 30 or 40 who did so. Mr. M. preached an interesting sermon. After the service was over, some of the Christian people of the congregation gathered round us, and showed much Christian love. I said a few words to them in such French as I could, and they each of them pressed forward to shake us by the hand. I never saw anything more near the spirit expressed in those words, "See how these Christians love one another!" We gave notice of an English sermon on tomorrow evening, at seven o'clock, and have reason to think that many will come who are not in the habit of hearing the word.

'*Friday.*—This holy day, on which the Saviour of the world died for sinners, Mr. Mayers went to Agincourt (*Query*, Was it the famous place of that name ?), to see a church assembled in that place by means of Mr. Pouchart, one of the agents of the Continental Society. The parish (*i.e.* the Protestants) is under the care of an ungodly minister, but the Christians there . assemble together through the means of the agents of the Continental Society. I did not like going so far, as I wished to hear Mr. M. Before the time of Protestant service, I went into the great Roman Catholic church of this place, and it being Good-Friday, it was a great day with them. There were many persons in the church. There were many priests chanting mass in many-coloured clothes; but the great business was kissing the cross. The people knelt down at the rails of the chancel, just as we do in succession at the rails of the communion-table; and instead of receiving the Holy Sacrament, according to our Saviour Christ's holy institution, two priests, dressed in white, carried two golden crosses, with images of Christ crucified on them, for the people to kiss. As they kissed they went away, and their places were supplied by others. Little children were made to kiss. I stood beside two men who seemed to be laughing at the unmeaning nature of the ceremony. They were probably quite infidel, and were confirmed in their infidelity by such unmeaning mummery. I went from that to the Protestant simple worship. There were but a few people. The service began by the chanter reading Phil. ii. and Ex. xx., and then giving out a hymn at the end of their Psalm-book. He then read Isa. liii., out of which chapter Mr. M. preached on verse 5: "He was wounded for our transgressions," etc. I dined with Mr. M. He had two young men of his congregation to meet me. The maid is a Christian woman, a child of Mr. Coligney's ministry. In place of soup we had rice-milk, which I was afraid to eat much of. We had some baked veal, which Mr. M. called beef, and a fricassée of frogs; of which last Mr. M. ate heartily, and said they agreed with him better than anything else, they were so light. I ate one leg, in spite of my dislike to try it, and found it not bad. After dinner

we had a prayer; and I should have said, that after grace
before dinner, Mr. M. read part of the 13th chapter of
Hebrews, as he said, to give us something profitable to
talk of. After dinner there was introduced an humble
young man, who is employed by the Continental Society,
and has been useful in gathering a congregation of converted Roman Catholics about two leagues from the
town. When I was going away, I shook hands with him
very cordially, when he begged to kiss me, to which I con-
sented, in spite of prejudice. This church has been proceeded against for holding meetings; and in order to get
the protection of the Consistory, they promised to join the
Established Protestant Church, and not to hear sermons
from any but ordained ministers. They found much inconvenience keeping to their promise, and were inclined
to break it; and I was much pleased with the way Mr.
M. spoke to this man of the need of strict truth. The man
had made, he said, no promise, so that he might preach to
them. "No," said Mr. M.; "if it is wrong in them to
hear you, you should tell them their duty as Christians to
keep truth; and if you preach to them, you are a partaker
in their sins." I went with Mr. M. to call on Mr. Juliet,
the chief manufacturer in St. Quentin, a Protestant, and
had some profitable conversation with him and his wife.
He told me that the immorality of the people was very
great; that half of them could not read, and those who
did read very hurtful books. I should have mentioned in
its proper place, that in the village in which the young
man I met at Mr. M.'s has been blessed, there had not
been worship of any kind for twenty-five years until the

Protestants collected their church, and then the Roman
Catholics sent a priest, and opened the church again.   In
St. Quentin there had been six Roman Catholic churches
before the Revolution, and now there is but one.

'*Brussels.*—We arrived at the hotel about four o'clock,
and were very comfortably lodged, and got a very good
dinner.   In the evening we walked out to call at the post
office, and see the town and parks, etc.   I found a bookseller that had some valuable good old books, which I am
to see to-morrow.   My God has been most gracious to me
in carrying me safely so far, and allowing me now to say,
" Hitherto the Lord hath helped me."

' *Thursday.*—We went to-day to see the field of Water-
loo.   I was surprised to find that I could feel as much as
I did then.   I caught a kind of enthusiasm, which very
much surprised me.   I felt for a moment as if martial
glory was something real; and then I went into the
sanctuary, and saw the end of these men and these things.
The ground really seemed as if it was made for the battle-
plain of two great armies,—two long ridges, one for each
army to encamp on, and a plain between for them to come
down on and meet in hand-to-hand.   There appeared to
be no advantage of ground.   It looked laid out as if for an
even pitched battle.   The Lord of battles had no doubt
greater results in His infinite mind than any of the parties
concerned dreamed of.   I got some buttons, and eagles,
and balls found on the ground.   The people in the neighbourhood are much injured by the crowds that come to see
the field, and who give them money, and encourage them
to lead an idle life.   The children and old people on the

road are all beggars.   Mr. Mayers and I had, in returning, some deep conversation on our mutual faults, which, though very humbling, was, I trust, calculated to be useful to us both.   I pray that it may.

'*Friday.*—I hired a carriage for 30 francs to go to Antwerp and back.   We went there to the Church of Notre Dame.   It is a most beautiful, simple church.   I never was so struck with any picture as Rubens' "Descent from the Cross."   I could stand looking at it for ever.   It is far more pleasing than the "Putting up of the Cross," which is its companion.

'*Saturday.*—After an uncomfortable breakfast without a table-cloth, we got a guide, and set out to see the things worthy of observation.   We went first to the Museum, and were highly interested with the pictures, especially seven or eight of Rubens', particularly "Christ between the Two Thieves."   The figures of the thieves are wonderful. There are also two very beautiful pictures by Vandyke. I could have enjoyed them more if I could have seen a few of the best pictures by themselves, but the eye is distracted by the number.   We went from thence to the Church of St. Paul.   At the entrance there is built a representation of Mount Calvary as it is at Jerusalem, and of the tomb of Joseph with the Saviour lying in it.   It was quite affecting to see the people kneeling round the tomb, and going through their formal round of prayers. When we entered the church, service was going on ; the priest was in his vestments reciting the mass, and a good many people were kneeling in different parts of the church.   They could not hear one word that the priest said; but when a bell was heard, they went through the movements suited to the time. We, as strangers, were not at all supposed to interrupt the service by going to every part of the church. The verger drew the curtain from the picture of " Christ being Scourged," by Rubens, which was on one side of the communion-rails; and he showed us through the chancel into the inner chapel, so that we went within five yards of the priest. The inside chapel is very beautiful, the altar all marble, with a very fine altar-piece. The carving in wood in all the churches here is very remarkable, but my spirit was grieved within me at seeing the corruption of devotion. We went thence to the Church of St. James, a most beautiful building. The service was over. We saw the tomb of Rubens, and the altar-piece painted by himself to be put up in the chapel dedicated to him. It represents the infant Jesus in the arms of His mother. The figures in the picture are por-traits of Rubens and different members of his family. Over the picture is a beautiful white marble statue of the Virgin, brought by Rubens from Rome. The aisles in this church are magnificent. There are splendid marble statues of the apostles, superior, in my mind, to almost any of the statues in the Louvre. We went from thence to see the private collection of a Mr. Lauker. There are about 130 paintings, some very beautiful, by Rubens, Vandyke, etc. I was perplexed by the variety and number, so that I could not enjoy them as I should otherwise have done. We went from thence to see the port, where there is a very fine quay, and much appearance of industry and traffic. The shops all about that part of the town have

English advertisements, showing plainly who are their
best customers.   Mr. Mayers was too tired to go on to see
the citadel.   He went home, and I went to the bookseller's; but I could not find any books worth buying,
except a Latin *Concordance*, for which I paid 15 francs.

'*Sunday.*—I had much pleasure in remembering my
dear flock before the throne of grace.   I hope the Lord
has been with them so far this day, and that He will be
abundantly present with them in the power of His Spirit
in the remaining exercises of this Lord's day.   What a
different thing to spend a Sabbath in a Roman Catholic
country, where the word of the Lord is a hidden treasure!
After breakfast, I went for a few minutes to the beautiful
Church of Notre Dame, where I found that immense area
almost entirely filled with people.   The organ was playing
and the choir chanting, but all was lost in the immense
space.   In the sermon, which was on Rom. vi. 4, there
was much truth upon which a mind used to it could feed.
I trust I did feed.   I heard of the corruption of man, the
atonement of Christ, the power of the Holy Ghost, and of
a spiritual and literal resurrection, though not put in a way
to rouse the unthinking.   I felt that, even such as it was, it
was useful, and I was thankful to be allowed to hear it.
I took a walk by myself almost round the town on the
ramparts.   On coming to the quay, it was cheering to see
the Sabbath honoured by all nations, at least outwardly,
by hoisting their flags.   The Sabbath does not seem nearly
as much profaned here as in Paris ; most of the shops are
shut.   I long for home.   Thanks to God, who has kept me
so far.   There was no English service in the evening or

afternoon, neither could I hear of French Protestant service. Mr. Mayers and I looked into some of the Roman Catholic churches. There were congregations in the evening, and well attended, which is not the case in France. I wish I could say they were well fed. In the beautifully-carved pulpit at one end of the aisle of Notre Dame, a priest dressed in white and gold was preaching to a very large congregation, as many as could hear him— about 1500 I should suppose. His sermon was in Dutch, so that I could not understand him; but I supposed, from the frequent use of the word Sabbath, that he was preaching on the observance of it. There were multitudes of other people in different parts of the immense and beautiful church, going through their different devotions. In the evening Mr. Mayers and I read and prayed together, and, walking out for a short time, fell in with the great promenade on the quay, which seemed' to be the evening lounge of all the townspeople. We were surprised at seeing many priests walking among them; their solemn dress, cocked hats, and gowns seemed ill to suit with their mixing in the profane crowd. I felt as if Mr. Mayers and myself were not in our places; and certainly nothing in my mind could have justified us but having no place of worship to go to, having joined the crowd unknowingly, and being desirous to know how different people in different countries observed the Sabbath.

'*Monday.*—We paid a parting visit to the church and pictures of Notre Dame, and I was increasingly delighted with the " Descent from the Cross," and increasingly grieved at the mummery I saw at all times going on. We went

also again to the Museum to see Rubens' pictures, particularly "Christ between the Thieves," which is one of his
best.   I was greatly pleased with three of Vandyke's,—
two of Christ dead, and one of Christ upon the cross.   At
half-past twelve we left Antwerp, where we had been
much pleased and well lodged, etc., at the Hotel St.
Antoine.   We reached the Hotel de l'Europe, in Brussels,
at five o'clock, and immediately set out to inquire about
coaches.   Mr. Mayers, having determined to go to Paris
to the meetings of the Protestant Religious Societies, took
a place in a diligence that set off at ten o'clock that night.
We accordingly parted, after having been allowed to travel
together and see much of each other's minds—much to
humble us, but, I hope, to prove us and do us good at our
latter end.   The more I know of myself, and the more I
am allowed to look into my fellow-men, the more am I
constrained to cry out in wonder, " Lord, what is man,
that Thou visitest him, or the son of man, that Thou so
regardest him ?" [1]

' *Wednesday.*—At five in the morning I set out for
Calais, only 84 miles distant.   Another gentleman, a
justice of the peace at Dunkerque, occupied the coupé.
He had been taken ill the night before with the gout, and
suffered much pain in his foot.   This gave me occasion to
speak of the origin of evil—sin, and the need of redemption from it.   In speaking to this gentleman, I found that

---

[1] This sentence explains an expression which the writer remembers to
have heard the subject of this Memoir make use of in after years, that he
was ' a very good *man-hater.*'   He certainly did not mean that he was
without love for his fellow-men, but that he was alive to their many faults
and shortcomings as well as to his own.

there was no provision for the poor, and that they suffer great distress. A provision has lately been made by the police in Paris, and the inhabitants are forced to contribute to a Mendicity Society, which accounts for what I remarked, that Paris was the only place where there are no beggars. I had the coupé to myself from Dunkerque to Calais, which I reached a little before eight o'clock, very thankful to the kind and gracious Providence which watched over me in my going out and coming in through France.

'*Thursday.*—This morning I left Calais at a quarter before nine, the wind blowing very hard from the west, and a very strong tide flowing the same way, so that we had a very rough, bad passage—five hours. I thought it probable one time that we should not have reached Dover, but must have put into Ramsgate, or some other port more to the east. However, the Lord carried me safely to the shores of England again, where I feel very thankful, and think it very probable that I shall never cross out of Great Britain again. I should be very ungrateful if I did not here raise mine Ebenezer, and bless the Lord for all His goodness to me, that I never had one moment's illness all the time I was from home, and, though travelling much in various places, never met with any unpleasant circumstance. I have never before been so long in a state of recreation or freedom from actual business; and I hope I shall be enabled to return to my work strengthened for it in body, and more than ever disposed in mind to work while my day lasts, for my night is indeed coming, when I cannot work; but I do hope to rest from all my labours.'

On Mr. Daly's return home, he did not forget the little society of poor persecuted Christians in whom he took so great an interest at St. Quentin. Among Mr. Coligney's congregation there were several persons, shopkeepers and others of a respectable class, who had been very much impoverished in consequence of the fact that, on account of their adherence to the Protestant faith, they were put out of employment. Mr. Daly procured situations for many of them; and as they spoke very good French, they were greatly sought after as nursery-governesses. Four of these were located in the parish of Powerscourt, and were greatly liked, on account of the simplicity of their minds and their Christian principles. When first they came over, not being able to understand English, Mr. Daly had a special service for them whenever they desired to receive the sacrament of the Lord's Supper, reading the communion-service in French, and administering to them in a language they could understand. This kind consideration for their feelings attached them very much to him.

One of Mr. Daly's journeys from London is recorded in a letter from the late Chief-Justice Lefroy, which has been published in his Memoir :[1]—

'LEESON STREET, *Thursday.*

'We had, thank God, a delightful journey, and the weather in the Channel very fine until we approached Ireland, when it became wet and windy; but we made an excellent passage of six hours and a half. Robert Daly joined us at Birmingham, and from Shrewsbury he, Jeffrey,

[1] *Memoir of Chief-Justice Lefroy,* p. 341.

and I had the coach wholly to ourselves, and so instructive
and delightful a day I don't know when I passed.   It is
remarkable that I laid out the two days of this journey
for going very minutely into the prophecies, which Lord
Mandeville and I had been reading together; and I made
it the subject of earnest prayer that I might be guided
aright, and profit by my search.   The first day I read
through the whole journey, but was more than ever
puzzled.   However, I was so prepared by my reading
to ask questions and receive instruction, that our dear
Robert Daly relieved me out of my chief perplexities,
and opened views of the subject so much more clear and
satisfactory than any I had met with, that I consider
myself to have had quite a gracious answer to my prayers.
On landing, Mr. Daly came home with us for breakfast,
and read for us in our family worship.   He is indeed a
true servant of God.   'T. L.'

On his return home from a visit to England, Mr. Daly
had an amusing passage-of-arms with one of the old
watchmen in Dublin, or 'Charlies,' as they were called;
it was an anecdote which he was very fond of relating in
after times.   It was late at night when he landed on the
quay near the Custom-house, and as in those days there
was not the same attention paid to the convenience of
travellers as there is now, he could not get any one to
carry his luggage.   He accordingly shouldered his portmanteau, which he was very well able to do, and was
walking off with it to the nearest hotel, when he was
stopped by one of the 'Charlies,' who desired him to give

an account of himself, and how he came by the portmanteau that he was carrying. On Mr. Daly's refusing to satisfy his curiosity, an altercation ensued, which ended by our friend being obliged to spend the night in the watch-house.

Although the Achill Mission was not the part of the Irish work in which Mr. Daly took the most lively interest, yet the following extract from the Rev. Edward Nangle's obituary notice of him will prove how heartily he joined in this as well as in other useful objects. Mr. Nangle says : ' The writer well remembers when, in the year 1831, he formed the plan of a mission work in the island of Achill, how on his return from a visit to the west of Ireland he called upon the Rev. Robert Daly, and communicated his purpose to him, the good man's countenance beamed with joy. He took down a large map of Ireland, and running his finger over the north-western portion of the county of Mayo, in the direction of Achill, he said with thoughtful solemnity: " I know all that country well ; I have traversed it over and over again, at a time when I thought that God had sent me into the world for no higher purpose than to slaughter grouse !" He then expressed his hearty approval of the missionary enterprise, confirming the sincerity of his expressed approval by a donation of fifty pounds to its funds.' Accordingly we find that Mr. Daly was the person chosen by a committee, which met for the purpose, to write to the Archbishop of Tuam to ask his sanction to the plan proposed—namely, that Mr. Nangle should settle as a missionary upon the island of Achill.

The Home Mission was the next object of public usefulness in which Mr. Daly interested himself. The state of
religious feeling in Ireland at that time called for some
such agency. There was not then to be met with in nearly
every parish throughout the land a minister who could
preach to perishing sinners the unsearchable riches of
Christ. The deputations sent about by the different
religious Societies had let the people hear just enough of
these precious truths to make them wish for more. Urgent
demands were made from various parts of the country for
itinerant preachers, who would go round once a month.
There were many difficulties to be overcome before this
plan could be carried into operation ; and so great was the
opposition given to it by many of the bishops, that after
some years the general Home Mission was given up, and
Diocesan Missions organized in its place wherever they
were found to be practicable. The bishops were not all,
however, hostile to the Home Mission. The Archbishop
of Tuam wrote to Mr. Daly on the subject ; his letter
shows forth the beautifully Christian humility of the
writer, and the high esteem in which Mr. Daly was held
by him :—

'THE PALACE OF TUAM, 8th *February* 1830.

' MY DEAR DALY,—I feel, and have reason to feel, very
thankful to you and Mr. Gregg for your late visit to this
place. Independent of the great gratification your sojourn
here (even for so few days) afforded to me and all my
family, I think (under God) the result will be beneficial to
my poor, ignorant population, and I *know* that your visit

has done me and my clergy much good. I made Potter
send a copy of your correspondence with Mr. Clowry to
each of our priests, who received them and returned thanks.
Dr. Kelly, in his chapel, cursed, on the Sunday after your
departure, from his altar, the persons who attended our
meetings and sermons; and on the Sunday following went
to a neighbouring chapel, frequented by your tenants, and
cursed them for listening to you.

'I feel truly thankful for your freedom of speech, and
shall always be obliged by receiving your kind counsel.
A man in his sixtieth year cannot hope much to promote
in his diocese the speaking to the people in their own
language, but I will (with the Lord's blessing) do what I
can, and trust that my successor may equally see the
necessity of it, and may follow up what I may be permitted and directed to commence. Feeling as I do that
the preaching the word is the means of grace upon which
more peculiarly the Lord's blessing is bestowed, I am disposed *heartily* to engage in the Home Mission in my own
two dioceses, but I have *almost* insurmountable difficulty
in the selection of proper persons. I have very few, if
any, clergymen well qualified for the important work of
home mission. . . . Could you recommend to me one or
two persons whom you would think qualified for this very
important work? I think I would enter into negotiation
with one or two *Greggs*, if such could be presented to
me; and your opinion, *founded* upon *your own knowledge*,
would be conclusive with me. . . . I am obliged to you
for all your kind advice upon this most interesting subject,
and will ever receive with thanks the benefit of your

experience and counsel. I am a man of very little talent, a poor man of business and arrangement, very unfit to direct or order, although I am awfully responsibly placed in authority; but if I know anything, it is my own imbecility and incapacity, which needs the assistance and prayers of all my Christian friends. The Lord be with you. Amen.—Yours, my dear Daly, ever most faithfully,

'POWER TUAM,' etc.

Mr. Daly frequently went on the Home Mission himself. On one occasion he had undertaken a tour through the distant parts of the county of Wicklow, when, as he was suffering from a sore throat, he engaged a young clergyman, who was on a visit with him at the Glebe, to accompany him, and to preach alternately with him. The first station at which this clergyman undertook to officiate was at Roundwood, where Mr. Daly proposed to join him the next morning. He has described to the writer the look of humour in Mr. Daly's countenance as he stood at the hall door to see his friend set out in a pour of rain, on a winter's evening, to drive up the 'long hill,' calling after him, 'Good-bye, M.; *endure hardness!*' There were overflowing congregations assembled wherever they went, in expectation of hearing Mr. Daly; and it was not a very agreeable task which his young friend had undertaken, to get up and preach in his place, amidst audible murmurs of dissatisfaction, and the frowns of the ladies, as they saw Mr. Daly quietly sitting by, heartily enjoying their disappointment, which afforded him great amusement wherever they went. Besides preaching the word, he may be said to have

N

obeyed St. Paul's injunctions to Timothy, to 'reprove, rebuke, exhort, with all long-suffering and doctrine.'

In the eyes of those who did not understand him, his reproofs sometimes seemed to be harsh, but he did not mean them to be so. His very energetic manner of speaking, particularly on subjects which he felt much about, made strangers sometimes think that he was intemperate and ill-tempered. Far from being intemperate, he never put forward an opinion which had not been weighed by a cool, sound judgment; and ill-tempered he certainly was not. His feelings were warm, his honesty and faithfulness were great, and we must confess that his manner of saying things was sometimes rough. It is the fashion to call every one who has not a gentle exterior a 'rough diamond.' Of the brightness with which he of whom we write will shine in his Redeemer's crown the diamond is but a faint picture ; he ' shall shine as the stars for ever and ever,' for he was one of those who turned many to righteousness. To any of his brethren in the ministry whom he thought in need either of reproof or exhortation, his faithfulness was very remarkable. To many amongst them, whose views on some subjects were not what he could look upon as thoroughly scriptural, he tried to show the way of the Lord more perfectly. It is much to be regretted that so few of his letters have been preserved ; but the answers to many of them, which were kept by him, prove the great influence which he possessed over their minds, an influence which was always used for good. He used the same plainness of speech towards his parishioners and friends, and never failed to tell them when he thought they were in the wrong. One of the very few in the parish who did not set much value upon his ministrations having absented herself for some time from Powerscourt Church, Mr. Daly asked her reason for doing so, and upon her giving some trivial excuse for going to a neighbouring church instead, he very honestly said to her, 'Well, I hope they may make a better Christian of you than I have been able to do during the fifteen years that you attended my church.'

His plainness of speech on another occasion took a more humorous turn. One of his 'young men,' trained for the ministry by him, preached his first sermon in Powerscourt Church. After the service was over, the mother of the young man, who was a great friend of Mr. Daly's, went round to meet him at the vestry-room door. 'I want to ask you how your cold is,' she said. 'You *do not*,' was Mr. Daly's answer; 'you want to hear me say that J. preached a very good sermon; and I *will* say it.'

Not a few of the young men who were instructed by him finished their course before him. They looked back with love and gratitude to him who had been the means, under God, of fitting them for His service, and many of them consulted him and asked his advice upon every step which they were about to make. The following is an extract from one of their letters :—

'MY DEAR MR. DALY,—I do owe it to you indeed to mention my contemplated change; and I owe you much more than this, for I feel I owe you (as the instrument) my "own self besides." I feel not only indebted to you for two years and upwards of unmixed enjoyment at K., but for the desire that first prompted me to enter the service I am now engaged in. When asked would I accept the curacy of D. if offered to me, I said I would, if Mr. Daly did not disapprove of it, for I felt I could not act against one who always acted for me. To say I did not wish to go to D. were to say an untruth. I longed for Mr. C.'s society; I longed for Christian co-operation in the work of the ministry; I longed to be (if I might) one of your Monday Evening Society; I longed to mix with Christians who know more of Christ than I do. But I am very happy at K. . . . My dear Mr. Daly, *you* sent me here; upon you it rests whether I shall go or stay. Determine for me. Settle all with Mr. C. . . .'

A great number of these clergymen are still alive who could testify what a blessing his 'Monday evenings,' as well as his other instructions, were made to them. We shall insert here a letter written to one amongst them on the occasion of his ordination. The person to whom it is addressed became acquainted with him very early in life, when a boy at Abbeyleix School. His mother afterwards brought her family to reside for many years in the parish of Powerscourt, and enjoyed the advantages of Mr. Daly's ministry and teaching. The friendship then formed continued unbroken through life :—

'POWERSCOURT GLEBE, BRAY, 17*th July* 1831.

'MY DEAR M.,—I was quite happy to get a letter from you, and do rejoice with you that, through divine providence and grace, you are a fellow-labourer in the Lord's vineyard. I do earnestly pray for you, that He that has called you by His grace, and put you into the ministry, may abundantly water your own soul, and make you a blessing to the souls of others. You are now engaged in what I deliberately think the only employment worth living for, that which is equally important and interesting in all times, bad times as well as good times. We are never to have one desponding thought from a sense of our own weakness; our God chooseth the weak things of this world to confound the strong. He puts the treasure in wretched earthen vessels, that the excellency of the power may be the more of Himself. I wish we all went about our work more in a sense of weakness, then we should find the power of Christ resting upon us. I trust I shall always feel an interest of the deepest kind in your personal and ministerial progress, and hope never to be forgotten by you in your prayers. It is a great encouragement to me to know that I have many friends that carry my name to the throne of grace. I often think what a delightful thing it will be when we shall meet before the throne of glory. There is nothing new in this place. The Lord has been very gracious in sparing us from the cholera; we have had but one case in our parish. There have been fourteen deaths in Bray.

'Our Monday evenings are very thin, all the candidates for orders having, thank God, entered the ministry. We never had such congregations. Our church was more crowded than ever last Sunday. I trust the Lord may bless His word to the souls of many. We are very quiet, and the people all disposed to remain so if not intimidated by agitators. When you write to your mother and sisters, give them my kindest Christian remembrances. I pray

the Lord to be abundantly with them. And now, my
dear friend, I commend you to God, and to the word of
His grace, which is able to build you up, etc. Be instant
in season and out of season. Preach the word, and draw
down upon it a blessing by earnest prayer.—Yours most
affectionately,   'R. DALY.'

Not long after the date of this letter, Mr. M. had the
pleasure of a visit from Mr. Daly at his curacy in the
County Down, and of hearing him preach in the church
in which he ministered. They drove together to a great
Protestant meeting, held at Hillsborough, under the patronage of the Marquis of Downshire. Here Mr. Daly showed
very remarkably the singular power which he possessed of
arresting the attention of a crowd chiefly composed of the
lower orders of people, and of carrying them with him.
The number assembled in the open air on this occasion
was so great, that those persons who were situated at the
back of the large platform, erected on the slope of a hill,
could not hear the speakers. Mr. Daly said to those about
him, that as they could not hear what was going on, they
might as well get up a little meeting on their own account,
and that, if it was agreeable to them, he would address
them. This proposal being warmly responded to, he got up
and spoke to them in a popular and animated style for
some time on the subject of religion, anxious as he always
was to embrace every opportunity that came in his way
of benefiting the souls of others. He was so warmly and
enthusiastically applauded by his hearers, that those who
were carrying on the main business of the meeting, at the

other side, called him to order, and he was obliged reluctantly to sit down.

In the year 1831 this country was visited by the cholera, which was more fatal in its effects than we have ever known it to be since that time. It was a very remarkable fact, that during the whole time of its prevalence in Ireland, there was but one Powerscourt parishioner attacked by this dreadful disorder, although two persons suffering from it were brought into Enniskerry, from the neighbouring parish, to the Cholera Hospital there.

Towards the close of this year Mr. Daly preached a sermon in St. Anne's Church, in Dublin, in which he dwelt upon the necessity of humbling ourselves, both rulers and people, before God, acknowledging that our national sins had brought the scourge of Almighty God upon our land. Archbishop Whately did not take the same view of this matter as he did, and a correspondence ensued, from which we shall give some extracts :—

To His Grace the Archbishop of Dublin.

'30*th November.*

'MY LORD,—I have been again honoured by your Grace's communication, and I beg to acknowledge with gratitude the kindness of expression used towards me.

'I think, however, the subject to be too important to myself individually, and too much connected with the ministry entrusted to me, to permit me simply to acknowledge your Grace's letter. I can by no means assent to the justness of the view that your Grace has taken of the extract of my sermon, nor of the line which you appear to me to mark out as a minister's duty with regard to national guilt. I feel assured that your Grace would not expect me to regulate the discharge of my solemn office by a blind submission to your authority, or to appear to yield assent to your arguments when in candour and honesty I am forced to say that I do not feel their force. I must beg most respectfully to dissent from the line which your Grace appears to me to mark out as a minister's duty with regard to national guilt. I should scruple as much as your Grace " to set forth health and disease, plenty and famine, and, in general, worldly prosperity and adversity, as sure marks of divine favour or disfavour respectively;" but I distinguish between individuals and nations in a way which seems overlooked by your Grace. With regard to individuals, there is an eternity,—space for the Lord's righteous dealings to be manifested; but nations have no national existence but in this world, and must be dealt with in time or not at all, and it is a part of God's righteous government of the world to pour forth His temporal judgments upon wicked nations. Though there were many circumstances in the Jewish polity which made their case a peculiar one, I would respectfully dissent from your Grace in supposing that this liability to national judgments was one of their peculiarities. The nations of Canaan met with the righteous judgments of God; the nations employed to chasten the Jews were themselves made signal instances of God's national judgments; and surely the page of Holy Writ is full of prophetic denunciations of God's judgments to be executed upon wicked nations. . . . I have, then, only one thing further to justify myself in. Speaking of the national sin which might lead us to expect this national judgment, I ventured to speak of the sins of the rulers and senate, as well as of the sins of others. . . .

'Do not rulers and senators need faithful rebuke as well as those in the humbler walks of life, and is it not the duty of the minister of religion to rebuke and exhort? "Them that sin," said St. Paul (1 Tim. v. 20), "rebuke before all, that they may be ashamed." Let it not be said that the maintenance given by the State to the ministers of the Establishment is a bribe to them to be silent as to the sins of those who rule in the State. No; the State has made the minister of the Established Church independent of both the ruled and the rulers for food and raiment, that he may be in a situation to be honest to both,—that, being independent of the people, he may not accommodate his teaching to their fancies; that, being independent of rulers, he may not flatter their vices. I thank God I am independent of both as a beneficed minister of the United Church of England and Ireland. I can without fear get up into the pulpit and deliver my conscience. I subscribe *ex animo* to the articles and liturgy of the Church of England; and whilst I preach according to her doctrines, and violate no law of the land, I court neither the people below me nor the rulers above me. I call no man master upon earth; One is my Master, who is in heaven. At the same time, I hope I shall not be wanting in respect to those who rule over me, either in State or Church. . . .— I remain, your Grace's obedient humble servant,

'ROBERT DALY.'

Mr. Daly took a very great interest in the success of the *Christian Examiner*. When at one period it seemed to be falling off, he undertook to be responsible for any sum of money required to keep it going, which proved during the first year a considerable expense, the deficiency being nearly £100. He prevailed upon the Rev. Charles Fleury to act as editor, and contributed to it largely himself in the way of writing. The papers upon prophetical subjects which appeared about this time in its pages, with the signature of R. D., would make an interesting volume in themselves. After he was made a bishop, when writing for that publication, he adopted that of 'Senex;' and from the articles written by him from time to time, his valuable opinion upon various important subjects may be gathered.

The Archbishop of Tuam felt so strongly that it would be an advantage to his diocese (being an Irish-speaking district) that the clergy should be able to preach to the people in their native tongue, that he at one time made a determination not to ordain any who had not learned it. To prepare the way for this, it was necessary first to facilitate the study of the Irish language; and for this purpose a Professorship of Irish was established in Trinity College, Dublin. Mr. Daly, though not the originator of this scheme, took much interest in it; and we find from a letter published by him in the *Christian Examiner*, dated 6th July 1832, that in the midst of his many avocations he found time to revise and reprint an Irish dictionary for the use of students. He begins this letter in the following humorous strain :—

'SIR,—There is by general consent a toleration given to

a man for a moderate enthusiasm upon some one subject. He is allowed to ride his hobby; and even if others will not mount it with him, yet, because it is his hobby, they will not quarrel with him.   Now the vernacular instruction of my native countrymen is a subject upon which I have fallen into an enthusiasm, which none, I believe, will consider to have been immoderate because it was my hobby, but which I seriously think to have been much less warm than the importance of the subject demands. . . .'

The labours of the Irish Society, which we have already had occasion to mention more than once during the course of this Memoir, had been so successful, through the blessing of God upon the reading of the Scriptures, that numbers of persons in different parts of Ireland embraced the Protestant faith.   Their sincerity in so doing could not reasonably be doubted, as they were invariably in consequence exposed to great persecution.   We read in the *History and Progress of the Irish Society* as follows :—

' In the winter of 1834, Mr. Daly, now Bishop of Cashel, a zealous member of the committee, and corresponding secretary for England, was pressed to visit Kingscourt.   A great object was in view, which required in its development prudence, experience, intelligence, and energy ; these were united in Mr. Daly.   A few extracts that have been published from his letters and other correspondence will best exhibit the movement that took place.   We shall commence with exhibiting an interesting letter to Mr. Winning from the teachers, to which it owes its origin :—

' " Rev. Sir,—We, the scriptural teachers in connection with the Irish Society, have, by the blessing of the Lord through that instrumentality, been brought to read, study, and learn the Holy Scriptures—to view them as the only rule of faith and practice—the supreme tribunal to whose testimony everything in religion is to be referred.

'"Sensible, from these Scriptures, that it is our duty and privilege to partake of Christian ordinances, and many of us for years being deprived of that privilege, and living disobedient to the command of Him who has said, 'Do this in remembrance of me,' we now, from sincere and conscientious motives, desire to have the holy ordinance of the Lord's Supper dispensed to us in a scriptural and Christian manner.

'"We believe the definition given of that ordinance to be truly scriptural,—'the outward and visible sign of an inward and spiritual grace given unto us, ordained by Christ Himself as a means whereby we receive the same, and a pledge to assure us thereof.' We believe that the bread broken is an emblem of our Lord's body broken and pierced for us; and that the wine in the cup is emblematic of Christ's blood, that was shed for us, poor, miserable, and wretched sinners. We believe, as the bread and wine nourish our natural bodies, that the body and blood of Christ spiritually (of which the bread and wine are emblems) nourish and feed the soul of the true believer. We believe that Jesus Christ has ascended with His glorious body into heaven, to remain there 'until that great day when He will come to judge the world in righteousness,' and that we are not to have His corporeal presence until then. We believe that as often as we approach the Lord's table with humble, contrite, and believing hearts, and with a sincere desire of holding communion with our Lord, and acting in all things to His glory, that our approach will be acceptable; and that, through 'the outward and visible sign,' bread and wine, partaken in faith, our love to God and man will be increased, our affections spiritualized, and Christ and the blessings of the covenant of grace represented, sealed, and applied to our souls.

'" With these impressions upon our minds, we entreat of you, Sir, to request of the Rev. Mr. Radcliff, or the Rev. Mr. Daly, or the Hon. and Rev. Archdeacon Pakenham (of whose piety and godly sincerity we can have no doubt), to come down to Kingscourt district one of the approaching Sabbaths of this very solemn season, and with you, Rev. and dear Sir, meet us and Mr. Russell as Christian brethren at the table of the Lord, that we may there solemnly partake of the emblems of the body of our Lord, broken for us, and of His precious blood, shed for us, in the hope that we may feed on Him in our hearts by faith, with thanksgivings; and in doing so you will, Rev. Sir, much oblige and, we trust, much spiritually benefit the souls of your humble brethren in the Lord."—*December* 1834.

'This invitation, it may be supposed, was joyfully accepted. Mr. Daly communicated the following account of the result :—

'" I have just returned from the most gratifying duty of preaching and administering the sacrament of the Lord's Supper, in the church of Syddan, in the county of Meath, to twenty-five of our Irish masters—I trust men of God, not only converted from the errors of the Roman Catholic

Church, but converted to God by a living faith in the Lord
Jesus Christ. There were, I understand, about one hundred
in that side of the Kingscourt district who were anxious to
receive the sacrament ; but as much persecution awaits
those who take such a decided step, it was thought better
to begin with only a few tried men, of whom we have no
doubt that they will, through grace, be faithful even unto
death. We are to have a quarterly sacrament for the Irish,
and at the next communion we hope to receive many
more."

' Mr. Daly neglected not to meet them at this next communion. His account of it is as follows :—

' " *29th October* 1835.

' " I have just returned from a most interesting and satisfactory meeting at Kingscourt. It commenced on Friday
the 23d October—Rev. Mr. Pratt in the chair. There
were about 300 teachers and about 100 visitors present.
Among the last, we had Lord and Lady Dunsany, the Hon.
Randal Plunket, Archdeacon Pakenham, Mr. and Mrs.
Fitzherbert, Rev. Messrs. Nixon, Noble, Radcliff, Cleaver,
Armstrong, Egan, etc. The meeting was opened with
prayer, and then a hymn was sung in Irish.

' " The first business of interest was an examination in
reading and translating Irish. There were some very
striking and interesting translations. Next there was an
examination of the Irishmen present as to their acquaintance with the doctrines of the Scriptures—such as the
sufficiency of Scripture as a rule of faith, the fall and ruin
of man, the salvation by Christ, the nature of justification,

and the righteousness that is by faith, the present and the future privileges of believers. Upon these subjects the men exhibited great acquaintance with the word of God, and the clearest insight into the grand fundamental doctrines of the gospel. In the evening there was a sermon by the Rev. Mr. Cleaver, which was heard with much attention by our Irish masters.

' " Saturday was a very interesting day. The masters and scholars were divided into classes, and examined by the clergymen present as to their individual acquaintance with the truths of the Scriptures. Their information and apparent deep feeling was most gratifying. Some persons were more particularly examined, who were considered qualified to be employed as readers of the Irish Scriptures in other parts of the country. But the most interesting and gratifying part of the whole meeting was, toward the conclusion of the day, the examination of thirty-six of these Irishmen who were anxious to receive, on the next day, the sacrament of the Lord's Supper. They were addressed collectively on the nature of the step they were about to take; and afterwards several of them were individually examined, and led to express their reasons for leaving the Church of Rome and desiring to join the Protestant communion. They were likewise strictly questioned as to their personal religion and as to their views of Christian truths. The result was most satisfactory. We had every reason to hope that they left the Church of Rome on a scriptural conviction of its errors, and that they now wished to approach the table of the Lord from a sense of their situation as sinners, and

from a value for the salvation purchased by the blood of
Jesus.

'"On the Sunday I had the pleasure of preaching to
these men, and administering to them the sacrament, in
the church of Kingscourt. All were new converts from
the Church of Rome, except twelve or fourteen who had
received the sacrament before, and all brought to the
knowledge of the truth by the Holy Scriptures in the Irish
language.

'"'This is the Lord's doing, and it is marvellous in our
eyes. He hath done great things for us, whereof we are
glad.'"

'There are facts connected with this first gathering of
the Society's harvest which require to be very particularly
noticed, for an alarm has been spread, in both Great
Britain and Ireland, respecting the great degree of scriptural reading and consequent knowledge that now exist
in the district, and the want of means, as is wrongfully
imagined, to direct it into a profitable channel. First we
urge the fact of the people themselves inviting, through
their superintendent, certain clergymen of the Church of
Ireland, "of whose piety and godly sincerity they could
have no doubt," to come and instruct and examine them,
and receive them into the bosom of that Church; and again,
their inviting their beloved superintendent, a Presbyterian,
not to take upon him these important offices, but to meet
them "as Christian brethren at the table of the Lord."
We would point out the assemblage of clergymen that
met and united with Mr. Daly in performing them; and
that while his letter comprehends others then present,

very many more such in the district might be added to the list. We should add the highly gratifying fact, that the first batch of twenty-eight converts was led by Mr. Winning himself to the communion; and after participating with them of the solemn emblems according to their desire, he presented them to these ministers as the first-fruits of a Church Society's efforts.'

Mr. Winning afterwards joined the communion of the Established Church, and was for many years its officiating minister at Kingscourt.

Mr. Daly alludes to his interesting visit to Kingscourt in a letter written at this time, from which we shall make an extract:—

'POWERSCOURT GLEBE, ENNISKERRY,
'9th January 1835.

'MY DEAR M.,—I am anxious to know how you all are, and particularly how Mrs. M. is after her heavy affliction. Oh, it is a world of death; but, blessed be God, it is the passage to life! How can I send to you my polyglot Bible, which I cannot now carry, as my eyes are growing dim? It may be of use to you; and yours, I remarked, was almost worn out. I have just returned from the neighbourhood of Kingscourt, where I administered the sacrament to twenty-five of our masters, all, I believe, Christian men; the first division of a large number who will, *D.V.*, openly join the Protestant Church. I had a most happy meeting with these men at Syddan Church, in the county of Meath. The Lord is doing a great work among the Roman Catholics in that large district. Remember me affectionately to your mother and sisters, and do not forget your engagement to visit me in May.— Wishing you many happy years, I remain, yours most truly,   'ROBERT DALY.'

On the promotion of the Rev. Arthur Wynne to the parish of Drogheda, the Rev. Henry Brien accepted the curacy of Powerscourt for six months.   He was succeeded by the Rev. John Grier.   The Rev. John B. Ormsby was Mr. Daly's last fellow-labourer at Powerscourt, and accompanied him to Waterford when he became a bishop.

Mr. Brien, who afterwards became his archdeacon at Emly, has favoured us with some reminiscences of the time he spent at Powerscourt, as well as of that in which he was associated with the Bishop in later years :—

'I arrived at the rectory of Powerscourt on a Saturday evening, and was received very kindly by Mr. Daly.   I found him in a very soft and tender mood, greatly affected by the death of one of his parishioners, the Lady E. S. There was no one present but Mr. Daly and myself, and he constantly alluded to her in his conversation, and always with great feeling, during the course of the evening.

'The next day being Sunday, I had an opportunity of hearing him preach for the first time.   It was a funeral sermon.   The subject was the death of the martyr Stephen and his dying prayer, practically and solemnly applied with reference to the case of her who had passed away. Of course I had heard much of Mr. Daly before my first interview with him—his name was at that time in celebrity in all the Irish Church.   He was looked up to as a man of wisdom, high-toned piety, zealous for the glory of God, and a distinguished champion for the truth of the gospel.

'I remember meeting a lady in Dublin as I was on my way to Powerscourt, and our conversation turning on Mr. Daly, she spoke of him as a man of *broad* understanding, a phrase I have often thought of since, and I have had abundant opportunities of verifying the truth of it. There was great instruction in his sermons, and they were characterized by good common sense. It was one of his strikingly sententious sayings, that the religion of the gospel was a religion of common sense.'

Archbishop Whately, on his first coming to the diocese of Dublin, expressed his disapprobation of many things which he was afterwards led to look upon in a very different light. In the year 1836 he gave notice to all candidates for ordination who wished to be admitted into his diocese, that he would require of them a sort of test of their opinions on some subjects which he thought to be of importance; and that they would be expected to sign a paper, promising, amongst other things, not to make use of extempore prayer in any of their ministrations. The clergy and laity of Dublin, who felt that this rule, if carried out, would virtually exclude from the diocese many pious men, got up remonstrances to his Grace which were very numerously signed. In answer to a circular sent by the Archbishop to all his clergy upon the same subject, Mr. Daly wrote a letter, giving his reasons for differing in opinion with him in a very forcible manner. This letter was afterwards published; and eventually the Archbishop, who in every instance where he felt himself to have been in the wrong candidly acknowledged it, withdrew the test alluded to which he had required from candidates for orders.

Mr. Daly showed much tender feeling and sympathy for those who were sick or afflicted in mind, body, or estate; he could wonderfully enter into their feelings, although he had not been called upon to experience them himself. For complaints which appeared to him to be either imaginary or fanciful, he did not, however, express much sympathy. On one of his friends complaining of a nervous headache, he laughingly said: 'And pray, will you tell me what *is* a nervous headache?' Sickness and trial, however, about this time came nearer to him than at any other period of his long and happy life. His eldest sister, Miss Daly, had adopted her sister Mrs. Godley's second daughter, and the family party at Bromley were much attached to her. She was early attacked by consumption of the lungs, which before very long proved fatal. During her illness an incident occurred, which was related to the writer of this Memoir by one who was present, and which shows how pleasant Mr. Daly made himself to young people. On the occasion of one of his frequent visits to Bromley, Miss Daly came into the room and said, 'Robert, Rosa is full of going in the gig with you after luncheon.' 'Very well,' said Mr. Daly pleasantly, 'and the gig shall be full of her!' The maid who attended upon this young invalid was afterwards attacked by consumption; and as hers was a lingering illness, Mr. Daly, after he was made a bishop, had her for many years, until her death, at the Palace at Waterford, where she was most affectionately and kindly nursed, the Bishop visiting her every morning in her sick-room, reading and praying with her. Miss Godley's death was soon followed by that of her kind aunt; and as the manner of her death was very sudden, it was a great blow to the whole family. Miss Daly was driving in a phaeton with one of her nieces, when the horse ran away while going down the steep hill in the village of Delgany; she was thrown with great violence out of the carriage. She was carried into Mr. Cleaver's house, where she died a few hours afterwards. This bereavement was deeply felt by Mr. Daly. He was very much attached to his sister, who was a most attractive person, beloved and esteemed by all who knew her.

His throat seems to have been more than usually affected by the damp of the winter of 1839–40. He mentions it in a note written about this time, in which he expresses his kind feelings of affection toward one who had been formerly one of his Powerscourt flock :—

' POWERSCOURT GLEBE, 31st *March* 1840.

' MY DEAR M.,—I rejoice to think that our dear friend is, through mercy, safe over her confinement. May the Lord restore her to her usual health, and preserve the child to His heavenly kingdom. May He make it His now and for ever.

' I am about to start for England, which I find necessary for the recovery of my voice, which has suffered much from the damp of the winter, then lately from the harsh east wind. I think of going the end of the week; this will prevent the possibility of my paying you a visit.

'It would give me great pleasure to take part in dedicating my friend's child to the Lord, and praying Him to receive it for His own child by adoption; but the thing of consequence is, that the Lord should receive him, put His hands upon him, and bless him. May the Lord be with you both—I must now say with you *three*—and abundantly bless you. So prays your affectionate friend,

'ROBERT DALY.'

When, in the winter of 1832, Mr. Daly had an attack of sore throat more than usually severe, upon his friend, the Rev. Denis Browne, afterwards Dean of Emly, writing to express his sympathy for him, his answer showed how he could be patient in tribulation, and could discern the hand of a loving Father in this, to him, unusual visitation of sickness. He also expressed his anxiety for the establishment of those annual meetings of the clergy in Dublin which were afterwards so much enjoyed and felt to be so edifying by them, and at which the Dean of Emly, and afterwards, when Bishop of Cashel, Mr. Daly himself, presided for many years :—

'POWERSCOURT GLEBE, BRAY,
'22d *November* 1832.

'MY DEAR DENIS,—I am very much obliged by your kind and affectionate feeling towards me. I am, thank God, now quite free from complaint, and only suffering from the cure rather than the disease. I never was, I believe, as ill as you seem to think I have been. My complaint was simply an attack in my throat, much more violent than I ever had it before, and extending to the windpipe in a way it never had done. The disorder was, through God's blessing on the means, overcome, when Dr. Gason thought it right to send for Crampton, with a view to future treatment for the sake of my voice. I suffered like, I should suppose, a drowning man for three days. I had much pain and much uneasiness of body, but much peace and quietness and stillness in my mind. I do really feel that I have reason to thank the Lord for the quiet and passive spirit He gave me. I feel assured He has been teaching me in mercy and in love what I trust may be useful to my soul, and through me to the souls of others. I know the value of peace with God through Christ for myself and others. I thought I had long learned that one thing is needful, but I have certainly seen it. May the impression be a lasting one; and when the Lord shall restore to me my throat to speak through, may I make better use of it, more singly to His glory and to the good of souls than ever. I thank you and Mrs. Browne for your kind wish to have me with you; I do not expect (*D. V.*) to be long an invalid, though I may be some time before I can use my voice, and I shall hope to pay you a visit and take sweet counsel with you. As to the meeting of the clergy, I am very anxious on the subject. I feel with you very anxious for something that shall draw the clergy together from the different parts of Ireland as one body. It is a great evil that the clergy do not know and help and encourage each other, as the men of other professions do. There is an *esprit de corps* in the bar and in the medical profession; not only the clergy of Ireland are not united as a body, but even the clergy of a diocese are not united. It would surely be well that we had an annual opportunity of uniting and conversing together, and contributing to each other's edification and strength, by a voluntary association for professional objects—that is, for considering how we may best advance the objects of our profession, which is the spread of Christ's kingdom, the saving of souls, and building them up in a holy faith. Surely, if the objects of the legal or the medical professions are of sufficient common interest to bind together the members of those professions, surely, I may say, the objects of our profession, if felt, can give us a common interest in each other's progress in the work. I know, if the Lord gives me health and strength, it would delight my heart to meet our believing brethren from north and south, east and west, once a year, to commune together of the common salvation, and also of the spiritual interests of our scriptural Church.

'The Lord has done more for the Church of Ireland than for any Church in the world in the last fifteen years (when there would have been indeed but a small meeting). How the fact that such a goodly company could now be collected of men made alive unto God, almost all within fifteen years, ought to cheer our hearts and make thanksgiving abound to God for His grace! I hope I may live to see a great number of them gathered around the word of God. The commencement time would have been, I think, most favourable for a blessing. May the Lord be in the midst of those who shall meet together, and may they find it good to be there. My Christian love to Mrs. Browne, my blessing on your children and flock.—Yours ever most affectionately, 'ROBERT DALY.'

Many years afterwards (about the year 1839), when the annual clerical meetings in Dublin were attended by the great majority of the clergy from all parts of Ireland, they were severely censured by the then Bishop of Down, in a charge delivered to his clergy, upon the principle laid down by St. Ignatius, that nothing should be done without the bishop. Mr. Daly, in commenting upon this in the pages of the *Christian Examiner*, gives it as his opinion, that the best way of obeying the injunction of the reverend father would be, that the bishops should take the lead in every good work, that thus much good might be done, and nothing done without the bishops. In a correspondence with Dr. Millar which arose out of this controversy, the following passage occurs in one of Mr. Daly's letters, which shows the high estimation in which he and those like-minded with him were held even by those who did not agree with him on every subject :—

'You will allow me to acknowledge with thankfulness the too flattering terms in which you have spoken of myself; to acknowledge with still greater gratitude the character which you have given of that portion of the clergy with which you have been pleased to join so unworthy an individual as myself, which, you say, "has been most commendably characterized by a superior zeal in the discharge of its pastoral duties, which has diffused new vigour through the whole Establishment, and fitted it for the more effectual discharge of its important functions."

'For this manly declaration of your estimate of the evangelical clergy, which I trust may be read and approved by the rulers of our Church, I beg to return you my cordial thanks, even though you should at the same time have described them by a name which they by no means acknowledge themselves to deserve, " a low-church party among the clergy." '

CHAPTER VII.

' A true bishop I esteem
The highest officer the Church on earth
Can have as proper to itself, and deem
A Church without one an imperfect birth.'

GEORGE HERBERT.

TOWARDS the end of the year 1840, the Deanery of St. Patrick's Cathedral in Dublin became vacant. The election of the Dean rested with the Chapter, and was open to members of that body only. Mr. Daly and Dr. Wilson (afterwards Bishop of Cork) became candidates. The latter, besides occupying a prebendal stall in the Cathedral, was a Fellow of Trinity College, Dublin. Mr. Daly seems to have looked upon the advice given him by many of his Christian brethren in the ministry, to become a candidate for the vacant deanery, as a token that the 'pillar of the cloud' was moving on, and that it was his duty, like Israel of old, to follow, trusting that the God of Israel would be his rereward. The following letters are very characteristic. They appear to have been written in answer to some which he had received, urging him to send in his name, and remonstrating with him for not being more conciliatory and popular in his manners. Mr. C. was perhaps nearly twenty years his junior, and one who had learned much from him; yet he allowed him to 'smite him friendly' :—

To the Rev. J. C.

'POWERSCOURT GLEBE, 28*th October.*

'MY DEAR C.,—I thank you sincerely for your very kind and warm letter, which I received yesterday. I do not set at nought the kind advice of my friends. I have declared myself a candidate, and will ask every prebendary for his vote. I have written to all to keep their votes disengaged until the meeting of the Chapter on Friday, when I shall personally seek their support. I trust this is according to the will of God. I should prefer staying where I am; I feel for my poor people. I have a conscientious objection to being a *seeker* of any position in the world; but when those I value seek me, and put the thing before me in a way that looks like God's providence, then I have no pride to hinder me from asking every man for his vote, and no pride to be hurt by refusals. I am perfectly aware I am not a popular person.[1] Many estimable people value me, and I value their esteem, but I know that with others I am far from popular. I speak too plain, perhaps sometimes unadvisedly, with my lips. Lord forgive me.— Yours, in the best bonds, very affectionately,

'ROBERT DALY.'

To the Same.

'POWERSCOURT GLEBE, *November.*

'MY DEAR C.,—I thank you sincerely for your friendly, faithful, Christian letter. I think I can say with David,

---

[1] Mr. Daly was mistaken in this, as he was decidedly a *popular* person, although he had some enemies.

" Let the righteous smite me, it shall be a kindness, and let him reprove me." I know there is much worthy of reproof in my manner, but there is much more in the " *matter* " that makes me unpopular with some. My manner is, alas, only expressing too plainly what I think and feel. I certainly ought to keep my feelings more to myself, but I cannot give a man my hand when I cannot give him my heart. With all my bad manner, I do not know one Christian man that I ever alienated from me by my rough, bad manner; so in this present business it is not my manner that makes me unpopular. If a man like —— was in my place, he would be returned ; but it would not be because he has a better manner (though he has), but because he does not take as decided a part. He will write a complimentary review of a bishop's bad book, which I cannot do.

' The Lord direct and sanctify me, and bring about His purpose in this affair.—Yours very truly,

' ROBERT DALY.'

Early in the year 1841 Dr. Wilson was elected Dean of St. Patrick's. The legality of the votes, however, of two of his friends was disputed by the opposite party. As the setting aside of even one of these votes would render Mr. Daly the successful candidate, a lawsuit ensued, which lasted for two years. The disputed votes were those of the Archbishop of Dublin and Dr. Todd. Many circumstances combined to make these two years a very trying time to Mr. Daly. To his ardent and energetic mind, the state of suspense in which he was kept was very galling ;

he was like a race-horse, fretting and fuming under the
curb, when longing for the signal to start off. There was
one consideration in particular which made the delay extremely irksome to him. It was well known to him that
Lord de Grey had set his heart upon making him a
bishop; but as Government wished the point of law at
issue in the deanery case to be decided, and that he
should fight it out, they refused to sanction his promotion
until the lawsuit should be at an end. In the meantime
two sees became vacant, either of which, if given his
choice, he would have preferred to that of Cashel. Meath
was nearer to Dublin. If resident at Stackallan, he could
have continued to take an active part in working the
different religious Societies in Dublin, the interests of
which he had always had much at heart. Ossory was a
fine diocese, with a great deal of patronage, in a more
Protestant country than that of Cashel, with part of
which (the diocese of Ferns) he had been early associated
when first he entered the ministry. He would often revert
to this fact in after times, as showing how frequently the
Lord, in choosing our inheritance for us, seems to go contrary to what we, in our blind judgment, would think
best, and, as a wise Father, does not always consult our
wayward inclinations. He said that he felt a great dislike
to go to Waterford, but that 'the Lord said, To Waterford
you must go.' He afterwards became much attached to
the people there, and was greatly beloved and sincerely
regretted by the inhabitants, of all classes and persuasions.

In this state of suspense he thus writes to one of his
former parishioners:—

'Powerscourt Glebe, Enniskerry,
' 16th January.

'My dear Miss P.,—. . . I am in a great state of uncertainty, but feel it happy to leave everything in the hands of the Lord. Did I only consider my own gratification, I should stay in dear Powerscourt, changed and desolated as it is. I like the very look of the country, and of the people of the country; but if the Lord by His providence says, Go and preach in another place, who am I to say no ? I pray, and call on you and my other friends to pray, that He may give me grace sufficient for the situation He puts me into. The deanery offers a great sphere of usefulness, particularly as affording a place to gather together young men training for the ministry, and try to lead them to all truth. Dublin wants something in the Establishment, and visibly connected with the Church. The proprietory chapels, though they have good ministers, appear but half churches. I would still hope to spend my summer in Powerscourt, and help the minister if he was disposed to receive my help, and help the poor people. . . . I would keep the schools in my hands, and carry on education in the parish for the sake of the young people, from many of whom I get very cheering accounts at different times. Remember me kindly to Mary. In about a year we may know something of the deanery.—Yours in the best bonds,   'Robert Daly.'

In December 1842 the deanery question was at length decided, and Mr. Daly was declared to be the successful candidate. The Archbishop's vote was declared to be a legal one, as the Archbishops of Dublin had been given a prebendal stall in St. Patrick's Cathedral in order to give them a vote in the election of a dean, as well as for other reasons. Dr. Todd's vote was set aside on the ground of his being only pro-treasurer at that time, although he was afterwards elected treasurer on the removal of the suspension. Although the decision of the court was destined so materially to affect his interests in after life, Mr. Daly had so completely committed his cause into the hands of Him who he knew would judge rightly, that he was able in a remarkable manner to obey the apostolic injunction, ' Be careful for nothing.' He could say with St. Paul, ' None of these things move me.' His brother, Lord Dunsandle, who had been a short time before raised to the peerage by the same Conservative Government which was now interested in Mr. Daly's promotion, was present at the trial upon the day on which the case was decided. When it was concluded, he went to look for his brother to congratulate him upon the result, and found him writing very quietly in an adjoining room. ' Well,' said Lord Dunsandle, ' you are the most extraordinary fellow in the world ! There I have been for hours in the greatest anxiety waiting for the decision of the court, while you are writing here quite unconcerned, as if nothing was going on.' ' In the meantime,' answered Mr. Daly, ' I have written a paper for the *Christian Examiner;* and what is more, I think I have written a very good paper, too !'

The paper alluded to was one of a series of letters, published just at that time by him in the *Christian Examiner,* in defence of the conduct of the Irish clergy in assembling together in Dublin, without their respective bishops, for the purpose of mutual edification and conversation on religious subjects. Mr. Daly, just on the eve of being made a bishop when this letter was written, proved to Lord de Grey that he had indeed chosen a fit man to fill the vacant see. He had a high standard of what a bishop ought to be ; and all who knew him in later years will agree that he did not fall short of the standard which he himself had set up.

On the 12th of December Mr. Daly was installed dean, and on the very same day was offered the bishopric of Cashel, which he accepted. Lord de Grey, as was generally supposed, had made it a condition, on coming to Ireland, that he was to have uncontrolled power in dispensing the patronage of the Government appointments in the Church during the period of his being Lord-Lieutenant. He highly disapproved of the manner in which they had been for some years bestowed almost exclusively on the supporters of the National system of education, thus excluding from any chance of promotion the large majority of the best men in Ireland. On his elevation to these high offices in the Church, Mr. Daly received many letters of congratulation, and not a few expressing sorrow at the prospect of his leaving Powerscourt. Amongst others, Lord Roden wrote to him on the occasion :—

'GENOA, 24th December 1840.

'MY DEAR FRIEND,—I have just seen in the papers that

P

you are elected Dean of St. Patrick's. I should be the first of your friends to congratulate you on any event that may add to your usefulness, or the benefit of the Church on earth. I owe you perhaps more than any one for me and mine ; but I know it was not you, but our dear Lord. I am sure you could not be placed in this new situation except by Him; and Maria and I both most sincerely pray that the Lord will give you many souls in Dublin, to the praise and glory of His grace. . . . I will be delighted to hear from you as to your health, your prospects, and *your thoughts*, when you can find time to write. A letter will find me, directed " Genoa, Italy, by France," till after the 1st of February, when we expect to leave this. So poor dear —— is gone ; and then you say you have every reason to think " in the Lord." *It could not be otherwise.* You have nearly outlived all those who were your first hearers in the parish of Powerscourt.

'I need not tell you that Lady Roden sends you her kindest love. . . . —Your affectionately attached friend,

'RODEN.'

'GENOA, 23*d January* 1841.

'MY DEAR FRIEND,—Although I have been premature in congratulating you on your elevation to usefulness, I trust it is only in anticipation of what will be ; yet I would leave it entirely where you do, in the hands of Him who knows how to use them for His dear people. For I am certain, if He has work for you to do in the Cathedral of St. Patrick's, He will put you there ; if not, He will leave you where you are, and bless you in either the one or the other. I am not surprised at your feelings about your dear parish of Powerscourt; even to me it is wonderful to think a little about it. What must it be to you? But oh, my dear friend, how much cause for thanksgiving you have when you remember all the scenes you have witnessed in the presence of so many who are gone; gratitude and praise to Him who privileged you by permitting you to tell them of Jesus; and humility when you think that He made you the instrument He chose to awaken some out of their sleep, and finally to lead them to the blessed end at which they have arrived, and which you have been permitted to see! I am sure you must be led to cry out in such thoughts, "Lord, who am I, that I should have been thus favoured and honoured?" But this is the way our precious Lord Jesus deals with His people. . . . Remember me to any friends left in the valley. . . . God bless you, my dear friend. May our precious Lord Jesus shine on you more and more, and make you happy in Him for ever.—Your affectionate friend, 'RODEN.'

To one of his parishioners he thus humbly speaks of himself:—

'MY DEAR ——,—Your too kind note quite overwhelms me. Oh that I were what you think me to be! I cannot tell you what I feel in leaving a scene of labour in which God has so much and so long blessed me. I could have preferred staying at the Deanery, ministering there, and occasionally visiting my friends in this place; but an unsought providence pushes me on, and I am

forced to say, "Here am I, send me." Pray for me, that
the Lord who has been with me for the last 29 years may
not leave me when I am old and grey-headed. . . .—
Yours gratefully and affectionately,   'ROBERT DALY.'

In February 1843 the subject of this Memoir was consecrated bishop in the cathedral church over which he
had for so short a time presided as dean. The following
is the account given of it in the *Christian Examiner* at
the time:—

'CONSECRATION OF THE BISHOP OF CASHEL AND
WATERFORD.

'The consecration of the Very Rev. the late Dean of St.
Patrick's to the united dioceses of Cashel, Waterford, and
Lismore, took place in the Cathedral on Sunday last, at
eleven o'clock. We have never, on any occasion of a similar
description, seen so large an assemblage of the evangelical
clergy and laity of the Church as were here congregated,
as well out of respect to the highly-esteemed individual
who was about to be consecrated, and whose elevation has
given greater satisfaction to those interested in the spiritual
welfare of Ireland than any appointment that has been
made to this important office for many years, as to witness
the important and imposing ceremony.

'Soon after eleven o'clock his Grace the Archbishop of
Dublin entered the Cathedral, preceded by the verger, and
occupied the throne. He was accompanied by the Bishops
of Cork and Ossory; the Bishop-elect; Dr. Radcliffe, the
Vicar-General; John Samuels, Esq., the Registrar; Rev.

Dr. West, chaplain to the Archbishop; and the Rev. Henry Irwin.

'The Rev. Dr. Marks read the morning prayers, and the minor canons, the Rev. J. M'Kee and the Rev. J. de Butts, read the lessons; at the conclusion of which the Archbishop, accompanied by the Bishops of Cork and Ossory, proceeded to the communion table, and read the second service appointed for the occasion. The Rev. Henry Irwin of Sandford, Archdeacon of Emly, then ascended the pulpit, and preached a most excellent and faithful sermon. He selected for his text 2 Peter, 1st chapter and 19th verse.'

The Bishop's venerable mother and several other members of his family were present, as well as a great number of his friends and Powerscourt parishioners. To the former it must have been a source of gratification of the highest order to see her son so worthy of this high calling, and to listen to his fervent and solemn responses when taking his part in our beautiful service for the consecration of bishops. It has not, perhaps, been allowed to many mothers to be present on such an occasion. Lady Harriet Daly had at this time exceeded what the Psalmist tells us is the age of man by fifteen or sixteen years; and yet her life was not labour and sorrow, her eye had not waxed dim, nor was her natural force much abated. She continued for some years after this time in the enjoyment of excellent health.

The Bishop gave an amusing account of his first interview with the Lord-Lieutenant after his promotion. Lady de Grey, who had long known and valued him, having

expressed her gratification on his appointment to the see
of Cashel, said to him: ' But come, let me look at you ;
they tell me that you will never dress like a bishop.' So
accordingly, as he expressed it, ' her ladyship proceeded to
examine me closely; and as I perceived that she did not look
quite satisfied with the lower part of my costume, I said :
" If his Excellency will allow me to put on my hat in his
presence, I will set you all at defiance !" ' He then, as he
related the story, put on his hat, to the great amusement
of the aides-de-camp and others who were present, when
Lady de Grey had to acknowledge that he looked very
like a bishop. A few days afterwards he met his former
curate in Sackville Street, when he said to him, ' Come,
now, I see you are shaping your mouth to call me " My
Lord," but never mind it ! '

As the Palace at Cashel was not at that time disposed
of, the Bishop was allowed to make his choice of a residence
between that place and Waterford. The County Tipperary
was at that time much disturbed, though it afterwards
became one of the most peaceable counties in Ireland.
In one of his letters written at this time he said he would,
as far as he was personally concerned, have preferred
Cashel to Waterford as a residence if he had not ' a throat
to cut.' The Palace was a fine house; the gardens and
pleasure-grounds were beautifully situated, stretching up
the side of the hill, which was surmounted by the pic-
turesque ruins so well known as the Rock of Cashel, of
which there was a beautiful view from the windows of the
Palace. But what influenced him most in making a
decision was the larger sphere of usefulness which Water-

ford presented to him, the Protestant population at that time exceeding Cashel in the proportion of ten to one.

The Bishop at first felt very much the separation from all his friends when he went to Waterford, and the change from the lovely scenery at Powerscourt to a town house. In one of his letters he described himself as 'like a lark in a cage, *barring* the sod.' It was not long, however, before he became thoroughly absorbed in the interests of his new sphere of duty, and warmly attached to Waterford and its people, with whom he completely identified himself.

By the County Wicklow clergy he was much regretted, although they rejoiced at his elevation to a higher sphere of duty in the Church. The following is an address of the clergy of Glandelagh to the Lord Bishop of Cashel and Waterford on his promotion, and his reply to the same :—

' *To the Right Rev. the Lord Bishop of Cashel and
Waterford.*

' Deeply as we feel the loss which we have sustained in the removal of one from among us who has been so long a brother, a friend, and as a father to us, to whom we have been in the habit of looking as our counsellor and guide, from whom each month as we met together we have heard so much to instruct and edify us, who has been for so many years the mainspring and centre of every good work and labour of love among us,—while we cannot but feel deeply, more deeply than we can express, the separation from such a brother and companion and example in the ministry, we yet bless and praise the great Head of the Church for having called him to a station in it in which the gifts and graces which He has bestowed upon him may be yet more and more extensively and beneficially exercised.

'And it is a consolation to think that there is a relation subsisting between us which change of place and distance cannot affect; that, separated as we now are, there will still be a bond, a blessed bond, uniting us in spirit and at a throne of grace.

'Earnestly do we pray that the Author and Giver of every good gift will increase and multiply upon our revered and beloved friend His richest mercy; that in the arduous duties upon which he is now entering, the grace of his Divine Master may be sufficient for him; that He may send him wisdom from above, give him a right judgment in all things, make him ever valiant for the truth, and, in proportion to his greater opportunities and extended sphere, more and more an instrument of His glory and a blessing to His Church.

'Signed by

'WILLIAM CLEAVER, etc. etc.

'*February* 1843.'

This address being duly transmitted by one of the clergy, with an intimation that it would be made public if not objected to, the following reply was received from the Bishop :—

'DUBLIN, 18*th February* 1843.

'MY DEAR FRIEND,—I have received your letter (which reached me just as I was leaving Waterford) and the accompanying paper with no common feelings.

'I am firmly convinced that it belongs not to sinful man, conscious of his many sins, negligences, and ignorances, either to give or to seek praise. Yet I cannot but receive the address of my beloved clerical brethren with the highest gratification, as the expression of the affection and esteem of such a body of my old friends, among whom I have been going in and out for so many years.

'I consider it a subject of the most humble gratitude to God, that He should by His grace, in spite of all my evil, both of nature and manner, have enabled me so to walk in the county of Wicklow as after twenty-nine years to have received such a testimony from such men; and it is a great encouragement to me in my present more difficult circumstances, to be led to trust that He who has thus kept me in my younger days will not leave me when I am old and grey-headed.

'As to the publication of this gratifying testimony, it would be in vain to deny that the pride and vanity of the old man would be highly gratified by it; but surely on this very account a better spirit reminds us that, as the servants of God, we stand not at the bar of the world; and should we appeal to its judgment, or appear to value its opinion, we should be making light of the approbation of God and of the esteem of truly Christian friends.

'I can assure you, my beloved clerical brethren of the county of Wicklow, that I shall never forget the tie that has been formed between us, that I hope I may have grace to remember them at a throne of grace; and I beseech them not to forget to pray for me, that I may not be left to give occasion to the enemy to speak ill of the holy name whereby I am called, and to shame that character which their love and kindness has given me. — With every sentiment of affection and regard, I remain, my dear friends, yours affectionately in the bonds of the gospel,

'ROBERT CASHEL, etc.'

The affectionate congratulations of his former parishioners followed the Bishop to Waterford. One of them, who appears by his letters to have profited much both in temporal and spiritual things by what he learned at Powerscourt, writes to him thus :—

'ABERYSTWITH, 6th February 1843.

'MY LORD,—The receipt of your kind and affectionate letter gave me more satisfaction than I can express, not only on account of your preferment to that exalted station to which you have been appointed, but the fatherly affection which breathes throughout its lines. I was very forcibly struck with the similarity of your feelings to those of the great Apostle of the Gentiles. When he viewed the requisitions and tendencies of his ministerial functions, he exclaimed, "Who is sufficient for these things ?" and under similar feelings he makes use of those affecting and pathetic words, "Brethren, pray for us."

'You say you have need of the prayers of your Christian friends. I can only say on my part, that God has heard my prayer in that He has made you what you now are, and verified in you the fulfilment of that promise, "He that honoureth me, him will my Father honour;" and never, while I am able to raise my hands, shall I forget you at the throne of grace. I cannot; you are interwoven, as it were, in my very existence. Justly may I remember you, for you are bound to me by far stronger ties of affection, as the instrument by which spiritual life was bestowed, than those by whom natural life was given. Your letters I shall never part with; I have them all. I frequently read them, and fancy I hear as it were your own words; they are epistles indeed. I shall never lose sight of them till I exchange them for some token of approbation, which I trust will yet be bestowed on me as one of the unworthiest of the children of the Highest.

'Humbly imploring of Heaven to give me grace to abide by and follow the blessed advice contained in your last letter, and beseeching you for an interest in your prayers, I am, my Lord, your affectionate and grateful son in the gospel, 'JAMES MILLER.'

While the Palace at Waterford was being prepared for his reception, and in order to recruit his health before entering on his episcopal duties, the Bishop spent a few months on the Continent, and visited Switzerland, as he said he would like to see Mont Blanc before he died. In Cheever's *Wanderings in the Shadow of Mont Blanc* we find an interesting account of a Sunday at Geneva, from which the following is an extract:—

'The Sabbath evening before we parted, Mr. Bacon had gone with me to hear the Bishop of Cashel. The service was in the dining-hall of the Hotel de Bergues, a fashionable resort, where there were gathered as many of the votaries of rank and wealth from England as ordinarily are to be found in Geneva on any Sabbath. It was an unusual step for a bishop of the English Church—a regular conventicle, a Sabbath evening extempore sermon from a bishop in the dining-hall of the hotel. I love to record it, as a pleasant example of a dignitary of the Establishment using the influence of his rank to do good, to gather an assembly for hearing God's word in circumstances where no one else could have commanded an audience of half a dozen persons—where, indeed, the use of the room for such a purpose would hardly have been granted to any other individual.

'The hall was perfectly crowded. The preacher's sermon was a most simple, faithful, practical, affectionate exhibition of divine truth.

'He had just been made Bishop of Cashel, in Ireland; before, he was plain Rev. R. Daly. A Scottish clergyman of my acquaintance, who had formerly known him well, called on him in Geneva. "I hope," said he, when allusion was made to his recent elevation, "that you will find me Robert Daly still."'

On his return from the Continent, the Bishop took up his abode in the Palace at Waterford, bringing with him his Powerscourt servants, two of whom remained with him as long as he lived, and some of them died in his service. Their number was of course much increased from the number he had required in the small house at Powerscourt. Many people said that they felt sure he would continue to make use of his dinner-set of white delf at Waterford; but in this they were mistaken. He had too much good sense not to have everything in his establishment suitable to his position there. He was, as a bishop ought to be, 'given to hospitality,' entertaining at his house not only his clergy and neighbours, but the judges, etc., at assize time, and any military that were stationed in Waterford. In his own house he was remarkably pleasant, and was a most agreeable host. His nephew, the Hon. Bowes Daly, went to reside with him upon his becoming a bishop, and acted as his agent and secretary. His first summer in Waterford was that troublous period in Ireland's history when Daniel O'Connell, the great agitator, kept the minds of all loyal subjects of our gracious sovereign in a state of great alarm by his monster meetings in behalf of the repeal of the Union. In the beginning of July 1843 he held one of these meetings in Ballybricken, close to Waterford, when the Bishop was deeply grieved by the conduct of Sir Benjamin Morris— the mayor of the city of Waterford, and one of its most influential Protestant citizens—on the occasion. He went to the meeting (at which he afterwards presided) at the head of a large cavalcade from Waterford ; and as all this took place on a Sunday, the desecration of the Sabbath was very great. The Bishop, who never feared the face of man when he felt it to be his duty to raise his voice to 'reprove, rebuke, exhort,' wrote a letter of remonstrance to Sir Benjamin, which was printed and circulated in Waterford. What followed was a striking exemplification of the truth of God's promise, that 'when a man's ways please the Lord, He shall make even his enemies to be at peace with him.' Sir Benjamin Morris was at first very much annoyed by the Bishop's reproof, but he ultimately saw that he was right. He greatly respected and was most friendly with him during the rest of his life, attending regularly at the Cathedral.

The Bishop of Cashel held his first visitation of his dioceses in the month of July 1843. His primary charge was afterwards made a subject of debate in the House of Lords. Few people were so much misunderstood or so often misrepresented as the late Bishop of Cashel. We have said before that his manners were rough; those who sincerely loved him often felt it to be so; but knowing well the warm and true heart that beat within, they did not mind it. It could not be always so with strangers; and never did his unconciliatory manner appear to more disadvantage than at the beginning of his intercourse with the clergy of his new dioceses. He did not, however, always intend exactly what was gathered from his manner; nor was he always thinking of himself and of his own importance, and sometimes forgot the weight which would be attached to anything bordering on reproof which fell from him. The clergy, however, soon came to understand him, and to know and feel that he was their real friend. Many of them could bear testimony to the fact that in temporal matters he was their friend. To many a one among them has he ministered of his abundance when he came to know that they were in want of assistance, either from sickness or any other casualty. The following letter, written many years later, gives an instance of his liberality to his clergy. It is addressed to a rector in his diocese, whose curate, a truly Christian man, was dying of consumption:—

'My DEAR M.,—I am grieved, but not surprised, at the sad account you give of your curate, Mr. C.'s, health. At the time of his ordination I suspected that he was not to serve long; he had all the appearance of consumption. It is a trial to you, but a gain to him, as you represent him having found the pearl of great price. I cannot but feel for him and his sisters. His suffering will be but short. "He has fought a good fight; he has kept the faith," etc. As to what he may stand in need of while he remains here, I shall have much pleasure in taking the burden on myself, and off your hands, which have more than enough on them without this. I will pay for Mr. C. whatever you will say he wants, and you may consider what comforts his present delicacy requires. I hope all yours are as well as under the circumstances can be expected.— Very truly yours, 'ROBERT CASHEL.'

On the occasion of one of his ordinations, when an unsuccessful candidate seemed much depressed by his failure, the Bishop, on taking leave of him, handed him a cheque for a large sum of money.

The following characteristic letter was addressed by him to one of his clergy at a time when he suffered from acute illness :—

To the Rev. T. G.

'My DEAR G.,—I am truly sorry to find that you are ill. We are taught by our Master to bear one another's burdens. You want rest, and sickness is a time of expense and outlay. Will you accept the enclosed at my hands as from the Lord ? Do not send me any thanks, but simply acknowledge receipt.—Yours most truly,

'ROBERT CASHEL.'

Enclosed was a cheque for £50.

To another who was suffering from consumption of the lungs, he afforded the means of going abroad for the winter, in hopes of restoring his health, when he under-took to provide for his duty during his absence, that he might not be obliged to resign his curacy. To the widow of one of his clergy he gave £1000; and when the children of another were left without father or mother, he sent one of the little boys to a good school in England, and made himself liable for all expenses connected with his educa-tion. Who would mind a little roughness of manner when beneath it there beat so warm, so true a heart ? Are there many of whom it can be said that their only faults are faults of manner ? Yet so it was with the late Bishop of Cashel. He was one who spent his life in doing good to others, both temporally and spiritually, of whom it might truly be said, that 'he served his generation by the will of God.' He did not like, when a parish became vacant, to be asked for it; he wished to become personally acquainted with all his clergy, or to hear of them from others upon whose judgment he could depend, and his plain-spoken way of telling them so occasionally sur-prised them very much. He would sometimes tell them that he never took any man's opinion of himself. In his distribution of his patronage he was thoroughly conscien-tious; he could not be accused of 'Nepotism,' as he never gave a parish to one of his relations, although he had more than one nephew in the Church. In making an appointment, it was his earnest and prayerful wish to choose the man who was best fitted for the post. He may have sometimes erred in his judgment of men, and no doubt he did, but his motives were the best. On one of his clergy thanking him for having given him a good living, his answer was: 'You need not thank me; if I had known of a better man, and one more suited to it, I would have given it to him.' He had, generally speaking, great discernment of character; and few who were acquainted with him will forget the way in which he would take a look at a person, as if he would look into their inmost soul with his penetrating eye, which had a peculiar light in it. He was remarkably observant of what was going on about him; his hearing and sight were both very quick, and sometimes, in a large room full of people, he appeared to see and hear what every one was saying and doing. He was, however, sometimes mistaken in his estimate of people; but his mistakes generally leant to the side of charity—that charity which 'thinketh no evil,' which 'hopeth all things, believeth all things.' He did not often think people worse than they were, unless they were misrepresented to him by those on whose judgment he thought he could depend; but when once prejudiced against a person, it was very difficult, almost impossible, to alter his opinion. He frequently formed a better opinion of some than they deserved, —a mistake very often made by good people, who do not suspect others of being influenced by inferior motives, their own being high-minded and pure. The Bishop of

Q

Cashel had a strong way of expressing himself, often putting truths forward in a very striking and forcible way. He has frequently been heard to say that he thought it a very solemn reflection, on seeing a little infant, ' That child has begun an existence which will *never* end, whether happy or unhappy; we cannot cease to exist, we must go on.' At another time he said : 'Well, it's a fine thing to be *well* dead.' On a friend taking him over his house, he looked round it and said, ' Very good, very good for a worm.' On another occasion he astonished a gentleman very much, who was showing him a very fine house that he had just built, by saying to him, ' It will do very well to be burned,' reminding him that the world and all that was in it was to be burned up.

In the same straightforward way he would sometimes startle those who asked his opinion by telling them the plain unvarnished truth. During one of his visits to England, he spent the evening at the house of a friend, where the curate of the parish had been invited to meet him, and to conduct family worship, which he concluded by offering up an extempore prayer of unusual length. He afterwards said, 'I am afraid, my lord, that I was *too* long.' '*Three* long! *four* long!' was the Bishop's answer.

Of the Bishop's kind hospitality the writer of this Memoir can speak from experience, as she and her family have been several times under his roof for weeks, and on one occasion for months together. The first of these visits took place soon after his going to Waterford. It was indeed a privilege to be a member of his household, to join in his family worship morning and evening, and to enjoy his instructive and delightful conversation,—to witness the everyday life of this man of God. As to the former, one felt inclined to say, 'Happy are these thy servants which stand continually before thee, and that hear thy wisdom.'

There was nothing, perhaps, in which our revered friend excelled so much as in his short, familiar lectures at family prayer; they were simple, and yet striking. His words, coming from the heart, touched the hearts of all present; and his family altar, which he, as it were, set up each morning, seemed the very gate of heaven. He did not seem to want a cross to raise him nearer to God; perhaps that may have been the reason why he was so singularly exempt through life from the ordinary trials which Christians meet with. In his early diary, while yet a curate of Newcastle, he says that he enjoyed an abiding sense of God's presence; this feeling seemed to increase year by year, as 'the path of the just,' we are told, 'is like the shining light, which shineth more and more unto the perfect day,'—that perfect day which he is now enjoying, *His* presence, which is fulness of joy.

The Bishop was always his own private chaplain, and, after he went to Waterford, continued to read every morning the chapter for the day which was appointed to be read by the Powerscourt calendar. He found *all* Scripture to be profitable for instruction, etc., and no chapter occurred upon which he would not say some heart-stirring and profitable words,—not reading the whole chapter at once, but pausing whenever he came to a passage upon which he wished to comment. He always began by offering up a short prayer for the teaching of God's Holy Spirit to enable him to understand and profit by His word.

In reading one of the chapters of Ezekiel, which perhaps many persons might think did not afford material for a lecture of this sort, he on one occasion dwelt very solemnly upon the words, 'And they shall *know* that I am the Lord;' saying that there was no other expression in the whole of Scripture which appeared to him more awful than this one, showing how unrepenting sinners will at the last be forced by the judgments of God to feel His power, and to *know* that He whom they despised and rejected was the Lord Jehovah. In the evening he generally went through one of St. Paul's Epistles; and his prayers, morning and evening, were extempore. Like Daniel of old, he seemed then to be in his element; and when his supplications became very fervent, he would often add, '*Do, do,* gracious Lord!' as if to urge the petition with greater earnestness.

His habits of punctuality were well known. Precisely at nine o'clock in the morning the prayer-bell rang, when, on coming into the dining-room, we always found the good Bishop engaged in making tea, which, as well as pouring it out, he always did himself, even when ladies were staying in his house. After prayers, while waiting for breakfast to be quite ready, he would open some of his numerous letters and papers, and would pleasantly communicate anything interesting or amusing which they contained. The number of letters received by him was so great, that he always said that if a letter was not answered by him on the day that he received it, there was no chance of its being attended to afterwards. He was always remarkably pleasant at breakfast. He made it a very substantial meal, which, at the same time that it contributed to strengthen him for his day's work, was a sign of an excellent constitution with which he was blessed. On one occasion, when ready to pour out the tea, he found that he had neglected to put any water in the teapot, which amused him very much. He declared that he could not have been sane when he was capable of making such an omission. He had heard people say that every one was mad upon some subject, and he insisted that there must have been something astray in his mind when he was capable of putting the tea into the teapot and then sitting down to read prayers without having added the water. But though he turned this little circumstance thus pleasantly against himself, it was not his habit to be either forgetful or irregular in the discharge of the duties of the everyday routine of life. On the contrary, his great regularity was sometimes amusing, and what he did one day he liked to do every day; and a saying or anecdote which was called forth by any particular circumstance would be repeated by him whenever that circumstance occurred, in a manner which showed great simplicity in so great a mind. None of his guests have failed to hear him say, when eating an artichoke, 'I eat an artichoke because I think it's *as innocent* a way of spending ten minutes as I could possibly have;' or, when the second course consisted of a fruit-pie and a simple pudding, to be asked which they would have, ' wholesome or poison,' the former being invariably the one he would choose for himself.

His mornings, until two o'clock, were spent in his study, reading and writing; and this was the time when any of his clergy who had business with him would be sure to find him at home. He never ate luncheon himself, but was always at leisure to preside at it when he had friends staying in the house, to those with whom he was intimate generally giving the following invitation on coming into the room : ' Now for the great business of life !' When children were staying in the house, he would cut up the meat for their dinners himself, to save their mother the trouble; and the youngest (which was always his favourite in every family) must have her bowl of broth given to her in the parlour, sitting on her nurse's lap.

His afternoons were employed in working the various charities, over which, as bishop, he had much control. He took regular exercise on horseback. This was one great means of preserving his health, which was now quite re-established, and continued to be excellent as long as he lived. He would often ride out to ' Bishop Foy's School,' in which he took a particular interest. It was a fine institution, endowed by one of his predecessors in the see of Waterford, the appointment of the master and matron being left in the hands of the bishop for the time being.

Into this school the respectable citizens of Waterford were privileged to enter their sons, where they received a solid education, though not a classical one.

After the Bishop's death, the following lines were written by one of the boys who had been educated at this school:—

'Old warrior brave ! thou'rt gone to rest,
    Gone from earth's strife and sadness,
To the land where the upright and the blest
    Abide in peace and gladness.

'Thy battle is o'er, thy arms laid down,
    Thou hast long and nobly fought ;
Thou hast kept the faith, and gained the crown
    The Saviour's blood hath bought.

'The love of Him who gave His life
    A ransom for the lost,
Upheld and nerved thee in the strife
    'Gainst Satan's mighty host.

'Long hadst thou known that matchless love,
    It brought thee life and peace ;
Now thou dost taste its joys above,
    Where pleasures never cease.

'They loved thee most who knew thee best,
    They knew thy virtues great ;
A truer heart in human breast
    Hath never ceased to beat.

'Thy generous deeds, though oft unseen,
    They have not with thee perished ;
In grateful memories, fresh and green,
    Long, long shall they be cherished.

'A bold, intrepid heart was thine,
    No fear of man dismayed thee—
Ignoble foes could but malign,
    And o'er thy grave upbraid thee.

'Oh, base the foes that stab the dead !
    But they could harm thee not ;
Thy name in loving hearts shall live
    When theirs shall justly rot.

'Then rest thee still, old warrior brave !
  While angels watch shall keep ;
Though they reproach thee o'er thy grave,
  They can't disturb thy sleep.

' Let slander do what slander can—
  Impotently assail thee ;
Whate'er they say, a truer man
  Ne'er lived—than ROBERT DALY.

' WATERFORD, *Oct.* '73.   R. P.' .

The Fanning Institution in Waterford was one in which the Bishop took a great interest ; he was *ex officio* the chairman of its committee of management. He attended the committee meeting every week, taking much pains to ensure the election of the most deserving objects when there was a vacancy, and to benefit the inmates both temporally and spiritually in every way in his power ; amongst others, giving them every year a dinner at Christmas time. This house of industry, as it was sometimes called, was a fine building, bequeathed by a benevolent member of the Society of Friends, named James Fanning, as an asylum for those among the respectable inhabitants of Waterford, both male and female, who should be so much reduced in their circumstances as to need such a shelter, Roman Catholics as well as Protestants. Waterford is rich in endowed institutions, the greater number of which are very much under the control of the bishop. There is, among others, a fine orphanage near the town, houses for the widows of clergymen, and the Boucher Charity, which is an almshouse for elderly females.

The Bishop's dinner hour was six o'clock precisely,

except when he had company to dinner, when it was half-past six. During the visit of the writer and her husband to the Palace, on their children coming into the dining-room for the dessert, the little one would run over to him, passing her mother by, at which he was greatly gratified; he always received her with open arms, and set her upon his knee. He was remarkably fond of little children; if any one objected to their laughing too loud, he would say: 'Let them laugh while they can; they are happier now than they will ever be, until they come to enjoy the full con-summation of bliss in heaven.' At another time he said: 'I am never annoyed by children of this age when they are jumping over the chairs and sofas, and pulling the furniture about; it is when they grow older, and will go to the devil in spite of you, that they are a real anxiety.' He enjoyed most thoroughly having a romp with them, standing in the corner of the landing-place outside the drawing-room door making funny faces for them, and some-times pretending to be asleep, when, on his awakening up and trying to catch them, he was greeted with peals of laughter from the delighted children. Though he was anxious to store their memories with Scripture while young, he did not approve of bringing children to church before they were able to understand what was going on, saying that it was not proper to make a nursery of the church. The religion of children, he thought, was more a matter of feeling than what could be called real religion, as they knew nothing, he said, of what must be the foun-dation of all true religion,—a feeling of the exceeding sinfulness of sin, and therefore the need of a Saviour.

On these points, however, the writer was presumptuous enough sometimes to differ [in opinion from him. She was greatly struck on one occasion by his taking the little one, who was his god-child, up in his arms, to show her a picture of our Saviour which he had over his chimney-piece. On her asking, 'Who's that?' he compressed his lips, as those who knew him well will remember was his habit when speaking on any subject about which he felt deeply, and answered in a serious tone, 'The Man of sorrows.'

The Bishop was of a very sociable disposition; and as at this period of his life he did not study in the evenings, those who were privileged to be his guests had the enjoyment of his cheerful and instructive conversation. Every Wednesday evening he attended a lecture at St. Olave's Church, after which some of the clergy and their families would come in to tea at the Palace, when any among them who were musical were asked to join in singing sacred music. He was particularly fond of some of the stirring old tunes, such as 'Sound the loud timbrel,' 'Head of the Church triumphant,' 'The Lord my pasture shall prepare,' etc. When any friends dined with him for the first time at Waterford, he would never fail to call their attention, as soon as dinner was removed, to his table-cloths, which he was very proud of as a specimen of Irish manufacture. The pattern represented the arms of the see, beautifully wrought on a large scale, the rest of the cloth being covered with wreaths of shamrock. He had them manufactured for himself; and as the chief expense was the setting up of the loom, he had all his table-cloths of different qualities made of the same pattern. On the occasion of his clerical meetings, the first Wednesday in every month, his hospitality was on a large scale; not only his own house was filled for the two nights which preceded and followed this day, but beds were provided at his expense at the hotel for as many more coming from a distance as required them. The writer, when staying at the house, was allowed to be one of the party at the dinner-table the first day, when some of the clergy had arrived; but on the great day no ladies were present at dinner. The number attending these clerical meetings was, on an average, about forty, some coming from a great distance. Archdeacon Power, who was one who valued the Bishop for the truth's sake, frequently drove over in a drag from Lismore, with as many of the clergy from that neighbourhood as it would contain. No doubt many of those who were present at these meetings can testify that they found them to be 'times of refreshing,' and will acknowledge that it was good for them to have been there. The Bishop, though taking the chair, laid aside on these occasions his episcopal authority, and joined freely in conversation upon whatever subject was under discussion. It was often remarked that he at these meetings assumed a far less dictatorial tone than he had formerly done at the Wicklow clerical meetings. The old Dean (to whom he was made the means of much blessing) would sit out the meeting to the last, listening with avidity to whatever dropped from the lips of the Bishop; and when (being very deaf) he failed in catching the words, would call out, 'Speak up, my lord.' The Bishop, through the means of these meetings, became personally acquainted with all his clergy, with the curates as well as the rectors. They enabled him to form his own opinion of their abilities, and, what was more important still, of the soundness of their views of divine truth; while they on their part had an opportunity of profiting by the instructions of one who might indeed be said to be a scribe instructed unto the kingdom of heaven, who could bring out of his treasures things new and old, and give them the benefit of his valuable experience and advice in the working of their parishes.

In the evening, the Bishop and all the clergy attended service at St. Olave's Church, when one or other of the visitors, selected by the Bishop, preached. After service, the ladies staying in the house, and the families of the local clergy, joined them at tea. After breakfast the next morning, during which the conversation was often very delightful, the party separated, and those who came from other parishes returned to their homes. The Bishop preached every Sunday morning, either in the Cathedral or in some other church in the diocese. He did not wish to give up his work as a minister of the gospel, though raised to a higher office in the ministry; he wished, as he expressed it, 'to keep his old throat in wind.' He would frequently take the whole morning service himself, if one of his clergy was absent from home, or from illness unable to officiate, and could not otherwise find a substitute.

The famine with which Ireland was visited in the year 1846 called forth his kindly feelings and warmth of heart, and proved to the Roman Catholic population of Waterford that he was their friend. On his going there first, the Roman Catholics having no doubt heard of his campaigns at Carlow, as well as other controversies which he had been engaged in with the clergy of their Church, felt rather afraid of him, and slight attempts were made to annoy and intimidate him. When it was found, however, that they had not the effect of doing either the one or the other, they were very soon given up. He felt inclined, he said, when he heard the little street-boys calling out, ' Bob Daly,' ' Bob Daly,' to say, ' Where is the little boy who knows me so well ?' and to give him a shilling, but on reflection felt it to be a wiser plan to take no notice of them. The poor people who were not of his own persuasion grew to love him affectionately, and at his death he was sincerely regretted by them. They found him to be their friend in time of need, and that in the distribution of temporal relief in this their time of distress (in the famine of 1846), as he made no distinction in his charities in that trying time between Protestants and Roman Catholics.

The Rev. Thomas Gimlette, one of the Waterford clergy, writes :

' When Bishop Sandes died, there was, of course, great interest felt in considering who was likely to succeed to the vacant see. Several meetings were held for prayer, even by the Dissenting bodies, that the new Bishop of Cashel might be a man of God, thoroughly furnished unto all good works, and a faithful witness for Christ and His gospel.

'The nomination of Robert Daly, Dean of St. Patrick's, gave unfeigned satisfaction to those who were evangelical in sentiment, and who desired earnestly to contend for the faith once delivered to the saints. Many, however, of a latitudinarian spirit, and the Roman Catholics as a body, were not pleased. Robert Daly was known to be a man of such strong will and earnest purpose for the spread of Protestant truth, it was feared that a spirit of controversy would be fostered and encouraged by him amongst both laity and clergy. The general feeling, however, was one of satisfaction. It was felt that one was coming who was thoroughly in earnest in his work, who had high estimation in the Church, and who was a sound and faithful preacher of the gospel.'

The Protestants of Waterford were prepared to receive an evangelical bishop with open arms. They were people who knew the joyful sound of the gospel, which they had heard for many years from the lips of a devotedly Christian minister, the Rev. Richard Ryland, whose labours preceded those of Bishop Daly at Waterford. At the time we speak of, his health was declining; he lived, however, for many years afterwards. On hearing of his death, the Bishop wrote as follows in a letter to the Archdeacon of Waterford :—

'DUBLIN, 1st *January* 1867.

'MY DEAR BELL,—I thank you for writing to me to let me know the melancholy intelligence of Mr. Ryland's death. I was prepared for it. From what the doctor told me, I felt that he had not strength to recover. Well, blessed are the dead that die in the Lord; they rest from their labours, and their works do follow them. I cannot grieve for him—it is well for him; but I can mourn with and for his family, who lived for him. I can grieve for Waterford. Many a one in that city loved him and valued him, and are now grieving at their loss; for though latterly he could do very little, they liked that little. How can we supply his place?'

Amongst other fruits of Mr. Ryland's ministry was a most flourishing and interesting Sunday school, attended by about 500 young people of all ages, some of the classes being composed of young men engaged in business; and the young women frequently continued to attend even after they were married. Some letters which were addressed, soon after his going to Waterford, by the Bishop to one of his friends, show us how full his hands were of work at this time, although he considered himself to be too old for so arduous a post. He would sometimes remark, ' If they had made me a bishop ten years ago, I might have done something':—

'WATERFORD, 19th March 1845.

' MY DEAR ——,—It was very kind of you to write to me, and you must allow me to thank you for your letter. I feel an increased interest in the subject of prophecy. I would, if possible, command time to just gather my scattered thoughts into some tangible shape, that I myself as well as others might see them as a whole, and observe their consistency; but I am liable to such distractions, that I can look forward to no time very near that I could give to the subject. I shall, if the Lord permit, go next week to England for my Parliamentary duty, for which I have no appetite. When I return, I shall have to go through my diocese, to hold confirmations, which will consume the greater part of the summer.

'I expect a very interesting meeting of a little Prophetical Society in London, to which I belong. Mr. Bickersteth has proposed an examination of the sixth seal, on which subject he differs largely from Mr. Elliot, who is also to be there. I differ from both, so that I expect much to be brought out; and I hope, by the goodness of my cause, to gain ground, though it is very great odds to have against me authors who have pledged themselves to certain opinions in their books. They are hardly free to take up any new suggestion. The discussion will, however, be, I doubt not, very interesting. I do not think that I am quite as hard against Dr. Arnold as you seem to be. I was greatly interested by his life, and pleased to see how sterling truth bore sway in the midst of much political and religious error. He appeared to have a single eye to bring boys to Christ. His correspondence with them in after life showed his real religion. He had no zeal to bring them to his political views, but he had a zeal to bring them to Christ. My kind regards to your father and sister.—Yours very truly, 'ROBERT CASHEL, etc.'

In another letter to the same friend he says:
'I have my hands full here doing the Lord's work. I preach generally every Sunday to a crowded congregation,

besides many other useful employments. May the Lord give His blessing; without Him we can do nothing.'

To another friend, who had resided for a time at Waterford, he writes :—

'WATERFORD, 24*th December* 1844.

'MY DEAR MRS. S.,—I am very thankful that you are well after your confinement, and that the little one is likely to be strong and healthy. I cannot refuse your request, and to put *him* (as it appears to be) on the list of those I ought to pray for. May the Lord make him His for ever, and then it will be well for him that he was born! I have begun a clerical meeting. I had my first on the 1st of this month; the second is to be on the 8th of January, and the third on the first Wednesday in February. I had twenty-eight clergymen, and we had much profitable conversation. I trust the Lord will bless them for good. Our church continues very well attended, our singing very good, but I do not hear of any great work of grace. We must sow the seed, and wait for its growth. I hope you have marks of the Lord's blessing in your part of the vineyard. It is well to be employed in His service, and to wait upon Him for fruit.

'I do not relish the prospect of my Parliamentary campaign. We are very quiet; the mania for railroads has quite put Repeal into the shade. We had a Repeal dinner to O'Connell here, but it was a great failure. There were about 1000 persons assembled before the Town Hall. . . . —Yours affectionately,

'ROBERT CASHEL, etc.'

R

To the Same.

'WATERFORD, 14*th January* 1845.

' MY DEAR MRS. S.,—Easter is so very early this year, that I think it probable I shall not go over to England till after it, at the end of March. I think nothing interesting would be likely to come on in the early part of the session, and I might as well be with my large flock at the time when we are particularly called on to speak of a dying and risen Saviour. We are about making great improvements in all the schools here. We are looking for first-rate masters and mistresses; they have been very bad. We are trying also to make some arrangement about the pews in the church, so as to accommodate the many who, I am happy to say, are still anxious to come to our church. . . . Tell the children I would send them a biscuit a-piece, only I fear they would be broken in the post. Kind remembrances to all.—Yours affectionately,

' ROBERT CASHEL, etc.'

The next letters from which some extracts shall be given exhibit the depth and tenderness of the Bishop of Cashel's feelings, as well as the warmth and kindness of his affections. To parents mourning over the death of a little child of three years old, who was his god-child, he writes :—

'WATERFORD, 4*th February.*

' MY DEAR M.,—My heart bled for you and dear B. " The Lord gave, and the Lord hath taken away. Blessed be the name of the Lord," may you be enabled to add. It is most mysterious, but it is a Father, one that loves you and knows what is right, who has done it. Shall not He do right? Nothing ever gives me such a sense of the evil of this world as the power of inflicting a wound in proportion as there has been a blessing. I cannot but feel for the removal of the little dear child myself, having known her and loved her. How shall the dear, tender, weakly mother bear it? But the Lord will give her strength; I am sure He will. Cast thy burden upon the Lord, and He will sustain it. I commend you to God and the word of His grace, which is able to build you up. In a few days I shall hope to drive over and see dear B., but I think it better not just now.—Yours affectionately,

'ROBERT CASHEL, etc.'

Writing to a friend, he thus speaks of the death of one of his former parishioners, to whom he was much attached :—

'What a melancholy thing was the death of dear Mrs. S.! To her, no doubt, a great gain; but to her husband and six children, to be deprived of their mother—and such a mother! This is one of the features that stamps vanity in a peculiar way upon this world—that a pilgrim passing through it is in the way of suffering just in proportion as he possesses anything good in it. Poor S. never could be made to feel the pain he no doubt now feels had he not been possessed of such a treasure. What a meeting between her and her two sainted mothers! But can we conceive how she could be without pain whilst conscious of the bereavement of him and the children? I suppose a perfect acquiescence in God's will must be the antidote to all pain. He Himself will wipe away all tears.'

To the Same.

'WATERFORD, 19*th January* 1848.

'MY DEAR ——,—I have heard that it has pleased our heavenly Father to remove your venerable father out of the miseries of this evil world. I believe he was a shock of corn fully ripe. It is then his gain, though your loss. But we cannot expect all to move together; "One is taken, and another left." You no doubt, from his advanced age, must have expected and have been looking forward for it, and so prepared for the event; but nevertheless, when the separation comes, it is as keenly felt as if some strange thing had happened. And this is particularly the case when the age, or weakness, or illness of a friend or relation has made them for a long time the great object of solicitude and anxiety; the departure leaves such a blank. And at a certain time of life these blanks are never filled up. In the early times of life, young persons get new friends, new objects of interest; but as we advance, the old, long-valued friends are taken, and no new friends to supply the vacant place. Well, this is one of God's mysterious but wise ways of preparing us to use our wings and cheerfully fly. Like the balloon, one cord after another that has connected it with earth is cut, till at length the last cord is cut, and it ascends into the heavens. So the Lord cuts our ties, to prepare us to rise upward and fly away. How do you and your sister bear the heavy blow? How endure the wilderness? . . . As far as this world was concerned, you lived for him, and he is gone before. Well, if you have lost the tie to earth, you have a new tie to a better place. Remember me most kindly to your sister, and believe me to be, yours very truly,

'ROBERT CASHEL, etc.'

With the same friend he was called upon to sympathize some years later, on the death of her only sister:—

'WATERFORD, 3d *January*.

'MY MUCH BELOVED OLD FRIEND,—I hardly expected that you would have had nerve and spirit to have addressed me with your usual Christmas greeting, which I have always highly valued. I thank you much for your continued remembrance of me. Within this last week, I have heard of the loss of three Christian friends about contemporaries with myself. These things are slight in comparison of your bereavement, but they speak the same lesson. They say to us, Be ye ready, for the end is near. But surely these things say to us, not only, Look up, but, Look forward; look with more earnestness to that which our God has prepared for us, and to which He has brought our friends that have gone before us. Surely, my dear friend, you have an interest in the heavenly country such as you never had before. Before, you might have had a picture which at times pleased you, but now you have a reality. Nothing helps to give us such a reality in the eternal world as to think of those who were our companions gone before us, and now with Christ, which is far better. Surely there is everything to induce us to have our conversation in heaven—that is, our home where those are gone who were dearer to us than ourselves. And surely the removal of those we love acts in another world; it cuts the ties that bound us to earth. Now the tie is severed, the attraction is toward the country where they are, in the presence of our common Friend, our better Elder Brother. I have been feeling and saying for many years, that the common fault of real Christians (for Christians have faults) is, not cultivating hope which is engaged about the future. They have faith as to their standing accepted at the present with God, and they seem to be satisfied with that; but they do not press forward, and realize the happy presence with God in His eternal kingdom, to which present acceptance is but the prelude. My dear friend, look up, but also look forward; endeavour to realize the happy future. Enjoy it even now with her that is gone before; you will follow after. I hope the good Lord is collecting many lambs, young ones, that I know nothing of, for He is removing to heavenly pastures many old sheep, whom He has graciously fed in green pastures. It will not be Sabbath-breaking to give you a few sentiments from a sermon preached since I wrote the letter last evening,—Deut. xii. 9.: " For ye are not yet come to the rest and to the inheritance."

'It is as true of Christians now as it was of Israel when it was written. Israel had many sufferings, many imperfections, along with great manifestations of God's love in the wilderness, for they were not yet come to the rest, etc.

So we may expect much sufferings, many imperfections, along with great mercies and many manifestations of love, for we are not yet come to the rest. It was never expected, for never promised, that the Israelites should be as happy, as free from trial, while in the wilderness as they were promised to be in the land; so we are not promised to be as happy, etc., while here, as we are assured we shall be in the heavenly inheritance, for we are not yet come. But in this "not *yet*" there is not only put forward what should make us patient under present trials, but there is included a promise to Israel that they should in God's time be brought to the rest; so "we are not yet" gives a promise that we shall be brought into the rest. As Canaan was to follow the wilderness, so the perfect inheritance shall follow the unrest of the present time. Two things should follow,—patient submission for the present, and hopeful expectation of the future. Oh, what a wicked world it is that He is taking His sheep out of! What must pass in His holy mind when He sees the world—blood meeting blood, and His creatures destroying each other! And besides this wholesale wickedness, the immense quantity of sin and crime going on in every street and every lane. Wonderful the forbearance of our God—His love to the sinner, with holy hatred of the sin! Oh! to think of the place where there will be no more sin, and into which none shall enter that worketh abomination, or loveth or maketh a lie. Can we think of the happiness of a place in which there will be no sin?

'The thought of it ought to cheer us on our journey, and to make us try to prepare ourselves for the enjoyment of that holy place and holy company ; it might well lift us up above the trials of this life,—light, and but for a moment,—and also make us independent of the short joys and pleasures of this scene. In all these things we may be more than conquerors through Him that loved us. May we, through God's teaching, know the love of Christ, that passeth knowledge, and be filled with all the fulness of God. That grace, mercy, and peace may be abundantly with you this new year, is the fervent prayer of your sincere friend in the gospel of Christ,

'ROBERT CASHEL, etc.'

His watchful solicitude about the welfare of those young people who had been brought up in his parish at Powerscourt continued to be shown to them after he had left it. To one of them, who had freely opened her mind to him as to the state of her religious feelings, he thus wrote :—

'WATERFORD, 7th February 1842.

'MY DEAR MARY,— . . . I take a moment to say how thankful I am to you for your remembrance of me. You could not have written a kinder letter ; but I could have wished you to write a happier one, as far as relates to yourself. I hope yet to see you established in the faith, and abounding therein with thanksgiving. As you truly say, the door is open before you ; all that is wanting is, that you should press into it. You ought to look sharply, and examine what is the accursed thing that is in your way. Is it the world in some shape ? Oh, seek for it, and find it, and cast it out; if it is as dear as a right hand or right eye, pluck it out, and cast it from you. The Lord give me grace to pray for you; and pray for me in this dark place, this new sphere in which my God has placed me. I have no strength of myself; but I know in whom I have righteousness and strength.—Yours affectionately,

'ROBERT CASHEL, etc.'

To the mother of one of his god-children he wrote thus in answer to a letter telling him of her son's confirmation, in which she said that she felt assured of his god-son having been remembered by him in his prayers:—

'STRADBALLY, Co. WATERFORD,
'11th October 1854.

'MY DEAR MRS. C.,—I am verily guilty regarding your son and my god-son, in not having thought of him as I ought to have done. I feel very guilty with regard to you and my friend C. in the matter. How well it is that you and he are not depending upon an arm of flesh! Put no confidence in man. I shall write such a letter as you desire, and pray the Lord to forgive my neglect, and to bless a few words, though late, that I may be led to address to him. What a nervous position is that of parents bringing children, to whom is communicated their own evil nature, into an evil world! How impotent they find themselves for good; they may pray, they may advise, and warn, but they cannot change the heart. This is God's part, and the result must be left to Him who is a God of love. May we have grace to do our part; but alas! we do not that.

'We have great reason to be humbled to the very dust. Your letter has humbled me very much. May we all be driven to the throne of grace. Remember me most kindly to Joseph and all your family.—Yours in the best bonds,

'ROBERT CASHEL, etc.'

The promised letter was as follows :—

'MY DEAR YOUNG FRIEND,—I suppose you have been told that I stood sponsor for you, when in your infancy you were by baptism admitted into the visible Church of Christ. If I had known the time in which you were about to be confirmed, to renew in your own person the solemn vow, promise, and profession I made for you, it would have been a very suitable time for me to have addressed to you a few words of affectionate warning and advice. But having heard that you.have lately been confirmed, I hope you will take kindly, and consider seriously, a friendly letter from your god-father. I know, my young friend, what perhaps you are little aware of, the evil and dangerous tendency of the world, which you have entered, and into which you will be plunged ere long. Even in school, how many are the temptations to sin and wickedness! How many are the companions calculated to corrupt you rather than do you good! How much oftener do you hear a word likely to lead you to do wrong than a word likely to encourage you to do right! It will be much more so when really thrown upon that world which is before you. Then you have a corrupt nature, inclined to lead you to evil rather than lead you to good. This I am sure you have been taught by your good parents, but I would remind you of it. I would remind you of your danger, in order that, approaching the time when you will be your own director, you may be led to ask for and seek good guidance, even that of your heavenly Father, who is in Christ reconciling the world unto Himself.

'How happy I should be if I could persuade you to cultivate religion, to seek peace with God through Jesus Christ, to live the life you live in the flesh by the faith of the Son of God, who loved you and gave Himself for you! If I might offer you some advice, it would be : never pass a day without praying for pardon and peace with God through Jesus Christ; never begin a day without on your knees putting yourself under the protection of your heavenly Father. " Commit your way unto the Lord, and He will bring it to pass." Another piece of advice I would give you would be: never pass a day without reading a portion of God's holy word; as a new-born babe, desire the sincere milk of the word, that you may grow thereby. Remember what the Psalmist said: " Wherewith shall a young man cleanse his way ? Even by taking heed thereto according to Thy word." A verse, even, of Scripture, put into the mind in the morning, might be made a guide and a strength through the dangerous trials of the day. You have had an advantage which many young people, perhaps your companions, have not had; you were brought up by pious parents, who early trained you in the way you should go. Oh, seek strength, that when you grow old you may not depart from it! You have been taught the difference between right and wrong;

be on your guard against evil example and evil company.
Do not be ashamed of being conscientious and religious.
Don't be unhappy at being ridiculed for being righteous
over-much. Remember this is a state of trial. It is to
be tried who is on the Lord's side; and your everlasting
happiness is at stake. If you live with God through
Christ, you will be happy here and hereafter. If you turn
away from God and follow the world, you will perish with
the world. Meditate upon these things, and consider the
advice of your unworthy and sincere friend,

' ROBERT CASHEL, etc.'

On hearing that his god-son was about to enter the
army, the Bishop writes:—

' WATERFORD, 1st *March* 1856.

' MY DEAR Mrs. C.,—I shall have much pleasure in
sending your son (my god-child) a Bible with my name
in it. Your letter arrived here when I was in Dublin,
whither I had gone to preach for the Irish Society. If I
had received it before I went up, I should have got the
Bible in Dublin, and given it to your son. I am very
sorry that he has determined to go into the army, but I
have a hope that the peace which we are led to expect
will put a damp upon the warlike desires of many young
persons. I often think of what is recorded of St. Augustine. His mother, Monica, was anxious about her son, as
you are about yours, and going to some distinguished
father of those days, expressing her anxieties, he replied,
" The child of so many prayers cannot be lost." Continue

to pray for him and to strive with him, and your prayers will not be lost. You have a prayer-hearing God to go to. I hope you and your family are happy in your northern position. There are many cheery things connected with the North; and there is there, as well as elsewhere, the God and Father of our Lord Jesus Christ. To Him I commit you, your family, and husband. May He be your God and their God, now and for ever, is the prayer of, yours very truly,   'ROBERT CASHEL, etc.'

Upon the occasion of this young man's marriage, some years later, the Bishop says :—

'WATERFORD, 26*th March* 1863.

'MY DEAR MRS. C.,—I have received your letter, and have not in my morning prayer forgotten you and your son, and her who is by this time your daughter. I pray that the Lord may make her a helpmeet for your son, and a comfort to you and your husband. It is a very important step, and ought to be brought before the Lord with much seriousness. I feel that no persons have such trials as Christians with a large family. I often say, that if I had a parcel of children, I could never be off my knees, seeking from the Lord the help and protection they stand in need of, and which I could not give them. Well, it is happy that the Lord reigneth. That is our best hope, for ourselves and for the children. May you be enabled to cast all your care upon your covenant God, and find a peace of God passing all understanding keeping your hearts and minds. Remember me most kindly to your husband, and tell your son that I wish him all happiness, and that I pray for him that he and his wife may be blessed with the everlasting blessings of the gospel.—Affectionately and sincerely yours, in the best bonds,

'ROBERT CASHEL, etc.'

The following letter contains sound advice to young men. It was addressed to a mother who had informed him of her son's success in College:—

'MY DEAR ——,—Among the many letters I have had to write, I am at a loss whether I answered your letter of last week telling me of ——'s success. I think it better to run the chance of sending you a second letter than seem to be indifferent about him. I take a great interest in his real welfare, and I think industry and attention to literary improvement is a very valuable quality in a young man. A young man must be occupied; and good occupation is not only good in itself, but it is a security against evil occupation and bad company. Nothing produces so much temptation to young persons as to think that amusement and dissipation are the great happiness of life. Wholesome industry in mental improvement comes in most happily to supply a void they might otherwise feel. All that —— may learn by study at present may be, and will be, useful to him in after life; but I consider *that* less than I do the wholesome discipline and the self-control which studious habits confer. As he has begun so well, I have every hope that he will go on through life in a way that will be a comfort to you and profitable to himself.

If your dear mother is with you, tell her how much I feel about her. She must have been prepared for the event, so much in the course of nature, and accompanied by all the alleviations of grace; but still she must feel the separation, though but for a season. There is a place where we shall part no more.—Very truly yours,

'ROBERT CASHEL.'

CHAPTER VIII.

'A good bishop, as a tender father,
  Doth teach and rule the Church, and is obey'd
And reverenced by it ; so much the rather
  By how much he delighted more to lead
All by his own example in the way,
Than punish any when they go astray.'

GEORGE HERBERT.

THE Bishop of Cashel, on his first appearance in Parliament, was listened to with an interest and an attention which has not been often excited by a speaker rising from the bench of bishops. He was obliged to begin his Parliamentary career by repelling a most unfounded and unwarrantable attack which had been made upon his character as a bishop, by misrepresenting the sentiments which he had expressed on the subject of the Roman Catholic religion in his primary charge delivered to the united dioceses of Cashel, Emly, Waterford, and Lismore, in the year 1843.

A letter, from one who certainly was an impartial judge of the Bishop of Cashel's merit,[1] describes him as having 'boldly and triumphantly, in his place in Parliament, thrown back the malignant falsehood that was propagated

[1] The Bishop of Moray.

against him respecting the affairs of his diocese, and manfully dared his maligners to prove the accusation.'

The old Duke of Wellington stood up in defence of his charge, saying that he had read it, and that it was an *excellent* charge, a thoroughly ecclesiastical charge, and that it met with his most unqualified approval.

Some years afterwards, another unwarranted attack was made upon the Bishop of Cashel in Parliament by one of opposite politics—one who, although a Protestant, differed widely from him in his views on religious subjects. In refuting the charges brought against him on this occasion, the Bishop so completely floored his opponent, that the *Times*, in commenting upon it, observed that it was rather foolhardy in the learned gentleman to drive his little craft full sail against the ROCK OF CASHEL, or words to that effect. The simile was a happy one, and the name suited him so admirably, that it was afterwards constantly applied to him.

The subject so dear to his heart, that of scriptural education, was brought forward by the Bishop of Cashel on the 17th of June 1845, in a speech delivered by him in the House of Lords on presenting petitions on the subject of National Education. Of the effect of this speech on the House, one of his contemporaries remarks, in a letter addressed to the writer of this Memoir :—

' I remember hearing from an auditor of the speech that he made in defence of the Church Education Society in the House of Lords, that its arch-enemy absolutely quailed at the tempest of applause which its eloquence and power elicited at his expense.'

s

We may, alas, in these matters write upon our Church,
'Ichabod!' Our present excellent Bishop of Cashel has
it not in his power thus to raise his voice in the Senate in
defence of God's truth and of His word.

In the same year, 1845, the prelates of the Irish Church
(the Bishop of Cashel amongst others) issued a second
address to their clergy on the subject of the National
Board of Education. They continued every year to make
a requisition to Parliament for aid in supporting their
scriptural schools, but without success.

The year 1846 will long be remembered in Ireland.
The sad scenes which were witnessed in the time of famine,
caused by the total failure of the potato crop, upon which
a large portion of the poor people entirely depended for
food, can never be erased from the memory of those who
were spectators of the miseries of their fellow-countrymen,
without being able, even when doing their utmost, to ward
off this terrible calamity. The food of the people was
totally gone. It had disappeared so suddenly, and in so
short a space of time, that there was no opportunity of
supplying the want by bringing in foreign supplies of
provisions until thousands had passed into eternity. Of
Indian corn, now so generally made use of by the lower
orders, there was at that time in the country but a very
small supply, consequently its price was enormously high;
and the liberal aid given in money by our friends in the
sister isle went a fearfully short way in the purchase of
meal. This important crisis called forth at the same time
all the tender feelings and the active energies of the
Bishop of Cashel. He put himself in communication

with many pious and influential persons in England, allocating to each of them a particular parish or town in his diocese, over which they might exercise a special care. The town of Carrick-on-Suir was taken up by the congregation of the Rev. Mr. Fenn of Blackheath, near London, and a weekly correspondence kept up between him and the vicar of Carrick. Large collections were made in the church at Blackheath every Sunday, averaging from £30 to £40, and sent the following day to Carrick, with warm expressions of interest in their 'child,' as they affectionately called it. Carrick-on-Suir is, for its size, perhaps one of the poorest and most wretched-looking towns in Ireland, so much so that the Bishop could not refrain from humorously observing, ' I wish they could *see* their *ugly child !'*

In Waterford he took a personal share in the labours of the clergy in the relief of the starving population, and succeeded so well, that the distress was felt much less in that city than in most other places. No distinction was made between Protestants and Roman Catholics; and the latter, finding him to be their true friend, and a very pleasant one too, came to love him sincerely. He would often tell how cordially he was received, when, being crowded in the soup-shop, he would retire into the fish-market near it. the fish-women receiving him with the following kindly greeting, ' Come to us, my lord, and we'll take care of you !' The town was divided into districts, of which the Bishop took one, going from house to house with tickets for coal, meal, soup, or clothing, as might be required. When on these occasions they loaded him with blessings,

he would say to them : ' Why are you so fond of me now ?
When I came here first you used to hoot me and call me
Bob Daly, and now you are always blessing me. I am
just as good a Protestant now as I was then, and when I
came first I would have been just as anxious to do you
any good in my power as I am now, so what is the reason
of the change ? ' To which they would sometimes make
the following answer : ' Oh ! your lordship, we were told
lies of you, but now we have come to *know* you.'

One of the Waterford clergy[1] gives the following particulars of the famine year in Waterford, in a letter from
which we shall make an extract :—

' In this great strait few were more active than the
Bishop. Large sums were collected and sent to him from
England, and he was a judicious almoner. Many years
after, when he was preaching on behalf of the distress in
Lancashire through the cotton failure, he caused quite a
sensation by producing his account-book in the pulpit in
Waterford, and reading out from it the large and repeated
sums which were entrusted to him for distribution in the
year of famine in Ireland, sent to him from England.

' In Waterford, at this period, it was most remarkable
the confidence reposed in him by the poor. Whenever
the poor felt that an injustice was done to them, they
crowded round his door and demanded an audience, in
order that he might get them justice. Another strange
circumstance occurred in the early part of the work :—

---

[1] The Rev. Thomas Gimlette, D.D., one who was highly valued by the
late Bishop, and to whom we are indebted for much interesting information respecting him.

' When the Relief Committee was being formed, the parish priest of one of the most important parishes in Waterford, and he himself one of the ablest and most influential priests in the city,. rose, and after detailing the sad circumstances, and dwelling on the crisis at which they were arrived, said that this was a time when an able, independent, and honest man should be at the helm. He concluded by proposing that the Bishop should be chairman of the Relief Committee. Some that were present preferred that the Mayor should be president; on a division, the Mayor was elected by a majority of one. Father Sheehan and several influential Roman Catholics voted for the Bishop.'

In the year 1847 a correspondence took place between the Lord Primate of Ireland and Lord John Russell. On the refusal of the Prime Minister to give to the members of the Established Church in Ireland a share of the grant for education, the Bishop of Cashel addressed a letter of remonstrance to him, a copy of which we have been enabled to procure, as well as his answer to an article which appeared in the *Times* of 10th September 1856.

Some years later we find him again raising his voice in support of this cause, ' whether they would hear, or whether they would forbear ':—

To the Archdeacon of Waterford.

' LONDON, 30*th June* 1859.

' MY DEAR BELL,— . . . The committee of the Church Education Society are going to publish, as an occasional

paper, my speech at the meeting of the Society. I hope
it may open some eyes. We shall soon see whether the
Ministry will do anything for us. There will be a great
fight for the Bible in India, during which the temper of
the House will be tested, and I am afraid it will be found
on the unscriptural side. The *good* people here are very
jealous at my bringing forward our Irish demand. They
say to me, " Can't you let us get India first, and then
Ireland will follow ? " Many of them were annoyed that,
when I spoke at the meeting of the Society for Vernacular
and Scriptural Education in India, I introduced Ireland.
Colonel —— told me that, as soon as he saw me get up, he
said to his neighbour, " You'll see he will bring in Ireland."
I said to him, " Ought I not to have brought in Ireland ?
It was my having long acted on the principle with regard
to Ireland that brought me to the meeting, and made me
contribute to the Society." . . .'

That he advocated the cause wisely is proved by the
following extracts from letters :—

To the Same.

'KILLOUGH CASTLE, 24*th September* 1859.

'. . . I think it a delicate and difficult point to draw
up such a paper as ought to be sent out by the Church
Education Society. A printed proof of one drawn up by
—— was sent to me, but I objected to it, because it not
only said, " We did not ask for a separate grant," but
protested against it on principle, and I thought on bad
grounds. Whereas we always said, " We asked for a free

Bible," but never dictated in what way it was to be given.

'I do not prefer a separate grant, but I would not protest against it, because that is the principle adopted in England; and I certainly would not refuse to be put under the Privy Council in England. . . .'

'WATERFORD, 14th *January* 1860.

'. . . You have no doubt seen ——'s speech. It appears that this great stand *ad captandum vulgi* is to be taken on the point of parental authority, and we ought to meet it on that ground. I think we ought to speak out, and profess ourselves as great supporters of parental authority as they are, only in a different way. We would allow parental authority its full force in choosing the school to which the parent would send his child, but not to dictate the course to be adopted in the school. Surely we might ask ——, When he went to school, did not his parents choose the school, but did they prescribe the course of his instruction in the school? Did not his parents choose the University to which they would send him, but did they dictate what he was to read and answer in order to get a degree in that University? That subject of parental authority is chosen because it is likely to catch the ear of the public; but it is very insincere, and it only requires to be boldly met in order to take the sting out of it. . . .'

It was chiefly owing to the Bishop of Cashel's untiring exertions (in which he was joined by the Bishop of Ossory and others), that the Church Education Society not only outlived the storm which seemed to threaten it, but was greatly increased, both in funds and influence, by the liberality of the Christian public, both in England and Ireland.

The year 1860 was a trying year to the interests of this cause. Government continued to withhold any help from the clergy of the Established Church, who could not conscientiously avail themselves of the funds of the National Board. These funds enabled the Roman Catholic clergy, in some places at least, to offer an education so much superior in secular matters to that which the very limited income of the Church Education Society could afford, that many Protestant parents were tempted by the prospect of worldly advantages to send their children to the National schools. This so much disheartened our late excellent and venerated Primate, who had been the mainstay of the Church Education Society in Ireland, that he now withdrew from it, giving up the battle as lost, and advised the clergy—any amongst them who could conscientiously do so—to put their schools under the National Board. His advice was taken by a few, but not many. Amongst those who agreed with the Primate in theory, although they did not reduce it to practice, were two of the Bishop of Cashel's oldest and most beloved friends. He did not fail to tell them honestly that he thought they were in the wrong; but at the same time, he did not allow either his affection or Christian regard for them to be diminished by this difference of opinion, even though it was upon a subject which he considered to be of great importance. One of these friends thus writes to him in answer to a letter of affectionate remonstrance :—

'Your confidential and loving letter filled me with joy

and thankfulness. I reluctantly destroyed it, as you desired, as it would have been a perpetual memorial of your brotherly kindness; but as the loving heart that dictated it still remains, I am content.'

The storms which now gathered round this his favourite cause only tended to increase the zeal and earnestness with which the Bishop of Cashel embraced every opportunity which offered itself of seeking to impress upon all whom it was in his power to influence, both in public and in private, the importance of scriptural education for the rising generation, as being the only hope of improving the moral and religious condition of Ireland. With this in view, he spoke at meetings and preached sermons both in England and Ireland. He dwelt much upon the failure of the National system of education in Ireland in improving the moral condition of the people, proving by statistics, which he took much trouble to procure, that education without religion had only made them wise to do evil, as the number of criminals who had attended National schools was very remarkable. He also proved that it had quite failed to promote united education,—the schools patronized by Presbyterians in the North not having any Roman Catholics in attendance; whilst those in the South, which were in the hands of Roman Catholics, were very rarely frequented by children of any other religious denomination. The schools of the Church Education Society he found to be frequented in many instances by both Protestants and Roman Catholics. In his own diocese this Society was well worked. At the suggestion of the Bishop, a charity sermon was annually preached in every parish in behalf of its funds, and, with but very few exceptions, one school or more kept up in connection with it. To one of his clergy he thus expresses himself:—

'8 MOUNTJOY SQUARE, 25*th* *June* 1867.

'MY DEAR R.,—I am gratified by what you say about Mr. C. and a Church Education Society school. I shall have pleasure in giving you £10 per annum towards its support. I cannot conceive any other conclusion come to by a conscientious, godly man.

'Let him only realize you in the school with the children before you. You hear God's word saying, "Preach the word. Train up the children in the way they should go." The National Board says, "Hold your tongue." I know you could not be silent if you were there. May the Lord bless the good work, and those that are engaged in it.—Very truly yours, 'ROBERT CASHEL, etc.'

To one who had disappointed him by changing his views upon this subject, he closes a letter in which he expresses his regret by saying:—

'I thought we were too much of one mind on the important points of our common faith ever to differ upon a Christian minister's duty in his school. I have been disappointed, and have been pained; but I have no doubt it is wholesome for me.

'I pray that our heavenly Father may overrule all for your good, and for my good, and for the good of His Church generally.—Believe me to be, in spite of our differences, your sincere friend and brother in the common faith of Christ,   ' ROBERT CASHEL, etc.'

By his own example, and the pecuniary assistance that he liberally gave to many of the scriptural schools in his diocese, he reduced to practice the theories brought by him before the public. In some cases he built school-houses at his own expense. One of these was in Bonma-hon, the parish of Monklands, mentioned by him in his speech before the House of Lords as being a locality where such a school was peculiarly wanting. This schoolhouse he was obliged to build within the precincts of the church-yard, as he could not procure from the landlord a site for the building elsewhere. Bonmahon was within a few miles of Woodhouse, and during his residence there he frequently rode over to visit the school, which was a most useful one.

In the beginning of the summer of the year 1847 the Bishop removed to Woodhouse, near Stradbally, in the County Waterford, the residence of the Uniacke family, which, during their absence from home, they let to him for this and many succeeding summers. It is a beautiful place, situated in a richly-wooded valley, opening upon a sheltered little cove by the sea, upon the cliffs at either side of which the lovely walk on the breezy downs was much enjoyed by him. The writer of this Memoir has many delightful reminiscences of the happy weeks and months that she and her husband spent with him at this place, though not unmixed with melancholy feelings. How comforting is the reflection that the grave can only for a

little while divide us from his voice, his hand, his smile!
On the occasion of their first visit to Woodhouse, the
writer and her husband experienced such affectionate
sympathy and kindness in their time of sorrow and
trial, that they would be indeed ungrateful did they not
record it.

Their sorrow was one which he would not have been
expected to realize much; they had been bereaved of two
of their little children within the space of a few months.
In his kind invitations to visit him at Woodhouse, he
would not allow any child, however young, to be left
behind, saying, ' It would not do you any good to come
here if you were to be separated from the " angels;" so
bring them all.' He said that all mothers considered their
children to be perfect angels, and he playfully called them
so in his letters. In one of them he says, ' My blessing
upon the angels! Very presumptuous! Were I a Papist,
I would ask blessing from them;' and declared himself
at another time to be ready to ' entertain angels!' He was
always accompanied by one of them in his morning walk
before breakfast to a beautifully clear spring of water, his
little companion thinking it a great honour to be allowed
to carry his glass for him. And on one occasion an amusing passage-of-arms took place at luncheon between him
and a very little one, who refused to say her grace for the
Bishop, because the words were not quite the same as her
mother had taught her to use.

We have already alluded to the Bishop's natural propensity to contradict at times what was said in conversation; he did not, however, by any means expect every one

to agree with him, and much preferred that people should express their own sentiments, even though in opposition to his.

He did not like people to be afraid of him. On one occasion he volunteered to punish himself for what he humorously acknowledged to be too flagrant a case of contradiction.

One of his clergy, who was staying with him at Woodhouse, remarked one evening that he had seen the tower of Curraghmore from the top of a hill not far from the house. The Bishop said that it was quite impossible, and that he could not have seen it; however, Mr. M. said that he could not be mistaken, as it was a very remarkable object, a round tower on the top of a hill, which he knew the look of very well. The Bishop still contended that he could not have seen it. 'There's M., with his blind eyes, says he saw the tower of Curraghmore, which is nine miles off. He took the spire of the chapel at Stradbally for it.' However, the next morning at breakfast he was very penitent, and said: 'That was too bad, M., what I said about your taking the spire of the chapel for the tower of Curraghmore. Well, I'll tell you what; we'll go to the top of the hill you saw it from, and if you can show it to me, I will give you the new forms and desks for your schoolhouse at C. that you asked me for.' So, accordingly, all the party set out and walked across the demesne, and when they got to the top of the hill in question, they saw the Bishop riding slowly up, looking rather as if he knew he was going to be defeated. There it was, plain to be seen, and the Bishop had to pay his fine.

He would often illustrate this propensity in human nature to opposition by telling a story of Bianconi, the famous proprietor of Irish long cars. When he first set one a-going, he was very much disheartened at finding that he had no passengers. It then occurred to him that he would start another, in opposition to his first one. This plan he found to be very successful, as in a short time both cars were full. It was perhaps this spirit of opposition which made the Bishop always inclined to refuse to give anything to ladies who called upon him with cards collecting for charitable objects. A clergyman's wife in Waterford, who was a great favourite of his, and who understood him thoroughly, paid him a visit one day of this kind; he handed her a fourpenny bit, with which she went away quite meekly, supposing that it was all she need expect to get. The next morning, however, the kind Bishop sent her £5 to add to her collection. Another friend, on a similar occasion, 'caught him with guile.' She wrote to tell him that she felt sure that there would be no use in asking him to subscribe to the object about which she was interested, as he never gave anything to her. He immediately answered her letter by sending her a large contribution, saying, 'I don't know why you should say that I never give anything to you!' The Bishop was one of the few people to be met with who really disliked flattery; so much so, that any one attempting it must be possessed of a good deal of moral courage, as they would inevitably meet with a rebuff. A lady once poured forth a very warm panegyric upon him, comparing him to one of his brother bishops, when he very quietly said: 'That may be all very well; but at the same time, when the Bishop of —— publishes his charge, the price of it is 5s., whereas mine sells for 3d.'

The Bishop liked the situation of the house at Woodhouse, though some people thought it too low for health. He liked looking up at a view better than seeing it from a height, and did not much believe in one situation being more wholesome than another, probably because his health was so good that he felt well in every place. He said that ladies did not always understand cause and effect when they attributed their illness to the place they lived in, and thought they would be better anywhere else. He was sometimes very much annoyed by clergymen leaving their parishes because the air did not agree with their families, and would say, in a joking way, that we never would have the Church in true working order until the celibacy of the clergy was brought into fashion. On one occasion, when, in the course of reading at family prayer, the third chapter of the first Epistle of St. Paul to Timothy came to be considered, he very wisely dwelt upon the duty of a bishop to rule his own house well, addressing himself particularly to the servants, setting before them their duty, as forming the household of a bishop, to walk soberly, righteously, and godly, and to 'give none occasion to the enemy to blaspheme.'

Although he did not like people to be afraid of him, there were many who could never get over a certain feeling of awe which his presence inspired. Those, however, who were privileged to be admitted to the inner and more intimate circle of his friends could not have this feeling. He was at this period of his life a much finer-looking man than when he was younger. His white hair became him well. It was very thick; so much so, that he would often laughingly observe, on seeing younger men growing bald, that the present generation could seldom boast of as good a head of hair as their seniors could. He had a dignified air, which well became a bishop; and it would have been very difficult for any person to venture on an undue familiarity with him, if he chose, for any reason, to keep them at a distance.

He had been singularly exempt from family bereavements. Of so large a family, only one member had been until this time called away. In the summer of 1847, however, he was deeply afflicted by the loss of his only brother, Lord Dunsandle. He died of the fever which followed the famine year of 1846, which he caught when visiting the poorhouse in his neighbourhood. The distress of mind under which the Bishop suffered on hearing of the dangerous illness of his brother is well remembered by a friend who was staying with him at Woodhouse. His voice was heard while walking in the woods, as it were wrestling with the Lord in prayer. On hearing of his brother's death, he went to visit his aged mother, as he much dreaded the effect that the severe blow would have upon her health, and not without grounds. She was at this time eighty-seven years of age, and in perfect health, able to walk about her place, and still to take an interest in her farm; but from this time she began to decline, although she lived to the advanced age of ninety-two years.

The following notes show his affectionate anxiety about her:—

To Mrs. Hamilton Madden.

'BROMLEY, 18*th August* 1847.

'MY DEAR BELLA,—I hope to see you at Woodhouse on Saturday evening at tea. My dear mother is tolerably well recovering from her heavy blow, so that I can leave her for a little. I mean to go to Dublin to-morrow, and to Waterford on Friday (if the Lord permit). I am sorry to leave my mother and sister and H. without some more of the family to be with my mother, but I think it better to return and do some business in Waterford now, and come here again before the winter. . . .'

To the Same.

'WATERFORD, 20*th January.*

'MY DEAR BELLA,—I was glad to see your hand again, and to hear of your all being well in entering on the new year. Time is passing away, and we are moving on in the stream. It is a comfort to know whither it is carrying us, and to be able in some degree to lift up our heads, knowing that our redemption is drawing nigh.

'I am very sorry to hear that your aunt, Miss Mason, is so much laid by through illness. She was long a faithful, hard-working servant in the Lord's vineyard. She may expect to be called upon to rest, though no doubt she would rather not rest here, but whilst here work. . . .

'We have not good accounts of my poor aged mother.

T

She seems now to be growing weaker and weaker, and there is no ground for expecting that she, at her great age, may gather any strength; but she has no illness or pain.

'I expect to go to England in about a month, unless the Parliament is dissolved, which would save me the trouble of the session. . . .—Yours very affectionately,

'ROBERT CASHEL, etc.'

One of his confirmations the Bishop thus describes in a letter:—

To the Archdeacon of Waterford.

'STRADBALLY, 3d *October* 1851.

'MY DEAR BELL,—We had, in every sense of the word, a most glorious day at Dromkeen, in which church I held a confirmation for the parishes of Doon, Tuagh, and Pallas-grean. It was one of the most beautiful sunny days that ever came, and that fair country looked beautiful. The church would not hold conveniently more than 200, so that I had arranged to have two services, morning and afternoon. At the first service we had 164 converts for confirmation, and nearly 100 persons in the congregation. It was a dense crowd, and a most interesting sight. At the afternoon service we had 111 persons—three Pro-testants. We had been told by the priests from the altars that they would raise the country, and bring thousands from Limerick and Tipperary to prevent our holding the confirmation. We took the precaution of having a magis-trate and police force, but they had nothing to do. We never saw an angry look from the people as either I or the converts passed through the country. When, three years ago, I held confirmations in the same part of the diocese, there were not ten persons from the three parishes which now sent 375. I do trust it was a *confirmation* indeed, both of the people and the hard-working ministers.

'The priests and the Liberals cannot now deny the fact of the Reformation.

'There would have been a much larger number, but that I requested the clergyman not to seek for numbers to make a show, but to bring none but those of whom they thought well—to bring no children under fifteen years of age. I remarked one girl evidently below the age prescribed, and I spoke to Mr. D., the clergyman who presented her. He said she was indeed only in her fourteenth year, but if I would examine her, I should find that she was well instructed. I asked her, "Do you know how a sinner is to be saved?" Answer, "Believe in the Lord Jesus Christ, and thou shalt be saved." "Through whom can a sinner draw nigh to God?" Answer, "There is no other name under heaven, given amongst men, whereby we must be saved." "Give me some other text to show that there is but one Mediator?" Answer, "There is one God, and one Mediator between God and man, the man Christ Jesus."

'I said to Mr. D. I should have thought it wiser to have kept this child back, but as he had brought her, I could not refuse her when she knew so well what she was about. . . .—Very truly yours,

'ROBERT CASHEL, etc.'

This interesting scene was also described in a letter read by the Rev. Hugh M'Neile at a meeting held on the 30th of September 1851, in the Concert Hall, Liverpool, to discuss certain allegations brought against the work of Reformation in connection with the Irish Society in the district of Doon, diocese of Cashel, which were satisfactorily disproved. In his speech at this meeting, Mr. Atkinson, the then rector of the parish of Doon, read the following letter from the Rev. Mr. Hoare, incumbent of Christ Church, Ramsgate, to the Bishop of Cashel:—

'I arrived at Pallasgrean in the afternoon of Thursday, the 26th of June. Mr. Scott, Mr. Atkinson, and Mr. Darby very kindly met me at the station, and at once conducted me to the schoolroom, which I found full of men, women, and children, all converts from the Church of Rome. I was surprised at the respectability of their appearance, and at the number of well-dressed men amongst them. I was pleased also to observe that most of the men and children had Bibles in their hands, though I did not observe any Bible amongst the women. I spoke to them for some time on the great principles of the gospel, and questioned them carefully on the authority of the Scriptures, the atonement, and justification. I was anxious also to ascertain how far they understood the errors of the Church of Rome, and nothing could be more thoroughly satisfactory than their replies. They never failed in producing scriptural proof for any of the truths on which I examined them, and were always prepared with the chapter and verse to which they had occasion to refer. There was also such an appearance of heart and earnestness amongst them, more especially when I spoke of the great doctrines of salvation, such as justification by faith and a free pardon through the blood of the Lamb, that I can only say, that if they were not sincere converts, they were the most awful and successful hypocrites with whom it has ever been my misfortune to come in contact. I only wish that some of our cold, lukewarm Protestant professors could have witnessed the zeal and apparent joy with which these poor converts proved, from the word of God, that the only justification of the gospel is through the free grace of their crucified and risen Lord.

'After leaving Pallasgrean I went to Doon, about three miles distant, where I had the joy of meeting a similar assembly of converts; but there was this difference, that the room being insufficient for their accommodation, they were obliged to adjourn to the open space in front of Mr. Atkinson's house. There were persons of all ages and both sexes; but chiefly men,—some old men, just awakening to a new life as they approach the grave; and some most interesting children, whose prompt and accurate replies surpassed anything I have ever known in England. There were also persons of all ranks, including the intelligent gentleman, the respectable farmer, the comfortable pensioner, and the almost starving labourer, whose naked flesh appeared through the rags which hung in tatters upon his famished person; but in all, as far as I could judge, there appeared an accurate and intelligent acquaintance with the Scriptures, leading to a full determination to look to Jesus Christ as their Saviour, and to have done with Popery for ever.'

'The meetings,' Mr. Atkinson went on to say, 'have been held in the open air, partly because there was no sufficient house or church accommodation, and partly because there is a disposition in the clergy there to do everything openly. The Bishop of Cashel once said to a clergyman who consulted him as to the ecclesiastical propriety of preaching in the open air: "There may be canons against preaching in unlicensed houses, but there never has been a canon enacted against preaching under the canopy of heaven." '

'The work' (we quote from the Rev. W. A. Darby's speech) 'has been endorsed by our own Bishop, whose acute and scrutinizing mind, and whose stern integrity of character, are a sufficient guarantee to the world for the genuineness of any work that has his testimony. He has sent observing clergymen to see the work, and report to him concerning it. He has come himself and seen the converts at the confirmations. He sanctioned and authorized a deputation last spring (Mr. Atkinson and myself) to collect funds in England for the support and extension of this work.'

It may not be out of place here to explain the manner in which the Bishop of Cashel sanctioned the giving of employment to the converts of Doon.

He had always felt a great reluctance to give his sanction to any plan for the conversion of Roman Catholics which mixed up temporal relief with religious instruction, fearing that it might hold out an inducement to some to profess what they did not feel. In the year 1850, however, the sufferings of the poorer converts from Romanism in the district of Doon had become so severe, that he said he 'could hold out no longer, something must be done for them.' Several of them had died from actual want and starvation, as the persecution consequent on their change of faith was so bitter that they could not obtain any employment, and shopkeepers even refused to sell to them the necessaries of life. The Bishop accordingly became responsible for the rent of a large farm, about £100 per annum, in that neighbourhood, of which he obtained a lease.[1] The management of this farm he gave into the hands of the rector of the parish of Doon, with instructions to employ such of the converts in cultivating it as should apply to him for work, giving them a little less than the common rate of wages in the country (only 6d. a day without diet, and the women 4d.). A shop was also opened in the village of Doon, where they could procure at the usual prices such things as they stood in need of. The state of things in that district is now much altered. Many have emigrated; young people educated in the schools (which were of a superior character) have obtained situations in various other localities, so that the harvest of the good seed sown there may be reaped in far distant places; but no doubt it will be reaped, in fulfilment of the promise: 'My word shall not return unto me void, but shall accomplish that whereunto I have sent it.'

In the year 1852 the Bishop thought it a wiser plan to make the farm self-supporting. He accordingly raised the sum of £1200, to which he contributed largely himself, as farm capital, to be invested in the stock, crops, and cultiva-

---

[1] The rent of this farm was paid for many years by the late Lady Olivia Sparrow.

tion of the farm, to which he added one of sixty additional acres. He became personally responsible that this sum should always be forthcoming on the land; and in order to ease the local clergy from the burden of secular care which lay upon them, he engaged a skilful and experienced agriculturist, capable of undertaking the management of the farms.

Some years after this time, the Bishop deemed it wiser, for many reasons, to assist some of the converts to emigrate than to keep them at Doon. Referring to this, Mr. Fitzpatrick, who was the missionary agent of the Irish Society here, says, in a letter addressed to the writer of this Memoir: 'This plan the Bishop enabled me to carry out in 1863, by which a large number of them were sent as emigrants to Canada, and a few to Australia and New Zealand. In that year he gave me for this special purpose £177, and reproached me for not asking him for more. It was only those who, like myself, had such relations with him that understood the tenderness of his sympathies and benevolence. In a letter written at that time to me from London about the emigrants, he enclosed a cheque for £160. The letter was written late at night, in reply to one from me received too late for reply by the evening mail; but he wrote even at a late hour, in the hope of the letter being forwarded by the early morning mail. He was so anxious for the welfare of the poor people, and, I believe, to ease me of the burden of employing them, which he knew was too heavy for me, that he did not let a post pass without writing; and when a violent gale was blowing in London, he wrote to me mourning over the storms that were causing terror to those poor people, then on the Atlantic, and, breathing forth his prayers for their safety, he expressed the deep interest which he took in their welfare.'

The appointment of the Rev. Robert Bell to the Archdeaconry of Waterford was one of the first which the Bishop made in the diocese, and one of those which gave the most general satisfaction.[1] Archdeacon Bell was one who was highly valued by him, and was afterwards his chaplain. He had an intimate knowledge of the Bishop's manner of conducting his ordinations; we are happy, therefore, to be able to give his account of them in his own words :—

'I have much pleasure in complying with your request that I should contribute to your intended Memoir of our loved and honoured friend, the late Bishop of Cashel, some account of his manner of discharging that very important part of the duties of the episcopal office, namely, the ordination of persons to serve in the ministry of the Church.

'I had the great privilege of being associated with the Bishop in that solemn duty for five-and-twenty years, first as Archdeacon of Waterford, and afterwards as his chaplain; and I had therefore the fullest opportunity of knowing with what feelings he regarded everything connected with the sending forth labourers into the Lord's vineyard.

'To one who regarded, as he did, the preaching of the gospel of Christ as the great agency which God has constituted for the saving of sinners, and who so fully realized the necessity of a faithful discharge of that duty, as well for the ministers themselves as for those over whom they

[1] Now Archdeacon of Cashel.

are appointed ministers, an ordination was always an occasion of the deepest solemnity.

'The first object present to the Bishop's mind was, that, as far as in him lay, he might never be led to lay hands upon any who had not been called by the Spirit of God, and with whom it was not the chief desire in entering the ministry of the Church to testify to others the gospel of the grace of God, which had brought peace and comfort to their own souls.

'Personal religion was in his mind the first and indispensable qualification in a candidate for holy orders ; and it was his general habit to require, at the very commencement, an interview with persons presenting themselves to his notice, in order that he might be satisfied upon that point.

'At such interviews I have frequently been present. Many now labouring in the ministry of our Church will remember with what affectionate kindness the Bishop would converse with them about the great truths which concern our everlasting peace, and lead them on gently to unfold their own views and feelings and hopes, so as greatly to encourage young men who were really led by the Spirit, or to make those pause who might be conscious to themselves that some lower motive was the prevailing one in seeking admittance to the sacred office.

'Having satisfied himself as to the personal religion of candidates, he proceeded to ascertain how far they were possessed of those intellectual qualifications, whether natural or acquired, which the full and efficient discharge of the duties of the ministry require.

'It is a very great mistake to suppose (although it has

been said) that the Bishop was indifferent to qualifications of that kind, or that he undervalued the advantages of a collegiate course, and of that mental training of which a University degree may be generally accepted as sufficient evidence.

'It was very improbable that one whose own University career had been highly distinguished would undervalue such training in others; but the Bishop felt strongly that in a minister of the gospel, knowledge and love of the truth, and the wisdom that cometh from above, are the primary qualifications, without which all others would be little worth.

'In the earlier years of the Bishop's episcopate, candidates seeking to be employed in his diocese were required to present themselves to one or both of his intimate and valued friends, the late Dr. Singer, Bishop of Meath, then Regius Professor of Divinity in the University of Dublin, and the late Venerable Henry Irwin, Archdeacon of Emly. They were men who will not soon be forgotten in the Church of Ireland; and only such as were approved by them were finally accepted as candidates for ordination.

'The view which the Bishop took of the responsibility involved in the exercise of that part of his office was such as to cause him to decline to receive candidates with letters demissory from other bishops; and to that rule, I believe, there never was any exception. Upon two or three occasions, in consequence of the unexpected indisposition of a much-loved neighbouring bishop, he allowed him to send forward candidates already examined, and they were presented by the chaplain, who had examined and approved them. Under the influence of the same view, the Bishop never granted letters demissory, but invariably ordained those who were about to labour in his own diocese. That such was his rule I only mention as a matter of fact.

'To the season of ordination the Bishop always looked forward with much anxiety, and it was with him a time of very special thoughtfulness and prayer. The candidates were accustomed to assemble at the Bishop's house on the day before the examination commenced, and they were his guests until all had been completed; and I have no doubt that that important epoch in their history lives in the happy and grateful recollection of many who are now labouring within the bosom of our beloved Church. I shall not dwell upon the details of such examination, but merely mention how it was conducted. At the commencement the candidates assembled in the Bishop's library, his archdeacon and chaplain being in attendance; and special prayer was offered up, generally by the Bishop himself, for a blessing on the work in which all were about to be engaged.

'In the examination the Bishop always took a prominent part; and he felt special interest (increasing every year) in pointing out the perfectly scriptural character of the articles and formularies of our Church, and the deliberate intention of those who compiled them to purge out the leaven of Roman Catholic doctrine.

'The candidates were required to write a short sermon upon a text which the Bishop selected. One evening was happily spent in a simple analysis of the contents of some portion of Scripture, such as one of the Gospels or Epistles, in *viva voce* examination; and on the last evening the candidates read aloud the sermons which they had prepared.

'To those sermons the Bishop always listened with marked attention, often commending with words of kindly approbation clear statements of divine truth in such words as, "Thank you, Sir, for so much of God's truth. I hope that it will always be heard from your lips, and that God will bless it to the people amongst whom you minister."

'Many will remember how largely the work in which he was then engaged entered into those expositions of Scripture at family worship, for the freshness and power of which the Bishop of Cashel was so remarkable, and how earnestly he prayed for a blessing upon it. But none but those who were admitted to close intimacy could know how constantly that work was borne upon his heart before God throughout the entire season.

'On the morning of the ordination, all assembled again for special prayer immediately before proceeding to the Cathedral, and we went fresh from that appeal to the throne of grace to take our respective parts in the solemn service of the day.

'I need hardly say that the Bishop's part in that service was marked by the most impressive solemnity; and when all was happily concluded, he frequently gave utterance to his deep thankfulness that, as far as man's judgment could go, he had once more been engaged in sending forth worthy labourers into his Master's vineyard. I may say that he looked back upon the last occasion on which he exercised his episcopal functions in this great business with much of that spirit of happy thankfulness.

'I shall only add, that with all the solemnity which characterized such seasons there was mingled so much cheerfulness, so much freshness and vigour, in the Bishop's conversation and in his remarks upon the leading topics of the day, always tending to spiritual improvement, that many have in after life spoken to me of the pleasure and profit which memory recalled in connection with their ordination, and of the words of godly counsel or of special prayer which had made a deep and lasting impression upon their hearts.

'The great day of the Lord will make manifest how largely the Bishop's desire and prayer were granted in his being enabled to make choice of fit persons to serve in the ministry of the gospel, faithful shepherds of the flock, who, when the Chief Shepherd shall appear, shall receive the crown of glory that fadeth not away.—Believe me, faithfully yours, 'ROBERT BELL.'

It was the Bishop of Cashel's habit to give the young men ordained by him the benefit of his great experience in the work of the ministry, by affectionately giving them advice on various subjects. One of these young men described to the writer of this Memoir the impressive manner in which he spoke personally to him, together with another young man who was ordained with him. Taking a hand of each of them in his, he prayed fervently for a blessing upon them and upon their ministry. Amongst other things, he never failed to advise them' to write their sermons, at least for some years until their style was formed, and never at any time to preach without preparation. To illustrate the importance of this admonition, he would often tell them an anecdote of an extempore preacher whom he had heard many years previously. This young man informed the Bishop, that when he went into the pulpit he never knew a word that he was going to say. 'Well, my good friend,' the Bishop answered, ' that accounts for what some of your congregation tell me, that when you come out of the pulpit they do not know a word you have been saying!' The Bishop often remarked, that writing a sermon was a great safeguard against talking nonsense; and would say that he did not like to see a clergyman measure out his discourse by taking out his watch, as if to say, 'I can give it to you by the yard.' He thought that ministers ought to think more of the importance of, and spend more time in preparation for, making a profitable use of the only hour in the week in which he can have his people gathered together ready to hear, free from the distractions of worldly business, what he had to say to them regarding the things which concerned their everlasting peace. The advantage of not spinning out a sermon to such a length as would weaken its force and lessen its effect upon the congregation was in a characteristic manner illustrated by his relating an anecdote of a clergyman of his acquaintance, who, on going on the Home Mission for a tour of preaching, took with him but one sermon. At the beginning of the tour, the length of the sermon was an hour and a half; but it gradually diminished, until, on the last occasion of its being delivered, it had come down to half an hour. The Bishop said that it reminded him of a receipt for making soup: 'Put down two quarts of water, and boil it down to a pint.' He thought it probable that the pint contained more nutrition, and would be more easily taken in, than the two quarts.

A diocesan Home Mission was, soon after his appointment to the see of Cashel, set on foot under his immediate patronage. The Home Mission service was always attended by him in person, and the preacher entertained at the Palace. The same patronage was extended by him to all the deputations from Religious Societies which visited Waterford.

Many abuses had crept in, and much laxity was manifested in Church discipline throughout the entire diocese. In bringing about a change in this respect, the Bishop was most energetic. In many cases he himself paid the stipend for young, active, ardent, and faithful ministers, when the incumbent was aged or indifferent. He soon acquired a most intimate acquaintance with the circumstances of every parish under his jurisdiction.

In the spring of the year 1853 the question of the admission of Jews into Parliament was under consideration. The Bishop alludes to it in the following letter:—

To Mrs. Hamilton Madden.

'105 JERMYN STREET, 22d *April* 1853.

'MY DEAR BELLA,—I am obliged to you for your letter about your dear father. I had heard before of his death, and I did not need to hear any particulars. I had seen his life for many years bearing testimony to his faith. We can say of him, what sorrowing friends often find it hard to say of those that are gone, that he has entered into his rest. Wonderful change! Your dear mother must feel a great blank, but it will be but for a short time. He is only gone a little while before her; she will soon follow after. May we all be ready when the summons comes. . . . I am to go (*D.V.*) on Saturday to Winchester, to preach for the Irish Society. I must return on Monday, to be on Tuesday in the House of Lords to vote against the Jews' Bill, which I hope will be thrown out. . . .—Very affectionately yours,

'ROBERT CASHEL, etc.'

His reasons for voting against it he has recorded:—

'I do not vote against the admission of Jews into Parliament because I do not love the Jews. I can say, like the apostle, "Whilst they are enemies for the gospel's sake, they are beloved for the fathers' sakes." I would deal with them as with one whose father I loved, but who had disgraced that father, and had departed from the example which had been set by him. I would not admit a Jew into Parliament, lest he might take it as a proof that I did not consider that it was a matter of importance whether he was a Jew or a Christian.

'Another reason that I have for not consenting to throw off my Christian character in order to admit a Jew is, that a good Jew would not come into this assembly lest he should be defiled; just as the Jews, in the time of our Lord, would not go into the Judgment Hall lest they should be defiled, but ate the Passover.'

It is well known that the Bishop of Cashel was strongly

U

opposed to those views on religious subjects which are commonly called 'Tractarian;' but it is a mistake to suppose that he was so bigoted as to unchristianize all persons who held these views. Some of them he held very highly in esteem for their work's sake. He has been heard to say: 'I honour a man who will get out of his bed on a cold winter's night and lie on the flags, if he thinks it will benefit his soul, however mistaken I may think him to be; but I have no respect for those who adopt a religion of forms merely to cover their want of true vital religion.'

The Bishop of Cashel was not bigoted, but he was uncompromising. What he felt and thought to be error on so all-important a subject as that of religion, he would not go half-way to meet, although he did not allow this to alter his feelings of affection, and even of Christian regard, for the persons who entertained them. He was conservative in his religious opinions as well as in politics; and he wished to be able to say with truth, 'I have kept the faith.' The tide of public opinion, on some subjects, had ebbed away from him; but he stood still, unchangeable and immoveable as a rock. May the beacon-light kindled by his memory serve to warn any who are in danger of making shipwreck of their souls on the quicksands of error! He had seen so much evil brought upon his fellow-countrymen through the means of a system of religion which he agreed with Cecil in denominating 'Satan's *masterpiece*,' that he looked with a very jealous eye upon anything which he thought had a Romanizing tendency. This was his reason for so carefully excluding from his diocese any clergyman who held Tractarian views; which made some people think him narrow-minded, but he was very far from it. True, he was in one sense, perhaps, narrow-minded, for it is written, 'Strait is the gate and narrow is the way which leadeth unto life;' but his desire was that every one should find the right way, and in that sense he had a catholic spirit. In his own diocese he often said that he did not apprehend much danger from Tractarian views, as they had too much of the 'real thing' in that part of the country; but he felt it to be his duty carefully to guard against any attempt to introduce into it what he looked upon as dangerous. He was 'very jealous for the Lord God of Hosts;' and he considered himself as a watchman set over that part of His vineyard, to sound an alarm at the approach of an enemy. As it is said that no fortress is of greater strength than the weakest part of it will prove to be, so he carefully nipped in the bud everything which to his mind had a tendency to lead people to rest too much in forms and outward observances. Let it not be thought, however, that the Bishop of Cashel was not a good Churchman. He has been very erroneously classed among the Low Church party;[1] but people who give such names do not always reflect upon their meaning. That he sincerely loved and valued the services of that scriptural Church of which he was so useful a member and dignitary, was well known to those who had the privilege of being acquainted with his sentiments; and those who were not would be convinced of the truth of the

---

[1] In his letter to Dr. Millar, published a short time before he was made a bishop, Mr. Daly expressed his unwillingness to be classed among the Low Church party.

assertion by reading some discourses written by him upon
the services of our Church. They were found among his
manuscripts, and are well worthy of publication.

On his first going to Waterford, he found in use in the
Cathedral books of 'Altar Services,' which he caused to be
changed for others, as he objected to the name of altar
being given to the communion table. He also disapproved
of the practice of administering the sacrament of the
Lord's Supper first to any clergymen who might be present as members of the congregation. He thought that it
was too much making them 'lords over God's heritage.'
He wrote as follows to one of his clergy who asked his
advice upon this subject :—

'You acted about administering the sacrament according
to the principle I act upon. I never give the sacrament
to a clergyman not officiating before the rest of the congregation. On Sunday se'nnight I was at the parish
church here, sitting with the rest of the congregation. I
did not go up with the first communicants; and if the
clergyman had waited for me, I would not have gone
before others.'

He also very much disliked the practice of some communicants at the table of the Lord who do not take the
bread in their fingers, but hold their hand to receive it.
As he thought that there was a principle involved in this
matter, he felt it to be his duty to show his disapproval of
it on one occasion in rather a marked manner. At an
ordination held by him in the Cathedral of Waterford, a
stranger, an English clergyman, who was spending a few
days at the hotel at Waterford, presented himself at the

table of the Lord with the candidates for ordination. The
Bishop had known nothing of him previously; but as he
held out his hand to receive the element, the Bishop
repeated the words, 'Take, eat,' and at length said, 'Take,
eat; take it in your fingers,' which the stranger was un-
willingly obliged to do. On returning to his hotel, he
wrote a very long letter to the Bishop, remonstrating with
him; of which, however, the latter thought it wiser to take
no notice.

To one for whose welfare, both spiritual and temporal,
he was sincerely desirous, and who had joined the Tractarian party, he thus wrote:—

'3 HENRIETTA STREET, 24th *February.*

'MY DEAR ——,—I received your long letter with much
pleasure, from the proof it gave me of the interest you
take in the most important of all subjects; with some
uneasiness, from the proof it afforded of your being in
bondage to a system of human tradition, which almost
excluded from the world the light of God's truth, and
which does now keep the majority of the professing Christian world in idolatry and superstition. I am pleased with
the length of your letter, and yet not encumbered by it,
for the whole of the questions between us is found in the
first page, and is contained in what you say of the insufficiency and obscurity of Scripture, and the necessity of a
guide. I am writing without any books; if I had them, I
would give you a paragraph out of Milner's *End of Controversy,* in which he uses the very same arguments, almost
the very same words, to prove the existence of an infallible

Church. I do not bring this forward to put you down by
urging Popery, but to point out to you that your principles
are the same as the Papists'.' They lay down the same
principle, the necessity of a guide. Like you, they say *there
is, in their opinion, a want of a guide;* ergo, *there is a guide.*
But they work out their principle, and *prove* that the living
ministers of the infallible Church constitute at all times a
guide; whilst you, following their example in taking your
opinion that a guide is necessary as a proof that there is
in fact a guide, state that *the sense of antiquity, as collected
from the Fathers, is the most natural and eligible guide.*
Who told you, upon what evidence do you believe, that
the sense of antiquity, collected by fallible men out of the
voluminous contradictory writings of fallible men, is an
eligible guide ? God has nowhere told us to take them
for our guide, whilst He has said, " Search the Scriptures."
Is it treating God aright, who has given His word to be a
light to our feet and a lamp to our path, to take direction
from that word only as far as men guide us whom He has
not appointed as our guides ? The course adopted by you
and the Romanists, and the position which suggested that
course, is not new in the Church of God. He gave a
written word to His ancient Church of the house of Israel,
and there were those among them who, like you, thought
that word insufficient and obscure, and therefore considered
there was a necessity for a guide. Whatever you say as
to the insufficiency of Scripture would have had more
ground if said concerning the incomplete canon of Scripture which the Jews had ; yet let us consider whether
Christ or His apostles sanctioned their setting up a guide

which He had never appointed. If you say now that
there is a necessity for a guide, and infer from thence that
there is a guide, as you do, *à fortiori*, as there was a
greater necessity then, there is more proof that there *was* a
guide. But let us look to the fact. Is there any sanction
given to the idea that there is such a guide which it is
dangerous and criminal to neglect? I have never seen
such a sanction. But I have read our Lord's words: "You
make void the word of God by your traditions;" "In vain
do ye worship me, teaching for doctrines the commandments of men." Did our Lord direct the people of His
time to the consent of antiquity collected out of the Jewish
writers? Did He not, on the other hand, beginning at
Moses and all the prophets, expound unto them in all the
Scriptures the things concerning Himself? When Paul
would commend any doctrine that he taught, did he ever
consent to the Fathers of the Jewish Church? Did he not
say, "I continue unto this day, witnessing both to small
and great, saying none other things than those which the
prophets and Moses did say should come"? He certainly
paid no respect to such a guide as you and the Roman
Catholics say it is criminal and dangerous to neglect. His
language to Timothy is familiar to you: "The Holy Scriptures, which are able to make you wise unto salvation, by
faith in Christ Jesus." I confess I can see no countenance
you have for assuming that there is a guide, except your
own private judgment that it is necessary, from which you
unwarrantably conclude that there *is* such a guide. And
then let us consider what sort of a guide you have found
to supply your supposed necessity. "The sense of antiquity,

as collected from the early Fathers." This guide is to supply the insufficiency and obscurity of Scripture. In this collection, then, you must maintain that there is sufficiency and clearness. They must contain *the truth, the whole truth*, and *nothing but the truth*. If I admit that they contain much truth, as there may be a grain of wheat in a barrel of chaff, surely you would not say they contain the *whole* truth, the *whole* mind of God—that these uninspired men had written there all that God desired to reveal to His creatures. But last of all, do they contain "nothing but the truth"? have they error mixed up with their quantum of truth? Can you deny it? Have you ever read Chrysostom's comment on the parable of the "ten virgins," where he calls the five wise virgins men in a state of celibacy who give alms to the poor, and the five foolish virgins men in a state of celibacy who do not give alms to the poor? If there is a guide wanted to lead men in their searches of Scripture, do they not much more want a guide in their searches of the Fathers, to enable them to separate the chaff from the wheat, to distinguish truth from error? If you assist the obscurity of Scripture, and send us to the Fathers for guidance, it is certainly the figure of *ignotium per ignotius*. You speak of the numerous errors and sects flowing from men's private judgment on the Scriptures, and will you shut your eyes to the millions led to superstition and idolatry by fallible human guidance? The system you advocate covered the Middle Ages with darkness that might be felt; the principle you reject let in the light of the Reformation. There are but the two principles, that of Popery and that of the Reformation; if you reject the last, you must, if consistent, embrace the first. Rome works the principle of a guide thoroughly; you do it clumsily, lamely. It answers for a beginning, but you can never stop there. I shall give you a quotation from Bishop Stillingfleet, who is often referred to by the Tractarians : " Wise men, who have thoroughly considered of Vincentius, may, though in general they cannot but approve of it, so far as to think it highly improbable that there should be antiquity, universality, and consent, against the true and genuine sense of Scripture; yet, when they consider this way of Vincentius, with all those cautious restrictions and limitations laid down by him, they are apt to think that he has put men to a *wild-goose chase* to find out anything according to his rules, and that St. Augustine spoke a great deal more to the purpose when he spoke concerning all the writers of the Church, that although they had ever so much learning and sanctity, he did not think it true because they thought so, but because they persuaded him to believe it true either from the authority of Scripture or some probable reason."

' And our Church says she receives the three creeds not because they have the consent of antiquity, but because they can be proved by express warrant of Scripture. May the Lord direct you right, and keep you from forsaking the fountain of living waters, is the prayer of, yours affectionately, ' ROBERT CASHEL, etc.'

The case of the Episcopal Church in Scotland had been brought before him in the year 1845, when he received a letter from Dr. Low, Bishop of Moray in the Episcopal

Church, asking him whether he sympathized with some of his clergy, who had seceded from that body on account of not being able conscientiously to make use of the communion office, which had been lately introduced by the Episcopal Church in Scotland into their Book of Common Prayer. In answer to this the Bishop of Cashel wrote two letters, which were afterwards published, saying that he did sympathize with those who separated for the truth's sake. In the year 1849 a petition to Parliament was drawn up by members of the Church of England resident in Scotland, complaining of the manner in which these clergymen were dealt with in consequence of their secession. On the occasion of its being presented in the House of Lords by Lord Brougham, the Bishop of Cashel made an excellent and learned speech, in the course of which he quoted the following paragraph from one of his letters to the Bishop of Moray :—

'I find, I think, in our Church two things for which I love her,—SCRIPTURAL TRUTH and SCRIPTURAL ORDER. I love her for both; but when I shall find these two separated, and I shall be obliged to choose whether I will hold to the truth and give up the order, or hold to the order and give up the truth, I shall feel myself bound to hold to the truth.

'If my own Episcopal Church should turn away from the truth, should declare the doctrine of her communion service to be uncatholic, and should introduce a service that speaks more like transubstantiation than ever was spoken by any Church but the Church of Rome, I should feel myself bound to protest against her heresy and to separate from her communion, though that separation should involve the undesirable absence of episcopal superintendence and control. How much more must I sympathize with Church of England men in Scotland, who upon the same ground separate themselves from a Church which has no hereditary claim to their submission—which is not the Church of their fathers, and had not been the cradle of their youth! If asked my opinion, I must say, "Come out from her, and be separate." '

His diocesan charge for 1851 refers much to the subject which we have in hand; also a letter, published by him many years later, addressed to the Rev. Arthur Dawson, in reply to some remarks on the report of Master Brooke's Committee.[1]

The years 1848 and 1849 were eventful ones, both at home and abroad. The disturbance known by the name of 'Smith O'Brien's Rebellion' was followed by a visitation of that fearful disease the cholera. The localities connected with the former were many of them in the Bishop of Cashel's diocese,—the widow M'Cormac's cabbage-garden and the police-barrack near Carrick-on-Suir, where the only two scenes were enacted which at all bordered on a fight. On the Continent, the revolution in Paris and the flight of Louis Philippe were followed by insurrection in Rome and the banishment of the Pope to Gaeta. These remarkable events are commented upon in a very serious and edifying manner in the charge delivered by the Bishop to his clergy in the year 1849, which we regret that the limits of our Memoir will not admit of our giving here.

[1] See Appendix B.

CHAPTER IX.

' Friend after friend departs !
Who has not lost a friend ?
There is no union here of hearts
That finds not here an end.'

THE Bishop of Cashel's sentiments on various subjects are freely expressed in his letters to a friend who kept up for many years a correspondence with him.

We shall give some of them in this place.

' WATERFORD, *2d January* 1861.

' MY DEAR ——,— . . . It is pleasant to find that, cold as this world is, it is not with all " out of sight, out of mind," but that there is room in the heart for an absent friend.   I am, thank God, in very good health considering my years, which are very near that term when the Psalmist says it is labour and sorrow.   I am thankful to be able to say it is not so with me yet ; but we know not what a day, what this new year, may bring forth. We may be assured, that in whatever shape it may come, it will work together for our good.   Our language should be, " I will trust and not be afraid, for the Lord Jehovah is my strength and my song ; He is my salvation."   Now if the Lord is our salvation, surely He is and will be everything else. "He that spared not His own Son, but delivered Him up for us all, how shall He not with Him also freely give us all things?" What a word, "with Him!" Yes, all things are ours if we are Christ's; we ought to be cheerful, and hear the Lord saying to us, "Lift up your hearts, for your redemption draweth nigh." I remember that Richard Baxter says, when he was young in the faith, he thought the best thing he could do was to be looking at himself, and finding fault with himself; but now, in his maturer years, he was brought to see that one believing look up and on did him more good than ten gloomy complaining looks back to himself. Complaining of ourselves does not mend the matter, but rejoicing in the Lord does lift us up; and this is the reason that the apostle says, "Rejoice in the Lord always." The last year brought heavy tidings, yet we had what should make us rejoice, though now for a season we were in heaviness through manifold trials. What the new year may bring is happily hidden from us. I pray that it may not be war; it is the severest scourge with which an offended God can scourge a guilty world. I was reading the other day that chapter in Isaiah which says, "They shall learn war no more." It was forced upon my mind how different from the present scene. What are men about but learning war? and he is considered the greatest benefactor who invents the most destructive instrument of war. May peace be in your dwelling.—With kindest regards to your sister, I remain, in the best bonds, very sincerely yours,

'ROBERT CASHEL, etc.'

To the Same.

'MY DEAR ——,—I thank you much for your letter, showing that, whilst years pass away, kind recollections keep their place and do not pass away. There is no chilling frost there, cold as this world often is. Surely, when we are drawing nearer to that time and place where love remains, we ought to have more and more of warmth, even though nature is growing less sensitive,—the outward man decaying, but the inward man being renewed day by day. How much there is to chill us in this world! But there is in believers a fire within that keeps up the spiritual temperature, and keeps us from that which our God hates—that is, lukewarmness, neither hot nor cold. But as here we require to draw near to the fire when the coals are burning, so we must draw nigh to the great Source of heat, and receive out of His fulness grace for grace.

'It is unwise to live so much in the regions that are cold and dark, and so little in those that get heat and light from the great sun of the system. We are not straitened in our God, but in ourselves. We sometimes get a little heat from contact and company with our fellow-Christians, whose circumstances, blessed by grace, help to warm them. You have heard, no doubt, of the death of our valued friend and late neighbour, William Cleaver. It was very cheering and warming to hear of the support and victory he had at the latter end. His son told me in a letter that his last days presented a scene which he hoped that neither he nor his other children would ever forget. He was indeed more than conqueror, through Him that loved him. How gracious is our Lord, to make that as our day so shall be our strength, to give dying grace to dying people! Manifestations of that kind are very comfortable, and very seasonable to those who, like myself, are growing old. We are interested in what God does for a brother or sister who goes before us. It is a sample of the working of God's love, and shows us what we may expect in our own case when our time comes. I am very glad to hear so good an account of your sister's health, as well as your own. Faint, but pursuing.—Very truly yours,

'ROBERT CASHEL, etc.'

To another, who had asked his opinion of a book,— Martin Tupper on Faith and Probabilities,—he answers:—

'WATERFORD, 16*th December* 1858.

'MY DEAR R.,—I have looked through the book you sent to me. I like the author's intention, and I like some of his statements. There is a class of persons who have a proud mind, and an unwillingness to receive anything that does not commend itself to their reason. They are always hair-splitting and hole-picking. He tries to do them a service, but I think he goes too far. He encourages the idea that reason is to be satisfied. In this I think the author wrong. We must expect to find things *above reason*, but not contrary to reason. I was much struck with an observation of the late Henry Grattan: "It would be most unreasonable that God should have left His rational creatures without any revelation of His will. But it

requires the prostration of the human intellect." Every
man is not competent to comprehend everything in New-
ton's *Principia*. How should he expect to comprehend
everything in God's mind which He has revealed? Surely
man might expect to find things above his reason. I
think the chapter on the Bible is good, but I could point
out many silly probabilities in parts of the book, as at the
end of the Bible chapter, p. 171. When St. Augustine
was asked which was the first Christian grace, he said,
"Humility;" when asked the second, he said, "Humility;"
when asked the third, "Humility."

'An humble spirit, which thinks how high, how wise
God is, and how mean, how ignorant we are, is of great
value, and would solve many difficulties in God's dealings
and God's revelation. "Who can by searching find out
God unto perfection? It is high as heaven; what canst
thou do? deeper than hell; what canst thou know?"
(Job xi. 7, 8.) The important great points are very plain,
but not palatable to human pride,—that man is a sinner,
and that Jesus, the Son of God, is a Saviour. Lord, teach
us these truths!—Affectionately yours,

'ROBERT CASHEL, etc.'

Over the year 1857 there was a slight shade cast, as far
as the Bishop of Cashel was concerned, by an attack of
inflammation in his eyes, which, however, his wonderfully
vigorous constitution enabled him completely to recover
from, although a small ulcer had been formed upon one of
his eyes, which took some time to heal. Being laid aside
for so long a time from his usual occupations of reading

and writing, and partially confined to the house and darkened rooms, was, to one of his active mind and habits, no small trial. That he was patient in this tribulation, and received it as coming from the hand of a loving Father, is shown by some letters written during that year :—

'KILLOUGH CASTLE, HOLYCROSS, THURLES,
'*5th September.*

'MY DEAR ——,—. . . I should be very glad if the account you have had of the perfect restoration of my eye was founded on fact. I am sorry to say I was obliged to bleed with leeches again about a fortnight ago ; and though the bleeding was attended with good effect, I am unable to read or write half the quantity I should wish. I am thankful to be as well as I am. I suppose I shall not be quite well until my vile body is changed and fashioned like unto the glorious body of the Man Christ Jesus. There there will be no sore eyes, or such other ailments as you have often to complain of. The inhabitant shall not have to say, " I am sick." Glorious time ! We are not longing and looking for it as we ought. We have reason to say, " Lord, increase our faith." I fear England is about to be humbled and pulled down. She is, I fear, too proud ; and pride goeth before a fall. This India business appears to me to be the most fearful shake England has got. There is no saying how it will end. I feel for those that have relations in the army. The most of them will never return. We believers receive a kingdom that cannot be moved. Thanks be to God for His unspeakable gift ! . . .'

X

Again he writes as follows :—

'How thankful we ought to be that there is One that numbers the very hairs of our heads, and that there is no such thing as chance. We don't escape by chance; we don't suffer by chance. It is arranged by a higher and wiser Power, and He makes all things work together for our good. There is great beauty in many of the phrases of Scripture :—" work together "—the bitter and the sweet; " in heaviness, if need be." We don't see the need be, but a better Physician sees the need. It is all well, whether we see it or not. " There is balm in Gilead; there is a good Physician there." . . . I can say nothing about new books, I can read so very little. I am happy that I am able to preach in the neighbouring church by preparing a sermon to preach without book. I preach in small churches to great congregations; but alas! I see no fruit. We have need to pray much for the outpouring of the Spirit. . . .'

To the Same.

'WATERFORD, 12*th January* 1858.

'MY DEAR ——,—. . . . It is solemn and full of serious thought to find, as you say, that we are approaching the end, when time shall be no longer. Blessed end and blessed hope, that will not make ashamed! May we find that, though the outward man perish, the inner man is renewed day by day as we come nearer to the consummation. May we see it more clearly, and have it more continually before our eyes, looking for and hastening unto the coming of the Lord Jesus Christ.

'As you inquire about my eyes, you will be glad to hear

from me that they are free from disease, but not as strong as they were, and not able for as much work, particularly at night. I suppose they will never be as they were until the time when the Lord makes all things new, when, I presume, I shall have new eyes as well as new nature; and I shall have a new use of the eyes, to see the Lord as He is; for now, indeed, with our best eyes, we see as through a glass, darkly.

' I have read very little during 1857. I can recommend no new book, except that I have been surprised and gratified by a book published by Spurgeon. I expected nothing really solid from him; but I found, as far as I have read it, that it is more full of experimental religion than any I have seen for a long time. He exhibits an acquaintance with man and with God beyond what I had expected from him. . . . I am, I trust, doing a good work by circulating the Douay Bible among the Roman Catholics of Waterford. In the last two months I have sold 500. May the Lord bless His word! Remember me most kindly to your sister, and believe me, yours truly, in the best bonds,   ' ROBERT CASHEL, etc.'

About the year 1850, the Rev. Arthur Wynne, the Bishop's much-loved friend and cousin, who had been his fellow-labourer in the parish of Powerscourt for many years, exchanged the living of Drogheda for the precentorship of the Cathedral of Waterford, principally for the sake of enjoying the privilege of the society of and co-operation with one whom he had always loved and looked up to as a father in Christ Jesus.

This move involved a considerable sacrifice of income, which the Bishop managed to lessen by appointing him his private chaplain. He was the first who had filled that office, and as far as concerned the duties of conducting family prayer, etc., in the Bishop's household, it was quite a sinecure, as he continued to do so himself as long as he lived.

Of the pleasure and profit to be derived from Mr. Wynne's society and ministry, the Bishop and the people of Waterford were deprived by his death in 1854. His loss was keenly felt by his friend and patron, and his removal left a blank which to the Bishop was never filled up. His sister, in writing from the Palace to a friend soon after Mr. Wynne's death, says : ' The Bishop feels his loss extremely. Waterford is like a different place.' His feelings on this subject are expressed in the following letter :—

To the Rev. Joseph C——.

'WATERFORD, 14*th March* 1854.

' MY DEAR C.,—I thank you much for your very kind letter of sympathy. I have suffered a great loss, losing a Christian friend and relation, a gentleman in his mind and manners; but he was the Lord's. He lent him for a time, and He has taken him to Himself. He suffered much for the last fortnight from difficulty of breathing and want of sleep, but his mind was clear to the last. I have enjoyed much pleasure at different times at the bedside of dying believers, but I never saw a more calm, strong victory over death than in his case. He said to me that he never was so overwhelmed with a sense of sin as on that bed; but God had given him such a superabounding sense of the grace of God in Christ, that he had the victory,—" I am upon the Rock." I trust his death may do more good than we might have expected from his life. He spoke with wonderful power to his medical attendants. I trust they will never forget his dying words.

' At a certain time of life we do not get new friends. I cannot expect to find one to supply the vacant place he has left. Our gracious God cuts all our ties to this present world, that we may be the more ready at His bidding to mount up.

' I hope all your family are well, and that you find the Lord present with you in your new position. Remember me to Mrs. C.—Yours very truly,

' ROBERT CASHEL, etc.'

It was several years before the Bishop could bring himself to appoint a successor to Mr. Wynne. An old friend, he often said, was a blessing, which when removed, the vacant place could not be filled up. The truly excellent young man, however, who next acted as his private chaplain and secretary, the Rev. Richard Smith, was one for whom he had an affectionate regard, and over whose untimely death he sincerely mourned. His letters, both to him and afterwards to his young widow, sufficiently prove this.

It has been said of the Bishop of Cashel, and with truth, that his letters were not the best part of him. He had a certain difficulty at times in expressing his meaning with clearness and gracefulness in writing, which was never exhibited in the *viva voce* productions of his intellect. This was the more extraordinary, as he had an impediment (or, more properly, what would be called a stutter) in speaking. What this arose from it is impossible to say, as he certainly did not suffer from any constitutional nervousness. He was chiefly liable to be affected by it when conversing in private upon any subject that he felt much about, when his efforts to get out whatever word was backward in coming would often give additional force and emphasis to what he said. It never affected him in public speaking or in preaching; and as the gift of being able to influence others by public speaking has in all ages been considered to be the first of gifts, we do not detract from the honour of his memory by saying that his writing was inferior to his speaking. Many of his letters are, however, most characteristic; and they are in one respect invaluable to his biographer, as they prove beyond a possibility of doubt his tender sympathy for those in affliction, for which many persons who did not know him well would not give him credit. Such are his letters to Mrs. and Miss Smith, and to Mrs. Verschoyle, widow of his friend the late Bishop of Kilmore.

On hearing of Mr. Smith's illness having taken a fatal turn, while his poor young wife was in a state of health which caused great anxiety to her family, the kind Bishop thus writes to her sister :—

'WATERFORD, 21*st December* 1863.

'MY DEAR MISS SMITH,—I cannot tell you how over-whelmed I have been with grief and disappointment on

getting such a sad account of my valued friend. Your
letter yesterday morning had made me feel quite confident
about him; and then your letter by Dr. Mackesy so destroyed all my hopes. How I feel for poor Mrs. Smith in
her present state, without strength to bear the trial, and
in danger of getting injury by the distress she must be in.
Still we are in the Lord's hands; and He is a God of love,
a Father of mercies, and a God of all comfort, who comforts those that are in any trouble. May He comfort and
support you all, and give a happy issue out of the affliction. Will you tell me the truth, is there any difficulty
about money? I am ready to supply any that is required.
These illnesses cannot be without expense. We have but
one resource, to wait upon our gracious God. Oh, what a
world it is, to be liable to such awful visitations! Thanks
be to God, there is a better! May we realize it whilst in
this vale of sorrow, and joyfully reach it in God's good
time.—Very truly yours,   ' ROBERT CASHEL, etc.'

To the Same.

' WATERFORD, 23*d December* 1863.

' MY DEAR MISS SMITH,—I know not how to write to
you or what to say to you; we are here overwhelmed with
grief. We feel our own loss, but what is it to the loss sustained by his family and the parish? It is heartrending
to think of it. I am very uneasy about poor Mrs. Smith.
It was very providential that she had been removed out of
the house, and was with her father and mother. May they
be enabled to comfort her; but none can give consolation
but that gracious God who has struck the blow—oh, how

heavy a blow! I shall be very anxious to hear how she bears the sad intelligence when it reaches her. She had reason to fear the worst, but no doubt indulged in hope against hope. I never knew anything that put this world in such a sad light. It would be saying too little to say, Vanity of vanities, all is vanity. It is worse than vanity. Happy to think there remaineth a rest for the people of God; there is no rest here. May we all have grace to seek and lay hold on the true rest; there will be none of those heartrending scenes. Well, in the midst of all this painful scene, what a real comfort to know that he that is gone was a child of God; and if a child, then an heir of God, and a joint-heir with Jesus Christ! If he was permitted to speak to us, he no doubt would say, "Weep not for me who am taken away, but weep for yourselves and your children that remain in this evil world." There is an intense feeling about him and his afflicted family. He was beloved and valued. I hope his sister holds up well. The Lord be with you all.—Very truly yours,

'ROBERT CASHEL, etc.'

A few days later he thus sympathizes with the afflicted widow :—

'WATERFORD, 3d *January* 1864.

'MY DEAR MRS. SMITH,—I am sure you want no letter from me to assure you of the deep sympathy that I have towards you in your present bereavement. I really know not how to speak to one in your heavy sorrow. I feel my own loss and the loss to the Church generally; but what is all that compared to the loss you have sustained in losing

such a partner, such a companion, such a counsellor? We
have but one thing to look to, and that is to the hand of
that Lord who gave and has taken away. His ways are
unsearchable, and past finding out. He giveth no account
of His matters. We have no right to ask the Lord why
He afflicts, why He takes those we should keep. May the
Lord in His good time enable you to say, "Not my will, but
Thine be done." In the meantime, may He support you,
and comfort you, and preserve you and your little children
in health, to serve Him in the condition He has marked
out for you. . . . I commend you to God and the word of
His grace, which is able to save and preserve you, and bring
you to the inheritance incorruptible, undefiled, and that
fadeth not away. May the God of grace be with you and
yours.—Very truly yours, in the best bonds,

'ROBERT CASHEL, etc.'

Again he writes :—

'I can hardly realize such a change, such an overturning
in two or three weeks ; so bright, and now so dark. Well
may the apostle call this present state night, when he says,
"The night is far spent, the day is at hand." Oh that
we had grace to look to more and realize more the day
that is at hand! He has the day, we are in the night. . . .

> ' "Happy soul! his days are ended,
> All his mourning days below."'

To Mrs. Verschoyle.

'WATERFORD, 3d February 1870.

'MY DEAR MRS. VERSCHOYLE,—I do indeed feel for you.

The more valuable was your treasure, the more incalculable
is your loss. Among all my friends I do not know any
two that would feel a deeper pang at being separated than
you and my dear friend the Bishop. We were indeed
friends, joined to each other for many years, not only by
acquaintance, but by similarity of sentiments and unity of
religious faith. It could indeed be said of us, that we took
sweet counsel together, and went into the house of God as
friends. But what is the loss of a friend, however attached,
compared with your loss ? Yet you have not to sorrow as
those without hope when he sleeps in Jesus. You and
his many friends had not need of last words, uttered at the
last hour; you and we had a long life to testify to us his
faith. To him to live was Christ ; to die, then, was gain.
How many there are, who for so many years enjoyed his
ministry in Baggot Street Church, who can testify to the
faithfulness with which he preached Christ to them, and
besought them in Christ's stead to be reconciled unto God !
I am rejoiced at what you say of his children following
him as he followed Christ. They will know the blessed
privilege of having such a father to set them an example
as well as to give them instruction.—Your affectionate
friend in the Lord,   ' ROBERT CASHEL, etc.'

To a friend left alone by the death of her only sister:—

                                    ' DUBLIN, 24th April 1862.

' MY DEAR ——,—I yesterday heard the very afflicting
intelligence of the separation which our Heavenly Father
has in His wisdom thought fit to bring about in your

house. I feel deeply for you. To her that has been removed it has been, no doubt, an unspeakable blessing, a wondrous happy change; but to her that has been left solitary, it has been a most heavy blow, but from the hand of a heavenly Father, who does not willingly afflict His children. You both, no doubt, contemplated your end as not far off, but cannot but feel the separation, the snapping a cord that bound you so close together. If your remaining course may be solitary, yet it cannot but be short; and you are not alone, for your Father is with you, and no doubt will manifest His presence more than ever during the darkness of the night that precedes the coming day. You have only to do what we should all do, look forward to the time when the Lord shall come, and all His saints with Him, and there will be no more separation, no more death. Though He tarry, wait for Him; He will come, and will not tarry. With much sincere feeling I commend you to God and to the word of His grace, which is able to build you up and give you an inheritance among them that are sanctified.—Affectionately yours, in the best bonds,

'ROBERT CASHEL, etc.'

The following letter was addressed to a clergyman's wife on her recovery from a very trying illness :—

'MY DEAR MRS. ——,—I have been much gratified by getting a letter from you, and that one that testifies happily both to the health of your body and the health of your soul. I am thankful that you were able for the exertion of writing it, and that you could tell me that during the

illness you could feel the presence of your Saviour. This
is what St. Paul said (Rom. v.): "Tribulation worketh
patience, and patience experience, and experience hope."

'You have had experience in your trial, and I trust it
does work hope. Looking back on the experience of the
past enables us to look forward to the future with the
assurance of hope. Thus it is good to be afflicted. It
yieldeth a peaceable fruit to them that are exercised
thereby. You say that you are glad to "be raised up to
go forth into the world again." Paul had something of the
same feeling: as to himself, it would be better to depart
and be with Christ; but to remain was better for others.
I pray that your remaining may be a source of comfort and
good to others. I pray that it may be seen that this was
His object in leaving you for a longer time, and that He
may enable you to do good in two ways: first, as a light
so shining before men that they may see your good works,
and glorify your heavenly Father; and secondly, by doing
some actual good to those who may be set before you to
receive good, to comfort the heart and to strengthen the
hands of your husband and other fellow-labourers. But
remember, this may be the place of work for a Saviour,
but it is not our home. We should realize our heavenly
home more than we do. We ought to be like those
worthies we read of in the eleventh of Hebrews, for whom
God had prepared a city. They by faith saw it afar off,
and were persuaded of it, and embraced it, confessing that
they were strangers and pilgrims here. The state we
ought to be in is that of travellers, as one of our hymns
says :—

> "We are travelling through the wilderness
> To everlasting rest."

'Happy if we can say at all times, "Hallelujah! we are on our way to God."

'I expect to be in Waterford about the 4th of September, to transact business, and to prepare for receiving the Archbishop. I hope I shall find that you have made progress, and are gaining strength for any work the Lord may have for you to do. Remember me most kindly to Mr. ——.—Yours, with Christian regards, very truly,

'ROBERT CASHEL, etc.'

Of the Powerscourt Calendar he always kept a large store, which he gave freely when applied to for them. Nothing pleased him better than to be asked for them or for hymn-books; the latter was an enlarged edition of the Powerscourt one, published, with a preface written by himself, for the use of his diocese. He loved to do the work of an evangelist; and though now raised to a higher office in the Church, his delight was to minister individually to the souls of those around him. He taught a class in the Waterford Sunday school composed of young ladies, whose value for his instructions and personal affection for their teacher were very great. In order to become more acquainted with them, he gave them every year a tea-party at the Palace, a great part of the evening being spent in the singing of hymns and sacred music, in which he delighted. Archdeacon Brien, speaking of this class in his *Reminiscences*, says :—

'His class consisted of young ladies, to whom he expounded diligently the word of God, and tried to train them, by the blessed revelation of that word, for the kingdom of heaven. He had a very lively interest in that class; and I have good reason to believe that they who were taught by him entertained towards him warm sentiments of admiration and respectful love. For when some ladies connected with the Irish Society presented him, in recognition of his valuable services to that Society, with a very beautiful carpet, the work not of a mechanical loom, but the skilled fingers of the fair artificers, and which had occupied a place either in the first London or the first Dublin Exhibition as an attractive specimen of artistic skill, the ladies of his Sunday-school class supplemented the gift by working a rug to correspond with the carpet, which in due time they presented to him; and though the Bishop was not by any means very favourable to the presentation of testimonials, yet he received their gift very graciously, reciprocating the good-will and kindly feeling with which it was presented. He invited them to a tea-party at his house, and displayed both the carpet and the rug with great satisfaction and admiration. Very beautiful they were, and the Bishop was capable of appreciating the beautiful both in nature and art.

'Occasionally he made pastoral visits. If any one was sick, and expressed a wish to see him, he immediately responded. And there was no one who could speak with more unction and love to the sick than he could. He visited also those in health, and established an intimacy with some of the community of Friends. They also seemed kindly disposed towards him, and to value him for his goodness and the grace of God which was in him. He organized also a system of controversial sermons, which for many consecutive years were delivered, in the season of Lent, on Sunday evenings from the Cathedral pulpit. He always took part in them himself, threw his whole heart into them, and preached with amazing energy, though never with offensive asperity, for he was sincerely anxious for the good of the Roman Catholics as well as Protestants.'

In the year 1857 the clergy of Waterford applied to the Corporation of the city for a renewal of the lease which had been granted to them in the year 1831 of the Town Hall, upon which they (aided by subscriptions from the Protestants of Waterford) had laid out a considerable sum of money, and where they had for many years held their Sunday school and other meetings of a religious and useful character. Their application was refused, and it was accordingly determined, at a meeting held on the 13th of May 1857, the Bishop of Cashel in the chair, to erect a Protestant Hall in a suitable situation. The cost of the building was estimated at £2500, and the subscription-list was headed by the Bishop and the late Marquis of Waterford, who put down their names for £100 each. As the building was looked upon as a sort of memorial of the good Bishop's episcopate, many of the clergy of the other parts of the dioceses, who were quite unconnected with Waterford, gave their contributions towards its funds, so that it was not very long before a handsome and convenient building was provided for the use of the Protestants there.

The following description of the laying of the first stone is compiled from the *Waterford Mail* and *Clonmel Chronicle*, and is a faithful report of the proceedings of a day which will be ever remembered in the history of Waterford :—

'Thursday, November 3, 1859, must be a memorable day in the annals of our city. The first stone of the Protestant Hall was laid by our good Bishop, surrounded by the Mayor and citizens of Waterford. The clergy of his diocese were with them, and the ministers of the various Protestant denominations in Waterford also rallied around him, honouring him for his work's sake, and respecting him as the type of an evangelical prelate. Young and old assembled in crowded numbers. The gentry of the neighbourhood came in, to evince their attachment to the good old cause and to the principles of the Reformation.

'A spirit of earnestness and unanimity seemed to pervade all who took part in this great Protestant demonstration ; and it is most gratifying, that while the various speakers enunciated firmly, broadly, and fearlessly the grand principles on which the Protestant faith is founded and which it inculcates, there was nothing heard but what was consistent with the advocacy of civil and religious liberty, and with that feeling of love for their fellow-creatures which ever ought to be firmly implanted within the breast of every true Protestant. To the great champion of Protestantism within his extensive and important diocese— the Lord Bishop of Cashel, Emly, Waterford, and Lismore —the scene witnessed on Thursday must have been peculiarly gratifying. .

'The breakfast took place in the Town Hall. The number that sat down was over a hundred. The Bishop presided at the chief table. The Rev. Richard H. Ryland, Vice-President of the Institution, filled the vice-chair.

'The silver trowel which was presented to his lordship was beautifully wrought and chaste in design. The following was the inscription: "Presented to the Right Rev. Robert Daly, D.D., Lord Bishop of Cashel, Emly, Waterford, and Lismore, by the Protestant Freemen of the city of Waterford, on the occasion of his laying the first stone of the Waterford Protestant Hall and Sunday-school Institute, 1859." The medallion which was to be placed under the stone bore on one side the figure of a youth in full relief, reading an open Bible; beside him the globe and telescope, and this legend: "Thy word was a lamp unto my feet, and a light unto my path." On the obverse side, within a wreath, was the date. These, with a beautiful mallet, square, level, plummet, and apron, were exhibited on a table on the platform. A blessing was asked by the Bishop before breakfast, and thanks were offered by him after. The Rev. Richard Ryland then delivered a most interesting speech, after which Michael Dobbyn Hassard, Esq., M.P., addressed the meeting. He next handed to the Bishop the silver trowel. On receiving it, his lordship bowed his thanks, and amidst repeated cheers waved it round his head.

'Abraham Denny, Esq., honorary architect, on behalf of the committee, presented the chamois apron, trimmed with blue ribbon (which his lordship, amidst much laughter, "fitted" on him); also the mallet, square, level, and

Y

plummet, in polished mahogany. Mr. Denny said: "My lord, I have the honour to present you with these, and to express the hope that the work which we are about to raise will be found as firmly grounded, as consistent, and as lasting as your lordship's Protestant principles."

'The Bishop of Cashel, on rising to respond, was received with general applause. He said: "I cannot but say, my Protestant friends, that I feel exceedingly happy at being allowed (at having the privilege) to take part in that which I think will really uphold Protestantism in Waterford. I say Protestantism, not taking it in the sense of being hostile to any denomination whatsoever, but being in its principles that which is really good, and which stands against everything of error in doctrine and of viciousness in practice — true Protestantism. I have never been ashamed of it in my young days, and I hope I am not ashamed of it in my old age. When I use the word *true Protestant*, I mean one who takes the word of God as his rule of faith and of practice, and who stands out boldly against anything that would hinder the free exercise of man's judgment upon the Book of God. In supporting Protestantism, we are, then, supporting that which is for the good of society, because it does really uphold civil and religious liberty—real, **real** liberty! It is a great satisfaction to me to see such an assemblage as there is here present upon the occasion of laying the first stone of a Protestant hall in Waterford; and I hope that the example that has been set here, in seeking to have a place where unrestrictedly and freely our brethren may meet to advocate the interests of true liberty, religious and civil,

may be followed in many other places. In setting such
an example, I feel that we are doing good to the country;
and I am aware that there are other places that are at
present following the course we have adopted. We are
not first in the field in Ireland. Many are before us; yet
I find Cork is about to follow our example, and in Ennis-
corthy they have got a site from Lord Portsmouth to
build a Protestant hall there. There, too, the people will
be provided with a place of assembling, no one forbidding
them, and not being compelled to ask leave of those who,
perhaps, do not desire to assist them. I see these fine
things before me." (Taking up the trowel.) "This is not
exactly my *trade*; and if I were to attempt practically to
use them, I doubt not I would make a very poor operator.
But, my friends, we all know in the Scriptures Christians
are spoken of as *builders*, as well as everything else, and
the Church of Christ is a building which is augmented by
stone upon stone. It is not quite out of character, therefore, that I should appear as a builder. At the same time,
my great object is to build up, not dead stones, but living
stones. I pray that the Lord will enable me and make
me useful in adding many to the living 'corner-stone,'
upon which whoever builds shall never be confounded. I
am happy at being in any way enabled to assist in promoting the object we have in hand; and I trust that my
prayers will unite with the prayers of many here, that God
will give a blessing with this undertaking, and that the
hall which we are about to build will be useful in making
known the true principles of Christianity, and in proving
a blessing to society. I have to return to the Protestant

freemen of Waterford my thanks for their gift, and I pray that they may be fellow-citizens with those whose names are written in heaven, and stand fast in ' the liberty wherewith Christ hath made us free.' I will now conclude, as I must keep a little in reserve for the great *explosion*, which the secretary says we are to have in the open air."

' After the singing of a hymn, a prayer was offered up. The procession was then marshalled in front of the Courthouse, opposite Carlisle Bridge, which unites the Courthouse grounds with the park. It formed exactly at twelve o'clock. Immediately before this the gates of the enclosure were thrown open, and the children were admitted, headed by the band of the " Young Men's Christian Association."

' The school children came in as follows :—Bishop Foy's School; the Infant School; the Blue-Coat School; the Parochial School; the Abbey School; the Waterford Sunday School ; the St. Patrick Sunday School.

' The ladies and friends were then admitted, the band playing a selection of suitable airs.

' The Very Rev. Edward N. Hoare, Dean of Waterford, then received the Holy Bible from the Rev. E. F. Rambaut, and read in an audible voice the 127th Psalm :—

' " Except the Lord build the house, they labour in vain that build it: except the Lord keep the city, the watchman waketh but in vain.

' " It is vain for you to rise up early, to sit up late, to eat the bread of sorrows: for so He giveth His beloved sleep.

'" Lo, children are an heritage of the Lord: and the fruit of the womb is His reward.

'" As arrows are in the hand of a mighty man, so are children of the youth.

'" Happy is the man that hath his quiver full of them: they shall not be ashamed, but they shall speak with the enemies in the gate."

' At the conclusion of the psalm, the Dean and the entire assemblage, young and old, as if with one voice, joined together in the " Gloria Patri." The effect was most solemn and imposing, and a hearty and fervid " Amen" showed how deep was the impression and how feeling was the response.

' When the ceremony was concluded, the Right Rev. the Lord Bishop of Cashel, mounting the granite block, which lay firmly bedded in its position, addressed the vast assemblage as follows :—" We are assembled here, my friends, having laid the first stone of the Protestant Hall; and I would say a few words to you, to state why we lay the foundation of a Protestant Hall, why we want a Protestant Hall, and, in the next place, what should be the characteristics and the marked features of this Protestant Hall. In the first place, why we require a Protestant Hall. The Protestants of Waterford, my friends, want a place to meet in for many purposes, for the Protestants of Waterford are not an insignificant sect. They may be the minority in point of numbers, but I am bold to say they are the most important denomination, in consideration of their property, their position in society, their intellectual acquirements, and their character as members of the body politic. The country that they live in is interested in the progress and improvement of Protestants. If the Protestants of Ireland were to be diminished in numbers and lowered in character, the whole country would suffer by the event. The Roman Catholic portion of the community would suffer, as they would lose the benefit of their example, and would want the wholesome influence of competition with this good, sound body. They may be small, but they have, and ought to have, a beneficial effect upon the whole mass. How, then, is Protestantism here to be kept in health amongst us, as a light in the midst of a dark country? Certainly, my friends, not by putting it as you would put a candle under a bed. Not thus, my friends, but by placing it in a position in which men may see the light that is in it, and that it may increase and be made more powerful. Exposure to air and wholesome exercise tend to health, whereas being hid in a corner and consigned to sleep lessens vitality. Protestantism lives and grows by sound religious and secular instruction to all classes and all ages—by the sound and religious education of the young. That is the way to keep up Protestantism in a healthy state. Protestantism gets strength from the emancipation and improvement of the mind,—that improvement which sets it free from base subjugation to man, whoever he may be,—that subjugation which can, and does,

'Confine the intellect and enslave the soul!'

Protestantism is afraid of no height of intellectual attainments; Protestantism never says that 'ignorance is the mother of devotion.' But it knows that 'knowledge is power;' and therefore, because it *is* 'power,' it knows that it needs the highest wisdom to guide the movements of that power. No true Protestant, then, will desire to see secular instruction, which would increase the power of the intellect, without introducing that true wisdom which is to be found in God's word and from God's Spirit, which can sanctify the heart, and enable it to direct the increased powers of the whole man. No national system of merely secular instruction would suit the case and meet the wants of real Protestantism. The Protestants of Waterford want this hall, in the first place, then, for their Sunday schools, where the youth of all ranks of society can be gathered together, to be so trained up in the way they should go, that when they are old we may have the hope they will not depart from it. The Protestants of Waterford could not endure the thought, that when the Corporation would take from them the spacious and convenient room in which so many of them, and many of those whom I now address, have received instruction in their early days, —they could not endure the idea, I say, that the rising youth of this city should have no place to assemble on the Sabbath to read and hear God's word, and to sing His praise. So that they want this Protestant Hall, if there were no other reason, to have a place for collecting together all their youth upon the Sabbath day. But Protestants are not an unsocial community; they are not a community that think only of themselves, but they take an interest in their fellow-believers and in their fellow-creatures under all circumstances,—those that are lying in darkness and

in the shadow of death, and that whether they be Jew
or whether they be Gentile. The Protestants of Waterford wish to have a place in which they can receive deputations from any of those religious Societies that are
engaged in doing good to man—whether the Bible Society,
to hear of the spread of God's word ; or whether it be the
Missionary Society, to know the progress of missionary
work all over the world; or whether it be at home, to
know the advance made in giving ears to the deaf and
eyes to the blind. They desire to have a place in which
they can receive deputations from those useful Societies, and
from which they can send forth their expressions of sympathy, and, more than that, their contributions to carry on
the good work. These scriptural spiritual objects are first
in the minds of the Protestants of Waterford when seeking
to build this Protestant Hall. But Protestants also care
for whatever will improve the social interests of individuals and of society around them. Yes ; they are glad to
have a place that may be useful to all their fellow-citizens,
by having therein lectures on various scientific objects,
and upon those subjects likely to improve the social position of their country. They desire to have a place to
meet and receive any who shall come, and whose teachings
will benefit the temporal concerns of men. Such reasons,
then, are fairly sufficient in justifying us in desiring to
build this Protestant Hall. I would secondly, my friends,
just allude to what should be the characteristics of our
Protestant Hall. I would have inscribed over its entrance : ' Stand fast for ever in the liberty in which Christ
has made you free, and be not again entangled in bondage ;

and as you have been called into liberty, use it not as an occasion for the flesh, but by love serve one another.' We claim our privileges and freedom by the word and revelation of God; and what we claim for ourselves we would accord to others. We allow to others the *free* expression of thought, and all we claim is, that if they do differ from us, they shall differ in the spirit of forbearance and love. All who admit the paramount authority of God's word, and exercise their judgment in the interpretation of it under God's Spirit, will ever be welcome to this place of religious, social, and scientific meeting. As has been well said this morning by our faithful and respected friend, who has been long amongst us,—Mr. Ryland,—in this building we expect to see religion, charity, and science advanced, but shall exclude anything that would bring in the contending politics of the day. I do hope that this Protestant Hall may be the means of uniting fellow-Christians, by joining them together in those points on which they agree, rather than separating them in angry discussion upon points on which they differ. I have now given the reasons which have actuated those who have come forward to erect this building, and I have put forward what I conceive should be the spirit in which our Protestant Hall ought to be carried on, and ought to influence those who speak and teach within its walls. I hope that, as we have begun so auspiciously, with the bright sun coming out after the clouds and storms of which we have heard, that God's blessing will attend this place, and that we will often meet together for the good of our fellow-creatures, and not to do them harm. You have been told this morning that we want a large amount to complete the sum we require for the erection of the present building, and for that sum we must be *beggars;* but when we have got all we want for ourselves, we do not mean to be independent gentlemen, living self-satisfied within our means. We shall think it our privilege and our duty to be beggars still, and the instruments of raising funds for various religious and benevolent objects. At present we require £1200 to finish this hall, and I do hope that the good feeling and liberality of this neighbourhood, and of the many Christian and liberal people that do not belong to us, will help us to get this sum, and have this hall an honour and an ornament to Waterford, and a blessing to Protestants in general; for I do maintain that Protestantism goes not in the path of illiberal hostility, but in the free spirit of progress and improvement. Protestantism is calculated to be a blessing wherever it is; and where it is not, what do we find? In countries where Protestantism has been almost extinguished, we see them sunken in degradation and immorality. I hope, then, that this hall will be supported and carried on to the end by the liberality of the town and of the country around; and it only remains for me to pray God that He may pardon whatever has been done amiss in what has been undertaken, and make this building a blessed means for promoting His glory."

'His lordship concluded with a beautiful prayer, and during the entire of his powerful address was listened to with breathless attention. He stood down from the stone amid loud and continued applause.

' When the Bishop ceased, the precentor gave out the hymn—

"Lord, dismiss us with Thy blessing."

' The band played "God save the Queen," the whole company uncovered, and joining in the chorus. This part of the ceremony was peculiarly impressive. The little children took up the strain, and the sweet sounds were wafted on the breeze to a considerable distance, and it was indeed with "heart and voice" the words were repeated—

"Happy and glorious,
Long to reign over us,
God save the Queen."

' Mr. Abraham Denny then cried out, "Three cheers, boys, for our good bishop, the Rock of Cashel!" This was heartily responded to. Three cheers were then given for Mr. Ryland, after which the meeting separated.'

The Rev. Thomas Gimlette has given the following particulars relating to the Bishop's library :—

' The Bishop had a fine collection of scarce and valuable books. It embraced varied departments of literature, and some of his copies were unique, many of them most valuable. He continued to add to his library until the famine year, and after that he ceased to be a purchaser of old and rare books at fancy prices. Among his collection were Scripture and ancient liturgies, as well as some valuable editions of the Fathers. Amongst the versions of the Scriptures was a copy of Coverdale's Bible, printed at

Zurich in 1535, with wood engravings—the first edition of the entire Scriptures in English; the first edition of the Vulgate, which was suppressed by Gregory XIV. (this had had the arms of Pope Pius VI. on the side); several most rare black-letter copies of the Scriptures, printed in the earliest period; and some highly illuminated manuscript copies.

Amongst the Liturgies were several original copies of Edward the Sixth's First Book of Common Prayer, in black-letter, 1549; several copies of the Second Book of Edward VI., 1551 and 1552; a copy of the Irish Prayer Book; the first edition of the Liturgy printed in the Irish character, from the Irish types originally presented by Queen Elizabeth,—the first work ever printed in Ireland; a copy of the celebrated Bourdeaux Testament, described by Dr. Cotton; the first Prymer put forth in the reign of Henry VIII.; several other most rare editions in the time of the Reformation.

The chief treasure in the Bishop's library was a copy of the Gutenberg Bible, printed at Metz between the years 1450 and 1455, of which only seven copies now exist. The Bishop's copy was purchased for him at the sale of the library of the Duke of Sussex. His agent exceeded the Bishop's order in bidding for it, and the Bishop declined it in the first instance; but the bookseller being in a state of disappointment, the Bishop took it off his hands. The cost was £195.

In 1858 the Bishop disposed of a large number of his most valuable books, and gave away the proceeds to several religious and charitable objects. This book was bought for Mr. Perkins for £596, and was re-sold a few months ago for £2960.

The Bishop of Cashel was not guilty of the crime of ingratitude, with which the Irish people have been rather unjustly charged, and he may with truth be said to have been a thorough Irishman.

At the season of distress in Lancashire, in the year 1862, he expressed his desire that collections should be made for the relief of the sufferers there in all parts of his diocese.

To the Archdeacon of Waterford.

'*7th October* 1862.

' MY DEAR BELL,—There ought to be, and I am sure there is, among us a very strong feeling for the patient sufferers in the present distressed state of Lancashire. We ought not to, and I am sure we do not, forget the sympathy and liberality of the English population towards us in our time of need.

' We are now gathering in a much better harvest than some time ago we expected, and in the inland parts of the country there has been saved an abundant supply of good turf for firing. We have reason then to be thankful, and we ought to show our gratitude to a good Providence by contributing to the relief of those whom He has allowed to be afflicted. We have but little to give, but we may show our feeling and follow the example of those of old of whom it is recorded, " The abundance of their joy and their deep poverty abounded unto the riches of their liberality."

' May I request you to communicate to the clergy in

your archdeaconry my request that they will call upon
their congregations to make a collection for this purpose
on such Sunday before the end of November as they may
each think convenient.

'I feel we ought not to stand by and do nothing. I
know the money raised will effect next to nothing, but the
exhibition of brotherly feeling will, I think, be right. "It
is more blessed to give than to receive."'

The Bishop of Cashel was remarkably kind, and even
indulgent, to his servants. One little circumstance showed
his consideration for their comfort to a very great degree.
When at Woodhouse, they had been in the habit of bathing
every morning in the little cove close to the gate of the
demesne; and on their removal to Killough in the summer
months, thinking that they would feel the want of this
accustomed refreshment, he went to some expense to make
a bathing-place for them near the Castle, by damming up
a little stream which ran close by, so as to fill a reservoir
with water sufficiently deep for bathing in. A clergyman,
when visiting in one of the hospitals in Dublin, discovered
that one of the patients had formerly been a housemaid in
the Bishop of Cashel's service; he found her one day reading a letter from him, in which he enclosed her some
money, and addressed her as 'My dear Mary.' He was
indeed totally devoid of that kind of pride of station
which has its origin in low-minded feelings. On the death
of his good old housekeeper, who, he used to say, was one
of the blessings he had from the Lord, he writes to Archdeacon Bell, in answer to a letter informing him of it :—

'I thank you for having kindly written to me. I have suffered a serious loss, but the Lord gave and the Lord hath taken away; may we be always enabled to say, "Blessed be the name of the Lord!" It is a comfort to me to think that a child of God had for eleven years under my roof been happy, hearing and receiving the gospel. She showed its fruits in her life, and experienced its supports in her trying hour of death. She was one I could thoroughly depend on. I shall find it hard to supply her place.'

We have before spoken of his liberality to his clergy. His generosity was not confined to them; neither, when he sympathized with those in distress, was his sympathy of an unprofitable kind, which says, 'Be ye warmed and filled, notwithstanding ye give them not those things which are needful for the body.' The following letter was addressed to one of his former parishioners at Powerscourt, left in great poverty by the death of her husband, to whose necessities he had administered during his life :—

'WATERFORD, 24th October.

'DEAR ——,—I grieve for you under your present heavy trial. The Lord gave, and the Lord has taken away. It will require great grace to enable you to say, "Blessed be the name of the Lord!" You have lost a husband, but you have not lost your great Friend, who is better than any husband. He is a Friend that sticketh closer than a brother or any earthly friend; for He never leaves us, never forsakes us. Neither life, nor death, nor

any creature can separate us from the love of God, which
is in Christ Jesus the Saviour. May He support you and
comfort you. I will give you while I live a weekly pension.
I will pay it to you quarterly, on the 1st of January,
1st of April, 1st of July, and 1st of October. If I do not
remember to send it at those times, write to ask for it.
. . . You must manage to make this help you. May God
be your friend, preserve you while in this evil world, and
in His own time take you to Himself.—Your sincere
friend,   ' ROBERT CASHEL, etc.'

To one who had emigrated to Canada he thus expressed
his remembrance of a Powerscourt family :—

'WATERFORD, 30th September 1861.

' MY DEAR ——,—I have received your letter of the
14th of August, and am very glad to hear of a family I
care for, as having been under my care in dear Powerscourt. I am glad to hear of so many of such a large family
being preserved in life and health in this dying, suffering
world. I am glad to hear that a church is in progress in
which you can all worship God, and hear His message of
mercy in and through Christ Jesus our Lord. When you
write, you must tell me how much I promised to give when
the church is roofed. You must also tell me to whom the
money is to be paid. So that it will reach you, I will send
it in a letter of credit of the Bank of England, but I must
know to whom it is to be payable. If you are in the
diocese of Huron, I could send it to the good bishop, whom
I know, and to whom I send money for a church in his

diocese. I am sorry that you are not as happy as you could wish, and as I would desire you to be, but I would remind you that we are not promised perfect happiness in this world, which is under a curse for sin. The trials and annoyances of this world teach us that this is not our rest, but we should seek one to come. If you labour and are heavy-laden, remember what our Lord, while He was in this evil world, said: "Come unto me, all ye that labour and are heavy-laden, and I will give you rest." Do you remember a hymn we used to sing in the church and schoolhouse ?—

> " We've no abiding city here :
>   This may distress the worldling's mind,
> But should not cost a saint a tear,
>   Who hopes a better rest to find.
>
> " We've no abiding city here :
>   Sad truth were this to be our home ;
> But let this thought our spirits cheer—
>   We seek a city yet to come."

'I write this to you in the hope that, through the instruction you received in youth, and the study of the Bible since, you have sought and found peace with God through Jesus Christ. Then you are a child of God, and if a child, then an heir of God, joint-heir with Christ. Or if you have not sought and found that peace, I would call upon you, and all your brothers and sisters, to seek peace without delay, to come as sinners to the Saviour of sinners, and He will receive you. This is the one thing needful ; this will make you happy under all circumstances. As Peter said, speaking of the Christian's hope, " Wherein ye greatly rejoice, though now for a season, if need be, ye are in heaviness through manifold temptations." Your life in Canada, or in any other place, will be more than thrown away if you do not get the heavenly inheritance; but if you get that, all is well. "The sufferings of this present life are not worthy to be compared with the glory that shall be revealed." Remember me to your father, mother, brothers, and sisters; and believe me, my dear Arabella, to be your very sincere friend,

'ROBERT CASHEL, etc.'

How great was the amount bestowed by the Bishop of Cashel in these smaller charities is not known to any one; it was not his habit to insert them in the newspaper; he did not let his left hand know what his right hand was doing; but there is no doubt, from the number that have accidentally come to light, that they were very many. While at Woodhouse, he gave much pecuniary relief to the poor people in that neighbourhood, at a time when they were suffering much from the effects of the failure of the potato crop. To some he gave money to buy pigs to eat the bad potatoes; others he employed in salting a large take of hake, which had been brought in by the fishing-boats, and storing it for winter use; and others in making a good dry walk from the demesne to the church, which was about a quarter of a mile from the top of the hill above the house. He kept a store of clothing in the hall, ready to give to all who applied for it, measuring the material for them himself, from his mouth to the end of his arm, which he said was a yard. No doubt the people of Stradbally will long remember the sojourn amongst them of 'the Lord,' as they called him.

One poor man, on meeting him taking his accustomed walk on a wet day with an umbrella (as he never allowed the weather to prevent him from taking exercise), said to him, ' Well, you're the most *sinsible* man ever I met for a *great* man.' He used to say it was only a wise man who would be found to take his umbrella with him on a fine day, but any fool would bring it out when it was raining, adding, ' I never go without it, as I find that an umbrella makes a very good walking-stick, while a walking-stick would make a very bad umbrella.'

During part of his stay at Woodhouse he always insisted on the curate of Stradbally taking his vacation of a month or six weeks ; and as at that time the rector was absent on account of ill health, the Bishop undertook to act as curate during his absence, with the assistance of any of his clergy who might visit him during the interval—taking not only the Sunday duty, but the weekly visiting of the schools and of the poor people. The day appointed to be kept as a day of fasting and humiliation on account of the visitation of cholera, in the year 1849, occurred while the writer was staying at Woodhouse with the Bishop. She remembers being much struck by the way in which it was observed in his house. There were no regular meals on that day, but some simple refreshments were left in the dining-room, which any of the party who felt it necessary might partake of.

Upon the return of the Uniacke family to their residence at Woodhouse, in the year 1854, the Bishop fitted up and added to Killough Castle, near Thurles, which belonged to his nephew, the Honourable Bowes Daly ; and at this place he spent some months each summer for several years, accompanied by his sister, Miss Daly. Part of the building was an old castle, and in the upper part of the square tower the Bishop had his study, the stairs leading up to it being the stone steps inside the wall, which we often meet in these old buildings. It was conveniently situated for visiting the various parishes in the diocese of Cashel, with which he had not before been so well acquainted, as well as for attending clerical and chapter meetings at Cashel. While there he preached every Sunday, either at Holy Cross or in one or other of the neighbouring parishes, sometimes driving as far as Templemore for that purpose, a distance of 12 miles. On one of these occasions he wrote :—

To Mrs. Hamilton Madden.

'KILLOUGH CASTLE, HOLY CROSS, THURLES,
10th August 1855.

' MY DEAR BELLA,—I shall have much pleasure in preaching at Templemore, and baptizing your baby (*D. V.*) on the 18th. My sister is too delicate for excursions, and therefore would stay at home. I will drive over in time for service. I purpose, if the Lord permit, to preach in some church every Sunday while I remain in the neighbourhood, and I may as well begin with Templemore. We meet with an extraordinary difficulty here. We can find no washerwoman, and fear we must send our clothes backward and forward to Waterford. The population have all gone out of this neighbourhood. We are as unprovided as our poor soldiers in the Crimea, who had to wash their own clothes ;

but unfortunately they had no water; we have plenty that is good. I would make a bad washerwoman. I fear the corn has suffered much from the rain. It is a good prayer in our Litany, "Lord, give and preserve to our use the kindly fruits of the earth, that in due time we may enjoy them."—Yours very truly,

'ROBERT CASHEL, etc.

'Love to *men* and *angels.*'

These occasions were greatly prized and anxiously looked forward to both by the clergy and the people; there were always sure to be large congregations, many coming from the neighbouring parishes to hear the good Bishop preach. On two occasions he drove over to be present at school feasts at Templemore Rectory. He enjoyed the scene much. The children had their tea on the grass, and were delighted by the Bishop's kindness in helping to attend them, and in watching their play when the tea was over. It seemed to remind him of his 'Wednesday evenings' at Powerscourt; and he afterwards said, 'I do not know a pleasanter sight than to see a number of young people enjoying themselves, and to feel at the same time that they are getting some good.'

In those who were presented to him for confirmation he took a special interest. His addresses to them were most instructive; and to each person confirmed he always sent, before their leaving the church, a copy of a tract on the Lord's Supper written by himself, explaining the nature of the ordinance; and never failed to express to them his wish that they should present themselves on the earliest occasion at the table of the Lord. One of his confirmations, held in the church of Templemore, was a most interesting scene. It was during the time of the war in the Crimea, and Templemore being one of the military recruiting stations, called 'Depot Battalions,' which existed at that time in Ireland, about 40 young men, recruits, were presented along with the other candidates to the Bishop for confirmation. His manner of conducting this service was at all times most impressive, and this time it was doubly so. It was evident that, while laying his hand upon the head of each young person, he was engaged in earnest prayer, laying a peculiar emphasis on the words, 'Keep them Thine for ever.' On this occasion a great part of his remarks were particularly and most earnestly addressed to these young soldiers, who expected in a few weeks to join their comrades in the battle-field. For the brave men who at this time fought for their country and the cause of independence he had much sympathy. A detachment of the 87th Regiment, stationed at Waterford under the command of Major Hanley, having been ordered out to the Crimea, the Bishop gave them a public dinner at his own expense in the Town Hall, addressing them at parting in affectionate and stirring words, and giving them his blessing. The Bishop's nephew, the Honourable Charles Daly, held a commission in the 87th Regiment, and was one of the earliest victims to the unhealthy life in the trenches before Sebastopol.

The Bishop always showed kindness and hospitality to the military quartered at Waterford. At one time, when two of the artillery officers were pious young men, he invited them to dine with him every Sunday during their stay there, giving them classes in the Sunday school, and taking them with him to evening service at the Cathedral. With reference to a young officer to whom his ministry had been made a blessing, he wrote:—

To the Rev. Thomas Gimlette.

'WOODSTOCK, NEWTOWN, MOUNT KENNEDY, *22d July* 1869.

'MY DEAR GIMLETTE,—I am much obliged to you for your letter, and the very interesting enclosure, the letter of Captain T. In these bad times it is very cheering to see evident marks of God being present with us by His grace as well as by His providence. We grieve at times at seeing so little fruit from the ministry of the word—almost led to say that it does return void, and then the Lord gives for our encouragement an example of the life-giving efficacy of His truth. Such you have been allowed to see in Captain T. Change of place made no change in him; he had the same need of a Saviour, and the same view of the efficacy of that Saviour he became acquainted with in Waterford,—"Jesus Christ, the same yesterday, and to-day, and for ever." I have to dissent from one word in your letter. You say "*poor* Joe Browne;" you should rather have written "blessed Joe Browne," as our Book says, "Blessed are the dead that die in the Lord." He was rich in faith, and an heir of the kingdom. That little company to which he belonged will be probably broken up and scattered. . . . The Lords have done their duty well. It will be hard to say what

will be the final result. We have got time to breathe and
to think, to return thanks for our escape, and to pray for
protection and guidance for the future. I hope Mrs.
Gimlette and you get something out of my garden. . . .
Kindest regards to Mrs. Gimlette.—Very truly yours,

'ROBERT CASHEL, etc.'

We have before observed that the Bishop of Cashel was
very fond of the country, and had a thorough taste for and
appreciation of the beauties of nature. At Killough he
took much pleasure in walking through his nephew's farm,
and watching the growth of the turnips, etc. In the state
of the potato he took a special interest, as it so much
affected the comfort of the poor. He would always maintain that it was a most remarkable visitation, and could
not be accounted for by any natural causes; if any one
attempted to trace its origin to severe frosts, great fogs, or
any other atmospheric influence, they were sure to meet
with a flat contradiction. He had a farm at this time about
three miles from the town of Waterford, for the purpose
of giving employment in its cultivation to the poor people
in the neighbourhood. As it was his nature, whatever he
did, to do it well and with energy, he rode out constantly
to inspect it, and was very proud of his fine parsnips, which
he made use of to fatten pigs. He would sometimes amuse
his visitors by giving a particular account of the way in
which pigs should be managed, saying that he paid a woman
exclusively for attending to them, and told her that he
would expect to find that each of them increased in weight
at the rate of one pound per day, which he said they ought

to do if properly taken care of. In the autumn of 1856 the Bishop and Miss Daly went from Killough on a visit to the Lakes of Killarney, where they were joined by Dean and Mrs. Newman. They spent a week together at the Lake Hotel, where the Bishop enjoyed himself greatly. He was of a peculiarly happy turn of mind, and had naturally very high spirits; even when advanced in life, they were at times as exuberant as those of a boy. With his usual kind consideration for the feelings of young people, he on this occasion took with him a young man, the son of a rector of a neighbouring parish, who was a friend of his, making him one of their party at the hotel, and taking much pleasure in witnessing the gratification which he derived from the beautiful walks in the neighbourhood of that lovely spot.

Until the Bishop had entered upon his 80th year, he might be said to have been singularly exempt from any of those weaknesses or infirmities to which flesh is heir. His general health, until his very last illness, continued to be remarkably good, but in the winter of 1862 he was attacked by severe rheumatism in his legs, from which he suffered great pain. It was followed by a stiffness which gradually deprived him of the use of his limbs. This he felt very much, as after a time it prevented him from taking his accustomed exercise on horseback, which he had been in the habit of thinking so necessary for the preservation of his health. He was advised to visit Buxton, and to try what the warm baths there might do for him. From this place he writes to his old friend Dean Browne, sympathizing with him in his still more serious illness :—

'BUXTON, 21st September 1863.

'MY DEAR DENIS,—I have just received your letter of
the 19th. I am very sorry that your health is so unsatis-
factory, and that you are suffering pain. Your state is an
illustration of my interpretation of Rom. viii. 10: "The
body is dead because of sin." The believer who has passed
from death unto life because he has attained righteousness
in Christ is still liable to all the evil which sin has
brought upon the body. Its passage from death unto life
is yet to come, and will come when He shall change our
vile bodies, that they may be fashioned like unto His
glorious body. It is glorious to think that the spirit is
now safe, and to be able to look forward with happy
anticipation to the time when this mortal body shall put
on immortality, and this corruptible body put on incor-
ruption; and then, and not till then, shall be brought to
pass the saying that is written: " Death is swallowed up in
victory." We want not only a stronger faith in the aton-
ing work of the Lord, but a stronger hope of the great,
glorious things He has provided for us, "Wherein we may
greatly rejoice, though now for a season, if need be, we are
in heaviness through manifold temptations." As to myself,
my general health is as good as ever it was, but I have not
the use of my limbs. You would have laughed, if not
cried, if you had seen me yesterday going to church in a
wheel-chair. You would say, "How are the mighty
fallen!" The weather has been very unfavourable to improvement in rheumatic patients—cold and wet. I hope
your weather has been better. I propose leaving this to-
morrow. I shall go as far as Bangor (D.V.), and cross the

Channel on Wednesday. I hope I shall not have as much wind as there is here to-day. I am happy to say that in this important place, with a great concourse of people for a time, there is a faithful good man, who preaches Christ with power. When I was here many years ago, there was a sad Puseyite. I am going to print an extract from a charge lately delivered relating to the proposed revision of the Liturgy,[1] and I shall soon, I hope, send you a copy.— Sincerely sympathizing with you, affectionately yours,

'ROBERT CASHEL, etc.'

As the acute pain in his limbs after a time subsided, the Bishop was less annoyed by this infirmity than he had been at first. His carriage drives were now substituted for his afternoon rides on horseback. He would often pleasantly remark that his legs had done him good service for 80 years, and that he could not reasonably complain if they failed him now. 'They were only warranted to last a certain time,' he would say, looking down at them; 'and if I choose to live longer than that time, I have no right to expect to have the use of them any longer.' The weakness of his limbs did not prevent him from preaching, which he continued to do to the very last; it was not distressing to him to stand, but he could not mount up into a pulpit, and was obliged latterly to preach from his throne, and later still, from his chair by the communion table. Not being able to go about as much as formerly, he had more time in his later years for letter-writing, and has left us a few, which give us the benefit of his Chris-

[1] See Appendix D.

tian experience, and manifestly show us that his heavenly-
mindedness increased as he neared the haven where he
would be; while, at the same time, the vigour of his
intellect remained unabated, and his warmth of heart
unchilled. 'Age's frost' had not penetrated there; his
heart had lain always open to the life-giving beams of the
Sun of Righteousness.

To a Friend.

'DEANERY, CORK, 15*th January* 1864.

'MY DEAR ——,— . . . I came here to my poor sister,
Mrs. Newman, who has just lost her husband, the Dean of
Cork, after living with him for 40 years. A week before
I lost another brother-in-law, Mr. Godley, thus seeing two
sisters made widows within a few days. Within a few days
I lost the only cousin-german I ever had, the Rev. James
Daly, warden of Galway, and was also deprived of the
valuable assistance of an excellent chaplain and secretary.
This is all intended to cut the ties which bind us to earth,
and lead us, with all that are risen with Christ, to seek the
things that are above, where Christ sitteth at the right
hand of God. What a privilege to have our life hid with
Christ in God! There is a great deal in these words.
What security they set before us, what high spirituality!
They say, What manner of persons ought we to be, in holy
conversation and godliness? . . . Wishing you a better
year than you ever had, and an unending year still better.
—Yours, in the best bonds, very sincerely,

'ROBERT CASHEL, etc.'

To the Same.

' WATERFORD, 24*th January* 1865.

'MY DEAR ——,— . . . I was privileged to preach on Christmas day, and it was the 52d consecutive sermon I had preached at Christmas. This is a wonderful mercy of my God, and I hope I enjoy the glad tidings of great joy more than I did the first Sunday I preached, know more the need of a Saviour and the value of a Saviour, looking more to what He has done, to what He is doing, and what He will do when He comes again. He has not done with man ; when He was made flesh He began a great work, at the right hand of His Father He is carrying it on, and He will come again to complete it. It is incomplete until He restores all things ; and, having put all His enemies under His feet, He will sit down with His redeemed family in His Father's glorious house. There is a bright prospect before His believing people, and we ought to lift up our hearts with the thought that the perfect redemption is drawing nigh. As He said to Abraham, " Look north and south, east and west, and all that land will I give you ;" so He tells us, if we have by faith joined Christ, " Look all around, and you shall inherit all things." When we arrive there we shall be able to say, " All things are ours, for we are Christ's, and Christ is God's." This ought to cheer our old hearts, and enable us to say of our weaknesses and infirmities, We rejoice in them, for they are bringing us nearer home. Our path should be like the shining light, that shineth more and more unto the perfect day. The night is far spent, the *day* is at hand. I trust, my dear friend, that the Lord blesses you by enabling you, being justified by faith, to rejoice in the hope of the glory of God. It is our privilege. The times are very strongly marked; more evil, and more good, the conflict becoming more decided. The devil is very busy, because he knows his time is short; he will soon be shut up, and a happy period will come. Infidelity and Popery are very bold, and will join together to make up the man of sin, who will be revealed in the very last days. Woe to those who receive his mark! Upon them will be poured out the vials of God's wrath, not one drop of which shall fall upon any of the believers in Christ. They shall be separated, as Lot was before the fire fell on Sodom and Gomorrah. We may not, perhaps, meet face to face in this scene, but we shall meet in that day of rejoicing, and sing together the song of Moses and the Lamb. May the Lord enable us to realize the prospect of those happy scenes, and may they be our cordial and support when we are old and weak.— Your very affectionate friend, in the best bonds, those of the gospel,   ' ROBERT CASHEL, etc.'

To the Same.

'WATERFORD, 4th January 1866.

' MY DEAR ——,—I thank you for thinking of me, not forgetting an old friend. I value old friends more than ever I did. It is one feature of old age to lose old friends and to get no new ones. The young people would not be bothered with old incurables. They are like horses in a team; they are looking before them, never behind them. Oh that they would act up to the principle, and, forgetting the things that are behind, press forward toward the mark for the prize of the high calling of God in Christ Jesus. They act on the principle when it is wrong, but do not act on it when it is right, and would make them have their conversation in heaven, from whence expecting the Saviour, who shall change their bodies of humiliation, that they may be fashioned like unto the body of His glory. This is a great principle that God has implanted in man, to look into the future; but it was intended to lead us to look into eternity, but here man does not use it. We ought to look into eternity with an appropriating faith. You say you long for faith to be able to realize that beautiful passage, "Ye are come unto Mount Zion." Why, all Scripture speaks of our being in possession of the future inheritance, though not now dwelling in it; just as, when a lease is signed, we are in possession of the place though not yet residing in it. You were in possession of your "dear little home," though you were residing for eleven weeks in Dublin. It is in the same spirit the apostle says, "We know that though our earthly house be dissolved, *we have* a building of God, a house not made with hands, eternal in the heavens." You ask about a book. I have met with a book I think good,—that does not mean endorsing everything in it,—*Voices from the Valley*, by Whitfield. He says in his preface, what I fully agree with him in, that Christians are advancing towards the world, and that the world is taking steps towards the Christian world. They both are moving towards the line of demarcation,— Christians getting worldly, and worldly people getting some religion, yet a religion that won't save them. I wish

I could see Christians, what Peter says they are, a peculiar
people. What communion hath Christ with Belial? I
am very glad you are not to be moved out of your dear
home (yet it is not your home; you would be sorry it was).
I should like to see you, and was sorry when I was in
your neighbourhood that I had to pass your gate; but it
does not signify where we are:—

> "While place we seek, or place we shun,
> We shall find happiness in none."

I must take another half-sheet of paper, to tell you what
you are so kind as to inquire about,—how I bear the winter,
whether it has brought on rheumatic pains. It has not
brought them on, for I brought them to the winter. I
have, through rheumatics, almost entirely lost the use of
my limbs. I can hardly walk, and I cannot ride; I cannot
get up on a horse. This is a great trial to me, who always
used to take so much exercise; but it is all well. I
expect the Saviour, who shall change the body of humiliation. There will be no rheumatism, no pain. But my
general health is very good, and I can enjoy myself. I
can preach, though not as often as before. Last Christmas
day I preached the 53d consecutive Christmas day sermon,
and with as loud a voice and as earnest a heart as ever.
As you ask my opinion about the Fenians, I will tell you
I do not apprehend any danger from them. They have
done poor Ireland immense evil,—put her back 100 years;
no one will come into it. I fear the cattle-plague a great
deal more, and am very thankful for our exemption from
it. . . . I sympathize with you in your admiration of

Mr. Day.[1] If you had not been hearing him, I should have said, Buy his sample sermon.—I remain, very truly and affectionately yours,   'ROBERT CASHEL, etc.'

To his Sister, Mrs. Godley.

'WATERFORD, 27th October 1865.

'MY DEAR CATHERINE,—Time is passing on with both of us; mine, though I am older, rather slower than yours. With both of us the period is approaching when time shall be no more. We have always been taught this, but the lesson is taught more plainly when the effects of age are manifest. There is a text that I dwell much upon of late; it applies to both you and me: Rom. viii. 10, "If Christ be in you, the body is dead because of sin; but the Spirit is life because of righteousness." This puts before us a truth which I feel in degree, from the comparatively small trial that I have from losing the use of my limbs; but you feel in a large measure, from the infirmity with which it has pleased your heavenly Father to visit you. But this text teaches us that neither the little trial nor the greater trial is inconsistent with our being at peace with God through Christ. Christ may be in us; and that brings life, though our bodies may be sufferers. But as Paul says afterwards, "The sufferings of this present time are not worthy to be compared with the glory that shall be revealed in us." I would not make little of any fellow-traveller's sufferings, but I would wish to lead him or her to dwell more upon the glory that is to follow, if at peace with God through Christ; as Paul adds, "If the Spirit of Him that raised

---

[1] The present Bishop of Cashel.

2 A

up Christ from the dead dwell in you, it shall quicken your mortal body, by His Spirit that dwelleth in you." Now, the quickening of the Spirit; then, the redemption of the body. In my ordinary course of reading the Bible, I read this morning Rev. xxi. 3: "A voice out of heaven saying, Behold, the tabernacle of God is with men, and He will dwell with them, etc.; and God shall wipe away all tears from their eyes; and there shall be no more death, neither sorrow nor crying, neither shall there be any more pain: for the former things are passed away." With such words addressed to us, such promises in His word, we may well say to the sufferer in Christ, to the believer at the approach of death, " Lift up your heart, for your redemption draweth nigh." In this spirit, Peter, speaking of the inheritance incorruptible, etc., reserved in heaven for us, says, " Wherein ye greatly rejoice, though now for a season, if need be, ye are in heaviness through manifold temptations, for the trial of your faith." Look back to what Christ has done, making atonement for sin; look up to what He is doing, making intercession for us; and look forward to the completed redemption which He will perform for all His believing people when He shall come again, to that perfect consummation and bliss in His eternal kingdom. May God, by His Spirit, be very present with you, is the prayer of your very affectionate   ' ROBERT CASHEL, etc.'

To the Same.

'WATERFORD, *5th November* 1865.

'MY DEAR CATHERINE,—It is my general principle not to write letters on Sunday, but I do not think I shall break

the Sabbath by writing to you. I have a cold, which keeps
me from going to church, and I think I may spend the
time of service in sending to you some of those thoughts
which I might preach if I was in church. I was able to
read your letter, and very much gratified by getting it.
You want to get the truth you have in your head more
into your heart. I have one receipt for that. Compare
yourself and your life with the holy law and nature of
God, till you get a deeper sense of sin,—not only of acts of
sin, but of sinfulness pervading all our actions, even those
called good. The entire absence of religion comes from an
entire absence of a sense of sin. Those that think themselves whole have no feeling of a want of a physician, and
thus a slight sense of sin brings with it a very partial
apprehension of the saving doctrines of the gospel; but
when a review of heart and life, compared with the holiness of God, brings a real sense of our sin and consequent
lost state in ourselves, the heart flies to the remedy revealed to us in the gospel of Christ. The deeper the sense
of sin, the more earnest will be the laying hold of the
sufficiency of the salvation of Christ; the more deep is
our despair as to ourselves, the more joyous will be our
rejoicing in Christ Jesus. Those ignorant of human
nature and of the gospel of Christ would attempt to
comfort a person by telling him, " You are not as bad as
gloomy people would tell you ;" but one who knows the
truth would say, "You are in God's holy eyes worse than
you are aware, but the blood of Jesus cleanses from all
sin." He has said, " Though your sins are as scarlet, I
will make them white as snow." Persons will never get

comfort from looking for any good in themselves, but they will get such a conviction of sin as shall drive them to Christ, in whom there is plenteous redemption to save from all sin. If the head only assents to the charge of sin, the head only will lay hold of the remedy; but if the heart, under the teaching of the Spirit, says, "I am vile," the heart will rejoice in Christ the Saviour; it will be a heart-work throughout. May you experience that to your comfort in your present extremity. And then, what happy things are before the dying believer; his *night* is far spent, his *day* is at hand! And what a day it will be, without a cloud, eternal sunshine! no more curse, no pain, all tears wiped away from all eyes! But we are authorized to expect not only the absence of all evil, but the presence of all good. Christ has said, " Father, I will that those that Thou hast given me may be with me where I am, that they may behold my glory, and the glory that Thou hast given me I have given them." This is a glorious prospect, and ought to bring comfort, and will do so in proportion as it is believed, and especially when we are suffering in this present scene. What are the sufferings of this present life in comparison with the glory that is coming to us ? But after considering those happy things, the heart may ask the question, "What right have I to lay hold of these things for myself ?" Simply upon the proclamation of God Himself, " Ho, every one that thirsteth, come ye to the waters, and buy wine and milk without money and without price !" " Be it known unto you, that through this man is preached unto you the forgiveness of sins," etc. This gives to every one that hears it an undoubted claim to every blessing contained in the gospel of Christ. It authorizes us to say, " The Lord Jesus has died, and so I have died in Him, and paid the penalty due to my sins ; the Lord Jesus has obeyed the law, so I have obeyed in Him ; though in myself I am unrighteous, yet I am righteous and accepted in Him." Our faith in Christ makes us one with Him ; as the Apostle Paul expresses it, " We are members of His body, of His flesh, and of His bones ;" and as members of Christ, we come in for the benefit of all that He has done, and joint-heirs of every-thing of which He is possessed. Blessed be God, we have " an inheritance incorruptible, undefiled, and that fadeth not away, reserved in heaven for us." I may well say, then, to you, as the Lord said to His disciples, " Lift up your heads, for your redemption draweth nigh." May you be enabled to do so, and to be more than conqueror through Him that loved you. The time is short; He will come quickly. May the Lord support and comfort you with these truths of the gospel, is the earnest prayer of your affectionate ' ROBERT CASHEL, etc.'

To a lady at Clontarf, whose charities to the poor people around her were annually assisted by him, he writes :—

'8 MOUNTJOY SQUARE, DUBLIN,
11th November 1869.

'. . . There is a pure gratification derived from being actively engaged in alleviating the bodily wants, and aim-ing at the spiritual good, of our fellow-creatures, fellow-sinners. This you enjoy, and I have great pleasure in

assisting you at the work. . . . I have been here to
attend the funeral of my sister, Miss Daly, who died of the
effects of a long paralytic attack. It was a comfort to
know that she had been for a long time a child of God, by
faith in the Lord Jesus, and, as the apostle says, if a child,
then an heir, a joint-heir of Jesus Christ. We can thus
indeed say, " O death, where is thy sting ? O grave, where
is thy victory ? " We are in very critical and awful times,
when we do not know what a day may bring forth ; what a
comfort in the truth—the Lord reigneth ! Oh that He
would soon come, and sit upon His throne, and judge the
world in righteousness ! '

In the beginning of the year 1867 he seemed to have
impressed upon his mind the duty of setting his house in
order, feeling that he must soon die, though he was
graciously left with us for five years after that time. He
had always had a taste for collecting rare books of ancient
divinity. He was well read in the Fathers ; and when at
Powerscourt, his library contained a considerable number
of their writings, besides many curious old books. When
he became a bishop, and had more money to spare, it was
perhaps the only way in which he gave himself any personal indulgence, to add to his collection of quaint old
volumes. His friend the late Duke of Manchester sympathized with him in this taste, and on hearing of his
promotion to the bench, said, ' What books he will buy ! '
The Bishop felt, that as he alone knew the value of those
books, it would be his wisest plan to dispose of them
during his lifetime, which he accordingly did some years

before the time we speak of, giving a large share of the profits to some of his favourite religious Societies. One of these books, a rare copy of the Bible, sold for nearly £600. No doubt it was not without a pang that he parted with the cherished treasures of a lifetime; but his face was set Zionwards, he laid aside every weight, cut every cord that would needlessly bind him to earth, and in a most remarkable manner awaited patiently the call to 'go up,' as he expressed it, so much so that he did not like to be asked whether he was growing stronger. 'No,' he would say, 'I am growing weaker.' On one occasion, a friend who was in a delicate state of health said to him, 'They tell me that I shall come round in time;' he made the characteristic answer, 'Well, I am going up, and that is better than *coming round !*' On the 4th of January 1866 he writes from Waterford:—'It is wonderful that I should have been left so long in this world of death, when almost all my contemporaries have been one after the other called.

> "The time my God appoints is best,
> And His to fix my time of rest."

'The Fenians will do the poor people no good. Political troubles will only bring suffering on them. We must try to do good to the poor ignorant people while they are left among us. Happy if we could get any of them, though poor in this world, to be rich in faith, and heirs of the kingdom. What a wonderful thing, that a sufferer in a cabin should be a joint-heir with Christ! Lord, give some of them to know and believe this great truth !'

He began this year by circulating a lithographed pastoral to his Waterford people, copies of which he sent to many of his friends in other places. This touching letter did not fail to draw tears from many an eye, reminding them that the time of his departure must be near :—

' To my much esteemed Neighbours residing in and near the City of Waterford.

'*1st January* 1867.

' MY DEAR FRIENDS,—At the close of the past and the beginning of a new year, I am led to reflect upon the many years that have passed since I first came among you as the overseer of the ambassadors of Christ in this city, set over those whose high office it is to beseech you, in Christ's stead, to be reconciled unto God. I am now, I may be assured, very near drawing to a close the days of my office, very near finishing my course. The time of my departure being at hand, I desire to say a few words to you in faithfulness and affection. I cannot, in the presence of God, look back upon the past time without deep and sincere acknowledgment of deficiency, of having left undone much that I ought to have done, and done much which I ought not to have done ; but with all my deficiencies, my conscience bears me witness that in the main I told you the truth. I preached among you "repentance towards God, and faith in the Lord Jesus Christ." I spoke to you, both in public and in private, as (what I know myself to be) sinners in the sight of God ; and it was my happiness to tell you what was the comfort of my own soul, that Jesus came into the world to save sinners. I called on you to look back to Him bearing our sins in His own body on the tree ; to look up to Him where He is now, at the right hand of God, making intercession for us ; and to look forward to Him when He shall come again, with ten thousand of His saints, to receive to a participation of His glory all who trust in Him—to receive to Himself all those who, through faith, have been drawn out from the mass of a sinful, perishing world, and led to join His little despised flock. Standing on the borders of eternity, I have no new truths to put before you. I have only, as a parting word, to repeat to you the same important truths, and to press them with all earnestness and affection on your attention. I think of the many that from among us have passed out of this world in the past years. They all of them, whether lost or saved, know now the importance of those truths. There are many, I am happy to think, who are now thankful for having heard of God's inestimable love in the redemption, and have through it entered into the rest that remaineth for the people of God. There are many of whom I cannot think but with extreme pain, who have learned the value of these truths by experiencing the misery which has been the result of having neglected them. But I turn from the crowds that have passed away, to address myself to the many that still remain amongst us, and to the flock that has grown up in the midst of us in the interval. I would speak to them as divided into two classes, into which the Scripture constantly divides the dwellers on this earth.

'First, I would speak to those who are still walking according to the course of this world, according to the spirit that worketh in the children of disobedience. I would say to this class, as I have said to them before,

" Repent, and believe the gospel." I would entreat them,
" Seek the Lord while He may be found, call upon Him
while He is near. Now is a day of salvation ; now, if ye
do hear His voice, harden not your hearts. Let the wicked
forsake his way, and the unrighteous man his thoughts ;
let him return unto the Lord, and He will have mercy
upon him ; and to our God, and He will abundantly
pardon him."

' To the second class I say, in all earnestness and affection,—to those who were by nature dead in trespasses and
sin, but have been quickened and raised up, and made to
sit in heavenly places in Christ Jesus,—Be thankful for
your fellowship in the gospel ; be thankful that, by grace,
ye have been saved through faith ; that you, through
mercy, have passed from death unto life. I entreat you,
my Christian friends, to live close to Christ ; to live up to
the full privileges of the gospel as pardoned sinners accepted in the Beloved, heirs of God, and joint-heirs with
Jesus Christ. As risen with Christ, seek the things that
are above, and not those that are on the earth ; cultivate
and exhibit no friendship with the world ; come out from
among them, and be separate ; touch not the unclean
things ; be as God's witnesses ; shine as lights in the
midst of a crooked and perverse generation. Let your
light so shine before men, that they may see your good
works, and glorify your Father which is in heaven. Thus
shall you give diligence to make your calling and election
sure, and an entrance shall be ministered to you abundantly unto the everlasting kingdom of the Lord and
Saviour Jesus Christ. Live as new creatures this new

year, looking, according to His promise, for a new heaven and a new earth, wherein dwelleth righteousness.—I remain, in much sincerity, your unworthy bishop, but affectionate and faithful friend, 'ROBERT CASHEL.'

On the back of it he writes to his annual correspondent:—

'WATERFORD, 8th January.

'MY DEAR ——,—I write to you on this paper, that while I thank you for your kind remembrance of me, and your interesting letter, I may let you see that we are in some degree alive still. I have, by rheumatism, almost lost the use of my limbs, so that I cannot move about as I used to do, and call upon my neighbours. I therefore speak to them by letter, and ask the great Head of the Church to bless this mode of putting forth His truth. Our God changeth not. Jesus Christ is the same yesterday, to-day, and for ever. As far, then, as I have been taught of God, I change not, but speak the same warning and comforting truths that I did at Powerscourt.

'We have, both in Church and State, the sea and the waves roaring, with, I think, much more to dread in the Church than the State. It is wonderful, it is lamentable, to find the tendency to go back towards Popery, and the rulers of the Church not united to stamp out the pest. Oh, how we want the spirit of our Reformers, to be ready to go to the stake for truth! I fear more for our Church from the enemy within than from the enemy without. As to the State, the panic has subsided. I never was afraid. No one that meant to rob and murder me would tell me beforehand that he was coming. As the Fenians said they were coming, I never was afraid that they would come. It has done, however, infinite injury to our country; it has kept men and money out of it, and put us back half a century.

'As to prophecy, the year-day prophets, who announced that the year 1866 was to bring the consummation of all things, are trying how to get out of the scrape. I do not know what Dr. Cumming will say now for his calculations. I say we know not the day nor the hour. Be ye ready, prepared for whatever the Lord is preparing for us. We should be looking forward with hope; and if we are to be down in the grave for a time, those that shall be alive shall not be before us. The first thing the Lord will do when He comes will be to speak to us with a shout, the voice of the archangel, and trump of God. Fare you well till then.—Your sincere and affectionate friend,

'ROBERT CASHEL, etc.'

To Mrs. Madden.

'WATERFORD, 19th January 1867.

'MY DEAR B.,—I thank you for your kind letter. I was sorry to find by it that your health was much worse than I had thought. I knew that you were not well, but I had no idea that you were so seriously an invalid. You have high authority in St. Paul for being desirous, if it is the will of your God, to remain for the good of others. His, to be sure, was a higher motive than we can pretend to. He could say that to him to live was Christ. It would be better for his account to depart; but for the cause of Christ, and the building up of His Church, it was needful that he should continue with them, and for that object he was willing to stay away from his heavenly rest. I wish we could have more of that Christian motive and desire to remain with our families and friends, not only for their temporal advantage, and their and our gratification, but to promote their spiritual good, and thus be working for the glory of Christ. It is an humbling thing to think how low are the motives of our best actions, and that there is sin mixed up with and spoiling them; that we have need to bring the best things we do or think to be washed in the blood of Christ. And how comfortable to know that it is there that Christ washes our feet, which gather dirt while we walk through a dirty world. My general health, thank God, continues very good; but I have almost entirely lost the use of my limbs, and the fine clear frost we have had certainly did them no good. But I have no more right to expect that I am to pass through this sin-cursed world as active as I used to be than you to pass through it without sickness. These are part of the curse; but, blessed be God, there is a time and a place where there will be no more curse, and your sickness will be turned to health, and the body of humiliation will be changed. My kindest regard to all of yours.—Yours affectionately, ' ROBERT CASHEL.'

To Mrs. Verschoyle.

' WATERFORD, *5th June* 1868.

' MY DEAR MRS. VERSCHOYLE,—It was a great gratification to me to get a letter from you, in which, though you said nothing about your health, I gathered that you had returned home in renovated health and strength. I am very glad that I have a few copies of my address, so that I can send you six copies. I am much gratified by your approval of it. It has been made useful through divine grace to some; and I hope it may be in some little degree made useful yet to others, both as warning and as comfort. I am glad that you can give a tolerable account of my dear friend the Bishop. You speak of his escaping from the London heat. We know nothing of that. We complain rather of cold, and are looking forward with hope to some of the heat of summer. We have, however, much reason to be thankful that the country looks very well, and promises a good harvest. Our ecclesiastical prospects are very dark. I wish our religious state was improving under the Lord's chastening hand. We have no might against that great company that is coming against us. May it lead us to look up more singly to Him that can help His people. May we get more of a spirit of prayer and supplication, and trust more to God and less to man; and may we look forward with more hope to our heavenly home.—With warm affection to you and the Bishop, I remain, very truly yours, 'ROBERT CASHEL, etc.'

To a Friend.

'WATERFORD, 4th January 1868.

'MY DEAR ———,—It cheered me much to see your handwriting as young as in former years, and your mind apparently as fresh and as vigorous as in former new years. What a gracious dealing of our God and Father, that He leaves us the use of our mind and intellect, though He is pleased to begin the dissolution of our earthly tabernacle in another part! It is by our minds, and not by our limbs, that we make progress towards the kingdom of peace and glory. I can say of myself, that the state of my mind is to be looking forward more than I ever did, as your letter shows that you are doing, to that world full of peace and good-will, instead of sin, murder, hatred, and strife; that is the character of the world under the present dispensation. I have been finding fault with myself and fellow-Christians for being so, as it were, satisfied with faith, and not adding to it the grace of hope, as if Paul had written, "Justified by faith, we have peace with God," and had not added, "Rejoice in the hope of the glory of God." The Israelites ought, while in the wilderness, to have been heartily thankful for the bread from heaven, and the water out of the rock, which their heavenly Father gave them on the way; but they ought not to have been satisfied with those blessings, and to have said, "It is good to be here." They should have been looking for the good land flowing with milk and honey. What would the manna and the water be worth if they were not means towards the better land? To think of being joint-heirs with Christ! "The glory which Thou hast given me, I have given them." You tell me of new neighbours; I hope you may find them profitable and pleasant. But in this sinful world I shrink from an increase of neighbours; I am afraid of them. I would not go into Bray on any account since it has been so improved (as many call it).

It is bringing the town world into the country, spoiling our green fields with their artificial flowers. I love nature, but I have no taste for the many-coloured garments of the dissipated world. May we be content with our white robes and the palms in our hands.—Your sincere and affectionate friend, 'ROBERT CASHEL, etc.'

To the Same.

'WATERFORD, *4th January* 1869.

'MY DEAR ——,—I thank you very sincerely for your letter of the first of this year, proving to me that I have left among us a true old friend, who remembers the intercourse of former years, and has a pleasure in renewing it. Every year removes some of those with whom we took sweet counsel, and went into the house of God as friends. As one Christian brother said, speaking of another about the same age with himself who had lately been called up higher, "We often talked of our ages, but he won the race, and reached the goal before me." Happy the intercourse of friends that has this element in it, being on the same journey, and going to the same end. Happy thought, that while the true believer has to ask for many things on the journey, he has not in a state of uncertainty to ask about the end; that has been settled long ago. God has prepared for him an habitation, and that is in His presence, where is fulness of joy, and at His right hand, where there are pleasures for evermore. When I was in the habit of going to London, I always had prepared for me a lodging, an habitation, so that my mind would be quite at ease, assured that when I came to the end of the road I should have rest. Such views give great peace to the mind amidst the talked of disestablishment and disen-dowment of our Church. It may be indeed, as you call it, a disgraceful proceeding, and we cannot but utterly condemn all those who would be the authors of it; but it cannot shake our kingdom. *It* cannot be moved, for indeed it is founded upon a rock, and that rock is Christ. We are forewarned that in the latter days perilous times will come; and I cannot but think, if not come, they are coming, and we may expect a time full of evil and full of good. That movement in Spain is very remarkable, where the most Popish country in Europe has come out more decidedly against Popery than any other. It appears to me like the fulfilment of that prophecy in Rev. xvii. 16. The horns of the beast that was seen carrying the woman is set before us as hating the whore, and making her desolate and naked. It will be most interesting to watch the progress of the movement, and to see what it will do to promote truth. How sad it is that England should be strengthening Popery when other countries are pulling it down. I pray that the Lord may keep you, and me, and our fellow-believers, in all the troubled scenes that we may expect.—Believe me, yours most sincerely and affectionately, in the hope of the gospel,

' ROBERT CASHEL, etc.'

The following letter is extracted from the Memoir of the late Chief-Justice Lefroy, and was addressed to his son on hearing of the death of his old friend :—

2 B

'WATERFORD, *7th May* 1869.

'MY DEAR LEFROY,—It has pleased our gracious God to take to Himself the soul of your dear father, and my oldest, most valued friend. We cannot say that He has not done all things well. He lent him for an unusually long time to his children and his friends, and then He said, "Come up higher." When we think what He that giveth grace and glory did for him, and what in consequence He is doing for him now, we cannot think of offering the common consolation to those who feel his loss, but must realize his unspeakable gain. No; we say with warm feeling, "Blessed be the God and Father of our Lord Jesus Christ, who, according to His abundant mercy, hath begotten us again unto a lively hope by the resurrection of Jesus Christ." We bless God, on the part of our departed one and ourselves, for the inheritance incorruptible, and reserved in heaven for him and us who are partakers of the same faith. It is promised to us left behind, that we shall be kept by the power of God, through faith unto the salvation ready to be revealed, and we greatly rejoice in the prospect. But he is beyond it; we are to be kept for it, but he has been put into possession of it. Shall not we, then, on his account greatly rejoice, though now for a season we may be in heaviness? He is, indeed, taken away from evil to come, and from what an extent of evil we do not know. We may well be led to offer up the beautiful prayer of our funeral-service, that our God may speedily accomplish the number of His elect, and hasten His kingdom, that we, and all those who are partakers of the faith of the gospel, may have our perfect consummation of bliss, both in body and soul, in Christ's kingdom. . . . I never shall forget the pleasure and profit we had for many successive years in having your father speaking at the meeting of the Wicklow Bible Society, which, by his presence and spiritual addresses, he was instrumental in establishing and confirming. I look back with a most pleasing recollection to a journey I took with him in the Holyhead Mail from Birmingham. I had come to Birmingham the day before, and had taken a place in the Mail to Holyhead. I went in the morning to the office just before starting, anxious to see what company I should have, and I found your father, and I think one of you his sons, and a stranger, and myself. When he came into the coach he had his Bible in his hand, and he put it into the pocket of the carriage at hand for use, and a most delightful searching of Scripture we had on the road. He loved his Bible, and I remember a saying of his that struck me much at the time. He said, "I sometimes read the Bible on my knees—not that I am making an idol of the book, and falling down to worship it; but I am in a position to say, 'Give me understanding, that I may see the wondrous things that are in Thy book.' Deal with me according to the favour Thou showedst unto Thy people." Will you give my kindest regards to your sisters, who must feel more than any others the gap that has been made ? I pray for you all, that grace may abound to you through Jesus Christ.—Yours most affectionately in the gospel of Christ,

'ROBERT CASHEL, etc.'

CHAPTER X.

PARTING DAYS.

'Say not it dies, that glory ;
  'Tis caught unquench'd on high ;
  Those saintlike brows so hoary
  Shall wear it in the sky.'

KILLOUGH CASTLE did not now suit the Bishop as a residence, when no longer able for country walks and drives. He expresses this in the following letter to Mrs. Hamilton Madden :—

'BUXTON, 31*st* *August* 1863.

'MY DEAR BELLA,—I am very much obliged by your very kind and affectionate letter of inquiry as to the state of my limbs. I came here ten days ago, and have consulted the doctor and taken four baths. I cannot say that I am any better. I have very little use of my limbs; I do not suffer much pain, but I have no strength in my legs from the hip downward. My legs have carried me for 80 years, and if they are to do so no more, I have reason to be thankful for what they have done. I am thankful that the little pain I have does not keep me awake at night, and in all other respects my health is very good. Of course I can say nothing about the time I may remain here; that will depend upon the effects of the baths, and the desire of the doctor to have the pleasure of my company and the profit of my fees; but I am in no hurry to get back to Killough if I can neither walk nor ride. We have had very changeable weather—a great deal of damp and wet, not favourable to getting rid of rheumatism.

'I know that the earthly house of this tabernacle is to be dissolved, and the beginning of the dissolution may be in my limbs. What comfort to have ground for an assurance that we have a building of God, an house not made with hands, eternal in the heavens! It is the character of this state, that while in this tabernacle we may groan, being burdened. The burden I have had has been very light. May grace, mercy, and peace be with you all.— Very truly and warmly yours,

'ROBERT CASHEL, etc.'

His heart returned in a remarkable manner to the scenes of his early youth, and to those among the number of his old friends who were still to be found there. In the County Wicklow he spent some months every summer of his later years, within reach of Bromley, Delgany, and Bellevue, and near enough to Powerscourt for some of his old parishioners, whose hearts he had won in their youth not only for himself but for God, to visit him. In a letter to Archdeacon Bell, dated 6th September 1864, he expresses his gratification at being able again to take part in the meetings of the Bible Society at Wicklow, at which, from this time till his last year upon earth, he was heard to speak every year. He says: 'I am expecting on Thursday to attend the meeting of the Wicklow Bible Society, the formation of which I attended fifty-two years ago, and I acted as secretary for thirty years; and now, at an interval of twenty-two years, I hope to be there again. It is cheering to find it so well kept up in the interval.'

Friar's Hill, near Wicklow, was the first place which he took in that neighbourhood. In the summer of 1869 he spent some months at Woodstock, and in 1870 at Clonmannon, near Ashford, and returned again to Friar's Hill in 1871, the last summer of his long and useful life. Here he was still able to enjoy much the society of and intercourse with Christian friends like-minded with himself, many of whom were invited to dine or spend a few days with him. Miss Daly joined him at these summer residences as long as she was able, and he had visits from his sister, Lady Croften, as well as from his nephews. Delgany Church, which had been his place of worship for so many of his earliest years, could not be looked upon by him with the eye of a stranger. In answer to a request from Miss La Touche of Bellevue for a contribution towards its alteration, he wrote the following characteristic note:—

'WATERFORD, 14th January 1871.

'MY DEAR MISS LA TOUCHE,—It gave me much pleasure to receive a letter from you, giving as favourable an account of your dear mother as could be expected at her time of life. It is no wonder that she should not have the pen of a ready writer.

'I am sorry that you cannot give a good account of the health and strength of the roof of my old acquaintance, Delgany Church. This, too, is a very unfortunate time in which to look for large contributions, there are so many pressing demands. I can give you but little, as almost every letter that I get says, "Give, give!"

'I send you a cheque for £10; at another time I might have given more. I am longing for and looking for that time and place where neither our bodies nor our churches will be falling into decay. There is such a time and place for all that, convinced of sin, believe with the heart in the Lord Jesus Christ.—Very truly yours,

'ROBERT CASHEL, etc.'

The interests of the Church occupied the greater part of his thoughts during the retirement consequent upon his advanced age. In his younger days he had said that he was married to the Church, and he now continued to love and to cherish it. 'I have it in my head,' he writes to Archdeacon Bell in September 1864, 'to go to the Bristol Church Congress, but I rather think I may start back from it when the time draws nearer. It is rather interesting to speculate what such meetings will produce. I suppose active spirits set it a-going because the Convocations are not allowed to do anything. Our Primate got a very decided answer that the Crown will not sanction the meeting of the Irish Convocation.' Again, a few years later, he says: 'You have no doubt been pleased by the bishops' admirable letter. I think they have taken the first step well. When the Convocation assembles for the province of Dublin, I shall make it a point to attend, though at much personal inconvenience.'

Of the Church Congress in 1868, the Rev. Thomas Gimlette has given the following particulars :—

'In the year 1867 the Church Congress met at Wolverhampton. It was proposed that the next meeting should be held in Dublin, and a telegram was sent to His Grace the Archbishop of Dublin, asking whether he would sanction the meeting, and give it his approval. His Grace was at his country seat in the county of Wicklow, and the Bishop of Cashel was dining with him, when the telegram arrived. The Archbishop, on reading it, handed it over to the Bishop, saying, "What would your lordship advise?" "Sanction and encourage any movement, your Grace," was the reply, "which draws the bonds of union closer between the Churches of England and Ireland." "If I consent, will your lordship attend and take part at the Congress?" "I will most certainly, if the Lord enables me," was the answer. This decided the Archbishop; an affirmative answer was sent to Wolverhampton, and the Church Congress was fixed to be held in Dublin, commencing on the 29th day of September 1868. It was most successful. The number of tickets sold amounted to 2261, being 300 more than at Wolverhampton. The Bishop of Cashel, with his wonted liberality, gave free tickets to any of his curates who desired to attend.

'He attended first on the evening of the 29th of September, and spoke with much power on the subject of National Education, or rather, the relative functions of Church and State in National Education. The introductory paper was read by the Rev. R. Gregory, and in the discussion that took place the speakers were Archdeacon Denison, the present Bishop of Cashel, the Dean of Clonfert, the Bishop of Oxford, F. S. Powell, Esq., M.P., Dr. Webster, the Dean of Waterford, and the Bishop. His reception, when he made his appearance on the platform, was most enthusiastic; and as he took his seat, cheer after cheer came from the whole assembly.' The following is an extract from his speech :—

'I might well be expected to make an apology for standing up to address this meeting. For a person of my age, and to a great extent of my infirmity, it might be considered more than I ought to do to stand up at all before such an assembly. But considering that this is a subject upon which I have held very strong and earnest opinions, in the sight of God, for the good of my country, I would desire—if it be the last time I shall ever appear before a large assembly of my fellow-creatures and fellow-sinners—to advocate the cause of scriptural education. I feel that it is a most important subject that is put before us on the programme this evening,—the connection that there should be between the Church and the State in this important matter of national education. I would remark, as it strikes me very strongly, that we are not to consider the State and Church as if they were two opposite and antagonistic powers, the one against the other; for they are only parts of one great whole, both acknowledging one common Master and one common Lord, to whom they are both responsible for doing their duty. The first thing, therefore, which each has to do, is to consider what is the duty it owes in this matter to that common Master, what that common Master requires of both; and if both would consider that seriously and earnestly, it would, I believe, bring them to unity and agreement upon this point. If those governing in the State would consider what is required of them by God, and if the Church asked the same question as regards herself, it would be the means, I do believe, of bringing us all into unity of mind and unity of purpose on this great subject; and I would certainly say, that both State and Church should desire to cultivate and advance the education of the people.'

Archdeacon Bell writes, in answer to a letter from the writer of this Memoir :—

'I think that the interesting scene to which you refer took place at the assembling of the provincial Synods of Armagh and Dublin, at St. Patrick's Cathedral, in September 1869.

'I met the Bishop, by appointment, at the robing-room of the choir, near the entrance, and he walked up the nave leaning upon me. As soon as we entered the chancel, several of the bishops advanced to greet and welcome him, and he took his seat amidst a general and cordial reception on the part of all assembled. . . . On one occasion I accompanied him to the Metropolitan Hall, and on his entrance he was most warmly welcomed, not only by the bishops and others assembled on the platform, but also by the whole body of the clergy and laity in the body of the hall.

'I have reason to know that his advice and opinion were held in high esteem by the bench of bishops, and his presence greatly desired by them, during the difficult and anxious scenes of the earlier meetings of the General Synod.'

At the General Convention of 1870 he was present only one day. He came into the meeting at the same time as the Duke of Abercorn. When the Bishop was recognised, his appearance was hailed with loud and long-continued applause. He, however, took no part in the proceedings.

On the 23d of November 1869 the following notice of his generosity appeared in the newspapers :—

'The venerable Bishop of Cashel has done an act of thoughtful kindness to the curates of his diocese, which will endear his name to the poorer clergy of the Irish Church. He had made arrangements for giving them each, by his will, a token of remembrance; but, in the altered circumstances of the Church, he thought it better (and the curates will not question the wisdom of the more mature decision) to hand the gift over to them at once. He has accordingly directed the amount to be paid over. It is varied in proportion to the claims of the respective recipients, some receiving £50, others £100.'

To the Sustentation Fund of the Irish Church the Bishop gave £5000, to be appropriated particularly to assist in providing an income for his successor. He did not wish to die rich, but preferred distributing what he had to give during his lifetime; he left, however, to some of the religious Societies considerable legacies.

On the 5th of January 1870 he writes from Waterford to a friend :—

'. . . You wish to know my opinion of the present state of things, especially in relation to our Church. The State has been, like the Assyrian of old, the rod of God's anger. I am much more reconciled to what has happened (the disestablishment) when I consider the religious (or rather the irreligious) character of our Government now. At the time of the Reformation and the establishment of our Church, the Crown and the Parliament belonged to our Church. But what are they now? The Crown almost blotted out of our Constitution, the House of Lords afraid to act, and the Commons composed of Jews, Turks, heretics, and infidels. What right have they to interfere with our Church, to which they do not belong, and to which a majority of them is hostile? They were the lay element that had a right to take a part; but it is not so now, and I cannot but see good in the future by getting free from Gladstone and the like. May the new lay element that must now take a part in the proceedings of the reorganized Church prove a better fellow-worker than we had before. The ministers of our Church are, as a body, sound in the faith, and will, I trust, be blessed in their work when they outlive the present shock, which has unavoidably led them for a time to think more of the external than the spiritual part of their office. It is painful to me to be unable to take my part in the several meetings that are passing to carry on the work of reorganization, but I am not equal to the exertion. There is a most important meeting going on to-day, to consider a draft of a constitution for the governing body of the Church. I could not go up to it, but I can pray the Lord to be among the few that will be gathered together in His name. May He give them wisdom and faithfulness and His blessing, without which all will be vain. I condole with you on the loss of a good neighbour, Miss H.; such as she was are scarce. We should not grieve that they are taken away from the evil to come. We do not know what evils are coming upon this world, but we know that in the last days perilous times will come. Thanks be to God that there is a hiding-place to preserve us from trouble, to compass us about with songs of deliverance.

'I may well say to you, my dear friend, Fare you well. We can hardly expect another annual greeting, but what a greeting there will be when the Lord appears with all His saints! Grace be with you till then, and then glory. —Affectionately yours, 'ROBERT CASHEL, etc.'

The Bishop having been called upon publicly to express his opinion on a subject which caused much division and bitterness of feeling between two parties in the Irish Church at this time, he endeavoured to heal these divisions, and to restore confidence in those who had been appointed to administer the affairs of our Church under its altered circumstances. Referring to this, he wrote as follows to a member of the representative body :—

'WATERFORD, 31st May 1870.

'MY DEAR MR. ——,—I must begin my answer to your letter of the 28th by expressing the great gratification it has been to me that you should acknowledge that the clergy and laity of the dioceses under my charge have been of one mind with me in all questions affecting the Church organization. And I think it an additional source

of gratification that we have been, and are, of one mind on
the great Protestant doctrines of our Reformed Church, and
that the bishop, clergy, and laity of our united diocese
continue our protest against what we consider the soul-
destroying errors of the Church of Rome, which intercept
the sinner in his access to Christ, and that with equal
determination we continue our protest against the dis-
honest half-Popery which is put forward at the present
time. . . . It is the wonderful prerogative of our almighty
and all-wise God that He can bring good out of evil; and
He has so overruled the deplorable evil that has grieved
and tried us in the present day, that it has produced such
a united declaration of Protestant scriptural truth as has
stamped unmistakeably the character of the Church of
Ireland, so that she shall be a witness and keeper of Holy
Writ in the midst of the abounding iniquity which we have
ground to expect in the last days, when perilous times will
come, until we shall be blessed by the glorious appearing of
the Lord and Saviour Jesus Christ. We may even hope,
that as in early days the Church of Ireland was a source
of Christian light to other countries, so she may be an
example of a pure Protestant Church, and thus be made
useful to sister Churches, that seem now to be halting
between two opinions.

'I did not feel that I was called upon to publish my
sentiments, as I considered my long-known character, as a
sincere Protestant bishop, and the character of my dioceses
as untainted by Popish or semi-Popish doctrines, rendered
it unnecessary. Before concluding, I would mention that
I have devoted a sum of money to the Sustentation Fund

of the Church of Ireland; and I have paid it to the Representative Body, because, having well considered the character of the members that compose it, I think them sound, trustworthy, intelligent men, so that we have every reason to expect from them the faithful and effective discharge of the very arduous and important duty committed to them.

'It has been a great grief to me that I was unable, from age and infirmity, to attend and take part in the discussions at the Convention; but if I was absent in body, I was present in spirit. And I have prayed, and I do pray, for you and your worthy fellow-labourers, that the Spirit of God may instil and maintain in you and them true scriptural Protestantism, that shall make the word of God the light to your feet and the lamp to your path; that as to faith, you may have before you the injunction as to Babylon, " Come out of her, my people, and be not partaker of her sins, lest you be partaker of her plagues;" and as to manner of life, you may have set before you, " Be not conformed to this world," which, according to the apostle, " lieth in the wicked one." Concerning both the word says, "Touch not the unclean thing," and "I will be a Father unto you, and ye shall be my children."—I remain, my dear Mr. ——, your unworthy bishop and humble fellow-servant,

'ROBERT CASHEL, etc.'

His opinion and advice were highly valued and sought after by those in authority in the Church. One of his brother bishops, who was also his personal friend, writes to him from London, at the time of the conference of all the bishops at Lambeth Palace :—

'It will be very gratifying to me, my dear bishop, to have your Pisgah views of these matters which are in progress in the plain below. When days and years, which should speak and teach wisdom, are in conjunction with the Spirit of the Almighty, we may expect to hear something to the purpose.'

To the Archbishop of Dublin he thus expresses his sentiments as to the spirit in which the liturgical revision should be undertaken, if carried on at all :—

'WATERFORD, 22d *May* 1871.

'MY DEAR LORD ARCHBISHOP,—Your Grace some time ago, in a letter addressed to me, very kindly expressed a desire to be able to take into consultation such a useless individual as myself on points connected with our Church. On the great mass of details that come before the Church in synods and councils and elsewhere, there would be no room for profitable consultation, except there was a personal meeting of the parties; but there are some subjects that are so important and self-dependent, that it may not be time thrown away or labour wasted for an individual to set before those who are more active labourers in the cause the convictions that have been formed in his mind. The subject I allude to is "the Book of Common Prayer." The revision of it, bringing it into a form that shall make it a suitable instrument for carrying on the common, intelligent, and spiritual worship of God by the Church, is the most important, and, I would add, the most difficult work that can be undertaken by those who are reorganizing our Church. I was much struck with the wisdom and large-heartedness of his Grace the Lord Primate, who, speaking of the character that would ·be necessary to have maintained in the Book of Common Prayer, said it must be that which would suit the Topladys and the Wesleys, and he left it to be inferred that it was no common book that would answer this end. Within the limits to be considered between these extremes of religious systems there were various opinions to be taken into account, and various professors to be thoughtfully and tenderly dealt with ; but we cannot but say that his Grace stopped short. Outside of those he mentioned, there is a large class of persons who will have their share in the revision or composition of the book, and for whose use it is intended. I mean the large class the apostle speaks of (1 Cor. ii. 14),—the natural man, who receiveth not the things of the Spirit of God, for they are foolishness to him; neither can he know them, because they are spiritually discerned. Of the existence and largeness of this class your Grace is well aware, and you would say that they were ignorant of the first principles of the doctrine of Christ who, looking at the great mass of mankind, or at the smaller number in the Church of Ireland, would deny their having fallen "longissime" from original righteousness. This corruption exists in a proportion of those who are selected to revise or compare a Book of Common Prayer, as also in that larger company of men for whose use it was intended, in whose hands it will be placed, and who are expected to receive it. This presents a difficulty which we should say that, but for the blessing sought from God, it would be impossible to overcome,—a difficulty which should be seen and felt beforehand by those who are associated for the revision, as also by those who are expected to welcome the completion of the work. There was no difficulty such as meets us now at the first composing, and afterwards revising, of the Prayer Book. The compilers, martyrs and confessors, among whom were Cranmer and Ridley, were not divided among themselves. There was not even the difference that would exist between the Topladys and Wesleys. There were taken into their councils none belonging to the natural man, who receiveth not the things of the Spirit, counting them foolishness; neither was the book referred to such a mixed body for emendation or alteration, as the Prayer Book, in whatever shape it comes from the committee of revision, will be submitted to the Synod, composed as it is of various shades of religious professors, and in a large proportion of the natural man, to be modified by them to suit their various discordant views.

'But how can we expect to see the revised Prayer Book come out of the hands of the mixed committee? How can we expect to see a consistent, evangelical, devotional form, except by the blessing and overruling control of the great God of truth and light, by the same wise and powerful influence as He makes the several prismatic shades in the sunbeam combine to give us the one uniform light that illumines our path and directs our way?

'It is, my dear lord, of the first importance that this difficulty should be seen and acknowledged, in its real extent, by all parties employed and interested in the revision of the Prayer Book; that it should be felt and acknowledged by the mixed body by whom the revision is to be undertaken,—a body which, though small, has in it some of whom the Lord has promised that He will give them the Spirit to lead them into all truth, and, led by the Spirit, are the children of God. But in the same body, and engaged in the same work, are some who are natural men, who receive not the things of the Spirit. They are foolishness unto them. They cannot know them, for they are spiritually discerned.

‘There is a necessity for a revision, a demand for it at the present time, so that it must be undertaken; but the difficulty is of such magnitude that it is impossible to see how it may be brought to a happy issue.

‘There never was a time in which all in our Church who ever pray were more called upon to go to the throne of grace, and pray that God's grace may be made perfect in our weakness. He hath said, “Call upon me in the day of trouble, and I will answer thee, and thou shalt praise me.”

‘Entreating your Grace to pardon my intrusion on your rest, praying that our God may overrule all things to His glory and the good of His Church, I remain, my dear lord, your weak fellow-servant and your unworthy brother,

‘ROBERT CASHEL, etc.’

It is a great mistake to suppose that the Bishop of Cashel would, if now amongst us, sympathize with those who are plucking down the hedges of our Church, laying it open to be spoiled by every ‘wild boar out of the wood,’ or to class him with the Low Church party in the Irish Church at the present day. Happy would it be for us, though not for him, if we could have him live his life over again—if we could have his sound judgment, his power of influencing the minds of others at our Synods ; but he, being dead, may yet speak to us in the language of wisdom and advice.

With regard to the question of the revision of the Book of Common Prayer, it was always his opinion, which he has often been heard to express, that it was not called for. He thought our liturgy to be as nearly perfect as any human institution could be, and that the objections raised to it were of so unimportant a character, that it would be far wiser, as he expressed it, to 'let well enough alone.' The greater number of these objections, he thought, would vanish, if the persons deliberating upon them were able fully to enter into the spirit of the compilers of our liturgy.

He was, as we have said before, a Conservative in matters of religion, just as much as Lord Eldon was in political matters when he was cheered by the youth of Oxford. ' Three cheers for old Eldon !—*he* never ratted ! ' If the Bishop did not give in to novelties brought in by the Tractarian party, neither would he have joined with those who seek to unchurch our Church. Having 'proved all things,' he sought to ' hold fast that which is good.' [1]

Having been asked by a friend how she ought to answer those who found fault with the form of absolution in our service for the Visitation of the Sick, he wrote in reply :—

[1] For an extract on the subject of Liturgical Revision, from the charge delivered in 1863 by the Bishop of Cashel, see Appendix C.

To Lady Harriet Monck.

'WATERFORD, *17th November* 1858.

'. . . The language in the absolution in the Visitation of the Sick is not, perhaps, as cautious as would be used now. If, however, you look at what goes before and follows, it will appear evident that our Church never meant to assert a power in her ministers to forgive sins, but only to declare for the sinner's comfort the forgiving mercy of the Lord. The form begins with a prayer that the Lord " may forgive thee thine offences;" afterwards there is a prayer, " Open Thine eye of mercy upon this Thy servant, etc. ; and as he putteth his full trust only in Thy mercy, impute not unto him his former sins." That the words used are intended only as declaratory appears from other parts of the Prayer Book,—as, for example, the absolution in the Morning Service: " Hath given power and commandment to His ministers to declare and pronounce to His people, being penitent, the absolution and remission of their sins, HE pardoneth," etc. etc.

' I hope this will be satisfactory to your mind. It is very different from what the Romish Church says, which declares that if any one shall say that the sacramental absolution of the priest is not a judicial act, but barely a ministerial one, in declaring that the sins of the person who confesses are pardoned, etc., let him be accursed.'

As to whether it would be desirable to revise our English translation of the Holy Scriptures, the Bishop of Cashel has been heard to say, that he thought the marginal readings in Bagster's *Comprehensive Bible* supplied any corrections which were wanting in order to make the meaning of some passages more clear.

For the Archbishop of Dublin he had a sincere regard, and felt towards him that spirit of love which one true Christian bears to another. This sentiment was no doubt reciprocated. It was indeed a touching sight, at the last triennial visitation of the dioceses of Cashel, etc., at which they both were present, to see the Bishop walking slowly up the aisle of the Cathedral leaning upon the arm of the Archbishop, whose bearing towards him was one of filial tenderness and respect, obeying the injunction of St. Paul with regard to an 'elder,' to 'entreat him as a father.'

The following letters show us how cordial was the feeling that existed between them :—

To His Grace the Archbishop of Dublin.

'WATERFORD, *27th April* 1870.

'MY DEAR LORD,—In acknowledging your Grace's letter, received this morning, I have in my own name and that of the Church of Ireland Protestants in my dioceses, to thank you for the increasing attention to their interests which you have manifested.

'There may well be ascribed to your Grace, what Paul could say of himself, " In labours more abundant ; " and you have my prayers that our gracious God may so strengthen you, both in body and mind, that neither may be overpowered by the burden laid on you.

'My clergy will no doubt have pleasure in complying

with your Grace's wishes, and reading in their churches
the paper you will send.

'When I receive the appeal from the Representative
Body, I shall have pleasure in responding to it.—I remain,
my dear lord, your sincere, unworthy fellow-labourer,

'ROBERT CASHEL, etc.'

To the Same.

'WATERFORD, 8*th May* 1871.

'MY DEAR LORD,— . . . I feel much for our Church,
and I pray for it.

'I feel especially for the bishops, because you are put
in the fore-rank, and have many shots directed against
you. I pray for you generally, but I also pray for you
individually, because there is more violence and bitterness
exhibited against you than any other. I thank the Lord
that the violence of your enemies does not lead you to
forget your high and holy position, and that you are
enabled to keep your temper under great provocation.
May the Lord continue to keep you strong in the Lord
and in the power of His might.

'I thank you for your nice prayer. Some individuals
got copies of it, and used it yesterday. As I conceive the
Synod is near its closing, and that next Sunday might be
the last, I shall not send it round my diocese till before
the opening of the next Synod, that it may not be thrown
aside now, and perhaps forgotten, but begin afresh. I
wish it was in my power to take counsel with you
and my other brethren; but I am so entirely a cripple,
that I cannot leave my own room and my own carriage.

I have also for the last few days become so deaf that I can hardly keep up a conversation with anybody. The Lord is pulling down my tabernacle of clay ; but, blessed be His name, He has for me " a house not made with hands, eternal in the heavens." Glorious it will be when I am clothed upon with this house from heaven.—Very truly and warmly yours, 'ROBERT CASHEL, etc.'

To the Same.

'DEAR LORD ARCHBISHOP,—I consider that it is settled for me, in the providence of God, that I should not go to Dublin at this time to attend the National Conference. I had much satisfaction in attending the Synod, as my presence was necessary. I took the chair, and having friends and helpers at hand, I got through it without inconvenience; but I shrink from going from home to a meeting which it would be a gratification to me to attend, but where my presence would not be required.

'I feel that I need hardly assure your Grace and the Lord Primate, and through you the large number of laymen and clergy assembled, that I am not absent from want of sympathy in the movement. I most highly approve of your Grace's having invited laity and clergy to come together to this Conference.

'I can, in the language of the apostle, say, " Though I be absent in the flesh, yet I am with you in the spirit, joying and beholding your order and the stedfastness of your faith in Christ." I admire the determination with which you maintain the primitive discipline and the Protestant doctrine of the United Church of England and Ireland,

and I pray to our God by His Holy Spirit to give
to your Grace and to your companions in trouble the
spirit which He gave to a sufferer in former times, who, if
we cannot say of him that he was threatened with disestablishment and disendowment, was forcibly separated
from the house of worship which he loved, and deprived
of the ministry that he valued; who thus said to Zadok
the priest: "Carry back the ark of God into the city. If
I shall find favour in the eyes of the Lord, He will bring
me again, and show me both it and His habitation; but
if He thus say, I have no delight in thee, behold, here
am I, let Him do to me as seemeth good unto Him."'

At the first meeting of the General Synod of the Irish
Church held in Dublin, the Bishop of Cashel was present.
His reception there was warm and enthusiastic; not less
so was the feeling shown on the occasion of his appearance
at the Waterford and Lismore Diocesan Synod, only about
three months before his death, at which he spoke with
warmth and energy, and at considerable length, on subjects
which had been always dear to his heart. Having enlarged
much upon that of scriptural education, he went on to
say: 'There is another matter, and it is a delicate one, as
to which I desire to make a few observations—that is, the
action of the Church with regard to vacant parishes; the
evil that may arise from a bad mode being adopted, and
the good that may arise from a good system being followed.
There are a good many vacancies in these dioceses, and
there has been set up a very general canvass on the part
of the clergy with regard to filling up those vacancies. I

say that carrying on a largely extended canvass with regard to this matter is not, in my mind, the most likely or the best way of providing for such vacancies, nor is it most creditable to the character of the clergy. There are many things that might be said to apologize for it, but many things that might be said against it. The question is, whether that sort of active canvass as soon as vacancies arise—whether it is the most likely way to get the best men to fill the several appointments. I know many who from conscience would not canvass for themselves; they have a feeling that such a course would not be consistent with their position and duty as ministers of the gospel. . . . In many things we may clearly see a remedy; but as regards this, I must confess that I am not prepared to suggest any. I think the system of canvassing is a very evil one, and very unsuited to the feelings of religious, serious, nice-minded men; but I don't say that I have in my mind any way by which that evil could be got thoroughly rid of. It just occurs to me, that if parochial nominators, whenever a vacancy arose, would keep their ears and their eyes open—if they would ascertain for themselves where good men were to be had, then they might come to some determination to offer the vacant post to such an one who had not offered for it. I shall not detain you longer; I am sorry that I should have occupied so much of your time; and now we shall proceed to business in the regular course.'

After the meeting of the Synod was over, a large number of both the clergy and laity were entertained by the aged Bishop at the Palace, as many as the house could accommodate remaining for the night. He had already undergone more exertion and fatigue than was prudent at his advanced age. His friends, therefore, tried to dissuade him from lecturing as usual at family prayer, but without success; the Bishop was not one to hold his peace while he could speak a word in season, and his words of warning and godly admonition were even more than usually forcible and energetic. The excitement was too much for him, and the following night he was very unwell. When leaving Dublin to return to Waterford a short time previously, he had expressed himself in the following remarkable manner: ' Now I have nothing to do but to die, and then to live for ever.' His clergy now feared that the time was come when their master would be taken away from their head; but the great Head of the Church, whose he was and whom he served, had still something more for him to do. His wonderful constitution recovered from this shock, and held out a little longer. His County Wicklow friends have pleasing though sad remembrances of his last summer spent amongst them. One in an humble walk in life, who had been one of the young people so carefully instructed by him when at Powerscourt, well remembers the last time he met him. The good Bishop took him by the two hands, and said to him affectionately, ' Well, John, I hope we shall meet in heaven; believe on the Lord Jesus Christ, and we shall be sure to meet there.' One of his former flock at Powerscourt walked the whole way to Friar's Hill and back again, in order once again to have the pleasure of seeing him. A friend, when staying with him there for a few days, was greatly impressed by his expression of longing to depart and be with Christ. The last evening that she and her husband, who had been one of his clergy at Waterford, spent with him, after pouring out their tea for them, he leant both his hands upon his stick, and resting his head upon them with his eyes shut, as was often his habit when speaking upon solemn subjects, he addressed himself to them in the most impressive manner, and ended by fervently exclaiming, 'Oh! I *long* to realize the joys of heaven!' He wished before leaving Friar's Hill to dine at Bellevue with his old friend Mrs. La Touche, between whose age and his own there was only the difference of ten days. He said it had been the first house in which he ever dined out, and he would like it to be the last. When setting out from the hall-door to return home at night, the present Bishop of Cashel, who stood upon the steps to bid him farewell, after speaking of attending the Synod, made some inquiry from the Bishop as to what he intended doing after that. His answer was, 'After that I shall *go up*.' 'Oh, my lord,' said Mr. Day, 'we should like to keep you a little longer amongst us.' 'I dare say you would!' replied the Bishop; 'but that does not make the least difference— drive on!' A short time afterwards he addressed the following note to Miss La Touche :—

'FRIAR'S HILL, WICKLOW,
26th September 1871.

'MY DEAR MISS LA TOUCHE,—I heard yesterday from John Scott that your dear mother was able to leave her room, and that I could see her about three o'clock.

' I determined to lose no time, but go immediately to see her. This day has turned to rain, so that I cannot go.

' Both your dear mother and myself are a year nearer our release than when I last saw her. I am more afraid of a bad day than I was, but I hope we may have some good days before I leave the country. Let all of us lay hold of peace with God through Jesus Christ, and then we may feel assured of a country where there will be unchanging fair weather.—Most sincerely yours,

'ROBERT CASHEL, etc.'

The letters written in his later years show a ripeness for Paradise rarely to be met with. At the opening of the year 1871 he thanks an old Christian friend for her continued remembrance of him, and goes on to say :—

' It is one of the gracious promises of our heavenly Father, " I will not forget thee. Thou art written on the palms of mine hands." It belongs to the children of God to have some of the spirit of their Father, to remember those with whom they have taken sweet counsel, and who are called in one hope of their calling. This unity of spirit and sameness of hope should be a great bond to unite the Lord's children while they are together journeying through the wilderness. But I think believers make the hope of joining their friends in the heavenly country too prominent a feature in their expected happiness. There is too much of earth in this. We see at times a godly family, a church in the house, where the whole family may look forward to meet before the throne; but much oftener we see a godly parent with a large family, the majority of whom are determined to walk according to the course of this world. This parent must have sorrow in this world; and if his happiness in the next depended on meeting his children, there must be a mixture of pain. There must be something from being joint-heirs with Christ that must ensure all happiness. " Father, I will that those whom Thou hast given me be with me where I am, that they may behold my glory;" and, " The glory Thou hast given me I have given them." There is nothing of earth in this. For a long time my mind dwelt much upon the signs of Christ's coming, and what we might consider as preceding Him; but now I feel that I have so short a time to remain here, that I think little of what will precede His coming, but seek more than ever to realize the coming itself. As Simeon was assured that he should see the infant Saviour, so I wish to realize that I shall see the glorified Saviour—"the King in His beauty." In the thought of it I should greatly rejoice, though now for a season I may be in heaviness. That thought should satisfy me as to the future, and ought to make me say, "Come, Lord Jesus, come quickly!" I trust, my dear friend, that is your mind.—Your affectionate friend,

' ROBERT CASHEL, etc.'

From the time that the Bishop was unable any longer to attend evening service in the Cathedral on Sundays, he spent that hour in compiling the ' Sunday Readings' for the Waterford newspaper the *Standard*, and sent them in his own handwriting. He continued to do so as long as he lived. Some of them were his own composition, and

others were extracts copied out by him from the many
excellent books of divinity which his library contained.
The last of these, which was published only a few days
before his death, was in beautiful harmony with the rest
of his life. In it the following passage occurs:—

'Reader, seek Christ, and light is yours; seek Christ,
and all perfection is yours. Is He not glory? Is He not
beauty? Who will not love Him? Who will not praise
Him? Who will not pray, Glorify me in Thy glory,
beautify me in Thy beauty, for I am Thine?'

The following is another extract from Archdeacon Brien's
reminiscences:—

'There is no man from whom I have gathered so much
benefit, religiously and intellectually, as the late Bishop
of Cashel. Not that I coincided with every sentiment he
uttered—there were many things concerning the which
I differed, and he was not the man to find fault with any
one for independence of thought and judgment; but he
gave an impetus to my mind, and started in me trains
of thought and reflection, which certainly, as far as I am
capable of forming a judgment, tended to the enlargement
of my mind.

'It was when I found the Bishop quite alone that he
was specially interesting in his Scripture conversation.
He was intimately acquainted with the word of God. He
had not only read it diligently, but thought deeply upon
it, and was quite prepared to speak on any subject which
might be suggested in connection with it; and it was then
specially I saw how highly scriptural was the tone of his

mind. Indeed, I do not think that I have ever met any one whose mind could so quickly pass from the most purely secular matter to the most deeply religious subject. His was a mind that seemed never out of tune. His heart was filled with the love of God, and the marvellous grace of Christ had complete possession of his soul.

'He had great delight in the Psalms of David, and often expounded them in family worship, though I have heard him say again and again, that he thought that there was no portion of the word of God which it was so heard to expound—that is, with an assured conviction that one was setting forth in his exposition what the Spirit of God intended.

'He was one who could weep with them that wept; he had the sympathizing spirit of a Christian, but all his feelings were under strong control. If it had been other-wise, he never could have had that massiveness and majesty of character which he exhibited, and which was so highly beneficial in his administration of the affairs of the Church of God.

'When last I saw him, his intellect maintained all its pristine energy, and his zeal in the interests of divine truth remained unabated. The very last lecture which I heard him deliver at family worship, which was about two months before his decease, was full of earnestness. It was on the eve of a Board of Nomination, which was to be held next day in connection with the reorganization of the Church of Ireland. Oh, with what earnestness he pressed the importance of choosing for the ministry of the Church in vacant parishes men of God, men into whose hearts God had shined, to give the light of the knowledge of the glory of God in the face of Jesus Christ! For he had read for the Scripture of the evening in the family worship the beginning of the 4th chapter of the 2d Epistle to the Corinthians; and even after the service was concluded, again and again he said, showing the estimate he formed of the importance of the ministry, and the character of the men thereunto appointed—again and again he said, "Men into whose hearts God hath shined." His spirit was earnest, full of zeal for the glory of God and the interest of His Church, but the flesh was failing.

'In the days of his office on earth, like a distinguished high priest of ancient time, " he shone as the morning star in the midst of a cloud; and as the sun when it shineth, so did he shine in the temple of God;" but in brighter splendour he shall come forth again. When the Son of God shall call him from the dust of death, the body of his humiliation shall be made like to the glorified body of his loved Lord and Master.

'Is it a partial opinion? Yet I thought he always looked comely and dignified in the robes of his earthly office, as he walked with his clergy to the hallowed service of the sanctuary of God. Ah! when he is seen again, shall he not be clothed in vestments of dazzling whiteness, so as no fuller on earth can white them? Shall he not come in robes washed and made white in the blood of the Lamb, which they wear who stand before the throne of God in heaven? But has he not left his name as a heritage to the Church of God on earth? The name of Robert Daly, sometime rector of Powerscourt, sometime bishop of

2 D

Cashel, it is a name of power to stir the heart of all who know and value the pure truth of the holy gospel of Christ.

'What were any little failings the Bishop of Cashel may have had, in comparison of his distinguished virtues and his blessed goodness? What are the spots on the sun, in comparison of his glorious brightness? Why should we seek to search out the shortcomings of the servants of God, instead of contemplating for our profit and example what is bright and beautiful? Let the enemies of the Bishop of Cashel, with beams in their eyes, search out if they can the mote that was in his. But I will write of him, and all the lovers of the truth of God will endorse what I write, while I proclaim, as my parting testimony to his blessed memory, that he was a great-hearted man of God.'

After his return to Waterford at the close of the year, the Bishop preached a charity sermon, 50 minutes in length, for the Church Education Society, with much of his former warmth and vigour. On Christmas day he preached in the Cathedral Church. In the beginning of the year 1872 he wrote, as his barque neared the heavenly shore :—

'WATERFORD, *4th January* 1872.

'MY DEAR ——,— . . . I cannot tell you how I value my old Christian friends, and the more because there are so few remaining. It is one of the trials of old age that we are left so alone in this world. And yet we are not alone; the best Friend never leaves us, never forsakes us, and He says, "Look unto me, and I will refresh you." He refreshed me by your letter, realizing to me one kept by the power of God, through faith, unto salvation. You write as if you were disappointed at not enjoying the serenity you expected in old age; you are pained by the view of your deficiencies and shortcomings; and it is well that it should be so when you look back and look in. But we have other, more elevating prospects, which we ought to enjoy. I remember reading in an old Father, that he found one look up do him more good, and humble him more, than twenty looks backward and inward. If our bodily health requires that we should take medicine, and at times very ill-tasted medicine, we have also food to take, both palatable and healthful. Take and eat of the food given to us. Feed on Him who has revealed Himself as the bread of life; and the more we are cut down by the sight of our spiritual deficiencies, so much the more take of that bread on which whosoever feeds he shall never hunger and never thirst. I must give you a couple of verses that I particularly value :—

> "Just as I am, without one plea,
> But that Thy blood was shed for me,
> And that Thou bidst me come to Thee,
> O Lamb of God, I come.

> "Just as I am, and waiting not
> To cleanse my soul from one dark spot,
> To Thee, whose blood can cleanse each blot,
> O Lamb of God, I come."

'I conceive there are two great subjects for our constant thoughts here—sin and salvation; we should think much of both. If we think only of sin, we do not listen to Jesus, who has said, " Lift up your heads, your redemption

is drawing nigh." If we thought of salvation forgetting
our sin, we should have a wrong conception of it. When
we reach the heavenly country, into which we shall not·
bring sin, we shall still see the use of the dark ground in
the picture, in order the more visibly to bring out the light.
The idea that is most happily present to my old mind, and
which I desire to realize more and more, is that beyond the
Jordan is my home. I wish to feel as if in a passage-boat
returning home. I could not think of remaining in the
boat; it does its part when it brings me home. It is better
to depart and be with Christ.—Wishing you a truly happy
New Year, I am, sincerely, your affectionate friend,

'ROBERT CASHEL, etc.'

His heavenly Father did not leave him much longer in
the 'boat,' as he expressed it. The Rev. William Sandford,
who was one of the first of the many useful and active
clergymen whom the Bishop introduced into his diocese,
thus describes the last time that he was able to entertain
any of his clergy at dinner :—

'THE RECTORY, TRAMORE,
5th January 1874.

'MY DEAR MRS. MADDEN,— ... Never on any other occasion did I see the characteristics of his vigorous mind, and
deep, manly piety, more strikingly exhibited. The dinner
party included six in all, and so the conversation was not
divided. Apparently in his usual health, the Bishop took
the lead. The topics introduced were varied and interesting.
At length the good men among his early friends who had·
been called away from time to time were passed in review.

I can see him (after the cloth was removed), with his arms resting on the table supporting his head, bending downwards, and as the names of Archdeacon Irwin, and Arthur Wynne, and others, were introduced, with a few graphic touches bringing out each character into full relief; and then, with solemn tone and characteristic movement of the head, speaking a word of counsel or encouragement or warning, as each suggested. And there was such calmness and softness, mingled with holy fervour, in all he said, that we felt as in the presence of one in very close fellowship with God, and caught all of us, I trust, a spark of his heavenly spirit. It was as if, now nearing the confines of the world within the veil, he rose sensibly above the fogs and mists of this lower world.

'We adjourned to the drawing-room for tea. Again the dear old Bishop took the lead, starting this time as a subject for conversation the life of Daniel Wilson, the late venerable Bishop of Calcutta. He had been now reading it with great interest, as if it had been but lately published. The higher life of the Christian, as developed in the good man, he seemed to think was pitched on too low a key. The absence of "the rejoicing of hope" in his case was canvassed; and the difference betweeen healthy self-examination in the Christian and morbid introspection were discussed. The conversation became general and animated. Very forcibly did the Bishop speak of the importance of hope as a great element of the Christian life, in which many true Christians are deficient, owing partly to defective views of the gospel of the grace of God in all its breadth and fulness, and partly to natural temperament, etc. etc. With an intellect as clear and a heart as warm as ever beat within his bosom in the vigour of youth, he maintained this as a glorious privilege of all God's children. He gave me a cordial shake of the hand with the "Good night, God bless you, and I am very glad to have you amongst us."[1] I never saw him more. Ever treating me with fatherly kindness and confidence, these his last words are written indelibly on the tablet of a loving, grateful heart.—I am, my dear Mrs. Madden, yours most sincerely,

'WILLIAM SANDFORD.'

That night, or early the following morning, two doctors were summoned to attend him. From this last attack, which was only three weeks before his death, he never rallied, but gradually declined in strength.

He had often said that he would wish to die suddenly, and would not like to have his friends worn out in attending him through a long and protracted illness; neither did he desire what is called a death-bed scene. Although often most edifying and instructive, he did not think it was what people ought to look to for comfort respecting their departed friends. 'People,' he would say, 'generally die as they live;' and he looked upon it as one of the ways in which Satan tries to deceive, that those who have lived for the world are often said to have died in a happy state of mind if they express a little penitence at the end. In his case, to him to live was Christ; and to die was gain to him, though loss to us. One part of his desire was,

---

[1] Mr. Sandford had lately removed to Tramore from a more distant part of the diocese.

however, granted to him. He did not linger long after he was unable to leave his bed. From that time he did not suffer any pain.

His nephew, Mr. Bowes Daly, was with him in his last illness, and before the parting scene came, was joined by one of his brothers. Nothing was left undone by him and his attached servants that could smooth his dying pillow.

His faithful servant and attendant writes :—

'For some months before he died, I had to attend him going to bed and getting up; but I had to leave him while he was communing with his heavenly Father. Before he went to bed, and the last thing before lying down, he would say, "Lord, take care of me;" and then, "He will, He will take care of me." He *felt* underneath him the everlasting arms. Dr. Elliott was his only physician after Dr. Mackesy's death, and he, being a very serious man, used often to draw conversation from the Bishop.'

In a letter addressed to the writer of this Memoir, Dr. Elliott says :—

'The impression he made on me during these years of intimate intercourse with him was that of a sincere believer, cheerfully bearing painful infirmities, deeply thankful for such alleviations as were granted, and looking forward with joyful hope and confidence to the rest and inheritance which remain for the people of God.'

He had a deep sense of the Saviour's abiding presence with him. One expression of his to a clergyman whom he much regarded, and who was admitted to his bedside, was as follows:—'I am not alone. My Saviour is with me. He is beside me. He never leaves me. I fancy Him constantly at the foot of my bed.'

For the last day or two he grew weaker. The vital principle was, however, strong, and at times he wonderfully rallied. At last the time of his departure came, and he fell asleep. It was about eight o'clock on Friday morning, the 16th of February 1872, when the great bell of the Cathedral gave out its mournful peal, and, full of faith, full of years, and full of honours, his great spirit was parted from the earthly house of this tabernacle, to enter into the joy of his Lord. 'Blessed are the dead which die in the Lord.'

Thrice blessed must be the portion of one who had, while here, so great a capacity for the enjoyment of heavenly things. If there are degrees of happiness in heaven, his must be a very high one. If the vessels which are 'made to honour' differ in size, some being large enough to hold much more than others, his must be an abundant portion. 'They that turn many to righteousness shall shine as the stars for ever and ever.' If one star differeth from another star in glory, bright must be the radiance that will surround him through all eternity.

It has not been given to many, during their lifetime, to reap so abundant a harvest of the seed sown by them as the late Bishop of Cashel was privileged to do; but the effects of his labours are not over yet—his works do follow him. Surely we may say so when we take a retrospective view of what the state of religion was in Ireland at the beginning of his ministry, and compare it with what may be met with now, and trace the part which he took in every good work, in every religious Society which has, under God, been the means of effecting this happy change.

We need hardly say that the Bishop of Cashel was sincerely regretted at Waterford by both Protestants and Roman Catholics. To his friends, the news of his removal seemed almost like an unexpected blow. So great, even to the last, had been the energy of his mind and the vitality of his spirit, that they could not bring themselves to realize that the vital spark was so soon to quit its mortal frame. The Church mourned over his loss.

At the meeting of the United Synods of Dublin, Kildare, and Glandalough, held in Dublin on the 17th February, the following resolution was moved. The Dean of St. Patrick's said it was fit the Synod should take some notice of an event which had just occurred, and which was of great moment to the Church. It had lost one of its best friends by the death of the Lord Bishop of Cashel. His name was in all the Churches in the land. He had won the highest repute, and was revered and cherished for his stern and strenuous championship of the cause of the Church on all occasions when he had an opportunity. He thought that some record of such an event should appear on the books of the Synod, and he would therefore move : ' That the Synod of the three united dioceses desire to express their deep sense of the loss which the Church of Ireland has just sustained, more especially the united dioceses of Cashel, Emly, Waterford, and Lismore, by the death of the Right Rev. Robert Daly.'

A very large number of clergy and some Dissenting clergymen attended his remains to their last resting-place, under the Cathedral at Waterford, in which his voice had been so long heard preaching the unsearchable riches of Christ. Amongst the foremost in the procession of mourners were two of his faithful servants, who had lived with him, one for forty years, and the other for thirty-six.

On the Sunday which followed his death, the subject was dwelt upon in almost all the pulpits in his diocese.

At a meeting held in St. Mary's Church, Clonmel, on the 19th of March 1872, for the election of his successor, His Grace the Archbishop of Dublin made the following mention of him:—

'My dear brethren of the clergy, and my dear brethren of the laity, I am sure it does not need any word of mine to remind you of the very great and solemn task which has this day brought you together. An episcopate of some thirty years, or nearly so, has just come to a close. He who was your revered chief pastor during all that time has now passed away—full of years, and full of that honour which cometh from God—to his rest and to his reward. Let it be granted that we did not all of us, in all things, see eye to eye with him; and yet I am sure that no one could have ever come to any near contact with him without feeling in his heart of hearts *this* was indeed a man of God, a man rooted and grounded in the faith; one to whom heavenly things were very near; one whom no favour would ever flatter, whom no fear would ever have terrified from that which he believed to be the right and the truth. Such a man has passed from among you. To me, if I may speak so much of myself, it is a very grateful memory that all my relations with him were cordial.

Towards myself, I would almost venture to say, though late in life we knew one another, they were affectionate. To him I ever rendered that reverence and respect which on so many grounds he had a right to claim ; and it is pleasing to me to know, and I treasure it up with thankfulness, that he would speak to me in terms of kindness, and, I would almost say, of affection. Such a man has passed from us, and your task is now to find a fitting successor for him—for him who can no longer go in and out amongst us as he did for so long a time. . . .'

The present Bishop of Cashel, who wishes to have his name linked with that of his revered predecessor, paid the following tribute to his memory when delivering his primary charge, in the summer of the year 1873 :—

'I cannot meet you for the first time, in this regular assembly of the clergy, without a reference, however brief, to my honoured and loved predecessor. I need not speak of his personal character ; it was known to you all, and known throughout the whole Church. Bold and fearless in the statement of his opinions on all important matters,—holding them not merely as things which he assented to, but as part of his very being, acting them out in his daily life, in private and in public,—no one who had any intercourse with him could be ignorant what were Robert Daly's sentiments as regards the great and vital doctrines of the gospel. They were strong and decided, firmly held and plainly stated. But there was nothing extravagant about them. They were the great truths which our Reformers held, and which our Church has embodied in the Articles and Homilies as the truths which its ministers are to teach. With that form of doctrine as he held it, I desire humbly to express my own heartfelt sympathy; and I am thankful to find that in this respect he has, through the grace of God, left his mark deep upon the diocese over which he presided for so long a time.'

A memorial-pulpit has been erected in the Cathedral Church, Waterford, to his memory. It is a very handsome piece of work. It is supported by four polished Cork marble pillars, with carved capitals, and surmounted with elaborate block cornices. There are four panels, inlaid with green polished marble, bearing the following inscriptions :—

'We preach Christ crucified.'

'The power of God unto salvation.'

'In Memory of ROBERT DALY, D.D., Bishop of Cashel, Emly, Waterford, and Lismore, MDCCCXLIII. to LXXII.'

'This tribute of loving respect is erected by his brethren in the ministry.'

APPENDIX.

———◆———

APPENDIX A.

A Speech at the First Meeting of the Church Education Society.

At the first annual meeting of the Church Education Society for Ireland, held in the Rotunda, Dublin, on Thursday the 24th of April 1840, His Grace the Lord Primate in the chair, we find Mr. Daly speaking as follows:—

'I rise to second the resolution that has been moved by the Marquis of Downshire. It is very gratifying to see the great landed proprietors joining with the clergy of the Established Church in striving to promote the scriptural education of the people. There was much room for hope that, when the great landed proprietors of the land followed the example that has this day been set them, we shall have a united force in favour of a true, orthodox, and scriptural education, which will carry us triumphant against all opposition with which we may expect to contend. . . .

'We are met together on one of the most important objects that could be set before any people—namely, the education of the people of Ireland. With regard to education itself, there seemed to be no difference of opinion—

there seemed to be a common unity of sentiment, and
every one cried out, "Educate the people, educate the
people;" and, indeed, I would ask, how could there be a
second opinion with regard to the subject of educating the
people? Is there a second opinion with regard to the
cultivation of the land? Who was bold enough or foolish
enough to stand up and say there was no use in cultivating the land? When the curse that sin brought into the
world declared that the earth should bring forth thorns
and thistles, who would for a moment advocate the principle that it was not necessary to cultivate the land? And
surely if the mind of man, and if the heart of man, had not
suffered less from the Fall than the ground from which he
produces the food he eats, who was there among them bold
enough, who was there mad enough, to deny the necessity
of imparting education to the people? But education
without religion was like turning up the ground with
the plough, and manuring it, without casting seed into it,
and leaving it there to bring forth thistles and thorns.
Such, my lord, I conceive to be the principle of education
without religion; and I think that man would err from
common sense who would set about the education of
children without religion; he would be turning up the land,
but casting no seed into it. Then comes the question, if
we are to cast seed into the ground, what kind of seed is
it to be? Some people say, and I believe the advocates of
the National Board had sometimes said, that they were in
favour of religious education; but do they tell us what
that religion is? what is the seed of that good tree from
which they expect good fruit? No; they talk of religion,

but they not only leave out, but I must say they exclude, that which God Himself has said was the good seed. "The seed is the word of God;" and therefore I maintain, that if we educate the children, and do not cultivate the heart as well as the ground, and cast the good seed therein,—and there was but one good seed, and that was the truth, the word of the eternal God,—we educate them in vain. In a conversation I had on this subject with a friend of mine who was tinged with liberalism, the latter exclaimed, "Why, you are a quack; you have but one cure for all disorders." Now, however much I dislike the word, yet I have no objection in this instance to acknowledge myself a quack, so true was it that there was but one cure for all the evils of mankind, and that was God's truth brought home with power to men's hearts. That, and that alone, could ever make a man what all men wanted to be—namely, new creatures in Christ Jesus. If we are to cultivate the heart of man, it must be by pouring into it God's truth; and that truth is to be found, in all its original brightness, in all its fulness, its vividness, in the revealed word of the living God. There it was to be found uncontaminated, incorrupted, undefiled by the world. Just, my lord, as on a thirsty day, if we wished for the refreshing water in its purity and refreshing influence, we would go to the fountain where it springs up and is yet uncontaminated, where its freshness is not taken away by having passed through a defiling and corrupting world, so we go to the fountain of living waters; and oh that we had that spirit which animated the Psalmist when he said: "As the hart panteth for the waters, so my soul panteth for Thee, O God"!

'The reason why I advocate and would support this Society is, that it gives an opportunity of putting the undefiled word of God into the hands of little children—those of whom our Saviour said, "Suffer the little children to come unto me, and forbid them not, for of such is the kingdom of heaven." This Society desires not only to give to the children the Scriptures, the truth of the living God; but, in order to establish and preserve men in that truth, she would put the formularies of the Church—for every Church has some formularies—into the hands of the children, not because they are the formularies of the Church, not because the Church sanctions, but because they are conformable to the Holy Scriptures, and are therefore profitable for instruction. But, making a true distinction between the word of God and anything from the hand of man, the Society gives those formularies to those who belong to the Church; but to those who dissent from the Church of England, the language of the Society still is, "Come along with us and read the Scriptures,"—those Holy Scriptures "that are able to make wise unto salvation, through faith which is in Christ Jesus." This Society puts no work of man, however conformable to the unerring standard of Holy Writ, in comparison with that word, which has emanated from the pure mind of God Himself. The Society addresses all men thus: "If you do not like our formularies, come and read with us what you will like better than any formularies, that is, God's eternal word." Feeling perfectly assured as I do that the more we are really conversant with the Scriptures, the more we have really the spirit of the Scriptures in our hearts, the more will we be led to approve of and value the discipline, form, and doctrine of our venerable Church.

' Yes, we are not guilty ; and if this Society did put the formularies of the Church on a par with God's holy word, I would separate from it as I would from the National Board, whose great sin is that it excludes the people from the sight of the word of God, which they did from the time of putting forth their prospectus. My great complaint against the National Board is, and I will continue to raise my voice against it until it is changed, that at its very setting out it endeavours to bring about, to secure, that the light of God's word should be excluded from the Roman Catholic population of the country. If all the Protestants of Ireland joined with the Roman Catholics in the system of education adopted by the National Board, the effect would be that no portion of God's word would ever be seen by the Roman Catholic child, except what its priest would allow it to have, and that would be none at all. The Roman Catholic priests, wise in their own generation, knowing their system cannot stand the light, will not allow the people to read the word of God. That was the principle of the Roman Catholic Church, that no one should read the Bible that was not duly authorized. Now, to show that this is the principle of the Roman Catholic Church, I will just read to you their authorized statement with regard to the Scriptures, and just say that I dissent from the National Board because it gives its assent and consent to this which I am going to read, a document published and sanctioned by three Popes,—Pius, Sixtus, and Clement,—as well as by the Council of Trent, which prohibits the reading of the Holy Scriptures by any lay person without a faculty had for that purpose. The document states that, "since it was manifest, by experience, that by the promiscuous reading of the Bible, by the temerity of some men, greater detriment than advantage had arisen, such matters should be referred to the judgment of the bishop or inquisitor, and that the confessor should give leave to read the Bible only to those whom he knew would not receive damage, but increase of faith thereby; and that such leave or faculty should be in writing; and that whosoever, without such faculty, should presume to read the Bible, should not receive absolution of his sins until he gives up the Bible." Now there is their principle, utterly opposed to all veneration, respect, and value for God's holy word. In my little experience, I have found that the wicked people were those who did not read the Bible, and the good people were those who read it. Now Roman Catholics say that we Protestants tell untruths of them—that we malign them. I only read their own authorized documents, and there we will find that if a man has not " *a faculty* " from the priest, who does not like that the man should have more light than himself, he is not to get forgiveness of his sins till he gives up the Bible. The great evil, in my mind, is not alone their bad translations, but that the working of the system helped the Church of Rome to accomplish her wish of preventing the children ever having an opportunity of reading God's word.

' On that principle, my lord, I dissent from the National Board; and I say that if I have love for my neighbour, a value for God's word, or any deference to Him who gave that word as "a lamp unto my feet and a light unto my path," I dare not, I cannot join in a system that gives that unholy facility to a corrupt and unholy Church. With respect to the junction of the Presbyterian body with the National Board, whatsoever good they might have done for themselves, they had helped to bind the system of darkness upon the Roman Catholic people of Ireland. I know there are hundreds and thousands of the Presbyterians who would not, if they knew the object of the National Board, join it in shutting out the Scriptures from the Roman Catholic children—they would put their hands in the fire sooner than be found in such an unholy combination; and this makes this meeting and this Society the more important. The situation in which the Society was placed was certainly an awful one; but it was also a glorious situation for the Church of Ireland, which, in the midst of all her deprivations, of all the wrongs inflicted on her, was still willing to take her stand alone (if she is to be alone) for the scriptural education of the rising generation.

'With regard to pecuniary means in order to secure them success, I know that England would soon pour in her contributions. When she saw the nature of the Society, she would rally round their standard, and would say to them, "Do you fight the battle, and we will find you the sinews of war."

'I will conclude with the words towards the conclusion of the Report, that I hope we consider ourselves pledged never to unite, for any offer of emolument, with a Society which would tie our hands, and prevent us educating our own children according to the Scriptures, and according to the formularies of the Church of England; never to join that system, that would bind us to give a stone instead of bread to the Roman Catholic population round us. I hope we never shall be a party in such a compromise. The Lord has said, "Preach the gospel to every creature;" and I could no more join any school which the Roman Catholic child attended, who departed when the word of God was opened, than I could live in a country in which a law was passed that every man should go to bed as soon as the sun was up; and I never could be a party to such a system. And again I would say, that I do not dissent from the National Board on the account of Protestants, because they could be taught at other times. I dissent from the principle because it helped to keep in darkness that part of the people that we wished to enlighten; and a blessed position it will be for the Established Church, that when others have given up the work, she should take it in hand, so that the light of God's truth may spread from the north, east, west, and south. The Lord grant this for Christ's sake. I have great pleasure, my lord, in seconding the resolution.'

The resolution was then put from the chair, and carried unanimously.

APPENDIX B.

A Short Criticism of the Rev. Arthur Dawson's Remarks on the Report of Master Brooke's Committee, by the Lord Bishop of Cashel, etc.

To the Rev. Arthur Dawson.

Dear Sir,—I, a few days ago, received from you a copy of your remarks on the report of Master Brooke's Committee, and in the title-page there were, in your hand, some kind words. This led me to conclude that more was intended than merely furnishing me with a copy of your pamphlet, and that probably you wished it to be understood that you would not be displeased if I gave you my opinion of its contents.

I shall therefore give a few words of criticism, not in the harsh spirit of controversy, but endeavouring to speak the truth in love, praying the Lord to lead us both into the way of truth, for the difference between us is vital; for if the system you hold and teach is the truth, and is the revealed way of salvation, I am not in the way of salvation; and on the other hand, if what I hold and teach is what God has revealed by His Son and by His apostles, then you are preaching another gospel (which is not another), in danger to yourself and endangering others.

You put the controversy very clearly in a short paragraph, which I transcribe :—

'These are the two leading points in the "heresy of

Sacerdotalism:" the power of the priest to consecrate the bread and wine, and thus make them the body and blood of Christ; and the power of the priest to convey to the penitent the absolution and remission of his sins.'

Such, then, according to your view, is God's machinery for the salvation of sinners. It is not, 'He so loved the world that He gave His only-begotten Son, that all that believe in Him should not perish, but have everlasting life;' but He has established a priesthood, taken from among men, who shall have power to change the bread and wine into the very body and blood of Christ, and, giving it, give Christ to be fed upon by the people.

He should have established a body of priesthood, taken from among men, to convey to the penitent the absolution and remission of sins, thus supplementing the priesthood of Christ, and supplying that without which it would have been of no effect.

That would be Sacerdotalism in reality. But the question is, Is that stated in the word of God to be His machinery for the salvation of man? Let us look to what the apostle tells us of the gifts that Jesus Christ received and gave to man. He tells us, Eph. iv. 11, 12, 'He gave some, apostles; and some, prophets; and some, evangelists; and some, pastors and teachers; for the perfecting of the saints, for the work of the ministry, for the edifying of the body of Christ.' You say this is Sacerdotalism. But can you give a reason, that will satisfy yourself or others, why, when He enumerated apostles, prophets, etc., He did not put into the catalogue 'priest,' 'ἱερεύς,' 'sacerdos'? You plead for Sacerdotalism; St. Paul excludes it.

And this is not the only place in which we might expect to find, on your system, priesthood—Sacerdotalism—presented to the Church as an essential part of God's machinery for the salvation of man. Let us turn to Heb. x. 17, etc.,—'And their sins and iniquities will I remember no more. Now, where remission of sin is, there is no more offering for sin. Having therefore, brethren, boldness to enter into the holiest by the blood of Jesus, by a new and living way, which He hath consecrated through the veil, that is to say, His flesh; and having an high priest over the house of God' (ἱερέα μέγαν, in the singular number, not a company of priests); 'let us draw near with a true heart, in full assurance of faith.'

I would direct your attention, and that of the readers of your remarks, to one passage, which is a gross *petitio principii:* 'If the due consecration of the bread and wine by a priest be a necessary preliminary to the body and blood of Christ being surely and indeed taken and received by the faithful in the Lord's Supper, this involves the whole principle of Sacerdotalism, or the need of the intervention of human agency, commissioned by Christ, to convey His graces to the souls of men.'

I would ask, On what ground do you assume the necessity of a priest to consecrate the bread and wine, when in the New Testament there is not one word that asserts that the office of priest is kept up in the Christian Church?

In the same strain, you speak of a priest endowed with power to absolve sinners, assuming and asserting that, besides the one great Priest, there is a company of priests.

I have only to repeat here what I said on the former question, that in the whole New Testament there is not a text asserting the existence of this priesthood, and consequently absolution by a priest.

If we turn to the texts that speak of the forgiveness of sin, we shall find the one Priest spoken of, and no other; as in Acts xiii. 38, 39, 'Be it known unto you therefore, men and brethren, that through this man' [in the singular number] 'is preached unto you the forgiveness of sins: and by Him all that believe are justified from all things, from which ye could not be justified by the law of Moses.'

Again, if we look at 1 John ii. 1, 2, 'These things write I unto you, that ye sin not. And if any man sin, we have an advocate with the Father' [one advocate], 'Jesus Christ the righteous: and He is the propitiation for our sins: and not for ours only, but also for the sins of the whole world.'

You deserve the praise of candour and open speaking. You defend Sacerdotalism in the features which are beautiful in your eyes, but are most ugly and distasteful to me and many others. 'The whole principle of Sacerdotalism is the need of the intervention of human agency, commissioned by Christ to convey His grace to the souls of men.' The first question with regard to this is, Is it true? Has the heavenly Father set up a human agency for conveying His grace to the souls of men? Was this Christ's last comforting words to His troubled disciples?—'I will not leave you comfortless. I will commission a large company of human agents to convey my grace to you and other men.' No; He said, 'I will not leave you comfortless. I will send the Comforter to you; and when He, the

Spirit of Truth, is come, He will guide you into all truth. He will show you things to come.' You teach a far lower system than that which was in the mind of David when he said, 'Let me fall into the hands of God, and not into the hands of men.' But let us shortly see what the Lord said to His apostles and ministers when He would urge them to do their duty: 'Preach the word, be instant in season and out of season; reprove, rebuke, exhort, with all long-suffering and doctrine.'

Let me reason with you as to the state that you are in, and also those who are led by you. You and they want for the life of your soul the bread which came down from heaven, of which it is true that whoso eateth it shall live for ever; and of which it is equally true, except ye eat it ye have no life in you. But according to your doctrine, you cannot have this life-giving bread except through a priest, a human agent — first to make this bread, and then to convey this grace to you. But in the Christian economy there are apostles, prophets, evangelists, pastors, and teachers, but no priests.[1] In what state, then, are

---

[1] There is a very remarkable corroboration of this in the fact that in the earlier days of our Reformation, when many editions of our Articles were printed,—some in English, and some with equal authority in Latin,—while they used the word 'priest' in English in many copies now extant, in Latin they used the word 'presbyter,' showing they did not acknowledge the sacrificing priest, the *sacerdos*, among their officers. For example, in the later edition of the Articles of 1553, we have—'Episcopis, presbyteris, et diaconis non est mandatum est cœlibatum voveant.' In the MS. of Convocation, 1562: 'Episcopis, presbyteris, et diaconis, nullo mandato divino preceptum est ut aut cœlibatum voveant aut a matrimonio abstineant.'—See Library T.C.D. I had some early editions of Articles, which I sold with other scarce books; among them one in Latin, in which the words were, 'Episcopi, presbyteres, et diaconi.' There is a

you, and those taught by you? According to you, as there
is no priest, there is no living bread. You, and those
who are led by you, stand in need of the absolution and
forgiveness of your sins; but as, according to you, none
can absolve but a priest, what state are you in when there
is no priest?—I remain, dear sir, with prayer for God's
blessing on His Church, on you and me, yours sincerely,

ROBERT CASHEL, etc.

APPENDIX C.

EXTRACT, ON THE SUBJECT OF LITURGICAL REVISION, FROM
THE CHARGE DELIVERED IN JULY AND AUGUST 1863
BY THE RIGHT REV. THE LORD BISHOP OF CASHEL,
EMLY, WATERFORD, AND LISMORE.

THERE is another quarter, of a very different kind, from
which, if not alarm, at least serious anxiety may arise. I
allude to the generally increasing feeling that there should
be some changes in our Liturgy and other formularies.

To some, not very careful observers, this might appear
a very simple proceeding, and carrying with it no very
great reason for apprehension.

But it is far otherwise when we consider the various
classes of men from whom the cry for change comes, some
desiring to lead us further from the Church of Rome, and

later edition of these Articles in Latin, printed in Oxford 1636, and there
is this title of one of the Articles: ' Libellus de consecratione archiepisco-
porum et episcoporum, et de ordinatione presbyterorum et diaconorum.'
They are the Articles of the London Synod of 1562.

some, in so doing, disposed to ignore all Church privileges and Church peculiarities.[1]

Others desire to see more clearly established their High Church principles; and whilst they would magnify the part which man has to bear, they would omit or soften those expressions which speak of the total fall of man, and tend to exalt the Creator and abase the creature.[2]

Perhaps a larger class are found complaining of the high religious tone of our services, as unsuitable for use by those whose standard harmonizes more with the spirit of the world than with that of the living members of the Church.

In their plans for attack, these have, with much wisdom, selected the Burial Service, as if it was the most evidently objectionable and the least defensible; and, as an unanswerable objection, it has been said of it, it is only fit to be read by a saint over the remains of a saint. This is its crime—this is its excellence. It will be well to keep in mind that the Prayer-Book was not compiled or intended for the use of the unconverted; and if we only consider that the Burial Service, according to the spirit of all our services, was drawn up with a view of its being read at the burial of a member of Christ, a child of God, and an inheritor of the kingdom of heaven, it will appear, perhaps,

---

[1] These demand not only the alteration of our baptismal service, but they would introduce changes into our Communion Office, and weaken some of the strong expressions in our Ordination Office.

[2] These would modify the strong expressions in the 10th, and 11th Articles, which speak of original sin and against the free will of man; and many of them would wish to remove altogether the 17th Article of our religion.

the most perfect and beautiful of all our services. It is in unison and keeping with the whole Book of Common Prayer, according to which the child of Christian parents is brought in faith in baptism to Christ, to be received as a child of God and an inheritor of the kingdom of heaven; he is afterwards brought, in confirmation, to take the baptismal vows upon himself; he is led during life to receive nourishment for his soul at the table of the Lord; and when he dies in peace, his body is committed to the ground, in sure and certain hope of the resurrection to eternal life, and with the hope that he doth rest in Him who is the resurrection and the life.

If such words, used in cases to which they are not suitable, and for which they never were intended, lay a burden on a minister of our Church, a similar burden lies much heavier upon the minister of a Dissenting congregation.

Our minister uses the language which our formulary prescribes, and he is in no way answerable for its being applicable in the particular case. If a leading member of a Dissenting congregation, who had been from his wealth or his station a chief support of the connection, dies and is buried, the minister is expected to prepare and preach a funeral sermon; and his conscience is sorely tried when he is, as it were, forced to use language that shall satisfy his people in eulogizing the dead, which is beyond, if not quite contrary to, his convictions with regard to the departed.

What, then, is to be done to relieve the complainants from the burden which oppresses?

Is there to be no Burial Service in our Prayer-Book?

Is there to be a Burial Service containing no expression

of Christian hope with regard to those concerning whom such hope may be entertained?

Or is there to be a discretion left to the clergyman to read or omit the expression of Christian hope?

Is there to be found anywhere a body of legislators, who, in the case of themselves or their relatives, would give to the clergy this discretion?

Or is there a body of clergy that would accept the discretion of expressing their hope of one individual, and, by silence, denying it with regard to another?

It is evident that introducing change that shall be satisfactory is no easy matter, as some have supposed.

The question naturally presents itself, Who is to undertake this great, important, difficult work?

There is no body now in existence that has the competence or the authority to undertake it.

A distinguished senator, looking at the question as a statesman, has said in the House of Commons, when the subject was introduced there, 'It must be referred to Convocation, formed upon a basis more comprehensive than that which now exists. You must associate with the Convocation of Canterbury that of the other province, and of the Church of Ireland;' and he adds, as his own opinion, 'There should be introduced that lay element to which the Church of England has been so much indebted.'[1]

The first step, then, towards revision, should be the exercise by the Crown of its prerogative, to call together such a Synod or Convocation as should be a fair represen-

---

[1] See Mr. Disraeli's speech on Mr. Buxton's motion, as reported in the *Times*.

tation of the United Church of England and Ireland; and to this Synod should be referred the dealing with this momentous question. It is evident that it will be no very simple, easy work to compose and institute such a deliberative body; and is it not a subject of deep anxiety to consider what may be the determination of such a Synod, composed as it would be of much discordant material?[1]

Is there not ground to apprehend that the Liturgy, Articles, and Canons, as they must come out very different, might be found worse than we have them at present?

Is there not ground to fear that within the body there might be exhibited a great and violent difference of opinion —a great proof that the Church was not at unity in herself; and as to what might be determined on by the majority, a greater and more violent difference of opinion might be felt by those without, and thence a disruption take place, which might endanger the very existence of our Established Church?

We have to acknowledge with thankfulness a gracious Providence that has watched over our Church in times

---

[1] It would be well boldly to look at the obstacles that stand in the way of a successful issue from the meeting of such a body. It has been well remarked, that when two parties of widely different sentiments meet to compile or to modify a book, and when both sides must exercise the greatest caution in giving expression to their views, lest they should be altogether rejected, and when at the same time they must be zealously on the watch to restrict the views of their opponents within the narrowest bounds, lest they should directly contradict their own, we cannot expect that there should be that richness and fulness of genial thought which flows from a heart that enters devotedly and without constraint into the spirit of the subject. There must be wanting that life and distinct character that would come from singleness of view and unity of purpose.

past, especially at the period of the Reformation by our honoured Reformers; and that same guardian care, we have no doubt, will be sought to guide us and carry us safe through all our dangers; but yet there is ground for deep anxiety.

I conceive there is danger to our Church whether we stand still or whether we move on. And if the question were put to me, 'To which of the dangers would you prefer to have the Church exposed?' I should give it as my deliberate opinion, that, considering the spirit of the times, and the uneasiness exhibited in many quarters, we cannot stand still—we cannot say we will do nothing; and I should prefer to see a comprehensive Convocation—a fair representative of the United Church—instituted and assembled, and thus a great and manifest evil got rid of— namely, our being without a governing body, authorized and competent to take in hand and deal with such subjects as the Church ought to deal with.' [1]

---

[1] Good men, who have formed themselves into an association for promoting the revision of the Liturgy, seem not to have looked very deep into the subject, or considered it in its several bearings. At a meeting lately held in Willis' Rooms, at which Lord Ebury presided, one of the speakers said that they had made known all the changes that they were seeking. It is very desirable that any individual, or number of individuals, should honestly and plainly declare what they are seeking, and with what change they will be content; but if they mean to convey to the public or to the Church that others will be satisfied with what will satisfy them, they are putting forward what is very far from the truth of the case. Many good men, who agree with them on the fundamental truths of the gospel, will seek many changes very different from those that they have stated as necessary; and those, again, who differ essentially from them on many doctrinal points, will differ equally widely from them; they will refuse to accept many of the changes they most ardently desire, and they will insist upon others diametrically different: so that whilst they very weakly flatter

themselves that if there are changes made in the Liturgy they will be just what they wish, they will probably find, that in proportion as opinions different from theirs prevail in the Church, so, if any changes be made in the Liturgy, they will be very different from those that they desire, and for the attainment of which they are stirring the minds of all around them to be dissatisfied with what they now have.

At the time of the Reformation, when our Liturgy was drawn up, the great principles of Popery and Protestantism stood out in such bold relief, that on the side of our Reformers there was that substantial unity which enabled them to bring to their deliberations a oneness of heart and purpose that secured a life and consistency in their performance which are not to be expected in our days, when there is no acknowledged common enemy to be opposed, no one common principle to be maintained.

THE END.

MURRAY AND GIBB, EDINBURGH,
PRINTERS TO HER MAJESTY'S STATIONERY OFFICE.

www.ingramcontent.com/pod-product-compliance
Lightning Source LLC
Chambersburg PA
CBHW031049110726
47900CB00003B/859